OPEN HOME MURDERS

A Novel

TOM KUNKEL

authorHOUSE®

AuthorHouse™
1663 Liberty Drive
Bloomington, IN 47403
www.authorhouse.com
Phone: 1 (800) 839-8640

Published by AuthorHouse 11/16/2017

ISBN: 978-1-5462-1726-8 (sc)
ISBN: 978-1-5462-1725-1 (hc)
ISBN: 978-1-5462-1834-0 (e)

Library of Congress Control Number: 2017917587

Print information available on the last page.

PROLOGUE

Henry "Hank" Pilcher was sitting at the kitchen table in his tiny one-bedroom apartment Friday morning reading the real estate section of the *Tribune*. *Interesting*, he thought, as he skimmed all the homes listed in the foreclosure section. Dozens upon dozens, even hundreds of available homes at bargain prices. Small cottage-type ranches right on up to million-dollar Tudors with beautiful views of rolling hills and woodlands scattered throughout the Chicagoland area, all to be had at a fraction of their original price. The poor slobs who had once occupied these homes—and some still did—filling them with memories of backyard barbeques and pool parties, were now probably living in cheap apartments or in their elderly parents' guest rooms, or worse yet, in their musty basements. Having done everything they could to save their dreams, they had failed. Mortgages, second loans, and equity lines had led to the same results, only more slowly than if they had left the keys on the counter with a note to the bank and just walked out months earlier.

Hank's apartment was located on the top floor of a three-story building in the crumbling section of Gilbert, Illinois. The kitchen window, one of only two windows in the entire apartment, looked out onto an alley where the trash containers for the building were stored. Every Friday morning, around six o'clock, he could hear the beeping of the backup horn on the large blue truck that had been contracted to pick up the decay of the thirty-six residents that called Humphrey Arms their home. The all-brick building had been built in the forties and had the same amenities now as then—boiler heat, gas stoves, and small bathroom with a tub-shower combination. People must have been smaller in the forties, because the tubs weren't even long enough to stretch out for a bath, had anyone the thought of relaxing in a chipped porcelain tub with a rusty drain, bowed pale blue ceramic tile sides, and permanently mildew-stained grout. The other window was in the flea-sized bedroom. The seal had broken long ago, and the pane had fogged over with moisture. No loss, really. The view was of the backside of another brick apartment building, with air conditioning units sticking out like broken teeth of an old boxer's smile. There was one living space in addition to the bedroom and kitchen. The carpet was so bare you could see the air underneath. A well-traveled pattern was formed from the television to the refrigerator to the bedroom. The upside was the plaster walls, which provided soundproofing between apartments. Hank had live in the Humphrey Arms for a little more than a year. He was on his second lease term and still had no idea who his neighbors were.

Hadn't we all been told, Hank thought, that "it was never a better time to buy," "money is cheap," "you can't afford not to buy that new home now." He believed it then as well. And why not? He had had a good job. Good, not great. He was successfully employed at Pearson's Plumbing and Supply as a salesman. In fact, he had even been sales associate of the month a dozen times in his eight years with the company. He knew the product line better than anyone else and had developed a strong and loyal client base of builders and homeowners alike. He had seen the trends move from shiny brass fixtures to chrome to brushed nickel. As the size and price of new homes continued to increase, so had the variety of luxury plumbing fixtures. No longer was a kitchen faucet merely a means of delivering water; it had become an artistic focal point in the kitchen. Dual- and single-swivel faucets had morphed into pull-out sprayers with multi-flow features. Extras now included soap dispensers and pot fillers with instant hot water. Bathrooms had become spas and were no longer just a place to shave, brush your teeth, and take a dump. Whirlpool tubs were still popular but were gradually becoming obsolete and were being replaced by state-of-the-art walk-in showers. Handheld spa heads, body jets, rain showerheads, and frameless glass hinged shower doors were all the rage. Hank's top-selling, most expensive shower fixture was the double-handle thermostatic valve with volume control, diverter, and lever handles. Now that was a beauty. He smiled each time he rang one up as he figured the sales commission in his head.

Hank had his regular builders and do-it-yourself home remodelers. The housing boon had been good for everyone. He was likable enough, knew what he was talking about and gave excellent customer service. His knowledge and sincerity were enough to keep them asking for Hank Pilcher when they called or entered the show room of Pearson's Plumbing and Supply.

One of Hank's new construction clients was Jackson Brothers Custom

Homes. In fact, Jackson Brothers built a brand-new home in a brand-new subdivision for him during the height of the housing boom. Why not? Money was cheap and it was a great time to buy. Plus, his Realtor and his lender, First Family Bank and Trust, had told him so. They were the experts in real estate, just as Hank was an expert in the plumbing supply business.

Hank and his family had finally moved in during the spring of 2004. The Pilcher's new two-story, four-bedroom, three-and-a-half bathroom home sat on a quarter-acre lot at the end of a premium cul-de-sac in Jordan Creek Estates. The "creek" was actually a small runoff tributary, but it had a name, and now so did the subdivision. Hank had even managed to have Jackson Brothers finish the lookout basement at cost. Yes sir, he had cut quite a deal. The American Dream was his.

The housing boom of the late 1990s continued right up until 2007, when everything came to a halt. The economy was showing signs of slowing. New home sales were stalling and interest rates were inching up. Hank had lived long enough to see these small blips on the radar before. It would surely pass by and regain momentum; it always had. His client list went from thirty builders to twenty-two the following year, and the year after that, down to seventeen. His commission checks began to get smaller and smaller at Pearson's as their business began to mirror the economy. The company had to let six sales associates go during this declining period. But things would have to improve, wouldn't they? They didn't.

In order to stay current with his bills, Hank took out a line of credit, which helped temporarily. They had put a large amount down on the home, so it was really like taking a loan from himself, wasn't it? He knew how to budget, but his family was another story. Lydia, Hank's wife, had a love affair with credit cards. And she never denied their daughter, Samantha, ten, or their son, Tyler, eight, anything. Summer camp? Sure, why not. They deserved it. All their friends were going to camp. iPods, Xbox, flat-screen plasma TVs, computers for everyone, all the necessities to live in Jordan Creek Estates. Ten-year-old Samantha had even talked her mom into getting her a cell phone, for crying out loud. Many evenings, after Samantha and Tyler were tucked into bed, ended in arguments between Hank and Lydia about money.

"Do we need a cleaning service every week?" Hank would ask. "Can't we get through one more year before we need a new car? Why don't you do my shirts instead of sending them out? No, we can't afford a pool. We'll take the kids to Florida for spring break next year." And on and on went the conversations. It was a struggle to keep up with the other families moving into Jordan Creek Estates, but Lydia was determined to have it all and then some. Image was a driving force in her life. Hank wondered how many other families in the new shiny subdivision were having similar late-night discussions. The money rift had spilled over into other aspects of their marriage. The lack of communication and affection added to the growing depressive atmosphere in the Pilcher household.

Hank was in trouble financially and was the only member of the family who seemed to acknowledge that fact. They had bought in over their head. He even talked to his Realtor about the option of selling their four-year-old home without Lydia's knowledge. "Timing is bad," Hank was told. "Not a good time to sell. Prices have fallen dramatically, and they don't look like they're going up anytime soon. In fact, the numbers suggest that you couldn't sell it for what you paid for it." The timing was terrible. Not only had they paid a premium for the lot, but the house was loaded with amenities. Plus, Hank had paid to finish the basement (at cost, of course). And then there was the landscaping: patio, extra trees and bushes, sod instead of seed, hard scape, and fire pit. Lydia had gone all out on the window treatments. Holy God in heaven were drapes, curtains, blinds, and sheers expensive! How had this all happened? Hank agonized almost daily. While at work, on the drive to and from work, and worst of all during his restless nights, all he could think of was the building debt and how to get out from under the growing situation.

He didn't know how to solve the problem. It felt as though a shovel of wet sand was tossed onto on his chest every time he let his mind wander to the bills. It was hard to breathe, as if someone was sucking the air out of his lungs with a vacuum hose. Waking up exhausted each morning did nothing for his mood. Lydia certainly didn't want to worry the children or deny them anything, and it would surely be all right eventually. It wasn't.

His bills equaled more than his income. Hank suggested that Lydia look for a part-time job. She worried what the other wives would think if they saw her going to work every day. This was not the marriage she had dreamed of as a little girl growing up in a well-to-do upper-middle-class home. After some hesitation and self-doubt about her qualifications, she hit the streets in search of employment. Not a career, just a job. Her skills were fifteen years old, and apparently being a supportive mother and spouse didn't count for much to the outside world. Meanwhile, Hank's list of builders dropped to eleven, and his commission checks were skimpy in comparison to his mounting debt. He was behind on credit card bill payments, barely making the mortgage payment, and to make things worse, he now couldn't cover the repayment of his draw at work.

Hank also began to look for part-time employment to supplement his meager wages at Pearson's Plumbing and Supply. Weekends, evenings, any spare time he could carve out was devoted to other employment opportunities. His only background had been in sales, and sales-oriented companies were not hiring. He tried other fields as well, but at age forty-two, his resume lacked appeal. Luckily, Lydia had found a part-time position at a local real estate office. She was guaranteed thirty hours a week as the receptionist. Her duties included answering phones, filing, making brochures, and doing any other tasks that the Realtors might need. The position offered flexible hours, slightly better than minimum wage, and proximity to home. Great news! No.

Six months into the new job, Lydia asked Hank for a divorce. It seemed her tasks involved sleeping with Thad Essington, managing broker and owner of Essington Realty. And Lydia excelled at that job. Seeing no future with a deadbeat plumbing salesman who was constantly in a sour mood, and tired of worrying about money, Lydia jumped ship and took the kids with her in the little lifeboat known as Thad.

Thad was infatuated with Lydia from the start. In fact, he had hired her with the subconscious idea of a little friendly flirting and maybe a short office romance. He fell head over heels in love with her. It didn't matter that she was married or even that she had children. What they had discovered in each other were true passion and real love. As Lydia was not going to change her mind, after much pleading and even begging, Hank agreed to the divorce request and moved out and into an apartment, close enough to be near his children. The salt in the wound was when Thad Essington planted his sign in the front yard of Hank's house two months later. FOR SALE. Not only had Thad taken Hank's wife and children; he had stolen the American Dream from him, and now he was going to have to pay Thad a commission for doing so!

In Hank's mind, Realtors and lenders were the causes of this whole mess. They drove up the housing prices, convinced people to overpay for homes, and got them into financial hardships. The lenders gave money away, often with no or little documentation for the loan. Who invented the no-doc loan anyway? Greedy lenders who were only after the fees and interest associated with creating mortgages, whether you were qualified or not! Who needed Realtors anyway? They drove around in fancy cars, opening front doors and convincing people to buy homes. And they got paid big bucks for doing nothing. Realtors were lowlife scum who slept with the money handlers, and neither served any worthwhile purpose in Hank's mind. They had ruined his life. His home was sold for a pittance compared to what he had paid. After the sales costs and commission, and the split with his wife, he was left with a negative balance with his lender. First Family Bank and Trust had worked out a deal with Hank on the sale, which left him owning nothing but with no proceeds. The American Dream had become a short sale. No home, no wife, no money, no dignity.

Hank moved on with the life he had been dealt, but not without an inner rage that gave him perpetual red-rimmed eyes, taut jaw, and slumped shoulders. He often found his hands clenched into fists. Most days he didn't bother to shave. When he went to work, which was now as a part-time salesman at Pearson's Plumbing and Supply, his shirts looks as though he had slept in them. The once colorful ties were dulled with age and frayed at the tips. The fresh crease down the front of his trouser was long gone. He drove his beater of a car, a 1998 Chevy Malibu, to work three days a week and did his best to budget what little money he did bring home. Thankfully, Lydia and Thad had agreed to not pursue the delinquent child support payments. He hadn't been able to pay in over six months, and the future didn't look much different. He stopped seeing his children on a regular basis. There was no room in his one-bedroom apartment for Samantha and Tyler to sleep over on weekends anyway. Plus, they seemed thrilled with their new life.

When he went to pick up the kids, pulling into the driveway of his ex-wife's new home, which she shared with Thad Essington, destroyed any remaining self-worth he had. Well, at least Lydia had the lifestyle she had always wanted, and then some. The new Mr. and Mrs. Essington, along with Hank's children, lived in a five-thousand-square-foot Tudor that had been built seven years ago in a tear-down area of Gilbert. The old section of town, where there once stood modest single-family homes, ranches, split-levels, and Cape Cods, had slowly transformed into an upscale Mecca of the nouveau rich. The four-car driveway was laid with distressed red paver bricks. The front door was encased in a two-story turret, with lead glass windows. When he went to pick up the kids, Hank never made it much past the spacious foyer with its travertine tile from Mexico, and nor did he want to. He heard plenty about the house while he and his children discussed their lives. He would take them out for a lunch or a big breakfast at the pancake house that had been his family's favorite in happier times. He still took the kids there, but it seemed like an entirely different restaurant now. The conversation eventually turned to Samantha's bathroom paradise, or the theater room in the finished basement, or the pool party for Sam's thirteenth birthday party. It made Hank sad and angry behind his fatherly eyes and plastic smile. Well, he would have his revenge.

The phone on the dingy yellow kitchen wall rang. It was 10:30 on Friday morning. As Hank got up to answer, the *Tribune* fell from the table to the floor. The pages of the real estate section floated to the grimy, cracked linoleum. Circled in red were two scheduled open houses for Sunday.

CHAPTER 1

The victim's name was Sara Donoghue. Thirty-four years old. Wife, mother of two boys: Bryan, age seven, and Nicolas, age five. Real estate agent for three years. She went back to work to supplement her husband Brad's income as a sixth-grade school teacher in District 38. She lived in a northern suburb of Chicago and worked for a large national real-estate franchise. Last year's production was eleven homes, and she had hoped to increase that to seventeen this year. Her main business was holding open houses for other agents on weekends. She had procured a bounty of buyers with this method and had even sold one property during an open house last year. Her current year was off to a fast start thanks to an early spring and cooperative weather.

She was a perky five feet five (five three without the Prada knockoffs) and 133 pounds. Short, curly brown hair worn in a flyaway style, and always smartly dressed, very professional. She put together her wardrobe from discount stores, accessorizing with expensive jewelry to create a high-fashion look without the price tag. Sara drove a ten-year-old four-door Lincoln Town Car, which she bought from her dad at a bargain price. It floated down the highway like a large boat. Given Sara's stature, it often looked as though no one was driving. She gave it love and care and regular maintenance, keeping it looking practically new. Black exterior with gray cloth interior, low mileage, terrible on gas. A very big trunk, plenty of room for her "Open Home" event signs.

Sara was in charge of planning her parents' fortieth wedding anniversary celebration. Her two sisters lived out of state and just couldn't help with local arrangements. The big surprise party was to happen exactly twelve weeks from her Sunday open house.

The Donoghue family were outdoors people. They loved to go for bike rides and hiking, and they took camping vacations in the days before the boys were born. Real camping, with a tent, no Winnebago for Sara and Brad. A day at a nearby forest preserve was more exciting than a trip into the city. It was simple and pure, a day filled with laughs. Sara was the soccer mom who brought juice packs and homemade cookies, not for just the team but for the coaches and the other parents as well. Each three-by-five-inch juice carton had one of Sara's business cards taped neatly in place. After all, these people might someday want to sell or buy a home. Why not mix business with pleasure? Sara had read in a real estate book—purchased at last year's annual conference in Springfield—that success was based on self-marketing. Every chance you have to put your name in front of someone, do it.

"Welcome. Come on in. My name is Sara. Are you familiar with the neighborhood? No. Well, let me tell you a little bit about the local parks, shopping, and where the schools are located. Do you have children in school? This is a four-bedroom Cape Cod with two and a half baths. Wait until you see the potential for finishing the basement. Follow me."

Sara was sweet, informative, and naive. Her unassuming nature was part of her charm. It was no act for Sara to be open and overly friendly—it was who she was, and it served her well in the real-estate business.

Brad Donoghue had reported his wife missing when she failed to return home late on Sunday, well after her scheduled open house should have ended. He and his sons spent a terrifying twenty-four hours waiting for news of their beloved wife and mother. He drove by the house where Sara was to have held her open house, but there was no sign of her. The managing broker of her office as well as several concerned agents drove to the house, but no one did a thorough search. No one even checked the garage until the police decided to pop the trunk of a late-model Lincoln the next day. Everyone assumed that the previous owner was storing the car there or that a neighbor had permission to keep an extra car out of the elements. No one thought it unusual that a vacant home had a car parked in the garage.

And so Sara Donoghue was found in the trunk of a ten-year-old black Lincoln Town Car, parked in the garage at 1214 Mission Hill Court, the site of her last open house. Neighbors reported seeing the light on through the windows of the garage door. This was odd, as the previous owners had moved out months earlier. The bank was foreclosing on the house. The

Robbins had simply said their goodbyes to neighbors, packed what they could in a rental moving truck, and left the right after the first of the New Year. It had been important to Mr. and Mrs. Robbins to spend one last Christmas together in the home where their four children had been born. It was a sad, cold day in January when the six Robbins drove away down the street—a two-vehicle parade of minivan and a rental truck.

Local Glenburg police had come to investigate. Looking through the window of the garage door, they saw the car and ran the Illinois license plate. It came back as registered to a one Sara Lynn Donoghue. The stench was powerful when they opened the trunk and found the decaying body of its owner. Her light-blue oxford-cloth blouse with the Peter Pan collar was unbuttoned and spread wide. Written on her chest, over her heart, in the same rose-pink lipstick she had put on fresh the morning of the open house, was the word *LYER*. Her lips, no longer pink, were caked with a dried powdery white substance. Taped across each eye was one of Sara's business cards. A picture of Sara—smiling, as though a bright future lay ahead of her—stared up at the policeman from the floor of her trunk: *Call Sara—I make dreams come true.* The patrolman on the scene gaped at the stark difference between the smiling image on the cards and the waxen, bloated body of Sara Donoghue.

CHAPTER 2

"Congratulations, Kurt."

A good marriage gone bad. I don't actually believe there is such a thing. I hear it all the time from friends describing other friends' divorces. "They were a fun couple, just a good marriage gone bad. Gee, they seemed happy—minivan, kids, and that big, loveable dog. What a shame—a good marriage gone bad."

"Don't know how you stayed sane for a decade."

I believe there are good people who are good their entire lives and go on to celebrate their fiftieth wedding anniversary surrounded by their children and grandchildren. Balloons covered in gold spray, an overly rich three-layer cake with old farts on top, and thoughtful but meaningless gifts to the "happy" couple. A celebration of commitment and love, honor and thoughtfulness, celebrated in a sterile rental hall.

"Nice job, Kurt. Keep it up."

Then there are bad people who should never have gotten married in the first place. Even in the early stages of dating, when we're all on our best behavior, the signs are evident. Physical attraction should be taken for what it is—lust! Lust won't last, because it costs too much.

"Where would you like to go for dinner?"

"Chin's House of Rice would be nice."

"Again? We just ate there last week."

"You asked. I'm hungry for Chinese."

"Well, I'm not."

"Fine."

"I'm going down to Larry's Pub for a burger and a beer."

"Have a good time. Don't wake me when you come in."

No lust, just lost.

These were my thoughts as I contemplated the demise of my own marriage more than twelve years earlier. My ex and I were neither good nor bad, although at the time I was certain we were both good. I found out it was just lust. Over our fourteen years together, we became complacent and compromising and uninvolved with each other. The marriage had served its purpose, and there was nothing left. It wasn't a good marriage gone bad, just lust lost.

That was the road that brought me to my current station in life: Kurt Banning, Realtor extraordinaire. I may be taking some liberty with the "extraordinaire" part, but in my little part of the world, I was making a comfortable living fulfilling other people's dream of home ownership. I was considered successful by my peers.

The accolades continued as I sat in the small cubicle I called my office. Ten minutes earlier, we had been cramped in the small kitchenette in the back of the office. Ten balloons were tied to the back of an aging card-table chair, one of four that serviced the four-by-four-foot card table. On the plaid vinyl-covered tabletop was a store-bought sheet cake. Too much butter cream frosting hid the chocolate cake beneath. Powdered-sugar rosettes were planted at each corner. Rope lettering squeezed out of a tube said, *Thanks and Congratulations*. Below that was a huge number ten. No candles. We had long ago given up the tradition of blowing out candles on cakes celebrating a variety of accomplishments at the office. A few years ago, when we were celebrating Marge Linkus's eightieth birthday, her bottom denture flew out as she blew and landed in the center of the zero. Too many hackers and sneezers spreading their cold-and-flu-season germs, SARS, bird flu virus, and so on. Marge Linkus ended a century-old tradition. Not surprisingly, since the no-candle policy went into effect, a lot more cake was consumed during company events.

It was ten years ago today that I jumped into a career that I knew very little about, with the exception of my own previous home purchases. Real estate had and still does intrigue me. It is an interesting fact that before the technology boom and the likes of Microsoft, Google, Amazon, Facebook, etc., 90 percent of America's millionaires made their fortunes in buying, selling, owning, or having rights to dirt! It is a simple yet complicated process of risk and reward. That's where I come in; I simplify the risk-reward proposition for clients and reap a portion of the reward. I am certain that mine is an honorable profession, but not all participants are honorable. Some are just lustful.

"Way to go, buddy," Mark said as he walked behind me. His attempt at a pat on the back resulted in bumping my chair, causing a rogue wave of lukewarm, hour-old coffee to splash over the lip of my cup and on to my littered desk and freshly pressed slacks. Thank you for cold coffee and dark brown pants. I swiveled in my chair to give Mark a deserved ugly face, and I struck my knee on the inside second drawer of my genuine Steelcase desk. And I do mean steel case. I had been sitting at the same desk for ten years, and at least once a day I would slam my left knee into that damn drawer.

You see, although we guide people through the vagaries of buying that first home or upgrading their family domicile, we aren't high on the professional food chain. At last ranking, we were still above lawyers, car salesmen, and insurance agents, but I doubt we'll ever come close to the firefighters, doctors, teachers, and police, and nor should we. Although, I suppose that depends if your house is on fire or you need to have a fire sale on an overpriced home in a down market.

As a Realtor, I sell homes, land, and multi-family buildings. I assist hardworking folks in getting a good deal on the perfect home, whether it is a starter condo, townhouse, four-bedroom traditional, or McMansion dream home. I help landlords fill those vacant apartments and squatty little homes buried deep within downtown heritage zones. My responsibilities include selling that overpriced home because I feel sorry for the thirty-year resident who "needs" the money to move to Phoenix or Miami. Yes, people still move to Miami. Selling a home of a financially strapped owner is gut wrenching. There is no place for emotion in a business transaction, but as much as you try to be the eternal optimist, it can be tough. I guess that's what I love about this business: different people with different needs, challenges, properties, and stories. Oh, and the money's not bad!

As my previously-discussed marriage was falling apart, slowly sinking, I knew I would need a fresh start, and likely a better income. Real estate seemed profitable from the standpoint of an investor as well as an agent. I had always been intrigued by the sales process. I witnessed my first transaction when I was eight years old. It was a Saturday morning in September. I remember because school had just resumed, and that morning the sun shined bright. The sky was a see-through blue, and the air was just crisp enough to burn if you took the biggest gulp you could. Dad asked me to ride along on an errand with him. As this was an unusual occurrence, I gladly skipped Bugs, Daffy, and Roadrunner. I jumped up onto the seat of his old '47 Ford pickup. He had owned that truck for as long as I could remember. He said it was a fond memory from his teenage years, and it is now one of keepsakes as well.

That old Ford was darker than Army green. Half green and half blood red Bondo that covered where the rust would appear every year. Dad was great at patching that truck together. There wasn't anything he couldn't do mechanically. He never painted over the Bondo, because he said it was just for driving around and having fun and running errands. I can still see and smell that truck. The inside was huge and empty, nothing but a dash over which I could barely see and a steering wheel as big as an oak barrel. It smelled old, like dust mixed with rain. And it was loud.

On that Saturday in September, we drove to the nearby farm of Mr. Smith. Mr. Smith owned a lot of farm acreage in the county and the rumor was that he might be willing to sell off some of the land as he grew older and farmed less. My dad had wanted us to be able to move out of the small two-bedroom home that he and Mom and I shared and build a new modern home with all the conveniences of the late seventies.

I sat in the front seat, watching through the enormous windshield as my dad and Mr. Smith leaned against the hood of the Ford and chatted, pointing this way and that way. Then my dad took a piece of folded notebook paper from the front pocket of his plaid work shirt and a pencil from under his stained cap. He wrote, holding the paper firm on the hood, and showed it to Mr. Smith. The old farmer looked at it through squinty eyes and a creased face, leaned over the hood with the paper and pencil, and wrote something as well. When he handed back to my dad, I think I saw a small smile at the corner of his mouth. I noticed it because he didn't smile all that much. My dad was all business. They shook hands, and Dad came around the truck and got in. He didn't say anything, and I didn't ask any questions. We drove about two miles and turned onto a gravel road. Another mile down County Rd. 40, we slowed and drove through a rolled-back opening in the chain fencing. He stopped, and we both got out. He hoisted me up onto the hood of the Ford so I could get a better view. The metal was warm through my jeans.

He drew an arc in the sky with his left hand and said, "Your mom's going to be very happy. I just agreed to buy these fifteen acres from Mr. Smith. This is where we're going to build our new home." I was amazed that, just like that, someone would give you property for money. I never knew how much Dad paid, and I didn't know anything about formal paperwork and bank closings, but from that day on, I thought of that land as our new home. Just like that.

I glanced past the cluttered desks of my fellow Realtors, worn chairs from years of use, and stacks of banker boxes. The sun had set, and a slight spring drizzle had begun. The light of day was replaced by fluorescent office lighting. It was 6:30, and tiny rivulets of rain were racing down the front windows of Prescott Realty, distorting the store lights from across the street.

As I stared out the window, I contemplated my ten years in the business. Flexible hours, easy work, fancy car, and the many rounds of golf where you do your most important selling. Drive pretty divorcees around town showing the "beginning over" homes where they would enjoy their newfound freedom. Sleep in, cocktails at five. This was going to be a leisurely work life. Wrong! Those of you who are Realtors, married to a Realtor, friends of a Realtor, or lucky enough to have a Realtor in your family can stop laughing now. The down and dirty is long hours, unfaithful customers who never develop into clients, no time for golf, a mountain of paperwork crammed into a small, windowless office (if you're lucky enough to get an office), and holes in the heels of your socks from taking off and putting on your shoes twenty times a day. Keeping a late model car as clean as possible to make it look as new as possible is a feat in itself. Buyers who don't show up, clients who are late (or really late), a cell phone that rings at seven in the morning, because everyone starts work at seven, right? Being rained on or snowed on all day long, enjoying the screeching baby in the backseat that the client has brought because her sitter cancelled at the last minute. Cute kid, smart babysitter. A true joy of mine is finding a fossilized French fry under the back seat floor mat or the occasional sunbaked Pink Rose Number 4 Crayola stuck between my genuine leatherette seats.

Not that I'm complaining. I absolutely love this profession and wouldn't trade it for any other. I wish I had gotten into the game earlier in life. This is where I fit. I love being a real estate agent. Lustfully.

CHAPTER

"Kurt, Robbie and I are going over to Abby's for a drink. Come with us?"

Dex Bradley is probably the closest thing I have to a best friend. He's a third-generation Realtor, although he's taken a step or two back from the business his grandfather founded and his father grew. It's not that he doesn't try—he really does—but he doesn't have the drive of old Pops and Gramps. They made quite a name for themselves during the building boom and built a respected business in the Hamilton area. Dex's grandfather was a founding member of the Elms Country Club in the 1940s, which is where Stuart Bradley cultivated many of his early real estate clients. The club still exists, and Dex is one of its youngest current members. However, the Elms is now mostly populated with crimson maples, silver maples, king maples, and spruce pine. The Dutch elm disease of the sixties wiped out all of the trees that lined the fairways a long time ago. Not so for the current members, who, unlike the old gnarly elm, are ancient and craggy and still standing. These are the old money people of Hamilton.

The Hamilton Country Club, where I am also not a member, is a newer addition to our city. Built in the early nineties, it is much more family friendly, with an average member age in the mid-forties. HCC offers a modern atmosphere, with a sprawling clubhouse, shiny pool, and cabana, along with championship tennis courts and a meticulously groomed eighteen-hole course. This is where new money goes to play and relax, those with above-average incomes in tech and software. Elms members would never think of setting foot on their grounds, as this would be an act of treason.

"Can't. I promised Liz I would meet her for a light dinner when she gets off her shift," I replied, packing up my briefcase.

"Are you two starting up again? I don't think you have the energy for the break-ups and make-ups you two seem to enjoy."

"Not that it's any of your business, Dex, but no, no relationship. Just a nice dinner with a friend."

"Yah, okay, just a friend. You can't be friends with a boss, or a rabid dog, or an ex-lover."

"Thanks for the offer, Dex. Next time, okay?"

"Sure. Be careful and skip dessert."

Such a wiener, but a lovable wiener.

The wealth came steadily over those first two generations for the Bradley family, until suburban blight stalled things in the late seventies and interest rates went sky high. They sold the business but kept the wealth. By the time Poindexter Bradley (his actual name) was an adult, the patriarchs had long since retired. Dexter (to his acquaintances; Dex to his friends) never had the drive or need to stick with a chosen field. He always had the silver spoon of life next to his plate. After another failed attempt in corporate America, dad had suggested real estate. I think ol' Dex had the same misguided perception about the housing business that I originally had. But something clicked, and he has been at it nearly as long as I have. He might be a bit lazy and cut a corner here and there when the consequences are minimal, but he's an all-around good guy who would give you his last ten bucks if you needed it. He is enjoyable to be around (usually), and his clients love him. He thrives on a satisfied customer. He's found his niche. With Mother and Father Bradley departed, Dex could probably afford to buy the entire city of Hamilton, but you wouldn't know it. He limits his extravagances are usually keeps out of the public eye.

My commute home is easy. I rent the apartment above Prescott Realty, where I work. I know what you're thinking. A Realtor who rents! Quite the oxymoron. I actually do own a home; in fact, I own five houses. Sorry, homes. A dog lives in a house; people live in homes. I rent all of them to hard-working families, who mostly pay their rent on time. I think of each of them as a mini 401k. When that glorious day comes and I turn in my Realtor license, I plan on divesting each home, one at a time, to fund my retirement. And, as cash flow provides, I plan on adding to my pension, one home at a time.

Besides, my lifestyle doesn't give me the time to mow a lawn, paint, or attend to other weekend time-wasting projects. I don't own a cat or a dog or a fish. I send my laundry out and rarely cook. I do own a cookbook, called

International Cuisine. I use it to hold my local take out menus, organized by ethnic cuisines. Pizza and pasta in the Italian section, burgers and ribs in the American section—you get the idea. I had my fill of honey-do projects when I was married. I'm actually quite handy and have a complete set of tools stored in my rented garage. I have built decks, rewired old electric outlets, fixed the constantly running toilet numerous time, put in new garbage disposals, and even installed a doggy door through drywall, insulation, and ten-gauge aluminum siding. And although I could, I no longer have the desire to be Tim the Tool Man Taylor.

I spend an average of sixty-seven hours a week maintaining my career. I know this number is accurate, because each year I do the math for my accountant. He doesn't always buy in to my large amount of business expenses. Hopefully his skepticism doesn't show up in my returns with the IRS. I spend most days preparing for listing presentations for hopeful home sellers, searching for and showing properties to prospective buyers, and filling out paperwork. I work Mondays, Tuesdays, Thursdays, Fridays, Saturdays, and Sundays. I reserve Wednesday for Kurt. This schedule is purely voluntary. I love what I do and want to be the best I can be. Other Realtors I know put in less time and are just as successful, sometimes more so. I'm not antisocial by any means; in fact, the office has become my extended family and social circle. I'm as close to most of them as anyone can be without sharing the same mother or father. I guess being the only child of Martha and George Banning gave me the independence to enjoy my own company without the need for dozens of friends and acquaintances.

Prescott Realty owns the building where I live and work. They are terrific landlords. The rent is cheap, and they attend to repairs as needed. Mine is a fourteen-hundred-square-foot one-floor apartment with two bedrooms, two baths, and an enormous kitchen, which by now you know gets hardly any use. I use one bedroom as an office. The layout is perfect for me, with one exception. The building is older, built in the sixties, and has a small bathroom. The shower is built into the sloped side of the inside wall. This allows me to wash approximately five feet, six inches of my six-foot, two-inch frame without stooping like a retired stone mason. It's convenient when I'm too lazy to trudge down the back stairs to the real office or when I feel like working in my boxers. My front window has a nice view of the quaint main street shops and maple trees that line our thoroughfare. At certain times of the year, my view is almost Norman Rockwellian. In the spring, budding flowers send their aromas up through my windows, and in the fall, the leaves turn magnificent colors as though I were looking down on spilled cans of earthy paints. Winter is a festival of thousands of tiny white lights, strung by the city just before Thanksgiving and kept there until the first of February.

Hamilton hosts two parades a year, Fourth of July and Labor Day. My apartment view is perfect for enjoying the floats, vintage autos, and marching bands. As these two holidays get nearer, I become very popular with my friends. Fat, balding Mayor Dudley is ever present at the head of each parade, riding in a brand new Cadillac, courtesy of Bowers Cadillac, New and Used.

Stairs lead down from the back door off my kitchen to the alley, where my two cars are garaged. Another set of stairs leads up to the roof. There's really not much up there, and I seldom climb those stairs. But on an occasional starry night I have been known to ascend with my large tumbler of Ketel One to contemplate the universe. Contemplating is always better on the rocks with two olives.

I have a nice patio setup on the roof top that a client gave me. They were moving into a condo and wanted me to have the set to thank me for selling their home quickly for $11,000 over asking. It is rather a nice set. The four swivel chairs are draped in striped material of beige, red, and brown, which match the umbrella that fits through the hole of a five-foot circular table with a Plexiglas top. I rarely put up the umbrella, due to the wind that blows over the roof. Besides, if I want to sit in the shade, I'll stay indoors.

When I began with Prescott Realty ten years ago, fresh off a divorce and with limited funds, the owners made me a great offer for the upstairs flat. A reduced commission split off set the minimum rent. Today, as I am doing quite well, I have no desire to leave my comfortable den for a more conventional dwelling. The commission split is up, and so, unfortunately, is the rent.

James Prescott began his real estate venture in the 1960s as an ambitious young man who carved out a niche as a boutique real estate company. He catered exclusively to high-end clientele who came from his circle of country club friends and their friends. He built a reputation as an honest man in a dubious field. He went above and beyond to serve his clients and soon added the moniker of "exceeding expectations" to his marquee and letterhead. It's still there today. PRESCOTT REALTY ... EXCEEDING EXPECTATIONS. Of course, over the years, and through changing markets, we serve all types and sizes of real estate clients. No longer are we just the agents to the wealthy, with 5000-plus square feet and a million-dollar minimum home to buy or sell.

Mr. Prescott and his wife, Elle, were killed in an RV accident twelve years ago. Having borne no children, and with no surviving Prescotts to be found, the company was given to the agents who had faithfully worked for Prescott over the years. According to his will, all agents who had been at the firm for at least fifteen years were to be given equal shares of the company. This provision was added as the Prescotts got older and began spending time together traveling across the United States in their Winnebago. So the ten-member ownership contingent was the one who not only hired me with no experience in real estate but also provided me with an affordable living arrangement. I later realized that for most real estate brokerages, the only requirement for employment was that you could walk, talk, and breathe. At Prescott, we do believe in providing a superior service, and we are thought of as honest, ethical, and unwavering in providing due diligence. We seek out those potential candidates that exhibit these qualities. Usually we succeed. If we won't, this usually becomes obvious during the first twelve months, and another nametag disappears from the wall directory.

The sound of a phone ringing at home usually sends a jolt up my sphincter, as few people call or even know my home number. This shouldn't bother me, as I'm surrounded by ringing phones all day long.

"Hello, this is Kurt. May I help you?" I said, forgetting that I was at home and off the clock.

"How's the best real estate salesman in all of the county doing?" she purred.

"Well, I was just getting ready for a quiet, laid-back dinner with the hottest police lieutenant in the county. But I have a feeling she's about to blow me off. Better offer?"

"Not a better offer," she said. "Work, sweetie. A last-minute detail I need to finish before morning. Boss's orders. The report needs to be done in time for tomorrow's squad meeting."

"I haven't heard that in a while, but sure, that's okay. Maybe this weekend. Give me a call?"

"I will, and thanks for understanding. That's what I love about you, Kurty. Bye."

Liz and I have had an on-again, off-again relationship for more than six years. Lately, off. We met on a setup, but we were both blind to it. Roger and Janice Portman invited each of us separately to your all-American backyard barbeque. The group was all couples, except Liz and me. That should have been the tipoff, but we didn't make the connection until sometime later. Some cop! I had sold the Portmans their home, and unlike most clients, they had become good friends. I form a bond during the buying/selling period with most of my clients, and we do in fact become friends, but once the transaction has been completed and the obligatory after closing dinner has been eaten, we drift our separate ways. When we bump into each other around town, we say we need to get together, but know we probably won't. We do, in fact, like each other, but not in a social way; it's more business than pleasure. And I like it that way. It is much easier to work for a past client or referral than a "friend."

Roger and I play golf together a couple of times a month during the season. His handicap is higher than mine, but I usually miss a putt or two. It's good for business. Janice met Liz shortly after they moved in to their new home, at a charity bike ride for cancer. After that, they would see each other riding the many trails that branched out from the main parks in Hamilton. They became fast friends.

Sparks flew at the barbeque. Liz and I were so completely enamored with each other that we risked being rude to our hosts. After the introduction, we settled into nonstop talk. We had so much in common. I was drawn to her long, wavy ashen hair and crinkling eyes. And what a smile! It's the kind of smile you see and can't help but smile back, even if she isn't looking at you. I was smitten on the spot.

Our interests ran side by side. We both enjoy the outdoors—golf and bike riding are our two favorites. We both enjoy baseball, although for different teams and different leagues. She favors the want-to-be Chicago Cubs, and my dream team is the Detroit Tigers, a result of my growing up in Michigan. We are both only children. That should have been a clue to the ups and downs to come. We love the Sunday crossword puzzle, red wine, vodka (with or without olives), pepperoni pizza, the beach on Lake Michigan, either coast, and dogs. Her dog, not mine.

Our first official date was the next day for lunch. We picked up right where we had left off the previous evening at Roger and Janice's. If you're lucky enough to meet someone you feel as though you've known your whole life after just a couple of hours, then you understand how Liz and I became inseparable. The short courting period, not really getting to know each other, gave way to many ups and downs in our relationship. We dated, fell in love, moved in together, argued, made up, moved out, and moved on. It didn't take long to realize we wanted to be with each other. So after a cooling period, we dated again and then tried weekends at her place or mine. We loved each other, hurt each other, couldn't wait to see one another, and couldn't stand to be with each other. At some point during the final year of our six together, we decided there wasn't enough energy to keep us going on the rollercoaster and we would just wait it out to see if there was ever going to be a future. That was May 22 of last year. But I'm fine with it, or so I think. We don't need permission to date other people, but as far as I know, she hasn't, and I definitely haven't.

Lieutenant Elizabeth Colburn, the pride of the Hamilton Police Force, headed towards Capitan. She's hard charging, thorough, and decisive. I admire her ethical attitude and her basic life principles, which are work hard, honesty, and the need to do the right thing—always, not most of the time. She believes in herself and has the confidence to succeed without being cocky or bitchy. I think we might be soul mates, but more recently, it feels like a brother-sister act.

As my dinner date had cancelled, I decided to try and catch up with Dex and Robbie at Abby's before they tabbed out.

"Why would anyone need a prenup?" Robbie asked.

"To protect what you're bringing into the marriage," said Dex. "Do you want to end up like our good friend Kurt here? Take a decade to rebuild what you've lost? And for what, spooning and cooing and thanks a lot, see you around? By the way, I'm taking this and this and that and the other."

Dex was looking in my direction. I was beginning to regret my decision to join Dex and Robbie at Abby's.

"No comment," I said. "None of your business, really. A true friend wouldn't bring up bad moments in a guy's life every chance he gets."

"But it's fun, and you're so easy. I just can't turn down an opportunity to razz you a little."

"Okay, you've hit your limit. Let's talk about something else."

"So, Robbie, if you ever decide—or if *she* decides—that this marriage loses it lust, eh, luster, and one of you bails, you're protected," Dex continued. "Whatever you brought to the party leaves the party with you. None of that 'I gave him all I had to offer, and now I'm suffering from emotional abandonment. I feel an 80-20 split should help me get on with my life.' You'll end up living at the Red Roof Inn, wearing the same shirt and pants all week long. Isn't that right, Kurt?"

"Enough. And it was Extend-a-Stay, not Red Roof."

Robbie had announced his engagement to his long time live-in girlfriend, Olivia, just after my ten-year anniversary cake-cutting event at the office earlier in the day. Robert "Robbie" Ortiz was a nice kid and a pretty good Realtor. He had been in real estate for only three years and was making a consistent income. That's the key to success in a commission-based career, consistency.

"Last call. You want a nightcap, Kurt? Robbie? Dexter?" Abby's closes at eleven on weekdays.

"Not for me," said Robbie. "I told Olivia I'd be home an hour ago."

"Here we go. It's starting already. Prenup, my friend, or you won't even get to keep your pants—or the balls in them," Dex said.

"Ignore him, Robbie. He's jealous. He's got nothing waiting for him at home except a video library and cold Chinese in the fridge. Go home and give that pretty bride-to-be a hug from me. See you tomorrow," I said as Robbie stood to leave.

"Yeah, see you tomorrow, kid," Dex said.

"I didn't eat after Liz cancelled on me. How about a late burger at Roma's?"

"Did the fine lieutenant have a better offer?"

"Nope. She's working on a special report for Captain Dougan," I replied.

"What is it with you two anyway, Kurt? I've never seen two people more in love or more in hate. Okay, hate might be a bit strong, but what gives?" Dex said as we walked out the door of Abby's. He had generously picked up the tab for the evening's beverages.

It was only two blocks to Roma's from Abby's. That was one thing I really loved about Hamilton. It was quaint and friendly and navigable. Only thirty-two miles, due west from downtown Chicago, and yet it seemed like the heart of the Midwest. The 127,000 people who lived here, according to the welcome signs at the edges of our fine city, had the best of two worlds. The hustle and excitement of Chicago was only thirty minutes away by train, or up to two hours if you preferred to torture yourself by driving your car on the interstate. You could be anywhere in Hamilton in twenty minutes. However, with the recent explosion in our population growth, it took longer and longer to get from here to there. During the past five years, local politicians had convinced two large, one medium, and five small companies to locate headquarters, manufacturing facilities, and shipping warehouses within Hamilton's confines. You definitely felt the local climate changing, mostly for the good. I certainly wasn't complaining about new families moving into town. Other people from the Chicagoland area also had discovered Hamilton as a wonderful place to raise their families. We were known as a town of great schools and low crime. Our police department's emergency calls consisted mainly of kids smashing mailboxes, drunken fights on weekends, speeders, and DUIs. Sure there were two or three murders a year, and we had our share of youth drug problems, but we were rated as a "Hometown America" four out of the past five years in national publications. All in all, things were good in Hamilton. Mom-and-pop stores thrived alongside national chains. The brick paver streets were full almost every day with shoppers, diners, and bar hoppers. The brick façade storefronts gave our little town an almost New England feel, but with a Midwest smile.

Roma's wasn't very busy, as you might expect at ten o'clock on a Wednesday evening. A table of three, looking as though they might have drunk their dinner much earlier that evening, sat in the far rear corner. Two off-duty police officers were sitting at the counter up front, hot mugs in hand.

"Hey, Kurt," said one of Hamilton's finest, "I saw Liz as I was punching out. You're a lucky man, my friend."

"Just friends, but thanks for your vote. Appreciate it," I replied as Dex and I helped ourselves to a window booth.

"When are people in this town going to realize that Liz and I are just good friends? Does everyone have so much time on their hands that they must follow our lives?"

"Oh, probably when you start to realize it, my naive little nimrod. You don't seem to see what everyone else sees. You're so blind in love, you wouldn't see an elephant with a magnifying glass. You're a high-profile Realtor Kurt. Your picture is on signs all over town and Liz is climbing the ranks of the local police force. Makes for good entertainment, maybe a new reality cable show."

"Not anymore," I said. "That was a long time ago."

"Hi, hons. Something to drink?" asked Brenda, the waitress.

"Vodka" said Dex.

"Make mine a Ketel, two olives. Cheeseburger with American, medium rare, fries, and coleslaw."

"Ditto," said Dex, "but no olives, cranberry. Swiss cheese done well. No slaw."

"Ditto? I put up with smart mouth drunks every day. If that's ditto, then you're twins. Which you're not, thankfully. One Poindexter Bradley is more than enough for Hamilton."

Dex smiled as Brenda turned and headed for the kitchen. Brenda wore her red frizzy hair piled on top of her head, with loose strands falling practically everywhere. She had worked at Abby's for twenty years, starting right out of high school. She could handle the roughest of customers, and enjoyed bantering with the regulars.

We ate in silence, which was amazing considering my dinner companion. I was in a foul mood following the announcement of Robbie and Olivia's upcoming wedding, Dex's questioning of Liz and me, and comments from the peanut gallery when we entered Roma's. Anytime I allowed my mind to wander to Elizabeth Colburn, I found myself rehashing old arguments and conversations. She had to be the perfect woman for me, didn't she? I had already tried marriage and failed. Failure is not something I do very well or want to do again. But shouldn't we proceed on the basis of success as opposed to avoiding situations because of what ifs? Stay at home, be safe, and don't venture from the old comfort zone. Or get out there, see the world, take a chance. The older I get, the more I want to make up for any lost time and folly I may have missed. Not that I want to be juvenile, but I want real experiences, to step out of the box. Daily existence had become routine. I knew where I was going every day, what I would wear, how to find the shortest distance across town on a busy afternoon. There were no surprises in my life. That's what I needed, surprises, but I didn't have a clue how to get any. And that depressed me. I had now gone from golden anniversary boy at the office to a broken dinner date to hanging with Dex and from a foul mood to outright depression. Was this the dreaded midlife crisis I had heard of? Not likely, although I was nearing the correct age to be invited to the party. Was I going to be sitting in this booth a year from now, or five or twenty, with Dex, talking about enlarged prostates, comfortable shoes, and social security checks while staring at the nose hair and bushy eyebrows of one Poindexter Bradley? Oh God! Now I was slipping into self-pity.

"Dex, I'm going home. Been a long day, with the celebrating and all. Too much cake and too late of a dinner."

"You didn't finish your fries," he said.

"You're welcome to them." I slid out of the booth. "See you in the morning." I let a $10 bill float to the top of the table.

"See you, good buddy."

As I passed by the window, I saw Dex finishing my grease-laden fries that had been stuck to the bottom of the wrapper in the basket. I guess sometimes ignorance is bliss. Good ol' Dex. He would sleep just fine tonight, just fine.

I thought of giving Liz a call when I got home but thought better of it. She could read me like an hour-old crime scene, even over the phone. Bad idea. I tried channel surfing, but believe it or not, with my mid-level subscription plan, not one thing on 150 channels. Oh, I could buy stuff to make me look younger and feel more energetic, write down recipes I couldn't pronounce, watch old television shows I had already seen twenty-five years ago that I didn't think were funny then. I could watch the day's replays of college sports teams whose states I couldn't name. Weather was good, but I wasn't planning on traveling to Guam. I could have my problems solved and my soul saved ... for a small contribution. That was Pastor Mike's job on Sundays anyway, and who was I to put him out of a job? Besides, his handicap was a few strokes below mine, and I knew he never missed a putt he could make. Maybe it was time to give Mike a call and arrange our upcoming season's Wednesday golf schedule. If the timing was right, maybe I would bring up Kurt's obsession with the unknown, his lack of direction and rudderless nature. Pastor Mike was surely a man who did not judge but only offered an open ear, a concerned heart, and advice about getting rid of a bad slice. I put him on my mental to-do list.

Friday morning I slept in. My first appointment wasn't until noon. I was meeting with a mid-level manager who was being promoted and relocated to Denver. I had sold Nick and Connie Williams their home just three years prior. Four bedrooms, three baths, a flat-faced Georgian with a finished basement, a pool room, and a three-car side-load garage. Ah, you never forget a house. I think he has two or three kids. I never let relocation become too big a part of my business, because you can't count on it. Plus, the referral fees to the relocation company take a good cut out of your commissions, up to 40 percent in some cases. But I had met a lot of nice families over the years. Most had moved on once again, and the new ones would be coming and going in the future. In the heyday of the boom, Hamilton was a destination city for many relocating families. The average family in Hamilton moved every three and a half years back then. They moved in, moved up, or moved out. It was a beautiful situation for me, and I enjoyed helping families move to our wonderful city. Selling Hamilton on a daily basis is something I do very well.

I made a cup of instant decaf coffee and sat down to read the morning *Tribune*. I don't normally read the paper, but I still pay for an annual subscription. I love professional sports, but I find it boring to read about, except the box scores. I ignore politics and seldom go out to a movie. The business section concerns mostly Wall Street, whereas all my investments are in real estate. I still do the occasional crossword, but I usually forget to check for answers the next day for the ones that stumped me. On Fridays, I read the Real Estate section from front to back. Featured homes, new listings, foreclosures, ways to invest in any market, weekend open houses, current interest rates, and who's doing what. It's my way of keeping my finger on the pulse and find out what my competition is doing.

An article on the lower half of page 3 caught my eye. "MISSING REALTOR FOUND IN TRUNK OF CAR." The article went on to say,

"Sara Donoghue, age 34, failed to return home late last Sunday afternoon. Brad Donoghue, husband of Sara, contacted police to say his wife did not arrive home after holding an open house on Sunday. A call to her brokerage company confirmed that she had not returned to her office as well. Police found her open house signs still in place in the Glenburg subdivision on Chicago's far north side. The home where Mrs. Donoghue was working on Sunday showed no signs of foul play. The property, located at 1214 Mission Hill Court in the upscale Glenburg neighborhood, had been vacant at the time of the open house. Late Monday, police found the Realtor's car, a ten-year-old black Lincoln Town Car, parked inside the garage of the home where she had conducted Sunday's open house. The body of Mrs. Sara Donoghue was found in the trunk. She was identified by her husband. She apparently had been dead for 24 hours. No further details have been released at this time."

Wow! Now that hits close to home. Living in a large metropolitan area, murder is a frequent item on the evening news, but the killing of a fellow Realtor is especially haunting, even if it happened thirty miles away. I was sure it would be a topic of discussion when I got downstairs.

"Kurt, did you see the *Tribune*," Dex asked as I came into the office. Dex sat in the cubicle next to mine. As usual, his feet were propped up on his desk, his sickly white legs peeking between his cuffed pants and his trademark bright Kelly Green socks.

"I did." I put my briefcase on the floor next to my two-drawer file cabinet. "Lousy way to start the day. Did you hear any details?"

"Nope. The police are keeping them out of the paper. We won't hear anything until they catch the prick. They're probably checking out the husband. Family is always the first suspect, they say."

"Kurt, can you please step into my office." It was Bard Holmes, passing by with a fresh cup of coffee in a gallon-size mug.

"Sure, boss. Be right there. Give me just a minute."

Bard Holmes is our managing broker. He was chosen to lead the company after Mr. Prescott left this world in his Winnebago. It was a unanimous selection by the other nine co-owners. His reputation in the community was spotless. He was a member of the Chamber of Commerce, was a past president of the local United Way, coached Little League when his sons were young, and was a member in good standing at St. Paul's

Redeemer Church. His tall, lean frame and brushed-back silver hair gave him a regal yet grandfatherly look. But once you looked into his steel blue eyes, you realized he was all business. His strong leadership was what kept Prescott Realty number one in the market place as long as I'd been around. He was a natural and respected leader.

"What's up Bard," I asked as I entered his office.

"Did you see the *Tribune* this morning?" he asked as he hung up his sharp, light gray pin-striped suit coat. "Close the door."

"I did. A terrible thing. Any details?"

"None that I'm aware of, but I think that this would be an excellent time to address agent safety. We haven't really discussed the topic in a long time, if at all. We take so much for granted, and that leads to carelessness."

"You think Sara Donoghue was targeted because she was a Realtor?" I asked.

"Oh, I don't think so. Probably a case of being in the wrong place at the wrong time. But it would still be a good idea to go over the updated safety tips the board published last spring. At our sales meeting next Tuesday, I'll give you time to make a presentation to all our agents."

"Ah, but what, um … "

"Good. You're on the docket from nine-thirty to ten. Now go out there and sell something, would you?" he said, smiling.

"*Thanks*, boss," I said as I left his office. He didn't hear my intended sarcasm; he was already on the phone with the next piece of that morning's business.

"Hey, Kurt, any plans for the weekend?" Molly purred as she batted her eyes at me.

I was walking past Molly Peterson's desk on my way for a Styrofoam cup of real coffee from the kitchenette. She is our office administrator and the first person to represent Prescott Realty when someone enters the office from Main Street. I give her a lot of credit. She is in her late twenties and has to deal with all of the quirky personalities in the office. Although half a dozen of us bring the number down, the average age at Prescott Realty is 51 years old. Molly is efficient and pleasant and pretty in her own way. She handles our work load without complaint. At least to our faces. Her youth is good for the office. Her hairdos and wardrobe would never be confused with the conservative look of the women I work with. I call it the edgy business look.

"Only if it involves you."

"Oh, sure. You say that every Friday."

"Weekends are just like any other day of the week for me, Molly. I got to eat; therefore, I got to work. By the way, I have a little project for you to put together for me for next Tuesday's meeting. Have time?"

Molly had begun working at Prescott Realty while in high school as a weekend phone girl. College wasn't her thing, so upon graduating high school, she joined the office as a full-time receptionist. She was promoted to office administrator a little over three years ago and reports directly to Mr. Holms.

"For you, sure," she said as I left to get the file for my noon listing presentation with Mr. and Mrs. Nick Williams. Another fly-by corporate relocation relationship. Ah, they all leave so soon.

CHAPTER 4

"You really have done some nice things with your home," I said to Nick and Connie Williams. *Why didn't you replace that godawful brown carpet in the family room and repaint the purple hall bath?* The Williams had bought their home at 4147 Spring Garden Way three years ago at a bargain price of $345,000, a 10 percent plus discount, which was unheard of in that market. Thanks to the expertise of their knowledgeable and confident Realtor and a little inside information, we successfully negotiated a contract that made the Williams very happy. The home had been listed for $389,000 and was being sold by the original owners. The Thompsons were downsizing and wanted out of the cold weather. They had found their dream home outside Tempe, Arizona, and were very, *very* motivated to sell and get on with their lives. I had discovered the motivation during a very innocent conversation with the Thompsons, who had been at home when I arrived before the Williams. They had been chatty.

"Such a beautiful home," I had mentioned to Mr. and Mrs. Thompson as I waited for my clients to arrive. "I can image it's difficult to leave here, with all the memories you've made in this lovely home."

As Mrs. Thompson was nodding and agreeing with me, moisture pooling at the corners of her eyes, Mr. Thompson said, "Are you kidding me? I don't want to spend another winter shoveling the damn snow and freezing my ass off. This is the last one! We're moving to Arizona. Fact is, we already bought a home just outside of Tempe. You know, it's a dry heat."

Ah, the knowledge you get when you keep your mouth shut. I instruct all my sellers that if you must be home during a showing, which I prefer they don't, *do not* engage in conversation with anyone who may end up on the other side of the bargaining table. We made an insultingly low offer the next day, came up to a bargain purchase price after two volleys, and six hours later the Williams were the proud new owners of a terrific home and Mr. Thompson was mentally packing his U-Haul. That was three years ago.

"Thank you, Kurt," Connie said. "We really love it here and hate to move, but you know how the corporate world operates?" Oh, yes I do, thankfully. "Nick came home from work last Friday and said the company was considering promoting him and moving us to Denver. They never really asked if we would consider moving. It was more like, 'You should be thanking us for this enormous career opportunity.'"

New granite countertops in the kitchen. I thought it looked like St. Cecilia. Same oak cabinets but with all new brushed nickel hardware, very nice. New stainless steel appliances, Kitchen Aid, good, but not the top of the line.

"We took out that awful deck last summer," Connie continued as she drew open the vertical blinds, pointing outside. "We added this paver patio," she added with a sweep of her hand. "Nick did it himself over two weekends, didn't you, honey?" Connie smiled at Nick. "The hard scape is new. I planted those rose bushes and we added …"

The Williams had relocated from St. Petersburg, Florida, in the spring, three years prior. They and their children had come to house hunt right after the first of the year. I remembered the weekend vividly. Cold, with a wind chill in the single digits, eight inches of snow on the ground, with a forecast for more during the week. How do I remember? Isn't that the normal course of daily forecasts in January for the Chicagoland area? Yes. But the Williams visit was special. Ryan and Bethany, the cute, undisciplined children of Connie and Nick, loved the snow. So much that they insisted on bringing hard packed snowballs into my car after each showing of a home and stacking them in the back pockets of the front seats. Melting snow and genuine imitation leather do not go well together. Connie slipped on an icy spot in the sidewalk while leaving one of the homes we viewed. She caught herself but wrenched her back terribly. She spent the rest of the week getting in and out of my car looking like Herman Munster.

"… and we finished the basement since we bought the home. Nick's man cave." She gave an exaggerated chuckle. The basement really had been nicely and professionally renovated. This was not a Nick weekend project. Dry walled ceiling with plenty of pot lights gave the basement a natural glow. A built-in, dark oak bar with brass foot rails and matching oak stools was at the far north end of the basement. Lighting had been installed in the back bar, setting the mood for drinking. It shone through the glass front upper cabinets, which held a variety of highball glasses. Wine flutes hung upside down by their stems above the bar in slide racks, looking a bit dusty. Not much call for chardonnay in the Williams Tavern. Several neon lights displayed the names of half a dozen international beers.

"And over here," Connie said, ushering me away from the bar, "is where we curl up and watch family movies on weekends. I followed her around the corner from the bar to the theater area. It wasn't a true theater room but a useable setup nonetheless. A 70" screen was painted on the wall, with an overhead projector suspended from the ceiling. Expensive Bose speakers hung from the surround sound brackets at the four corners of the room, and a large subwoofer sat in the background. In the corner was the rack with a top of the line tuner and Blu-ray DVD player. At the opposite end of the basement was a standard seven-foot billiard table with green felt on the slate and rails, along with leather net pockets. Above it was a new, made-to-look-old, stained glass light with red and orange panels held in place by tarnished–faux gold solder. The layout was okay, but you could tell that the required four-foot perimeter around the table was a bit short because of the black and blue markings on the wall from tight cue shots.

"I can see a lot of good times in this basement," I said. "Football games, New Year's Eve parties, birthdays. Great fun. This will be an excellent selling point for your home." Connie was beaming, and Nick was quietly staring at the walls with his hands in his pockets. It's always easy to spot the decision maker. A key to being a successful Realtor is to determine the decision maker as soon as possible. Otherwise, you end up wasting a lot of time.

We continued the tour and Connie pointed out with pride improvements they had made to the home since making the purchase three years ago.

"So what do you think the market will bring us on our house Kurt?"

Depends if you want to paint the bathroom and replace the carpet, I thought.

"Well, we're entering the best five months of the year to sell, and the last four homes to sell in the neighborhood went in less than forty days for a reasonable price. The economy is sputtering a little, but interest rates are relatively low and your home is in a very desirable neighborhood, with great schools, and the inventory is pretty well balanced for this time of year. You certainly will be attractive to potential buyers. Plus, you made a very smart buy three years ago," I said, mentally patting myself on the back.

Connie and Nick were both staring at me as if I had just caught them coming out of the lake skinny dipping. Big eyed, quirky little smiles, waiting for what's next. I heard myself blabbing away and decided it was time to sit down.

"Let's sit down and I'll show you where your current competition is priced and where the market seems to be headed. Before I leave, I'll give you Fontana Welsh's number. She is a staging expert who will come over this week and give you ideas on furniture placement, de-cluttering tricks, and paint suggestions for areas that need touchups. I'll also give you a list of suggestions to get your home ready for the market. Basing your price on conditions is the key. The inventory is building, and we want to make sure we are the best-priced home in the range."

"Well now, Kurt, we're not just going to give our home away."

"Nick, when I say the best-priced home, I'm not saying cheapest. I mean the one that offers the best value. You can't compete with a home that's five hundred square feet. larger than you are, but we have the advantage with your finished basement and new landscaping. I call it doing the Ts. I'm giving you value for what you have and subtracting value for what your competition has that you don't. For example, the Martins' home around the corner, on Euclid, is similar to yours in many ways, but they have a three-car garage. So if everything else were exactly the same, we would have to compensate for the inequity. Does that make sense?"

Nick and Connie were nodding slowly, but they didn't buy in to the theory until I gave them a number. Every seller wants the number up front. I get it, but you have to build the story. You wouldn't go to a two-hour movie and want to see the last ten minutes first!

I give this little speech two to three times a week. I try to make it fresh so it doesn't sound rote. My clients can make all the difference in the world with their enthusiasm, or lack thereof. Everyone thinks his or her home is special. Sometimes that's true. Usually, it's just another three-thousand-square-foot house with four bedrooms, two and a half baths (not purple), full unfinished basement, and an attached two-car garage. Located on a charming, kid-friendly street in middle America, just blocks from everything. Even with my Super Duper Kurt Banning Marketing Plan to Get Your Home Sold, it's often difficult to make an ordinary property stand out. But I am ever the optimist; hence my successful career as a Realtor.

One time, I'd like to ring the doorbell and have Beer Belly Bob open the door, wearing a chili stained tee shirt, sporting a five-day beard, and say to me, "Hi ya, Kurt, old buddy. Good to see you. We've lived hard in this house since you sold it to us. It's worn out and used up. Kind of gone to crap, and I know it's a shit box, but what do you think we can sell her for? As is, of course!" Now that would be refreshing.

To be a successful Realtor, you need to be a counselor of sorts. You have to exude confidence without being cocky. You need to continually improve your knowledge base regarding housing trends, mortgage products, and tax consequences of home sales. The ability to stay on top of what the home buying consumer wants and expects is necessary to get your clients' homes ready for the market. Mr. and Mrs. Seller count on you to walk them through the process and take care of the details. Explain the contracts, cover their liability through disclosures, resolve home inspection issues, and have a stable of related professionals to assist in getting the job done. But most important is sincerity. You can't fake it in this business. You really truly must care. Greed and selfishness are two characteristics that will doom your career as a real estate agent. I never worry about the commission. If you listen to people's needs and then provide for those needs, the money will come and come and come. Referrals are the lifeblood of a Realtor, and it helps if you like your client. And I liked the Williams. There are more than 53,000 homes in Hamilton, and at that moment, the only home I cared about was the one with the god-awful brown carpet and purple bathroom. I made my follow-up appointment with the Williams for the following Tuesday and headed to the door.

I was thinking about my afternoon appointment as I backed out of the driveway at 4127 Spring Garden Way. I would spend my afternoon chauffeuring Anna Getz around town. I say chauffeuring, because Anna is a career looker. I've been showing her homes on and off for the past eight months. This is death to a Realtor, but in Anna's case, I don't really mind. She is a break from the mundane, a pleasure to be around and a knockout! Would I be wasting my time if she were a hag? Of course not, because I care.

Anna was in her late thirties, I'm guessing, and a lifelong renter. She had a great credit score, over eight hundred, and cash in the bank. You would think she would be a Realtor's dream. Well, she would be if I could just get her to commit. She had what I call the 'shoe store syndrome.' I named it after a condition my ex-wife had. You walk into a shoe store and find a great pair of shoes. The style, price, and comfort are all there. The salesman is just about to ring up the purchase and she says, "I'll be back." The buyer must see every home available, just in case there is a better one to purchase. And if we find the perfect home to purchase, we need to wait in case another absolutely perfect home comes on the market tomorrow.

Whenever I found the perfect home for Anna, she'd be thinking there might be a better home out there. "Let's keep looking," she'd say. "I'd like to see what else might be out there." And off we'd go, skipping hand in hand.

Anna was fun to be around and had a great smile. She has traveled to four continents and was what my Mother would call a free spirit. So when she called, if I had the time or needed a diversion, we spent a couple of hours on an afternoon shopping for homes. The calm and peace for me was equivalent to the silence you experience when someone turns off a car alarm. In a way, I hoped Anna and I never found the perfect home.

I have had all types of buyers. And over the years, I've grouped them into my own set of Kurt categories.

First-Time Homebuyer (No Kids): The process of finding their first home excites them. They are nervous because they are outside their comfort zone and my job is to make it fun and enjoyable. They revitalize me and renew my faith in my career choice. There is seldom a happier closing than that of a first-time homebuyer. They love every home we walk into and spend their time mentally placing their furniture. Usually they are in the first five years of their marriage and are still into each other without thoughts of a nursery. A side note here. It is dangerous to work with people who are engaged. The stress of home shopping can end the relationship. The wedding is off and the sale goes into the dumper. I tend to refer non-married couples to Dex.

First-Time Homebuyer (with Babies): These folks are *all* about the kids. The child is still breastfeeding and they are concerned about what high school he or she will attend, not understanding that they will likely be moving again in five years when they outgrow the home. They are often concerned that the baby's bedroom or closet is not big enough. Have you seen the size of infant clothes? Not all that big. These people will be moving before the next President of the United States will be elected, but baby has to have a suite with his own bathroom. That's okay, though. My job is to serve and provide choices, which I'm happy to do.

Engineers, Accountants, and Scientists: This is the most challenging group for me. It's all about the numbers. Cost per square foot, R rating of the insulation in the attic, average monthly utilities (broken out by winter months and summer months), BTUs of the furnace. Stats, numbers, and equations. Flow charts, graphs, and multipliers are deciding factors. Forget that the commuter bus stops at the next corner or that the neighborhood has organized play dates for all ages of children. It doesn't matter that the elementary school is walking distance or that the kitchen has recently been remodeled. It's all about the numbers. They end up with analysis paralysis and often take as long to make a decision as Anna Getz, but without the visual benefits for me.

Move-Up Buyer: These people realize the need for more space. Sounds easy enough, but to buy, we need to sell their current home. The home with a basement that you can't walk through because of all the plunder—a decorated Christmas tree standing in the corner and cardboard boxes from the Stone Age. A family room with more toys and games than Toys "R" Us, and a garage filled with bicycles, garden paraphernalia, six garbage containers, sleds, basketballs, tools, and flowerpots but no cars. Here's the amazing thing. In six months when I stop by to see the family in their new, more spacious home, it will look just like the tiny, cramped old home. These keep me in business.

The Downsizer: This is usually a couple, empty nesters, or newly retired. Sometimes it's a widow or widower headed to a beautiful condo or townhome or assisted living. They have spent most of their adult life in their current home. Lots of family memories, raising children, graduations, birthdays, anniversaries, weddings, and receptions in the backyard. There's a huge overgrown oak tree in the back that was planted as a sapling, a tire swing still hanging by a worn rope. Mostly we are looking for small bungalows or townhomes, preferably ranches that are easier for them to maintain. Often, the lawn is mowed and the snow is shoveled for you in these communities. Even though the objective is to downsize, the objection is that it's too small, not enough space. The fact is that the size is just right; it's just not large enough to hold the memories. These are the sweetest people in the world, everyone's grandpa and grandma.

Finally, the best category of all, the Transferee: This family has got to move and quickly. 'New job starts in a month' is music to my ears. Find a house, make an offer, move in, register the kids for school, make it a home, and remember your wonderful Realtor. I'm being transferred, I need to get the house on the market, I need a quick sale, thanks for being my Realtor. Great job. Well done, Kurt. The referrals from a transferee are a beautiful thing. I have past clients who I worked with when I first got into real estate who to this day to send me referrals of fellow employees who are moving either into or out of the area. Thank you, corporate America! This last group makes working with the Annas of the world financially possible.

Anna was on time, as always, leaning against the front driver's fender of her gleaming red two-seater Miata as I pulled into the lot next to Prescott Realty. She beamed her smile and held out two overpriced lattes, one for her and one for me, as I got out of my car. Her sunglasses were resting on top of a mound of short, curly blond hair. Her tight black jeans were tucked into knee-high leather boots, and she wore an old faded army jacket that used to belong to her brother. His name was still stitched over the right breast pocket—GETZ. She always surprised me with her ensemble.

"Oh, Kurt," she said, handing me the fancy cup of coffee as I approached her in the parking lot. "I'm so glad you had time for me this afternoon. I just love the little Cape Cod you sent to my email. I can't wait to see it in person. Thanks for taking the time. Maybe this is the one."

"Just could be, Anna." I couldn't stop smiling. "But if it's not, we'll keep on looking." I would have liked to have asked her out, but I feared it might end our current relationship. And I really enjoyed our current relationship. A shrink might have said that Liz was the real reason for not pursuing Anna. It didn't matter. Anna was here and so was I, and we were off to do some shopping.

CHAPTER 5

Tuesday Morning I was feeling a small case of nerves. I knew it was the presentation Bard had asked me to give that morning. I've given hundreds of presentations in my life. From Mr. and Mrs. Seller at their kitchen table to more than two hundred people at charity events. I've been told that I have a good stage presence, and I am often asked to host benefit auctions for local fundraisers. And it must be true; who else could coax $200 out of a slightly inebriated crowd for an ugly glass vase, hand blown in a remote village in New Mexico? It's a gift. And it's not as if I hadn't spoken at Prescott Realty. I still do, and on a somewhat regular basis, but that morning I was on edge. I think small nerves are necessary for a good performance, but these were slightly larger than normal nerves, so I was set to kill that morning.

It was awfully early for the phone to ring.

"Hello."

"Hi, Kurt. I'm headed into the office and needed to hear your voice before I started the day."

"Who is this?"

"Funny guy. This is Lieutenant Colburn, and you're under arrest."

"Again? I thought I had been released after a weekend of good behavior."

"I just wanted to tell you how much I enjoyed our dinner Saturday evening, and breakfast Sunday morning. The *Tribune* crossword puzzle was a nice touch too."

Liz and I had rescheduled our missed dinner date from last week and had made reservations for Saturday evening at LaToya, a French restaurant on the edge of Hamilton. It is located in a strip shopping center, and the atmosphere matches the mundane locale, but the food is awesome.

"Seemed just like old times, didn't it?" I asked. "Maybe next weekend we could—"

"Let's just enjoy the memory of last weekend and leave it at that."

"Sure, I had a good time too," I said, trying to sound upbeat. "Any news about Sara Donoghue, the Realtor who was found in her trunk last week?" I asked, changing the subject.

"Nothing much more than what was in the paper. Okay, sweetie. I'm at the station. Have a great day and knock 'em dead with your presentation."

"Thanks."

What a confusing relationship this was. She liked me enough to call before her day starts but not enough to commit to a second weekend date. She wants me but doesn't need me. We're on, we're off. Maybe Dex was right. Time for ol' Kurt to move on. There are plenty of attractive single women in Hamilton. You would think a guy who can raise $200 for ugly vases could find a catch of his own. But who am I kidding? I was crazy about Liz, and unfortunately, she knew it. I had turned into a romantic puffed pastry after years of reading novels about hard-living, thick-skinned washed-up detectives with hearts of Play-Doh. The soft stuff in the can, before it dries out due to too much of life's air.

Getting dressed for me is easy. I like blacks and grays and whites. Slacks and a button-down oxford cloth shirt are my favorite. Slacks and turtlenecks in the winter and slacks and short-sleeve golf shirts on Wednesdays. Simple is best. I once heard a story about Albert Einstein. Supposedly, he owned seven gray suits, all exactly the same. His theory was not to spend any time, energy, or thought when it came to dressing each day. I don't know if it's true, but it makes sense to me.

That day, however, I went with a muted blue tweed sports coat, a thin red striped power tie over a white button-down oxford cotton shirt, and my favorite charcoal grey slacks. I think of myself as a sharp dresser without being a prima donna. I love my loafers, five pairs in black, black with tassels, shiny black, light brown, dark brown. Easy off, easy on. The uniform was a nice change from my previous life in corporate America more than a decade earlier. Wearing suits every day made it hard to shed the crisp look for something more casual, favored by many of my contemporaries. Even my jeans have a creased ironed into them.

My first job right out of college was with a Fortune 500 manufacturing company, as a sales representative. In addition to wearing a suit every day, I wore wingtip shoes. I had two pairs, identical, one black and one brown.

Every morning while tying those shoes, I felt like my dad. I was twenty-two years old at the time, much too young for wingtips.

Today I wanted to look a little more professional in front of my fellow agents.

"Everyone take a seat please. Let's get started," Bard said from the front of the conference room.

The large conference room was located in the back of the office building. We had three smaller conference rooms up front, with full glass windows looking out onto Main Street. We used these when meeting with potential clients or small groups of four or five people. The large conference room in the back was windowless, with sterile white walls flooded with artificial light. It had a lectern at the front, a flip chart, and a pull-down screen for when we used the monitor. And of course, one large Bunn coffeemaker with all the accessories—fake creamer, fake sugar, plastic spoons, and foam cups. We sat in rows on padded folding chairs, as if we were at a school assembly. Fifty-six agents presently made up Prescott Realty, including our broker, Bard. A few new agents would join from time to time. Some made it; most didn't because of the inconsistent cash flow. It is very difficult to live month to month on commission. Some months were great, even outstanding. Other months were as dry as desert air. These were the months you went through your jackets, coats, and slacks hoping to find a $20 bill you might have forgotten there.

Our office, like most real estate companies, was primarily made up of women. Of the fifty-six full time Realtors, forty-four were women. Our age range was wide. Jane Stark, who was near seventy, but wouldn't say on which side, was quiet, almost shy. I was amazed at how she found success in a people business like real estate when it was difficult to drag more than a dozen words out of her at a time. The youngster was Robbie Ortiz, who was twenty-five. Robbie had majored in business at college with an emphasis on investing and financial planning. His goal was to be a Wall Street type, but along the way he discovered real estate. He took additional classes, got his license, and became a Realtor. He started with a large franchise firm but found it didn't provide the training or the right environment he needed to get off to a good start. He joined Prescott Realty two and a half years ago and was building a strong network of young first-time home buyers. And now he was about to get married. Lust!

Maureen O'Brien had seniority in the office and was one of the ten co-owner contingent. She had entered the field one year after her husband died at the early age of thirty-eight of a heart attack. She started part time while raising a family of four. She had a natural knack for the industry and was soon one of Prescott's top producers. Her insight and knowledge are unmatched. Maureen came off as unapproachable to those who were new, but deep inside, she was a wealth of knowledge that she gladly shared. However, she was no nonsense.

The Tuesday meeting started as it had every other Tuesday. Current sales figures for the company, year-to-date numbers versus last year, some individual sales recognitions, the state of the economy, and a couple of policy notices, such as a reminder about not using the company postage machine for personal mail, last one out needs to make sure the door is locked, all very routine.

"And now I would like to ask Kurt to come up front to discuss agent safety," Bard Holmes said. "The tragedy that occurred in Glenburg last week is a good reminder that we should always be aware of our surroundings and who we are dealing with, not just as Realtors but as human beings."

"Thanks, Bard." I rose and walked to the front. "It certainly was a shock to read about Sara Donoghue, the Realtor found in her car several days ago after doing an open house. As a Realtor, I feel as though we rarely think about our safety, especially in a town like Hamilton. We take our surroundings for granted because we have all become comfortable in how we run our businesses. But our safety is something we can always work on. I have prepared a list summarizing the bullet points on the board, which Molly is handing out to you now."

After shuffling some papers, I continued, "These are in no particular order. I'll go over each one briefly. If you have questions or comments, stop me."

I could tell by the sprawled legs and chair slouching that this was not going to be any revelation to anyone; all they really wanted to do was finish up and get out. On to phone calls and market reports. Some had client appointments, I was sure, and yet others would take the rest of the day off after checking their mail and emails.

"Okay, first," I began, "when meeting a potential client for the first time, it's a good idea to have them meet you here at the office. It is the safest and most professional beginning to your relationship. And before you take them out to show homes, have Molly make a copy of their driver's license. If they ask why, tell them it's company policy. You should know who you're working with. Second, before you leave the office, tell someone where you are going and, if possible, leave your itinerary of showings with that person. Also, it's not a bad idea to preset your cell phone to call a specific number with one push of the talk button. Never ride with a client unless you know them. Suggest that they follow you if they are persistent about driving."

Yawn.

As I stood there speaking about the best and right way to meet potential clients and conduct business, I couldn't help thinking that I never followed these rules myself. How many times had I received a call at the office from someone who had driven by one of my listings and called my number from the sign rider to say they would like to see the home? Suddenly, I became a Pop-Up Realtor. 'Sure, I can be there in thirty minutes.' Up I popped and off to the home I would go. I might be meeting the newest serial killer of the twenty-first century, but we're all too anxious to get that home sold, or at the very least to grab onto a new potential buyer.

"When actually showing homes," I continued, "let the client enter the home first after unlocking the door. Same goes for each room you enter. You should never let the person be behind you or blocking an exit way. If you're uncomfortable, let the client view the basement by themselves. This is particularly important if you are showing a property to a single man you have just met that day."

Blah blah blah. I'm pretty sure most in the room zoned out. But not Dex, my pal. He was sitting in the front row, staring at me so intently. He looked as though I were about to reveal the mystery of the universe.

"Now, in terms of holding open houses, there are a few simple rules to follow. First, never park your car in the driveway. You do not want your car blocked in. Again, preset your cell phone to dial with one touch of the button. If the home you are sitting has a rear entrance, a sliding glass door, a walkout basement, or whatever, unlock it when you get to the home. This will give you an escape exit should you need one. Never walk ahead of the guest, always follow them into a room first, and do not go to the basement with them. Allow them to view this part of the home alone. If you ever feel uncomfortable, tell the guest you are just locking up and escort them to the front door. And finally, if at all possible, do not hold open houses in vacant properties. It is better to know that the homeowner will be returning at some time, in case you do find yourself in an uncomfortable situation. Introduce yourself to the neighbors while setting up your open house signs. Let them know you are holding a public open house, from this time to this time. Invite them to stop by. This is also a great technique to get to know them, add them to your sphere mailing list, and list their home when they are ready to sell, whether next month or in five years."

Conducting open houses in our market was not a main tool for selling homes; more importantly, it was an effective way to prospect for new customers and convert them into clients. Roughly speaking, according to national statistics, only 4 percent of homes sell during an open house. The real intent is to satisfy your seller that you're working hard for them, because 90 percent of sellers are sure that their home will sell on a Sunday afternoon.

"Keep your cars at least half full of gas at all times. Make sure you have a flashlight somewhere inside your car. Make sure to have a phone charger in your car. Keep your pearl handled revolver locked in the glove compartment!"

Nothing. Jeannie is filing her nails. Craig is texting or playing Angry Birds on his cell phone. Jonathon has folded his handout into an F-15 replica. Several others are making their to-do lists. Bob is pouring himself another cup of tepid coffee. The few who were listening gave little snickers. And Dex was about to raise his hand with a question.

"Are there any questions?" Bard asked from the side of the room as I finished. He wasn't going to wait for any hands to shoot into the air. "Good stuff, Kurt. Thank you." Uncoordinated sympathy applause followed, sounding like rain that hadn't decided whether to pour or sprinkle hitting a tin roof. "Now, go out there and sell some homes today."

This was how Bard finished each meeting and in fact, most conversations.

"Kurt Banning, you have a call on line one," came Molly's voice over the paging system as we were breaking up the meeting. "Kurt, line one."

I walked back to my desk and picked up the phone. "Hello, this is Kurt. May I help you?"

"Kurt, it's me," Liz said in a heavy and serious voice. "They just found another Realtor."

"Who's they, and where did they find her—if it is a her?" I asked, my mind reeling.

"Wilmington, PD, and in Wilmington. And yes, it was a female."

"Wilmington!" I shouted. Wilmington is adjacent to Hamilton. The two cities share a common boundary. Wilmington's east border is Hamilton's west border.

"Who was she? Where was she found? When did it happen?" I rattled off.

"I don't have a lot of details at this point. It appears to be another open house murder."

Apparently we now had a name for these two killings.

"The Realtor was doing an open house on Sunday, according to the owner. When the owner got back home, she was gone and everything looked normal. Then, this morning, Mrs. Stuart, the owner, went down into the basement to look for some old photographs and smelled an odor. It was coming from the sump pump closet. When she opened the door, there was her Realtor. She immediately called the Wilmington Police Department."

"Oh my God! What else?"

"I don't have any more details. It just came across the wire about half an hour ago. We're meeting with a law enforcement team from Wilmington this afternoon. Because we're neighboring communities, Hamilton police are being brought in to discuss the situation."

"Let me know what you find out," I asked. I was hoping to get a little more information than what the local news reporters would receive by way of an official statement.

"Whatever I can, you know I will. Gotta go, call you later."

I sat at my desk, numb, still holding the phone to my ear. A murder this close, in geography and profession, was unnerving. I felt oddly excited and nausea at the same time.

My amateur detective brain started asking questions. Were the two murders connected, or was it a coincidence? Was the killer targeting Realtors? That seemed possible, but the two towns were easily thirty-five miles apart. Was this a killer who had something against Realtors or women or both? I like puzzles. More specifically, I like solving puzzles. However, this was more than I was used to, outside my knowledge base.

I needed some fresh air. Inside my cubicle it was getting stuffy and hard to take a full breath. I packed my brief case and was walking out the front when Dex came around the corner. "Hey, nice job this morning, you really … what's the matter? You look like the boss just slashed your commissions in half."

I wasn't sure what to say, or how much to say. "Bad eggs this morning. I'm going to take a stroll around the block and enjoy some sun."

"Want some company?"

"No thanks, Dex. I'd hate to spew on your new loafers." I gave a halfhearted smile and pushed open the front door to Prescott Realty.

The sun warmed my cheeks and made me feel as if I had a low-grade fever. It felt good in contrast to the chill that filled the rest of my body. I was clammy. I was anxious to talk with Liz when her afternoon meeting was through. I knew she couldn't tell me confidential information, but at least I might get a chance at the unofficial version of what was going on. In the meantime, I had a couple of hours to kill.

I really do enjoy living in Hamilton. The paver streets were lined with crimson maples that burned bright red in the fall and in their winter nakedness held thousands of Christmas lights, strung together. The city's utility trucks had just removed the holiday lights and ornaments from light poles, awnings, and street signs not more than six weeks ago. The fifty-year-old trees, our guardians of Main Street, had the beginnings of buds sprouting from the otherwise dead looking branches.

The bookstore was owned and operated by the Olsen family and had been for three generations. The McGuires operated the hardware store, and Bud and Besty Pruitt ran BB's Diner, which was open for breakfast and lunch only. In between these ageless establishments were the big boys. You could buy jeans and shirts at the Gap or grab a coffee at Starbucks. For the latest tech needs you could shop at the new Apple Store. Personally, I would never buy a phone that is smarter than I am. I have enough trouble operating the tech equipment at Prescott. If it weren't for Molly, I would probably be considered a dinosaur in the real estate world. It's all going high tech, and my learning curve is slow and steep, by choice. Paper jam, yes. Ink cartridges, maybe. JPEG a photo for the company web site, *no*.

Hamilton was anything but a sleepy little town, but somehow the city leaders had been able to keep that feeling alive while surging into the twenty-first century. The entire town was wireless, one of the high schools had won a Grammy for its music program, and three past graduates were playing in the major leagues, two in football and one in baseball. We had the distinct pleasure of having a state-of-the-art 911 call center that contributed to the quality of life for the entire county. Our jail facilities were bright and shiny and new. Of the seventeen pristine cells, only number one got much use. On a busy Friday or Saturday evening, or on St. Patrick's Day, it might hold three to five bleary-eyed drunks.

"Best Place to Raise a Family," "Top Schools in the Midwest," and "Lowest Crime Rate in Award Winning City" were all common headlines in regional publications when it came to extolling the virtues of Hamilton. Well, time would tell about this last one. I was itching to get details from Liz. I decided to go back to my apartment and wait for her call.

CHAPTER 6

The victim was Barbara Miller, forty-six years old, single mother of Brian, a freshman at college in down-state Illinois. Barbara had gone into real estate fifteen years earlier when her then husband, Frank, had needed the attentions of a petite coworker more than the strength of an eight-year marriage. He worked for an accounting firm where he was a midlevel manager. Apparently he had been counting more than beans. He left home on a cold but sunny fall day, never to return to Barbara and Brian. Lust lost, love loses.

After sadness, anger, and depression, Barbara had gotten herself together and looked for a career. She had been a receptionist at the accounting firm where Frank worked. The flirtation turned to romance, which led to an engagement and finally a marriage. It seems accounting is not as boring as one might think. Barbara continued to work until the ninth month of her pregnancy with Brian. For almost five years, raising her son and running an efficient household had become her career. The pay was lousy—actually, there wasn't any pay—but it was a loving marriage complete with a handsome and adoring husband and a healthy and energetic child folded into a lovely home in the suburbs.

Life in the post-Frank days had been difficult at best. Brian was too young to understand what happened to Daddy. Her friends, mostly married, had been there for her in the beginning, but gradually they fell away, two by two. Barbara found out after six days of crying that Frank had stopped by the bank as he skipped out of town. He wasn't a total monster; he had left a balance in their joint account of exactly $1022.56. The rest of the money, more than $25,000, had apparently left for the Bahamas with Frank and his young coworker. Five years ago, Barbara learned that Frank was broke, alone, and bartending in a touristy locale near Paradise Island.

After the divorce, real estate made sense. Flexible hours allowed

Barbara to take Brian to school and be there for him with snack in hand in the afternoons. Real estate also gave her the ability to earn a good income in the years plentiful with sellers and buyers.

Barbara was slightly overweight but with a frame that could easily conceal an extra twenty pounds. She still wore her mousy light brown hair in the style of the previous decade. She was the joy of her office. Barbara always had a smile and good things to say about clients and other agents alike. Her cackle of a laugh was very infectious, you knew when she was in the building, and her eyes sparkled with eternal optimism. She was everyone's friend. Now that Brian had gone off to attend college, she volunteered what free time she had to Wayside Memorial Hospital, as a greeter. Barbara never remarried.

Despite Brian's childhood illnesses, the death of her parents, which gave her a small inheritance, and an early onset of menopause, Barbara had persevered to carve out a nice slice of the real estate market for herself and was considered a top producer in the Wilmington area. She loved her clients, each and every one of them, God bless her. And they reciprocated by sending her all the referral business she could handle. Her picture was frequently in the real estate section of the newspaper. Her marketing also included the use of bus stop benches. In her smiling photo, her albino beagle named Sparky always accompanied her. The tag line under their pictures on her business card said, "Sparky speaks … and I listen."

Mrs. Ellen Stuart was the owner of the home at 113 Tesla Drive in Wilmington, Barbara's last open house. Mrs. Stuart had been arguing with her mortgage company for six months about her delinquency. Charles, her husband of thirty-two years, had passed away the year before, two days before the Fourth of July. It wasn't totally unexpected, as Charles had been diagnosed with liver cancer earlier in the year. The Stuarts had sought any and all treatments possible, running up huge amounts of medical debt, above and beyond what their insurance covered. In hindsight it was foolish, but they had remortgaged their home to take out the cash equity to help with the mounting bills. What little life insurance Mrs. Stuart received after Charles' passing was quickly used up. Now she had fallen behind on her mortgage and had been unable to keep current. As a last effort, before the bank foreclosed, Ellen Stuart had listed her home with Barbara Miller, a local Wilmington Realtor, in hopes of getting out from under her debt.

The mortgage company was sympathetic, of course, but "there's nothing we can do, ma'am."

Mrs. Stuart went to her basement on Monday morning to get the original documents she and Mr. Stuart had signed with the mortgage company. An odor was coming from somewhere in the basement. Mrs. Stuart followed her nose to the far end of the unfinished portion of the basement where the sump pump and water meter were housed, in a small closet. When she opened the door, she found Barbara Miller sitting on a small wooden children's play chair that had belonged to Ellen's daughter decades ago. She was puffy and grayish, and the smell was awful. Her hands had been tied behind her. Her purple tunic top with a mandarin collar had been unbuttoned to the waist, and LYER had been written on her chest just above the lace of her bra, in pink taffeta, the same color that was on her bluish gray lips. She and Sparky both smiled up from the two business cards covering her eyes. "Sparky speaks … and I listen."

CHAPTER

At 4:30, I was pacing the floor of my apartment. Fourteen hundred square feet can seem pretty small when you're walking in circles. My cell phone rang and I grabbed it on the first ring.

"What did you find out?" I asked a little too loudly.

"About what?" Dex said.

"Oh, sorry. I was expecting a call from Liz."

"Sorry to disappoint you, lover boy. You didn't come back to the office, and I was kind of worried about you …you know, in a manly way. It's not like you to skip out early. Everything all right?"

"Yep, just needed some fresh air. It was such a great day outside, I think maybe I have a case of spring fever. I decided to enjoy it while it lasted."

"So what was Liz supposed to find out?" Dex probed.

"Um, she was, er, getting some info on a new restaurant coming into town. Suppose to be a fancy seafood place from the East Coast. You know, something she read about in the *Tribune*. She was going to check it out and let me know when it's opening."

"Well, I'm glad you're feeling better. And by the way, Kurt."

"Yeah, what is it?"

"You're a terrible liar. See you tomorrow."

That's why they invented caller ID, you idiot, I thought.

The second time the phone rang, I checked the ID first. Elizabeth Colburn.

"What did you find out?" I asked, more calmly this time.

"No hello?"

"Hello. What did you find out?"

"How about dinner and I'll tell you what I can."

"Great. Where do you want to go? The new seafood place is supposed to great."

"What seafood place?"

"Nothing, a private joke. What do you feel like eating?"

"Tell you what. You come over to my place at seven and I'll cook for you."

"Should I bring a toothbrush?"

"Funny! Be there at seven and bring a bottle of wine. Red."

"Okay, but I thought—" She had already hung up. You've got to love that independence. Usually I did, but not always. That had been the cause of many arguments between us over the years. We were two strong-willed people who were independent enough not to need another person to go through life with but who enjoyed the twosome thing up to a point. Sometimes our arguments had nothing to do with being right or wrong. The banter can be fun—until one of us has had enough.

Although it would be a serious discussion tonight, I was excited at the idea of being with Liz. And it was a special treat for her to cook for me. Usually we went out or shared the dining experience at my apartment, not that we went out all that much anymore. Each time was a treat for me, and I hoped that Liz felt the same.

Liz lives in a small single-family home, a twelve-hundred-square-foot ranch with three bedrooms and two baths. It is situated on a quarter-acre lot on a tree-lined street, just north of the historical part of Hamilton. The remodeled kitchen includes maple cabinets, and new stainless steel appliances, including counter depth fridge with lower freezer and French upper doors. White trim and six-panel doors add a modern flair to this charming, mature home. New roof, poured concrete drive, and garage door add to the value of this "ready-to-move-in" home. Located conveniently near schools, shopping, and main highways. Low taxes and maintenance make this a great place to call home. Sorry, not for sale.

From my apartment to Liz's home took twelve minutes by car without stopping at Shorty's Liquor Mart for a bottle of Shiraz. I don't know much about wine—vodka is my game—but I do know that you shouldn't spend more than ten dollars if you're going to drink it yourself as opposed to giving it as a gift. Even though this would probably be a business dinner, I was almost giddy as I pulled into her driveway, like a high school kid picking up his date for homecoming. Liz and I had a long relationship that ran the gamut from thinking of marriage to "see you around." We were somewhere in between at present, and we were both okay with that—at least she was. Not that I was ready for marriage—been there, done that—but I feel better knowing where all parties stand. Give me a map so I know where I'm going is all I ask.

Liz met me at the front door with a glass of Ketel on ice, two olives.

"Thank you. Glad you remembered the olives," I said, taking the chilled glass and handing her the bottle of wine. I leaned in for a kiss and was given a cheek.

"But of course, dear. What would vodka be without the olives?" she teased.

"Boring. What's for dinner?"

"A surprise. One of your favorites."

"Funny, I don't smell anything." Liz is not a great cook, but she has a handful of recipes that will knock your socks off.

Then the doorbell rang behind me as I was still standing in the foyer.

Liz stepped in front of me and opened the door. Rudy's Pizza … You Order, We Deliver.

"Hi ya, Mr. Banning. Large cheese pizza, extra pepperoni, hand tossed crust, light on the sauce," Rusty said. He could find his way to my house at midnight without streetlights. I'm a regular Rudy's customer, at least once a week, and Rusty is usually the regular delivery boy. If you can call a twenty-five-year-old man with a full beard a boy.

"Perfect," said Liz as she took the box and headed for the kitchen. "Pay him, will you, Kurty?"

"Keep it," I said, handing Rusty a twenty. Mr. Big Spender.

I consider myself to be a connoisseur of not only vodka and olives but pizza as well. And Rudy's is the best in town. It is excellent for breakfast. In fact, it is better in the morning than it is the night before. You have to leave the leftovers in the box on a shelf in the refrigerator so the air can get to it. That way the crust dries out and turns up a little bit at the edges, making it a culinary treat. The grease has congealed and it makes for a perfect breakfast meal—protein, fat, and carbs all in one.

Pizza, vodka, wine, and Liz. I wish I had brought my toothbrush.

"Okay, so what do we know about the murders," I asked with a mouthful of cheese and pepperoni.

"Kurt, you know there are certain aspects that I can't discuss."

"I know that, but, hey, it's Kurty here. Tell me what you can."

She gave me the arched eyebrow look and said, "I can tell you that the two murders are connected. But I need you to promise me you will not discuss the details with anyone."

"I promise."

"Not even Dex or Molly or Robbie or Bard or—"

"I got it. I promise."

"It was a very interesting meeting this afternoon with the Wilmington Police Department. Their chief, Robinski, and my chief, Dougan, have no love lost between them. They were professional, but you could feel the tension. Robinski made it clear that this was his investigation and that Dougan and his team were asked to be there only as a professional courtesy. We were asked to keep our eyes and ears open and relay any information to Wilmington PD. We're not officially involved—yet."

"All right, protocol, I respect that. So what can you tell me?" I asked, wanting details, not inter-departmental procedures.

"Two murders. Both female Realtors. Both conducting open houses and supposedly killed on consecutive Sundays. Both had LYER written on their chests with lip stick."

"That's why you know they're connected."

"Right, Columbo. Plus they both had their business cards put over their eyes. However, there are some differences between the victims. One was married; the other was a single mom. One in her thirties, the other in her forties. No physical similarities, and geographically they were miles apart, in different cities. The first home was in an upscale neighborhood with homes well over half a million dollars. The second home, in addition to being far west of the first home, was in a tract housing development. You would probably equate them to the low two hundred thousand dollar range."

This was nice, under the circumstances. Liz and I were enjoying a meal and a drink, sitting on the floor, eating off the coffee table. It wasn't unlike conversations in the past, in the same living room, talking about a new book she had read or reviewing a movie we had just seen. Maybe we had been planning a weekend getaway and the coffee table had been covered in brochures of Midwest bed and breakfast inns or spas. Sometimes it was just talking about our day at the office. I guess that's what we were doing now, talking about her day at the office. I missed the routine we shared in that room.

"COD?"

She smiled. "COD. You're a regular Travis McGee. The cause of death is still pending the autopsy reports. At this time, it's only a guess. Both victims had a dry, white powdery substance on their lips and tongue, which appeared to be chapped and badly blistered, almost like a sunburn."

"So what's your guess?"

"I'm keeping that to myself for now."

"Come on, share your thoughts. Two heads better than one. Bounce ideas off each other. Toss it back and forth. Run it up the flagpole ..."

"No, Kurt, I can't. And I won't. So stop asking questions and enjoy your pizza."

"Last request. Can you at least keep me updated as the details come in so I'm getting them first hand? Not from 'reliable sources' quoted in the *Tribune*," I said, making air quotes.

"Deal."

The conversation over, we enjoyed our pizza and had no more talk about the murder victims. I opened the red wine and let it breathe while I finished the Ketel. We did talk about the two police forces, both Hamilton's and Wilmington's, as well as her career aspirations, which included becoming a captain someday.

Dougan and Robinski, although neighboring chiefs now, had both gone to the academy together over thirty years ago. They were in graduating classes one year apart. Dougan graduated first and took his first assignment with the Chicago Police Department, working a neighborhood foot patrol on the rough south side. It was an experience that would toughen Dougan and give him a special empathy for poor struggling families trying to make it through the week. As a white cop in a mostly black neighborhood, he was not to be trusted at first, but on three occasions during his first two years he had proven himself to be honest and trustworthy in the 'hood. He also received commendations on each occasion.

The first act of heroism occurred just six months into his tour. It was late afternoon, on a scorching summer day. A fire hydrant had been opened to form a river of respite so the local kids could splash and cool off. A Bemis Cab came around the corner, too heavy on the gas, slid out of control, and crashed into one Alessia Young. Six years old, playing in the water with her older brothers, she had stepped out in front of the cab as it rounded the corner. Dougan was half a block away on foot when he saw the accident. He raced to the scene and found Alessia unconscious, with a severe gash on the back of her head where she had hit the curb. He called an ambulance while holding her in his lap, applying pressure to her bleeding head. He talked to her, but she remained unresponsive. He held her hand in his. He smoothed the braids away from her forehead. Paramedics arrived and took her to the local hospital. She survived with no lasting effects, and Dougan was credited with fast-thinking action that may have saved her life. The white cop, Dougan, was okay in the books of many of those local residents.

The second event was your everyday purse snatching gone wrong for the thief. Dougan saw the punk running down an alley, emptying the contents of a ragged old black purse as he ran. Just like the movies, it was a dead-end alley. No way out except the way the punk had gone in. Dougan was waiting for him, and he gave up easily. He was a local miscreant with a long list of similar priors. The purse and its contents were returned to one Matilda Robinson, an elderly lady who had lived in the neighborhood since the 1960s, back when it was safe and respectable. Again, Dougan's credibility was kicked up a notch in the eyes of local residents.

Two years into his beat, he had earned a good reputation with local businesses as well as neighborhood families. On an early October morning, he passed Jimbo's Bar-B-Q. Jimbo opened early so to get the pork and beef and chicken slow cooking and ready by lunchtime. By ten in the morning, the entire street smelled so good that people would start planning their lunches. Dougan noticed Jimbo behind the counter, just standing there. On the other side of the counter was a guy who looked as though he was pointing his finger at him and shouting. Dougan stood off to the side, looking through the window. He hesitated as whether to enter or wait for the suspect to come out. If he waited, Jimbo might try to resist or defend himself or be shot just for the hell of it. If he went in, there could easily be shots fired. Before he could decide, the man in the gray stained hoody began walking towards the door. As he hurried out the door, Dougan was waiting. He grabbed him by the hood, twisted it tight, and pushed him up against the glass. Jimbo came rushing out, saying that he had been robbed and that was the rotten "sumbitch" who had taken his till. The money was returned, and Dougan's star rose even higher.

Five years later, the neighborhood threw Dougan a going-away party. He had made detective and was being moved uptown and assigned to the Gang Division. This is where he was reunited with Robinski. They worked together on and off for ten years. When a tired Robinski learned of an opening for chief of police position in the western suburb of Wilmington, he applied. Two years later, another position in the relatively safe, boring, crime-free burbs opened, and Dougan took it. He was assistant chief of police in Hamilton, and two years later he became its chief. Although professionally friendly, each chief ran his own turf and scorned outside interference. But the two cities' shared border required a certain amount of professional courtesy and communication between Hamilton and Wilmington.

Liz had grown up with police blood in her veins. Her great grandfather, Reginald, had been on the Omaha mounted police force early in the twentieth century. The family had settled in Nebraska after emigrating from Ireland at the turn of the last century. He was killed when he was thrown from his horse, which had been spooked by one of those new contraptions called an automobile.

Her grandfather, Stuart, moved his family to Illinois and was a constable in what was then a small hamlet west of Chicago. That hamlet, Hamilton, grew into a fair sized town after World War Two and exploded at the end of the twentieth century.

Dad went to the Academy and upon graduation joined the Chicago Police Department. He probably could have had a position with the Hamilton force, but Aaron loved the pace and grit of the big city. With his family tucked away safely in the suburbs, he did daily battle with the bad guys of Chicago. He had been offered several opportunities for advancement, but he loved the nitty gritty of the street. And that's where he stayed until his retirement following thirty-three years on the CPD. Aaron and Judith Colburn were now living the good life of a Florida retiree.

It was no wonder Liz became an officer of the law. What chance did she have really? It was in her blood. Growing up, table talk revolved around good guys and bad guys. Keeping citizens safe and removing scum from the streets. Being a protector of and advocate for the little guy, the innocent. The discussions never romanticized the job, so when Liz decided to go to the Academy, she knew what that life would bring. And she loved it, most days. She was fairly certain that today's cop was much more inundated with paperwork than old Reginald or Stuart. She set her sights high, aspiring to rise as high as possible in the ranks and go wherever the opportunity led her. So far, and hopefully for a long time, Hamilton was where she found the rewards of her career choice—as if she ever had one!

I helped Liz clean up the few dishes and glasses we had dirtied, corked the remainder of the Shiraz, and headed for home with three slices of wrapped pizza for my breakfast.

CHAPTER 8

Friday, Saturday, and Sunday are my busiest days with clients. This Saturday, I was meeting with the Murphy Family to give them a tour of available homes in Hamilton. I had selected eight properties that met the family's requirements, based on my telephone conversations with Jean Murphy.

The Murphys were transferring to the Chicagoland area from Steubenville, Ohio. Jean had felt Hamilton would be perfect to raise the family. Patrick, eight years old, loved soccer, baseball and, video games. Shannon was twelve. Number one in her sixth-grade class back in Steubenville, she loved animals, Girl Scouts, and helping her mother. She was not happy about the move, leaving her friends behind, and turning her top ranked academic and social spot in Mrs. Walcott's sixth-grade class over to Emily Horton. Her mother, Jean, had bribed her, promising a new home with a princess bedroom and her own bathroom. No longer having to share a sink, tub, and toilet with Patrick was a good incentive, but she still didn't like the idea of moving. Yin and Yang, the Siamese cats, and Buster, the droopy-eyed basset hound, rounded out the Murphy household. Luckily for me, only Jean, Pat, and the kids were scheduled to make the house-hunting trip to Hamilton.

Pat Murphy worked for a large national fertilizer company, with the tag line "We may smell bad, but watch us grow." He was being promoted to a divisional manager's job, which included a nice pay raise, along with stock options. Jean was ready to spend that money on a new home and all the extras that would fulfill her dreams. We had met over the phone after a previous client who worked for the same company as Pat had given her my name.

"Let me tell you what I'm looking for in a new house," she said after the initial small talk.

"Home," I replied into the receiver.

"What?"

"Home. People live in homes. Dogs live in houses," I said, finishing with a well-rehearsed chuckle.

I was still preoccupied with the recent murders of two fellow Realtors as I was making appointments to show homes to the Murphys.

"Hi, this is Kurt Banning with Prescott Realty. I'd like to show your home today between two and three o'clock. Great, I'll leave my card on the way out, turn off all the lights and make sure the doors are locked. No, thank you," I said for the fifth time that morning.

The Murphys were meeting me in the office at ten. I felt a little off, like the day after your favorite bartender has over-served you. Foggy brain. But I hadn't been drinking to excess, just my regular Ketel and olives, maybe two. I felt as though I had forgotten something. It didn't feel like a Saturday, or any particular day at all. I had made all but two appointments, and I had scheduled time for potty breaks during the day and a lunch stop at Abigail's Eatery. This would give the Murphys a genuine taste of the local flavor. My car was washed and full of gas. Hair combed, teeth brushed, and fly up. I had two appointments to make, and then I would be ready for the day with thirty minutes to spare.

The phone on my desk rang as I was reaching for the receiver, making my stomach bounce off the bottom of my throat. Few people called my direct line. Most came through the main number and were announced over the intercom.

"Hi, Kurty," cooed Liz.

"Hi, yourself," I replied. "What's up?"

"Well ... I was thinking. Remember the gift certificate I gave you for Christmas to the spa resort in Wisconsin?"

"Sure!" I said an octave higher than I intended.

"Can you get away next weekend? The weather's supposed to be great, and I thought it would be nice to redeem your gift. We could drive up on Friday and be back by mid-afternoon Sunday."

Oh boy! Even though Liz and I were currently in the neutral position, the thought of a weekend away together gave my stomach a whole new feeling.

"Ah, sure. I can keep my schedule clear. If anything comes up this week, I'll hand it off to Dex. Any special occasion?"

"No not really. I'm going to be getting pretty busy with this task force for the two murders. Captain said there would be no extra time off for the next couple of months or until this thing gets solved."

"Well, sounds like perfect timing. I'm really excited. Thanks for lifting the fog," I said, smiling into the phone.

"Did you say fog? What fog?"

"Nothing, just a figure of speech. I'll call you mid-week to firm up the details." We disconnected. The foggy brain was gone, and so was the feeling of being off by a step. That Liz Colburn was the cure for most any ailment I had. I was still staring at the phone with a grin on my face when Molly stuck her head around the corner of my cubicle.

"Kurt, the Murphys are here. I put them in conference room number one."

"Thank you, Molly," I said as I gathered up my "Murphy File." I was actually whistling as I entered conference room number one. The glare of the sun bounced off the windshield of a car parked outside on Main Street, temporarily blinding me as I looked for the Murphys. They sat huddled together at the far end of the rectangle table, looking as though they were waiting for the dentist. Ah, this won't hurt a bit. Open wide.

"Hello, Jean. Hi, Pat," I said, extending my hand as I entered. "I'm Kurt."

Jean was as small as a mouse. Her voice had sounded faint and echo-y when we spoke on the phone. I assumed she had a tinker toy cell phone. But now I realized that she had tinker toy vocal chords. She was a plain woman in a plain floral dress, which she had possibly sewn herself out of old draperies from Tara. She had a tired smile and, as I later learned, she hated to fly. Friday's flight into Chicago from Cleveland, under an hour from takeoff to touchdown, had been turbulent, so much so that they hadn't even served soda and pretzels. Her flat ballerina style shoes, although practical for viewing homes, didn't add any height to her five-foot frame. Her hand was slight, soft, and very cold.

"Hello, Mr. Banning," Jean said, reaching for my hand.

Pat was tall and thin, like a broom handle. He had a dark, drooping mustache that matched the color of his full head of curly hair. Even stoop shouldered, he was easily six feet tall, a couple of inches shorter than me.

"Pleased to meet you," Pat said in a drawling baritone.

"Pleasure's mine. Where are the kids?" I asked, looking around and over my shoulder, as though they were hiding in the hundred-square-foot room, somewhere among the single table, six chairs, and wall-mounted computer screen.

"Oh, they're staying with Grandpa and Grandma," Jean said. "That would be my folks. We thought it would be easier for us to come alone on this first trip. The kids get so antsy; it would be a long day for all of us. Plus," she said, with a shy upward glance at Pat, whose hand she was squeezing the blood out of, "we haven't been away, just the two of us, in such a long time."

Pat visually blushed. Egad, I thought. I had a quick flash in my mind of Mickey and Minnie here getting down to business back at the hotel.

"Molly would be happy to get you some coffee or tea while you wait. I've got two more appointments to set and we'll be ready to go. In the meantime, I have some brochures for you to look at," I said, spreading maps, flyers of local interest, and the current edition of the *Hamilton Herald* on the table.

"That would be very nice."

I left them in the conference room and went to find Molly. In spite of my sarcastic nature and first impression, they really were a sweet couple, I thought, still smiling. The Murphys were still in love and apparently lust as well. I would get them through the day, educate them on the area, and narrow the list of homes that best fit their needs. At the end of the day, I would turn them loose to return to their love nest at the Hampton Inn.

With the last appointment made and the Murphys' file in hand, we walked across the parking lot to my car. Pat and Jean held hands. A very sweet couple indeed. This was their first relocation move and the first time they would be leaving Ohio for parts unknown.

Pat held the left rear door open for Jean and then walked around to the other side. He opened the right rear door and slid in next to his wife. Well, this was going to be awkward. I should have brought my chauffeur's cap! Normally, the decision maker sits up front with me. If I haven't figured out who that is beforehand, it's the first thing I'll try to figure out. Usually the dominant personality sits in the front and asks most of the questions as we tour the area. The backseat client does most of the listening, shuffles through the brochures of homes we've seen, checks the map, and communicates mostly through rearview-mirror glances. I adjusted my mirror so I could see as much of both of them as possible. Shouting over my right shoulder was going to make for a long day, as well as a stiff neck.

The bright morning sun had warmed the inside of the car on that spring day. We pulled out of Prescott Realty's parking lot and headed east to begin the tour of beautiful Hamilton.

"Hamilton was settled in the mid-1800s by Scottish descendants moving out here from Chicago," I began my oratory. I had given this same speech, or some slight variation of it, hundreds of times in the past decade, and I never tired of doing so. I am proud of the city I live in and love to share the experience.

"We're thirty-two miles from Chicago, and it took those early settlers three days by wagon to arrive on the banks of the Walloon River. The river was a great source of power and provided a passageway to the south. Gristmills and lumber mills were the first industries set up in Hamilton. When the railroad came through, it gave an immediate guarantee of future growth to the community."

Pat and Jean stared at me intently through the rearview mirror, as though there would be a test at the end of the day. They nodded in unison to statements that required acknowledgment. While traveling through the historic areas of town, I pointed out the significance of this monument and that statue. We drove down tree-lined streets in the post–World War One neighborhoods, where many homes had been razed to make room for trendy McMansions.

"How much do these babies go for?" Pat asked from the back seat.

"Well they range between a million and a million three," I replied.

Pat and Jean whistled between their teeth.

"Oh, I know we're not in your price range, but I want to give you a representative feel for the community, the entire community."

"Would you look at that …" Jean's voiced trailed off as she glanced out the window, bony fingers at her lips.

We wound our way south of the downtown area to the first developed subdivisions of the sixties. More tree-lined streets, but much more affordable living. These homes were smaller and more dated, with detached garages and generous lots. Many of these homes are split-level, not for everyone's taste. We viewed two homes in the neighborhood without much excitement from either of the Murphys. We headed west to the early tract-home developments of the eighties and found it to be much more like Ohio. A homogeneous neighborhood—some would say boring. Two-story flat-faced Georgians with brick fronts. As a Realtor, I could drive down the street and pretty much tell you the floor plan of each home we passed. It added to my credibility that I could describe the homes to my clients before we went through the front door. I'm sure they thought I had spent hours previewing the homes on our list.

This neighborhood held some promise for the Murphys. Of the three homes we visited, one was a definite keeper and one other made the maybe list. I force my clients to limit the keeper list to only three homes. If a fourth appears on the radar, then we have to toss one; otherwise, they will never be able to make a decision. I also like to give the homes we view nicknames, especially when kids are involved. It's easier at the end of the day to remember the house with the large aquarium in the basement as the "fish house," rather than the one with four bedrooms up, two full baths on the second floor, and hardwood floors that need refinishing.

Abigail's Eatery is far from the nicest restaurant in town, but it is pure Hamilton. That Saturday was like every Saturday. The restaurant was bustling with lunchtime patrons and the background din of greetings from the serving staff. Decorated in the style of a diner, it has two rows of booths along each side of the interior, with red vinyl bench seats. Some of the bench seats have been repaired with duct tape to hide the splits and cracks. Eight tables fill the space between the rows of booths. Jenny herself waited on us to complete the experience.

After an artery-clogging lunch of bottomless French fries, grilled sandwiches, and homemade apple pie, we trudged back to the car to visit the final three homes of the day. Mouse and Mop really put away the food. I doubt if they weighed two hundred pounds combined.

We looped back around the downtown area and continued south and west until we came to the farthest section of Hamilton and the county. This area, the last to be developed, has homes built within the last ten years. These homes are larger than in the traditional neighborhoods, but the lots are smaller and the houses are tucked in close. Because they are newer, they have more amenities than the older residences. These homes offer skylights, granite kitchen and bathroom countertops, sunrooms, first-floor laundries, and spacious master bedrooms and baths and three-car garage. One of the three remaining homes made the maybe list, and after that we called it a day.

After eight homes and a carb-laden lunch, the Murphys were mentally fatigued as we drove back to my office. Jean took the down time and called her parents to check on the kids. The volume must have been turned to the max and I could hear both sides of the conversation. It sounded as though Grandpa and Grandma were having a great time with Shannon and Patrick.

"Don't worry about us. You and Pat just enjoy yourselves. We'll pick you up tomorrow night at the airport. Just Dad's coming, 'cause it'll be late. I'll stay with the kids and tuck 'em in," I heard through the tiny speaker on Jean's cell phone. Someone should tell Grandma she doesn't have to shout just because she's in Ohio.

We drove past one of five public golf courses sprinkled about Hamilton. Some eager golfers were on the course, wearing lightweight jackets. I parked on the street in front of Prescott Realty. I normally park in the lot, but as it was past 4:30 on a Saturday, I took advantage of the many open spaces on Main Street. I saw Molly sitting at the receptionist desk through the large front window. She was still smiling as if it was nine in the morning as we came through the front door. Both Pat and Jean took off for the restrooms at a sprinter's pace. This is another reason I have only one cup of coffee a day. When Pat and Jean returned, they look renewed, and we made plans to meet again on Sunday morning to see the remaining seven homes on our schedule.

"The good news is that we ended the day with a 'keeper' and two 'maybes,'" I said as they were heading towards the door. "By the end of tomorrow, I think you'll have narrowed your choices down to three or four homes. It'll be a good day."

"Um, Pat and I were talking and wondered if, um, it would be okay if we met you tomorrow at ten o'clock instead of nine?" Jean asked, blushing a shade.

"Sure, no problem. It'll give me a chance to read the entire newspaper, not just the Obituaries."

No response to this.

"Great," she said, obviously a bit relieved. "See you in the morning." She grabbed Pat by the hand and practically dragged him out the door.

Have fun, kids, I thought, smiling as I watched them almost skip down the sidewalk to the side parking lot. "Cute couple," Molly said from behind her desk.

CHAPTER 9

Annie Lawrence smiled shyly at herself in the mirror as she dressed for work. Not quite in her late thirties, her arms and legs still had that definition and muscle tone from years of bicycling through the countrysides of rural Illinois. Her abs were still tight but not rippled. She attributed this to not having had children; her only consolation was a firm gut. Her breasts were perky, without any sag. Although she was a lifelong B cup, she doubted that sagging would ever be a problem. How glad she was that her ex-husband, Ben, had not talked her into an augmentation years ago. He had even tried to present the idea of going to a C or D cup as his gift to her. *How generous of him!* Her auburn hair was cut in a Demi Moore bob and was as dark as ever. She had worn her hair in the same style ever since she was in the eighth grade. Her mother had insisted on keeping it short so it would be easy to take care of, save her time in the mornings before school. Annie had also been a swimmer, and the shortness had its advantages in the pool. Before the fifth grade, she had worn a massive mange of thick, wavy locks that couldn't be tamed.

Today was going to be a great day, she just knew it. In fact, the past year had been 365 great days. Her career was rolling, she'd once again taken an interest in her health and joined a gym, and her social life was moving at the perfect pace, with several dates in the past four months. She once again had balance in her life. She had come a long way up from her devastating divorce two and a half years ago. Back then she thought the world had ended, that she would never make it out of the black hole.

That terrible Friday, Benjamin Lawrence had come home in the afternoon, a few hours earlier than usual. When she heard him coming through the kitchen door, for a nanosecond, she thought he had decided to surprise her and start the weekend early. Maybe he had made reservations at the new Thai restaurant and they would be going out for a romantic dinner. Or possibly he had brought her a thoughtful "no reason" gift. He may have planned a trip for them back into the city for an evening of eating, music, and dancing. It had been so long since they had enjoyed an evening together, just the two of them. Just for a nanosecond that is, until he rounded the corner and met Annie coming from the living room. Annie saw Ben's face. His jaw was stone like and so stiff that the bones actually looked as if they might break through his skin. His forehead was furrowed like sheets on an unmade bed. The normal sparkle in his hazel eyes was missing and when he began to speak, his voice was a parched monotone, barely resembling that of her beloved husband of six years.

"Annie," he began, "I don't know where to start. I've been rehearsing the lines in my head for months and there's no easy way to say this."

Uh oh, no romantic evening or gift or surprise coming. Well, yes, maybe a surprise, but not in the good way Annie had thought. Had something happened at work? Ben had been required to take a company physical a few months ago. Did he have devastating results to share? And then the five most dreaded words in the relationship dictionary fell out of Ben's mouth.

"I don't love you anymore."

Wow, what a punch. Had she heard him correctly? It was hard to hear through the roaring in her ears. Was this a joke, a gag? What? It's amazing how much information can shoot through your brain before the second hand on the clock even moves. Forget about one Mississippi, two Mississippi. The words repeated themselves in her head, in slow motion, like a tape recording being played back at half speed.

By the time she could close her mouth, she felt the tears being squeezed out of her eye sockets by the tension in her temples. Ben was already going up the stairs, taking them two at a time. Annie stood there, in the foyer, still trying to process the thirty-second scene that had just taken place. She began to move slowly, like wading against the strong current of a river, until she reached the bottom of the stairs. She took them up, one at a time, trudging.

"What did you say?" Annie asked as she stood in the master bedroom doorframe.

Ben had taken the largest of the three suitcases they owned off the top shelf of their walk-in closet. The same suitcase they had used on their honeymoon to Aruba. The suitcase laid spread eagle on top of the striped, quilted bedspread. He was systematically removing the contents of his side of their dresser and dumping them into the red and black hard shell Samsonite.

"What didn't you understand? I think it was to the point," he replied irritably. "Please, let's not go into a long discussion about this. I don't have the energy and I've made my decision."

Annie blinked for the first time in several minutes. A tear from her right eye ran down into the fold of her cheek. "You made a decision! How can you make a decision that affects me? We need to talk. I don't even know what's going on here." She truly had no idea that there was trouble with her and Ben's marriage. No clue, no idea, no red flags. "You come home, tell me you don't love me anymore, and start packing your clothes, and I'm not supposed to want a discussion? Are you crazy?" She was screaming by this time. Her hands were clenched into fists at her sides. Ben continued to pack without looking at her. He took a final sweeping glance around the bedroom and then snapped the latches on the suitcase. Annie was hanging on the doorjamb, crying quietly in low sobs, as he brushed by her.

"Someone from the law firm will contact you about the paperwork. Goodbye, Annie," he said over his shoulder as he stomped down the hall and bounced down the stairs. After the front door slam shut, there was nothing, not a sound, not a breath.

Ben had been made a junior partner in a small successful law firm earlier in the year. His specialty was corporate mergers and acquisitions. And now some hotshot lawyer in the divorce department was going to represent him.

You bastard, she thought as she watched him from the upstairs bedroom window. Ben took the sidewalk to the street where his car was parked, the engine still running. She sat on the spot vacated by the suitcase. Now what? What just happened here? Her ears were still echoing, and the pain in her throat felt as if she had tried to swallow a granola bar without chewing first. Not even a "sorry" from the man she thought was her soul mate and best friend.

The weeks that followed were horrible, sleepless, and confusing. It was the proverbial dream from which Annie couldn't awaken. Daytime puffy eyes from nighttime crying. Lying awake at night, in her half-empty queen-size bed, counting the rotations of the ceiling fan. Annie kept going over and over the scenario, replaying the conversation of that Friday afternoon in October. She searched her memory banks for small signs. No odd cell phone calls, no tiny pieces of paper with names and numbers on them in his suit pockets, and very few late nights at the office. His humor and passion and handholding were there right up until the announcement: "I don't love you anymore." Sneaky bastard. What had happened? What had gone wrong with their marriage? She was sure it was something she had done, or hadn't done. Annie spent countless daytime and nighttime hours analyzing herself, but she come up with no answers, only a swirling funnel of depression. At a friend's suggestion, she went to a therapist.

Ben and Annie had dated for one year, followed by a two-year engagement and a six-year marriage that ended in the foyer of their home on a Friday afternoon. She was sure the date would be branded in her mind. Eventually, Annie didn't even remember that it had happened on a Friday.

She received the modest home they had shared in the divorce settlement, and little else. There had been no children (thank you, God), so the only money from Ben had been a small monthly sum for maintenance, for a two-year period. This helped Annie keep the house and pay off an old student loan that had been hanging around for a number of years.

At the time, Annie had been an event coordinator for a midsized company with seven offices spread throughout the Midwest. She worked in corporate, in downtown Chicago, just off Wacker Drive, an easy walk from Union Station. The job had been satisfying, challenging, and financially rewarding. Annie had started working for Bell & Bemis right after graduating from Northwestern University sixteen years previously. She met Ben through a mutual friend while he was finishing law school and studying for the bar exam.

Shortly after the divorce, Annie felt as though she had lost all control. She needed to take charge of some aspect of her life. With a concentrated effort and reevaluation, Annie wrote down a plan, listing her interests, talents, and experience. She love being around people, she could sell, sell, sell, and she had a knack for putting people together for their mutual benefit. After analyzing her career and industry opportunities, Annie decided to get out of the corporate world and go into real estate. It was a new challenge, the market was improving, and the income was unlimited. She signed up for a real estate licensing course at a local community college while still working at Bell and Bemis. Annie passed the six-week class and then took the state board exam. She passed that with ease on her first attempt.

The next question was, where should she practice her new trade? Annie interviewed several real estate brokerage firms and settled on Marshal and Montgomery Real Estate Company, located in the near west suburbs of Chicago. She had always thought the double Ms in old English script looked regal and classy on the signs that peppered the yards of suburban homes. She was familiar with the area, having grown up in the vicinity and graduated from Creighton High School. Many of Annie's high school and college friends still lived in the neighborhood, now raising their own families. Many of their parents were in the area as well and were prime candidates for down-sizing. She planned on making this her main sphere of influence in her new career. They would be a source of referrals that would propel her new adventure.

So, with her license in hand, Annie walked into her supervisor's office at Bell & Bemis and uttered the five most dreaded words in the human resources handbook: "I don't work here anymore."

That was eighteen months ago. Annie had made the right decision. She was a natural in real estate. Her friends and acquaintances knew Annie well, and referrals came in from the very beginning. She listened, demonstrated knowledge about the area, and won people's trust. She was named Rookie of the Year at Marshal and Montgomery last year and was on pace to double her sales this year.

As she finished dressing, Annie smiled back at herself in the mirror. She wore a white ruffled V-neck blouse that was cut low enough to be fashionable, but not so low as to be provocative. Certainly not as sensual as she had dressed the evening before when she had a fourth date with Jeff Majors.

Annie had met Jeff at a Chamber of Commerce social event six weeks ago. He was handsome and charming with a terrific smile. Jeff owned his own insurance agency and specialized in health insurance. Being self-employed, Annie was responsible for providing her own insurance and was in need of a better, lower cost policy. They agreed to meet for coffee the next day to discuss her options for health care insurance. Co-pay and deductible conversation quickly turned to hobbies and interests which led to date number 2. Last night's dinner date allowed Annie to dress up a little. Slinky black dress, 3" heels and a new bra that showed off the gifts God had given her. Jeff's smile had showed his appreciation. They ate and laughed and danced and Annie had felt happier in her personal life than she could remember.

She pulled up a navy blue A-line skirt, hemmed just a couple of inches above her knees and added a matching navy blue blazer. In her two-and-a-half-inch black pumps, she stood five feet, two and a half inches. Annie adjusted her blue and white nametag on her lapel and gave herself a final approving look in the mirror.

Yep, it was going to be a great day all right, Annie thought. It was her first Sunday open house of the spring season. The sun was shining and it would be the beginning of yet another successful year in her career. And the possibilities with Jeff Majors gave her the feeling of having balance back in her life.

CHAPTER 10

Liz and I worked our way through the early Friday-afternoon traffic headed north out of Hamilton. It didn't seem to matter what time of the year it was; Friday traffic was the worst. It was unseasonably warm for the first weekend in April as we slid in and out of returning lunch-goers and office slackers getting a jump on their weekend freedom.

The windows were down on my vintage MG, and the radio was playing loudly as we headed for the Wisconsin border. Liz had planned a weekend getaway as a Christmas present to ourselves over a year ago. That was back when we were 'on.'

Due to the careers we chose, we saw each other less frequently than either one of us would have preferred. As a lieutenant with Hamilton's Finest, Liz's shift rotated every other month between days and afternoons. When she was on a case, there was no regular routine.

But again, we're talking about Hamilton, one of the twenty safest communities in the United States with a population over 100,000. Our crime is mostly juvenile in nature, underage weekend parties when Mom and Dad are on a short trip out of town. The occasional mailbox gets knocked over by a bat-wielding passenger, and holidays bring the usual lawn ornament theft, where a baby Jesus ends up in the arms of Frosty the Snowman on the steps to the post office. We have the rare homicide or armed robbery, and the sale of narcotics is ever increasing, but in general, not a lot of investigations happen in Hamilton that require overtime.

After months of waiting, our weekend was here. The spa and resort in Kohler had a king luxury suite with our name on it, along with a four o'clock couples massage with Courtney and Alexia. Liz and I had been away together several times for romantic escapades. She is a great travel partner. I can't really relax and enjoy the vacation until I've reached the final destination, unpacked, and changed clothes. Liz, on the other hand, begins unwinding at the mere suggestion of an out-of-town adventure. Long lines do not frustrate her. "As long as we're together, what difference does it make if we have to wait?" She packs light, is ready to leave five minutes early and can sleep on planes and trains, and looks at the good in every situation. I, on the other hand, am always rushing out the door at the last minute, bring one entire suitcase too many, and have the patience of a dog at the impound lot. And even though we had plenty of time to make our way to Wisconsin, I was irritated at the pokiness of those less fortunate people who were going to less important destinations.

About two hours into the drive from Hamilton, the muscles used in everyday life at the real estate business began to relax. My back sank deeper into the seat cushion. My shoulders rounded slightly as I hugged the padded steering wheel of my car. Palms and pits were dry. No appointments or calls to return. Dex had offered to take care of my clients, and I left his number on my voicemail as a contact. I had let all my sellers know earlier in the week that their hard working real estate agent was going out of town for the weekend. Liz had put in for a weekend furlough from the Hamilton Police Department, and we were off for an amazing forty-eight hours. The sky was steel blue and cloudless. Trees, far from the freeway on the horizon, were beginning to leaf out, and the stark brown of branches and bark were tinged in varying shades of green. The roads were surprisingly smooth following such a harsh winter. Road crews put so much salt on the highways that spring usually brought cracks, crevices, and potholes large enough to hide a pony.

The traffic thinned as we continued north. We moved to the fast lane, and my little two-seater reached eighty with ease as George Thorogood's "Bad To The Bone" played with full bass. What's the use of being a cop's boyfriend if you can't speed a little?

Being a real estate agent, my hours are anything but regular. Office work takes place during what most would consider normal business hours. But listing presentations, buyer orientations, showing properties, writing contracts, and negotiating happen mostly in the evenings and weekends. And by evenings I mean up until 10:00 p.m. in some cases. And by weekends, I mean Saturdays and Sundays from sunup to evening. I'm not complaining. There are plenty of times during the week for Kurt time. I'm not bound to a desk or an office or even a boss. Production and results are what create job security in the real estate industry.

Traffic thinned as we closed in on the Wisconsin border.

"That's a great song," I said, turning up the radio. "I love Journey."

"Good for you," Liz said, "but that's Foreigner."

"No way!"

"I'll give you credit—you get the words right, but you're terrible at naming the bands," she said.

I knew she was right, but I wasn't about to give it up. "Absolutely not. It's Journey. You know, big hair, the eighties. They do all the reunion shows, summers at the fairs and festivals."

"Okay, you just described every band from the eighties," Liz said.

And on it went for another ten miles. This seemed like old times, and I really did miss them. This was good-natured jousting, which we both enjoyed. Not the everyday bickering that wedged us apart nineteen months, three weeks, and two days ago.

We stopped at the Welcome Center, getting off at the first exit in Wisconsin. I really enjoy taking my vintage MG on the road. I don't get to drive her that much. I keep her stored in an extra garage I rent down the alley behind my apartment above Prescott Realty. Real estate forces me to maintain my eight-year-old four-door Cadillac as my main means of transporting clients. A car with plenty of head room and easy access is an important tool for any Realtor. Today, many of my fellow Realtors have moved on to new high-end foreign cars as their staple of transportation. I prefer the broken-in feel of old Detroit. Really, I'm much too young to be driving around in a Caddy if I'm not working, so that's when the MG comes out. She's a 1979, forest green with a removable hard top. I had spent six months looking for just the right one. The company stopped manufacturing them in 1980, and parts finding parts can be a challenge. I found "Margaret" in an online auction. She was a one-owner automobile, living in north Alabama. With a few key clicks, she was mine in a matter of twenty-four hours. Matthew Johns was the owner, and he guaranteed the car to be in pristine condition. If not, I'd get my money back, no questions asked. I fell in love with the photos, bought her, and arranged for an enclosed transport to pick her up the following week in Huntsville, Alabama. Since that day over thirteen years ago, she has given me uncountable hours of driving pleasure. It was the only real personal item I demanded from my ex-wife during the divorce procedures. She could keep the tacky starter furniture we had purchased, stick by stick, when we first married out of college. The book collection was hers, and we split the albums, even though I didn't have a turntable on which to play them. It was a point of pride. She had used our dog, Brandy, as the bargaining chip, negotiating her custody for Margaret. I call her Margaret after my tenth-grade biology teacher, Ms. Margaret Hanks. She drove a fire engine red MG while I was in high school, and the truth is I had a crush on her *and* her car. Great lines, great legs!

Forty minutes past the Welcome Center, Liz and I pulled into the parking lot of the Green Springs Spa and Resort just after 3:00 p.m. on a glorious Friday afternoon. We were giddy and smiling like teenage kids sneaking away for a lustful encounter as we emptied the trunk. At least one of us was lusting.

"Welcome to the Green Springs," said Tiffany, the check-in clerk. Her giant smile almost matched mine. "We look forward to having you as our guests." Right out of the training manual. "If there is anything we can do to make your stay more pleasurable, please just ask." Tiffany was dwarfed by the enormous oak counter, looking like a high school student working a part-time job.

"Thank you," I said, pulling the confirmation out of my jacket pocket. I handed it over the counter to Tiffany, sitting on a high stool so she could see over the registration desk.

"You're all set, Mr. Banning," said the smiling Tiffany, handing us our keys. "Rooms 911 and 913."

"Two rooms?" I asked, surprised, looking from Tiffany, then back to Liz.

"Yes, sir," Tiffany replied. "Two adjoining king-size leisure suites, as requested. No smoking, of course."

"Of course," I replied glumly as I gave Liz a stare that could have melted the ice in Green Bay in January. "I just thought of something that would make my stay more enjoyable," I mumbled as I stooped to pick up our bags.

"And what is that, sir?" asked Tiffany, peering over her counter, still smiling.

"Oh, nothing.,"

I followed Liz to the elevator, carrying both our overnight bags. I could see her cheeks puffed up in her profile, grinning at my expense. She had been very clever with her little surprise.

"Cute," I said as the elevator doors closed behind us.

Liz pinned me against the side wall of the elevator, both my arms hanging straight down, holding our bags in my hands. I could feel the mild vibration of the elevator on my shoulder blades and the small of my back as she leaned into me and gave me the warmest, softest, slowest kiss we had shared in months. It was a nine-story kiss!

"Don't pout, little boy," she teased as she released me. "You won't be neglected this weekend. The rooms are connected so you can come visit … if you've been good."

The doors to the elevator opened onto a plush mauve carpet with a dark green flower pattern, right out of the eighties, when the Green Springs was built. The hallway was covered in ornate framed mirrors, giving a much bigger feel to the hall than the space allowed. When we came to the suite numbered 911, Liz, who was holding the keys in more ways than one, unlocked the door and gave it a playful push open with her foot.

"This one's yours," she said. "Get changed and ready for our massages and I'll meet you in the spa lounge in thirty minutes, second floor."

As Liz unlocked her door, I was still standing at my own with a dumb kid look on my face. She blew me a kiss, gave me a wink, and disappeared inside. What was going on? I wasn't sure, but the promise that I would not be neglected had certainly improved my mood.

I entered my room, flipped on the light switch, and dropped my bag on the edge of the bed as the door slammed shut behind me. I could hear Liz unpacking on the other side of the closed connecting door, humming a tune. I quietly tried the handle, and yes, it was locked. What a tease. She was certainly stirring up feelings in me. I glanced around the well-appointed room for the first time. The room was decorated in a tropical motif with dark wicker-framed palm tree paintings hung on the walls. The palms matched those on the king-size bedspread. The key attached to my door card opened the mini fridge to reveal an ample supply of shot and half sized bottles of over-priced booze, including Ketel One. The headboard was actually painted on the wall, as opposed to the real thing, obviously so that the more amorously involved would not disturb adjoining guests. I guessed that Liz's room was the mirror image of mine and that her painted headboard matched up perfectly. The floor-to-ceiling windows provided a beautiful view of the courtyard below. It was easy to imagine the deck chairs and swimwear-clad guests lounging in the pool during the summer. I left the drapes open and enjoyed the warmth of the sun streaming into the room. The bathroom seemed as large as half my entire loft back in Hamilton. It was decorated with rich granite in browns and golds. There was a bank of switches on the wall, inside to the left, their function indicated with individual labels. The light switch was obvious, as I had already turned it on. There was a switch for the heat lamp, one for the exhaust fan, one to turn on the jets in the whirlpool tub, and one for the heated marble floors. Fancy. However, being a knowledgeable Realtor, I know that marble is the most unsafe flooring for a bathroom. It becomes very slippery when wet, akin to being in leather soled shoes at a fifteen-degree incline on a solid inch of ice. Pretty but lethal.

I caught a glimpse of the bidet in the mirror. I had seen them of course, but having never been to Europe, I had never had the opportunity to try one out. Now, in the privacy of my luxury king suite, I was going to experience the kind of cleanliness reserved for royalty. On the back of the bathroom door, hanging on padded silk hangers, were two jumbo terrycloth robes. Attached to the neck of the hanger was a note card with typed print: FOR GUESTS. Wrapped in plastic, for my protection, were matching thong sandals.

I changed into my massage gear, robe and sandals and nothing else. Between the tour of my room and changing out of my clothes, I still had twenty minutes before our appointment at the spa. I decided to get a jump on my relaxing massage and cracked open a bottle of Ketel from the mini bar. Fresh ice sat in a stainless bucket, which room service had provided prior to our check-in. It was still mostly cubes, with a little water in the perspiring bucket. There were no olives to be found. I guess this was roughing it in Wisconsin. I sat in the overstuffed leather chair, staring at the blond hairs on my legs, sticking out from below the mid-calf robe. It was accompanied by a matching leather ottoman, complete with tarnished brass rivets outlining its edges.

I glanced at the digital clock next to the bed and decided to leave for the spa. I drained the remainder of my drink in one gulped, locked the mini fridge, and left my room. It is a very vulnerable yet erotic feeling to be in a public place, like a hallway or elevator, wearing only sandals and a robe. The front of the robe was pulled tight across the front of me, secured with the matching belt as I shuffled along the hall to the bank of elevators on the ninth floor. The terrycloth felt soft against my skin. I was relieved that no one was in the elevator as the doors opened. I pushed the second-floor button and received a static shock from scuffing along the thick carpet in my sandals. I was certain it had set my hair on edge. I held the button to the SPA all the way down in hopes the elevator would make it to the second floor without uninvited guest climbing on.

The ding of the bell announced my arrival on the spa floor. As the doors opened, I heard the distant sound of instrumental music. Etched glass doors provided direction to the spa lobby. As I pushed open the right door, I entered into a dimly lit lobby, with a dozen oversized chairs. The music was slightly louder here. Water trickled down an artificial stream from an artificial waterfall in the corner, conveniently reminding me I had not peed before coming downstairs. The smell of oranges and other citrus fruit floated in the air. Actually, there was a bowlful of fresh oranges waiting for us after our treatment, along with a supply of bottled water.

Liz was relaxing on a floral patterned chair. Her arms were stretched wide across the back, as if she were hugging two invisible friends on either side. Her feet were extended in front of her and crossed at the ankles. The robe had slid apart slightly, providing a sensuous view of her mid-thigh. Oh, those thighs! Maybe she was unaware, or maybe this was part of her game. Foreplay, if you will. She gave me a drowsy smile and got up to greet me with a peck on the lips. Her lips were warm and soft. Before I could say anything or react to the warmth of the kiss, another door opened and Courtney and Alexia appeared, wearing starched white tunic tops and matching white pants.

"We're ready for you now," they said in unison.

Liz took me by the hand and led me to our waiting masseuses. I should have peed.

CHAPTER 11

Annie Lawrence had just locked the front door to 2376 Willow Court and had snapped the key back into the lockbox hanging from the tarnished brass handle when she heard the low hum of an engine and tires come to a stop in the driveway behind her. Funny how this happened at every open house. Not just some or most but absolutely every single time. You could sit inside a home for an hour or five hours, and as soon as you turned off the lights and stepped outside with the key in your hand, some last-minute jamoke pulls up in front. That's okay, Annie thought. It was a lovely spring afternoon, just a few minutes after four o'clock. Why not take on one more potential client? After all, it only took one, the right one, to make a difference in your day.

"Hi, are you still open?" said a high-pitched male voice.

"Sure, come on in," Annie responded over her shoulder without even turning around. She was reopening the lockbox to retrieve the key.

"I was just driving through the neighborhood when I saw your signs," the male voice said, getting closer from behind as he approached the porch.

With the key in her hand, Annie turned around to greet the late home shopper. "Hi, I'm Annie Lawrence, oh ..."

He was so close that he startled her, and she instinctively backed up a step.

"Pleased to meet you, Annie Lawrence. My name is Ted, Ted Bell." He stuck out his hand. Annie took it with a firm, full grip, realizing too late it was clammy with sweat. She smiled pleasantly as she looked Ted in the eyes.

She surmised Ted to be in his late thirties, maybe early forties, thinning blond hair brushed sideways across his head, medium build, average height, nothing unusual except his eyes. They didn't match his expression or the friendliness in his voice. The eyes were milky blue and lifeless. Ted wore a brown checkered shirt, mostly covered by a solid brown suede sports coat and jeans. His skin was very white, almost pale, but hey, it was early spring; everyone was pale except those lucky enough to have gone somewhere sunny for spring break.

"How long have you been looking for a home, Ted?" Annie asked as she unlocked and pushed open the front door.

"To be honest, I'm just starting to look."

"Well, everyone has to start sometime and somewhere," Annie had been in the business long enough that she didn't believe anyone who started a sentence with "to be honest." "Where do you currently live?"

"I rent an apartment, so I'm flexible and not in any particular hurry."

Great, thought Annie, another tire-kicker. "Tell me, Ted, what are you looking for in a home?" Annie asked as they went through the foyer and down the hallway towards the kitchen. Ted closed the front door behind them.

"Oh, I don't need anything too big. It's just me right now. My kids come to visit some weekends, but that may change. I'm divorced, you see."

"Been there," Annie said, trying to form a common bond with a potential new client. "Well, as you can see, the kitchen has been updated with new appliances and lighting. The previous owners took exceptional care of their home as you can see."

Annie noticed that as she pointed out amenities of the home, Ted seemed to be staring at her, not taking in the selling points she was mentioning. So much for features and benefits.

"Ted, where did you say you currently live?" Annie asked, getting an odd cold feeling. She had had these feelings before in uncomfortable situations, but they had turned out to be nothing.

"Oh, I rent."

"I know that, but where, what part of town?"

"Hillshire Apartments on the far northwest side of Chicago," Ted answered, throwing in a smile. He sensed Annie was uncomfortable and didn't want to upset her. "Tell me about the area parks and schools," said Ted. "There's a good chance that my kids will be moving in with me. That's why I'm out here looking at homes. This is very close to where they now live with their mother, and I wouldn't want them to have to change schools. Right now they both attend Roosevelt Middle School. Sixth and Eighth grades."

Annie felt much better now. The staring was probably her imagination. Ted was just a single dad looking to take care of his children and was shopping for a new place for his family to call home.

"Miller's Park is just a block to the west of here, and Roosevelt Middle School is the designated school for this neighborhood, as you probably already know. The school bus stops just one block down from the corner of the cul-de-sac. It's really an ideal location. What do you think?"

"It could work. Let's see the size of the bedrooms. You know girls; my little princess is going to need space."

Annie relaxed as she led Ted down the hallway towards the bedrooms. "I know the carpet is old, but underneath are beautiful hardwood floors that would look terrific with a little buffing." She was now wondering how to approach the blue bathroom as they were nearing its doorway.

"Wow!" said Ted. "Are you kidding me? Look at that bathroom. Now that's what I call BLUE!"

"Well, you know, it's just some paint and—"

"My kids will flip over this! Blue is their favorite color. They both love blue. Their backpacks are blue, their lunch bags, gym shoes, hair ribbons, baseball cap, and on and on."

Annie was starting to have a good feeling about turning him from a customer into a buyer. No matter how many times you discover the "right" home for a client, it never gets old. The excitement of a buyer creates a sense of urgency with a Realtor. You want to get the offer written up and presented before someone else comes along and steals the prize. After showing the rest of the home, Annie suggested they take a walk around the outside and see just how large the yard was. She would also give Ted a view of the walking trails, and maybe they'd even take a stroll to the nearby park.

"Great," Ted agreed, "but can we look at the basement first?"

"Uh, sure," said Annie. "It's unfinished with a seven-and-a-half-foot ceiling. The furnace was just cleaned last winter, and the hot water heater was replaced in February. The washer and dryer hook ups are there as well." Annie turned on the light switch at the top of the stairs. She descended with Ted behind her. "The previous owners never had a problem with water in the basement, and the sump pump rarely runs." Annie halfway down the steps, holding the wooden handrail to the left. Ted's conversation had ended, and the only sound was that of Annie's high heels striking the wooden steps.

Annie felt pressure in the middle of her back and a thrust so strong that she lost her grip on the handrail. She pitched forward, landing on her knees and chin and sliding the remaining six steps on her belly, hands and arm spread forward.

Ted had used his size nine right boot to shove Annie down the stairs. He stood halfway up the steps, looking down on Annie as she lay moaning, trying to turn over on her back. She was crumpled into the fetal position, and she tried to right herself. Her blue blazer and skirt were scuffed and twisted. Ted was down the stairs in four long strides. Annie was conscious of him coming to her rescue. How could she have been so clumsy? What had she tripped on? How embarrassing. She was pretty sure she was all right, but boy was she going to be sore tomorrow. She could feel the sting on her chin where the skin had come off from having slid face first.

"I'm so sorry," Annie stammered while trying to get off the last two steps. Her right arm was stuck beneath her and her head was pointing down towards the basement floor. It was difficult to get up and gain any balance without sliding down the final two steps. She slumped to the basement floor as Ted arrived next to her, aware her skirt had slid up over her thighs.

"You should be sorry, you little bitch," Ted said through his teeth quietly.

Annie was very confused by now. What had Ted said? Her jaw hurt, and the pain in both knees was shooting down her shins. She needed to get up.

"Ted, help me up. I need to get on my feet."

"The hell you do. You stay right down there in the gutter where you belong," Ted said as he put his foot on her back and held her down.

"Ted, get off me," Annie screamed, realizing this had not been an accident.

"I'll get off when I'm ready, you whore."

Annie could not understand what had gone wrong, but she knew she was in trouble and had to figure out a strategy for getting away from Ted and out of that basement, and fast.

"Ted, what have I done to you? Why are you treating me like this?" She felt warmth on her upper lip. It was a trickle of blood coming from her nose. "Just tell me. I'm sorry." Ted released the pressure of his boot, allowing Annie to roll onto her back.

"You have no idea how sorry you're going to be." He jabbed her ribs with the point of his boot. A bolt of pain shot across her rib cage and took her breath for a moment. *Okay*, she thought, still curled up on her side, *pleading isn't working. What does he want? Am I about to be raped? What is my best defense? Time for plan B.*

"What the fuck do you want from me?" Annie yelled, attempting to sit up. It was not a scared voice but an angry voice. A "back off or else" voice.

Annie could tell by the look on his face, she had scored a point. There was a flicker of doubt in his eyes. She gain a little hope she could talk her way out of the situation. The thought was fleeting as he grabbed Annie by her short bobbed hair and dragged her to the corner of the basement, where the outside water supply pipe came into the basement through the foundation.

Annie told herself not to whine or cry. She didn't want to give this bastard the satisfaction of knowing that her hair felt like it was coming out a strand at a time. Once Ted had Annie by the water pipe, he let go of her hair. Annie was lying on her back, staring up at Ted through watery eyes. Not tears of fright but tears of anger and pain. It wasn't until she watched him undo the buckle on his belt and slip it through the loops that she became truly afraid.

"Ted, stop. You don't really want to do this. You'll get caught and you'll end up in jail. Ted, this is crazy. Just stop. Let me go right now and I promise I won't tell anyone. I promise," Annie was almost screaming now.

Ted smiled, but the milky eyes never changed. "Promise?"

"Yes, yes, I promise. Just let me go."

Ted held his belt in his left hand and reached towards Annie with his right. He was going to help her up. She reached up and took hold of his hand, pulling herself to a standing position. Annie was very wobbly and staggered back and forth, but she was up.

In a flash, Ted was behind her, pulling the collar of her blue blazer down over her shoulders, immobilizing her. Ted fastened her wrists together with his black leather belt. The jerking of her arms behind her sent sharp stabs of pain through both of her shoulder blades. Ted took the long end of the belt, after securing her wrists with the buckle, and threaded it between the water pipe and concrete cinder block of the foundation wall. He pulled it tight and upward, which left Annie in a standing position, on her tiptoes, lurching outward from the waist up. Her tied hands were pulled up almost to the middle of her back.

"Now, don't go away, you little bitch. I'll be right back," Ted said, and then he gave her cheek a soft pat.

Annie watched as Ted walked across the basement in large loping strides, taking the stairs two at a time as he disappeared up to the first floor. She could hear him walking across the kitchen floor and down the hallway to the front door. Then she heard the front door open and close.

Oh, thank God he's gone, Annie thought. She was definitely in a predicament, but at least she had not been raped. She was certain with a little effort she could loosen the noose around her wrists. It would take time, but she was okay. She was proud of her fast thinking and the part about jail. It probably saved her from becoming a victim. She knew that 60 percent of rapists were never caught, but she had been convincing enough to save herself. Now Annie had time to figure out her escape. It wasn't as though anyone would be coming home and she could just yell for help. The home was vacant, owned by the bank. She had to get out on her own; otherwise, it could be days before anyone missed her and came looking for her.

There was a noise and Annie froze. It was the front door again. She thought Ted had fled the scene. She heard his heavy boots walk down the hall and across the kitchen. At the top of the stairs she saw the boots, then the jeans with a crease down the front of each leg. The bottom hem of the suede sports coat came into view, along with a backpack hanging over Ted's shoulder. In his other hand he held Annie's purse by the strap. She had left it, along with her cell phone and keys, on the kitchen counter when they had reentered the home. He was smiling as he strode across the basement toward her. *On no. God, no. It's not over.*

"What do you want from me? I don't even know you."

"I want revenge," Ted said calmly as he sat the purse and backpack on the floor. "And you may not know me, but I know you and everyone like you. All Realtors are alike. Your only concern is your precious commission checks. You don't give a shit about the people who live in the houses you sell. Oh, you pretend to care about the schools and parks and what wonderful neighbors live next door," Ted said in mocking baby talk. "Bullshit!"

Annie's eyes were wide with fear as she watched Ted unpack the small backpack he had brought with him.

"You're all good actors, I'll give you that much," Ted continued. "You pretend to care about my needs. What am I looking for in a new home? How far of a commute am I willing to have to my job? What price range am I looking in? I tell you I can afford two seventy-five, tops. You show me three hundred, you little bitch."

"But I've never worked with you, Ted," Annie whimpered.

"You or the next slut down the road—what's the difference? You're all the same. Talk me into a home I can't afford and then happily sell it a few years later when I'm going broke trying to keep up on the payments. You tell me it's a bad market. 'Gee, Ted, sorry to tell you the market is soft. We probably can't sell it for what you paid, but I'll do my best.' Once you put the sign in the yard, I'll never hear from you. Could take months and months to get an offer. Right? Then the shitty offer does finally come in, and you say, 'Well, Ted, it's not what we were hoping for, but it's something. I think you should take it.' You're bloodsuckers, that's what you are. Well, little miss Realtor lady, I'm not taking it anymore."

All the time Ted was going on, Annie watched with horror as he laid the contents of the backpack on the floor of the basement.

"What are you going to do?" she asked, almost in a whisper.

"I'm going to rid the world of one more lowlife, money-grubbing, lying-through-their-teeth Realtor," he said with a slightly crooked smile and dull eyes, looking up at her from his crouched position on the basement floor. His teeth were crooked and stained a brownish yellow.

On the floor Ted had laid out a roll of white duct tape. Next to the tape he put a pair of scissors, latex gloves, a small bottle of water, a skinny plastic container holding some kind of pills, and a pair of long forceps. Next he emptied the contents of Annie's purse on the floor.

"You women are amazing. Look at all this shit you carry around with you everywhere you go." Ted scattered Annie's belongings until he found what he was looking for, her lipstick. "Nice shade. What do you call it?" Ted asked. Then he found her business card holder.

"Please, don't," Annie sobbed. "Please don't."

"I won't lie to you, Annie," said Ted. "This is going to hurt." For the first time, there was a glint in his pale blue eyes.

Ted put the latex gloves on, snapping them on his hands like they do in the movies, for effect. He then pulled a piece of duct tape off the roll, about six inches long, cut it with the scissors, and stuck it on the wall near Annie's head. Next he unscrewed the cap from the water bottle and set it on the floor near Annie's feet. Finally, the cap came off the plastic tube.

"You should thank me, Annie," Ted said. "Your pain will only last for a little while. My pain goes on day after day after month after year until I can barely stand to exist some days. But this makes it all worthwhile. I am doing the public a favor, preventing the likes of you from preying upon my fellow human beings. This is what keeps me going."

"Ted—"

"As I have been cast in the role of your executioner, you should know that my name is Henry, not Ted, but my friends call me Hank. You may call me Henry."

Hank stood up, took the forceps, and plucked a tablet about the size of a half dollar out of the plastic tube. He held it up so Annie could see. It was about the size of a poker chip, only a little thicker. It was white and chalky. He held it under her nose. There was no odor.

"You know what this is, Annie?"

Annie didn't answer. She was crying and wiggling against her restraint, to no avail.

"It's sodium hydroxide."

Henry squeezed her checks with his left hand. It forced her face into a pucker, the look of someone who just took a bite out of a fresh lemon.

"Open up."

Henry forced the tablet between Annie's lips with the forceps. Lodging the cake-like substance in the back of her throat, Henry quickly picked up the open bottle of water and poured a little in Annie's mouth. He grabbed the six-inch piece of white duct tape from the wall and smoothed it over Annie's mouth.

Annie's eyes exploded with tears as she shook her head back and forth violently. The burning in her mouth was unbearable. The tablet was foaming, filling her mouth with burning drool. The tape kept the liquid from escaping. It was boiling inside and felt as though it would soon be running out her nose. She couldn't hold the pressure any longer and was force to swallow. The pain and burning was too much to endure. She lost control of her bladder and felt the warm urine glide down the inside of her leg. Her chest was on fire. Instead of dissipating, the fire blast was building. She was coughing through her taped mouth and thought she might vomit. Liquid was spraying from her nose as she convulsed.

Annie stared at Henry like a trapped animal. Her eyes were wide with fear. Through the tears, she could see him readying another tablet, pinched between the tips of the forceps. Fear and pain gripped Annie as her final thoughts floated like feathers to the ground. *Who is this mad man ending my life? I'm glad I don't have children. This will devastate my mom. I guess it isn't going to be a very good spring market after all. Not now, not ever.*

Henry undid the duct tape, leaving it hanging from the right side of Annie's cheek, and forced a second tablet into her mouth, followed by a few drops of water. A quick slap and he put the tape back into place, sealing the burning sensation inside Annie's mouth. He fed Annie another tablet, followed by another few drops of water and more burning, until she eventually lost consciousness and the will to fight.

Henry always used at least two to three lye tablets to make sure the victim was good and bubbling on the inside. It was easier getting the second and third tablets down their throats, and sometimes a fourth was need for a particularly strong willed individual. If they weren't dead after an hour, they were surely unconscious, and it was only a short time later before they left this world. It was simple, remove the tape, inset the next tablet as deep as possible, add a bit of water, tilt the head back, and replace the tape—lights out. He put the cap back on the plastic tube, turned the latex gloves inside out as he removed them, and returned the tape to his backpack. He waited several more minutes, his eyes roaming the unfinished basement. It will make a great game room for some lucky family, or maybe the little kids will learn to ride their new Christmas bicycles down here before next spring comes along.

He gazed at Annie's face, gently stroking her cheek. A twinge of remorse filled his heart. But damn it, these people had to be taught a lesson. An example had to be made. And it was his job to make it.

Henry then took the scissors and, following the V-neckline of Annie's blouse, cut down towards where it was tucked into the top of her skirt. He parted the material, exposing Annie's lacy bra, and cut it in two at the breast bone. Henry reached down to the floor and picked up the tube of lipstick. Taking the cap off, he screwed the glossy point upwards. In large capital letters he wrote LYER on Annie's still chest, in pink organza.

He put everything back into Annie's purse except her business card holder. Henry withdrew two cards and looked at them. Sweet Annie's face, looking out from the card, a big smile, large white teeth, full of confidence. "Buying or Selling, Annie's the One" was written in old English at the top of each card.

Henry had some trouble getting the business cards to stay in place over Annie's eyes because she was hanging forward from the water pipe. He reached into the backpack for the duct tape. Using just a small, thin strip, he taped one card over each eye. When he was finished, Henry looked around to be sure he hadn't left behind any evidence. The belt would be useless to the police. It was from JC Penney and he had a dozen more at home. Satisfied with his cleanup and feeling as though he had done his part to better society, he went up the stairs, through the kitchen, and down the hall to the foyer. He stopped at the front door. It really was a nice house, but a blue bathroom—what were they thinking?

He paused on the porch with the door still open and said, loudly enough for a neighbor or passersby to hear, "Thank you, Annie. I'll discuss it with my wife when I get home and let you know what we have decided. You have a nice afternoon now."

Hank felt relief as he got into his car. The planning was exciting, but the execution could be tricky. You never knew what the situation might entail. There was only one time that he had planned an open house visit when he had failed to carry out his goal. He had gotten more careful in his planning after that. He would canvas the neighborhood ahead of time, check out the homes nearby, and have at least two routes out of the area in case he had to flee.

Hank looked over his shoulder as he back out of the driveway. No one was out and about and on such a beautiful spring afternoon. He drove off slowly, whistling nothing in particular.

CHAPTER 12

"How's your steak?" asked Liz.

"Mmm, good," I said, still chewing. "Charred on the outside, pink in the middle." Steak is without a doubt my favorite food. I could eat it every day and never tire of a good strip or ribeye. I prefer the fattier cuts for their flavor. Too much red meat is supposedly bad for the cholesterol, but every year when I have my blood work done, my count is the healthy range of around one fifty.

"And how's your salmon?"

"Delicious. Would you like a bite?"

"Absolutely not. You know how I feel about fish."

"Yeah, but salmon doesn't taste like fish."

"Yes, I know. And it's hot in Arizona, but there's no humidity. It only hurts if you think it's going to hurt. And oh yeah, I mailed you the check last week. Thanks but no thanks."

Liz and I were enjoying a wonderful meal at the lodge. It was a rustic building featuring urban cuisine, located on the property but in its own building, half a mile away. We were going to take the walking trail down to the restaurant but decided to drive Margaret instead. The night air had turned chilly, and after a relaxing massage, we decided to continue the pampering. The main dining room had an A-framed peak ceiling with massive hewn wood beams. In the center of the dining room was a see-through stone fireplace that was roaring with red embers. Tables and booths were generously spaced to give patrons ample room and private conversation. Liz and I sat in a small booth for two, midway along the north wall. The tablecloth and napkins were linen, the flowers were real, and the candle had been freshly lit when we were seated.

After a luxurious one hour massage, Liz and I had returned for hot, steamy showers—in our separate rooms, of course. The foreplay was stretching my limits, among other things. A few minutes before I was to call on Liz in her room, there was a knock on the adjoining room door. I unlocked my side and opened the door to find Liz standing there, dressed to kill.

"Wow" was all I could utter. She stood in three-inch black heels, which brought the top of her head to my eye level. She wore a flattering mid-thigh twirly red dress. It fit snugly in all the right places and flared at the bottom, giving a flirtatious view of her stunning bare and toned legs as she gave me a fashion spin. It floated up and down around her legs, causing a stir of emotion and an anticipation of an unforgettable evening. The deep red of Liz's dress set off her shoulder-length ashen brown curly hair. It looked almost smoky against the mandarin collared dress. She had selected just the right amount of bling to accessorize her outfit; silver hoop earrings the size of dollar coins, a long double looped necklace of jade and wooden beads, and a collection of solid silver bracelets on each wrist. Liz looked like a big-time Hollywood starlet.

"You like?" she said, twirling.

"Oh yeah! Kurt likes," I said with a huge grin. Liz is all woman, but I had grown so used to seeing her in her daily wear of cotton slacks and button-down denim shirts that I had forgotten how glamorous she could be. She normally wore her hair up or back or tucked under the navy blue HPD baseball cap. It was also nice to see her without a police-issued.38 revolver holstered under her arm.

"You look beautiful," I said, gazing up and down her five-foot-eight frame, including heels. "I will be the envy of every man at the restaurant tonight, possibly a couple of women as well."

"You're sweet, Kurty," she said, looping her arm through mine.

I tucked my money clip in my front pocket and picked up my room key from the dresser. I started to close the connecting door between our rooms as we got ready to leave.

"Let's just leave that open," Liz said with a husky voice.

"Certainly, Ms. Colburn," I replied with a mocking bow at the waist and a sweeping arm towards the hallway door. "Anything the lady requests, she shall have."

I'm not exaggerating when I say that turned as we walked through the lobby towards the parking lot. Liz was graceful and stunning and made me walk a little taller and straighter. We decided to drive Margaret, not only because the temperature had dropped but because it was a more practical solution than a half-mile walk in three-inch heels.

Our dinner conversation was full of laughs and old stories. We relived the day we spent at Megan's Bay, in the Caribbean. We were body surfing in blue-green waves, when Liz washed up ten feet from shore and stood up minus her bikini top. It was floating in the sandy water at her feet, which she quickly retrieved and put back on to the dismay of the two vacationing teenage boys and their family.

We laughed hysterically about the time we had taken a last-minute trip to St. Paul, Minnesota, to visit one of Liz's aunts. We booked a flight the day before and as a result didn't have seat assignments together. Liz sat behind me in row nine on the small 727 puddle jumper from Chicago to St. Paul. I was seated next to a large matronly woman who fell into a deep slumber almost immediately after takeoff. I was trapped between the window and a flatulent lady who most certainly had had burritos for breakfast. The sounds and smells brought tears to our eyes for the fifty-minute flight.

Liz reminded me of a day in summer when we rented bicycles in Lincoln Park, downtown Chicago. During our ride along the lakeshore and through the various parks, a small Hispanic boy had darted out across the bike path, chasing a Frisbee. Shouts of "On your right, on your right" disappeared into the wind coming off Lake Michigan and failed to get his attention. Unable to stop, I instinctively veered to the right and into a hundred-year-old oak tree. The front tire was bent so badly that I had to walk the bike back to the rental shack. I was assured that, although rare, the mighty oaks had claimed their share of riders over the years.

The conversation was light and easy. It felt like it had in the early days, when we had first met. At one point during dinner, Liz reached across the table and squeezed my hand, tilting head back with a throaty laugh. The dangling ruby earrings bounced off from her neck, laughing with her. The dark chocolate eyes were soft and sparkling. But don't be fooled. If you ever meet those eyes while on the wrong side of a conversation (or worse yet, the wrong side of the law), they can turn to solid black coal, igniting ants faster than a magnifying glass.

The evening progressed and we moved from the dining room into the Timbers lounge. An aging couple of rockers were playing acoustic versions of popular songs in the corner. Loud enough to enjoy but not so loud they prevented conversation. We sat and tapped our feet to familiar songs. We sang along, off key to some oldies but goodies from the eighties and nineties. We even attempted to dance to "Smoke on the Water" by Deep Purple on the small ten-by-ten dance floor. Sam and Dave, not to be confused with the real Sam and Dave, enjoyed our participation along with half a dozen other patrons who were there to kick back and enjoy the music of their youth and mellow out with after-dinner drinks. The evening was over, and last call was being announced before we knew what time it was. The last song by Sam and Dave was "You've Got a Friend" by James Taylor. Liz and I stood and danced slowly right there beside our table. We didn't need much room to rock back and forth. I stared into the dark chocolate and felt as though I was standing in a doorway, looking into our past. Knowing how it had run, I was hesitant to step across the threshold again. I wasn't sure. But my God, had this been a wonderful day, and it wasn't over.

The song ended, the lights came up, and we walked out of the lounge, arm in arm, giggling as if we were leaving the prom.

"What a great night, huh?" I said as we made our way to the parking lot.

"Mmm," Liz murmured, her head against the side of my shoulder. "What time is it?"

I looked at my watch, illuminated by the moon. "A little after two."

"Let's sleep in tomorrow morning. I guess technically it is morning. So let's sleep in today."

"Deal," I said as I opened Margaret's passenger door to let Liz slide in. Great legs!

We passed through the deserted lobby, still giggling and laughing over who knows what.

"Have a nice evening" came a voice from the registration desk. Marvin, according to his name tag, appeared to be a sixteen-year-old boy, towering a full six-five when he stood up from behind the counter. A fresh, bright pimple stood on his chin.

"We will. Thank you and you have a nice evening too," I said, flashing him a smile and a wink.

Liz gave me a soft kiss on the lips as I opened her door. The lips were warm, as if she had a fever, and slightly parted. "Give me a few minutes and then come over," she whispered in my ear.

I unlocked the door to my room to discover that housekeeping had performed their turn down service. One nightstand lamp had been left on to dimly light the room. Quiet music came from the clock radio. The day pillows and bedspread had been removed. The blanket and sheets had been folded back, and two foil wrapped candies lay nestled on my pillow. As I walked by the open connecting door to Liz's room, I saw her bathroom light on and the door half closed. I caught a glimpse of her reflection in the bathroom mirror. She was brushing her hair. I took off the sports coat I had been wearing all evening and hung it over the back of the desk chair. I removed the real estate–issued slip-on loafers as well as my socks and untucked the mock turtleneck shirt I had been wearing to give myself a more casual feel. In the few minutes I was to wait, I brushed my teeth, ran a comb through my still golden locks (although darkening from my teen and twenties), and fixed two Kettle Ones using the dwarf bottles from the mini fridge. I had splashed some cranberry juice left over from an earlier cocktail into Liz's glass. I couldn't find any olives, but I didn't really care. I was a schoolboy all over again. The thought of Liz and I reacquainting our bodies had my heart pounding in my chest like a jackhammer. I could actually hear the pulse in my ears. It had been almost six months since our last conjugal visit. After a gentlemanly amount of time, I knocked gently on the open door, holding to the two high ball glasses in one hand.

"Come in, Kurty," Liz purred.

As I walked into Liz's room, I sucked the air in through my teeth. As beautiful as she had looked earlier in the evening, she now was the most sensuous looking woman I had ever seen. Liz was standing by the far side of the bed, next to the same dimly light nightstand that had been in my room. She was wearing a body-hugging one-piece satin nightgown that went from the spaghetti strapped top to the floor. It was clear to me that this was all she wearing by the silhouette from the lamp behind her. The snug fit showed off her sexy hip bones and the narrow waist she worked hard to keep. Her full breasts were barely concealed by the bodice and faded tan lines of last summer were still visible. I could see dark half circles of her nipples peeking above the lace. The straps were stretched taut over her clavicles like guitar strings.

"Apparently I'm over dressed," I stammered.

"I bought this for the occasion. I'm glad you approve," she said, motioning to me with her index finger to join her on the bed.

I sat the drinks down on the dresser and slipped out of my slacks. I tugged the turtleneck off over my head. So much for combing my hair. I could feel the static electricity spark as the cotton pulled my hair up into an imitation of Lady Liberty's crown. Liz laughed as the snap and crackle of ions filled the room and then jumped into bed. It didn't take long for me to lose the last of my clothes and join Liz under the covers. Her feet and hands were freezing as she reached out to me. I should have peed.

I could see daylight through the slit in the drapes as I opened my eyes for the first time. Liz was still breathing heavy with sleep as I slipped out of bed. We had forgotten to order room service seven hours before, so I decided to go downstairs and pick up something quick and easy. When I returned twenty minutes later, Liz was sitting up in bed, as if she had been waiting for the butler to bring her breakfast. I sat the tray, piled with juices, coffees, bagels, and an oversized blueberry muffin, the last pastry to be found for late risers, down on the side table next to her.

"Thank you, kind sir," Liz said in a raspy morning voice, the kind that comes from a late night of drinking and exertion.

"Oh, the pleasure is all mine. Last night was incredible." I almost told her that I loved her as I leaned down and kissed her cheek, brushing away long strands of renegade hair.

"Uh huh."

Uh huh? I was glad I hadn't let the "I love you" spill out. After devouring the carbs I had brought back, we changed into our swimming suits and headed down to the indoor pool. The laps helped loosen the tight muscles from the earlier acrobatics. We relaxed in the whirlpool until the echoes of late-arriving children splashing and screaming in the water shattered the silence. Shrill screams were magnified inside the aquatic center, bouncing from wall to water to ceiling. Liz and I toweled off and headed to the elevators specific to the indoor spa and took a ride to the ninth floor.

We planned the rest of our day while showering, together this time, and changing clothes. Liz and I took a short trip to a local vineyard for some sampling of merlots and Rieslings. Rosenberg Vineyard's tasting room sat high atop the farm, looking down on hundreds of acres of vines, growing up four to five feet high in neatly planted rows. The new crop of grapes was about to blossom. The tasting room itself was quite modern, with a long extended birch wood bar and floor-to-ceiling windows on all sides, providing a panoramic view of the vineyards. Knowledgeable salespeople poured one-ounce samples into small glass goblets. The goblets would have been a perfect match for the booze bottles in the mini fridge back at the hotel. Five dollars bought five samples of whites, reds, blushes, or dessert wines. The gift shop held an array of over-priced wine-related souvenirs. We purchased a couple of bottles to enjoy along with a variety of cheeses. You can't go to the dairy state without indulging in cheese, and what a variety of cheeses there were to choose from. Hard cheese, soft cheeses, yellow cheese threaded with salami, beer cheese, cheese curds, white farmer's cheese. You can buy cheese in a brick or a wheel or a wedge. There was a good chance I would be constipated for a week. It amazes me that the life expectancy in Wisconsin is so high. With all the beer, cheese, and brats they consume, not to mention the state pastime of cigarette smoking, you wouldn't expect anyone to live past fifty. It just shows how long a God-fearing, hard-working people can survive in spite of their diet. The frigid winter temperatures might also have something to do with longevity.

The late afternoon clouded over and a cold drizzle began to fall. We cut short the art gallery tour in the quaint farm towns sprinkled throughout the Wisconsin countryside. We returned to the resort very late in the afternoon and watched part of the Milwaukee Bucks game on the big screen in the bar. The day ended with an early dinner at a local eatery. The conversation was easy and comfortable, with not quite as many laughs as the evening before. But it had been a great day. The newness of being together again was wearing off, and we were settling into an old routine. By tomorrow we would both begin to feel a bit claustrophobic and would welcome the return to our individual homes. But for now, it was still all good.

The lovemaking was once again mutually satisfying, but less intense than the previous evening. We tossed and turned throughout the night, cuddling, reaching out in the dark to rest a hand on a hip or throw a leg over another leg.

I awoke the next morning to the sound of the door latching shut. I turned over to see Liz standing by the bed with a similar tray of goodies and beverages as we had had on Saturday morning.

"Good morning, sleepy head. I have a special treat," she said, unfolding an out-of-state edition of the *Tribune*. "Sunday crossword puzzle." Back when Liz and I were in the throes of cohabitation, the Sunday crossword was our special morning ritual. I would fix coffee and get the paper from the front porch. We would spend a good hour with clues and answers to start our day, before I ran off to meet with a client. Liz usually had Sundays to herself, which I know she looked forward to all week.

Liz and I lounged in the rooms until checkout time. Taking our time to pack and search for any left behind clues of our visit. Tiffany was at the counter as we settled our account.

"I hope you had a great stay with us Mr. Banning," she said, still wearing the ear-to-ear smile.

"We had a wonderful time Tiffany and look forward to our next trip. Maybe in the fall we'll be back and need only one room to make our stay more enjoyable," I joked.

Liz rolled her eyes and started towards the door, dragging her two-wheeled overnight bag behind her. I paid the balance due for incidentals and the now empty mini bar, turned in the keys, and followed Liz to the parking lot. I loaded the bags into the car. As I opened the door for Liz, she leaned into me and gave me a great big kiss.

"I had an amazing weekend, Kurt," Liz said, just a bit too seriously.

Wow, what does that mean? I thought. Are we stepping back through the threshold to start up the old relationship? I was not quite sure, so I said, "It was, wasn't it? Thank you for the idea and the gift and the gift and the gift." I was making fun to lighten the mood, which I thought had gotten a bit tense in the walk from the lobby to Margaret. "You're the best friend and lover, and I love you, Liz Colburn," I said matter-of-factly. She smiled and I closed her door.

"Best friend" was an idiotic thing to say, but I had to offset the "I love you" somehow.

The drive home was uneventful, and even though there were plenty of Sunday drivers on the road, none of it bothered me in the least. I dropped Liz at her house a little before five on Sunday afternoon. I declined to stay and gave her a hug and kiss on the porch. She was still standing in the doorway and gave me a wave as I headed to my own home. We had made no future date.

CHAPTER 13

Monday morning, several members of the Hamilton Police Department were gathered with members of the Wilmington Police Department, along with two agents from the Chicago bureau of the FBI and a smattering of officers and detectives from the surrounding areas police forces. There were twenty-five law enforcement officers assembled in the large conference room at Wilmington PD. The oblong oak table, scarred from years of use, seated sixteen comfortably. Folding chairs had been brought in to accommodate the other guests in the room. The florescent lighting in the windowless room cast a harsh glare that early in the morning, giving a gray cast to everyone's skin. Lieutenant Elizabeth Colburn sat at the conference table, wedged between her chief, Dougan, and another detective from Hamilton, Lance Boswell.

Wilmington's Chief of Police, Edward Robinski, stood at the north end of the room, next to a dry erase board and flat panel plasma screen. The bags under his eyes had bags. Wilmington is very much like Hamilton, in that there is very little crime and many of the investigations are minor. It was obvious that the recent murder of Barbara Miller, with its potential connection to an earlier Realtor murder, were taking its toll on the chief. The task force began its meeting at eight o'clock sharp on a dreary, overcast day in early April.

"I want to start by thanking everyone for their involvement on this case," said Chief Robinski. "It's not often we have a murder here in Wilmington, let alone one so brutal in nature. Seeing as we are neighboring communities, we have invited a select number of officers and detectives from Hamilton to join us. We are also fortunate enough to have two members from the FBI's regional office here to assist us with the investigation. I have asked additional local police departments to contribute a couple of officers as well. We are hoping this is an isolated event, but if turns out not to be, it's important for all of us in the area to be on alert."

The members of the task force were keenly intent and a bit fidgety as the opening remarks were made. Styrofoam coffee cups littered the table.

"As you know," Robinski continued, "a week ago today, the body of Barbara Miller was discovered in the basement of Mrs. Ellen Stuart's home at," he referred to his notes, "113 Tesla Drive. That home is currently for sale and the listing agent, Mrs. Miller, conducted an open house a week ago Sunday. Upon arriving home early Sunday evening, Mrs. Stuart did not notice anything strange. The home was left in the same condition as when she had left in the early afternoon.

"Ellen Stuart had decided to go to an afternoon matinee with her neighbor, Jillian Moss, to kill time while Mrs. Miller conducted the open house from 2:00 p.m. until 5:00 p.m. After the movie, Mrs. Stuart and Ms. Moss had an early dinner before returning home, around 6:15."

A hand was raised with a question. "There was no sign of a struggle, even though the body was discovered in the home?"

"That's correct," said Robinski. "We verified with Mrs. Stuart that everything was in place. Nothing had been moved, broken, or taken. The FBI crime team went through and did a thorough dusting for fingerprints. What did the results show, Agent Monroe?"

"The report came back with just three sets of prints in the house," said Special Agent Monroe. Ted Monroe was large, over six feet and 260 pounds easily, African-American, dressed in an expensive three-piece suit "The first sets of prints were obviously those of the homeowner, Mrs. Ellen Stuart." Special Agent Ted Monroe's booming voice matched his size and authority in the room. "The second set was identified as those of her neighbor, Ms. Jillian Moss. Ms. Moss is a frequent guest in Mrs. Stuarts home. They shared coffee two or three mornings a week. The last sets of prints belong to the victim, Mrs. Barbara Miller. Whoever committed the crime was very careful. They wore gloves, or did a complete wipe down before leaving the property."

Chief Robinski cleared his throat and began again. "Mrs. Stuart discovered the body approximately 10:30 a.m. Monday. She had gone down into the basement to retrieve a folder from the filing cabinet where she keeps records and personal papers. She smelled an odd odor and followed it to the closet where the sump pump is located. That's where she found Barbara Miller."

Liz took notes in her small spiral as Robinski laid out the details. These were details that the press had not received. Robinski wrote bullet statements on the dry erase board as he spoke.

"The victim's cause of death appears to be poisoning. Barbara Miller ingested a form of acid that aside from extensive burning of the lips, tongue, throat, and stomach, caused her internal organs to bleed out. Not a pleasant way to go, ladies and gentlemen. The victim would have spent thirty to forty minutes in excruciating pain before going unconscious and eventually dying."

Several people in attendance instinctively reached out and took a sip of their coffee to moisten their drying throats.

"Mrs. Miller was seated on a small wooden chair, similar to those found in elementary school classrooms. Her hands and ankles had been hog tied behind her. Her mouth had been covered with duct tape. When the coroner removed the tape, there was a dried white residue at the corners of her mouth, akin to dried toothpaste. And her lips were badly blistered. The coroner estimated the time of death sometime late Sunday evening. Most likely, Mrs. Miller was in an unconscious state, but alive, and would have died later in the evening, while Mrs. Stuart slept comfortably upstairs in her bed. In addition, the victim's business cards had been taped over her eyes, one over each eye. At this point we're not sure about the importance of the cards, but it is a signature of some sort. Lastly," Robinski continued, "Mrs. Miller's blouse had been unbuttoned to the waist, and the word LYER was written on her chest in lipstick."

Liz raised her hand. "Yes, Lieutenant," said Robinski.

"Was there any sign of sexual abuse?" Liz asked.

Robinski nodded towards Monroe. He rose to answer the question. "No, there was no sign of intercourse or bruising anywhere on the body that would indicate a sexual attack. The victim's bladder did release during her ordeal; otherwise, no indications of molestation." Monroe sat down.

Robinski drew a line down the center of the erase board and on the left-hand side he wrote Barbara Miller's name. "The victim was forty-six years old, divorced, mother of one son, Brian Miller, who attends college outside of the area." He paused. "We've checked, and he was at school that weekend and his whereabouts have been substantiated." He continued to write and Liz repeated the list in her own notebook. "As many of you know, she was a local Realtor and had been in the business a little over fifteen years. Mrs. Miller was of medium build with short brown hair, slightly overweight for her frame. Coworkers described her as jovial, helpful, and well respected. She was a community volunteer at the hospital as well as on several local committees." Robinski added each fact to the board in a descending pattern. When he was through, he looked in the direction of Special Agent Monroe.

Monroe stood and replaced Robinski at the front of the conference room. He certainly looked the part of an FBI agent, either that or a retired NFL linebacker or a Hollywood leading man. Once again his baritone filled the room. "Ladies and gentlemen, I'm sure many of you have wondered why Special Agent Wilcox and I are present here today. As you may know, just over two weeks ago, a Realtor was discovered murdered in Glenburg. We believe these two homicides are connected and may be the work of the same individual or individuals." Monroe's voice was steady and almost a monotone, as if it was just another day at the office for him. Working out of the Chicago office of the FBI, it probably was just another day at the office—not so for the officers sitting in that room on a Monday morning.

Murmurs went around the room. Liz, and most everyone else in the room, had heard about the body of a Realtor found in a northeast suburb. But until now, it had been considered a random killing, not one specifically targeting Realtors. Living in the Chicagoland area, murder was almost an everyday occurrence, and the memory of a two-week-old murder had faded from most people's mind. Now a profile was emerging. On the right side of the erase board, Monroe wrote the name Sara Donoghue at the top and began a similar list to that of Robinski's.

"The victim, Sara Donoghue, was a thirty-four-year-old white female. She was married and had two children. She had been a real estate agent for three years. She failed to return home after hosting an open house three weeks ago. Her husband reported her missing that same day and she was discovered four days later, at the residence of the home where she was last seen in Glenburg. The home was vacant and therefore the discovery was not immediate. Mrs. Donoghue was found in the trunk of her car, which had been parked in the garage of the home at 1214 Mission Hill Court, where the open house was held. Although her hands and feet had not been tied, there were abrasions on her wrists and ankles indicating that she had been restrained. This also would indicate that she was murdered somewhere else and then put into the trunk of the car. A sweep of the interior of the home revealed nothing to suggest a struggle took place. Similarly to Chief Robinski's case, the only fingerprints in the house belonged to Mrs. Donoghue and the members of the Robbins family, who had vacated in early January."

Liz was now on page three of her own notes. She had entered questions in the left margin in case they were not answered during the meeting.

"The similarities are stunning," continued Monroe. "That's why we believe these two homicides are connected. First, the victim's mouth was sealed with duct tape, and when removed by the Lake County medical examiner, a white dried residue was also found around the mouth. The same blistering of lips, mouth, and throat was discovered, as with Mrs. Miller. Toxicology revealed an acidic substance had been ingested. Cause of death was poisoning. To complete the comparisons, Mrs. Donoghue's blouse had been unbuttoned and the word LYER was written on the victim's chest in her own lipstick. Finally, two of Sara Donoghue's business cards had been taped over her eyes. Therefore, we believe that the two murders were committed by the same person or persons, therefore it is either coincidence or they are intentionally targeting Realtors. The motive is unclear at this time, but we are hopeful of getting a profile put together in the next day or two from our department downtown. We have plenty of evidence from the victims but little to none of the assailant. We would ask that you keep your eyes open for any information that may help with this investigation. Thank you." Monroe returned to his seat.

Without getting up, Robinski introduced Dr. Sam Turnquist. He had been the local coroner since Regan was President of the United States. Dr. Sam, as most people referred to him, had been a lifelong resident of Wilmington and had returned after medical school to begin his practice. His professional status was unmarred, and he was highly respected in both the medical and criminal fields. He had moved through the ranks of the medical examiner's department and on to county coroner. He had held the current title for over three decades, with no interest in retiring or slowing down, in spite of his age.

"Thank you Special Agent Monroe," Dr. Sam said as he got to his feet slowly and moved to the front of the room. "I know most of you in this room, and it's always a sad occasion when I see you." He offered a tired smile, with wrinkles at the corners of his mouth and across his forehead. "I won't keep you long, but I would like to relay the tox screen findings to you. I've had a chance to review the Lake County coroner's report, and the findings for Mrs. Donoghue are identical to those of Mrs. Miller. An endoscopy performed on both victims revealed poisoning by way of sodium hydroxide—NaOH for any chemistry buffs here today. The more common name would be lye, a toxic acid if ingested. The amount of blood would indicate the cause of death was internal bleeding, initiated by the lye. No one would voluntarily eat or drink lye, so we determined that it was force fed. During the internal probing of the victim's stomach and other organs, undissolved crystals were discovered, leading me to believe the lye was administered in a powdered form. In summary, these two women met with the same horrible death. They were surprised, restrained, and forced to swallow large amounts of sodium hydroxide. Death would have taken several hours. This would have been preceded by agonizing pain. It would take approximately an hour or less to succumb to the pain and lose consciousness, depending on the individual's personal threshold. The sodium hydroxide, or lye, would have eaten away at the stomach lining and other organs as it was transported throughout the body's system. During ingestion, skin, lips, tongue, gums, and esophagus would have experienced surface burns. Think of the worst case of heartburn you've ever had and multiply by a hundred." Dr. Sam glanced around the room, "Any questions?"

After scanning the left margin on her notepad, Liz raised her hand. "Dr. Sam, how would one be forced to ingest lye? And if it wasn't a liquid, how could the perpetrator get the victim to swallow enough to kill them?"

"Good questions, Lieutenant Colburn," Dr. Sam said. "The quantity of poison needed to cause death would have been substantial, five to seven grams in solid form. The substance would need to be forced into the mouth, then swallowed, with the mouth covered to prevent spewing it back out. The size and weight of the individual would also determine the quantity and time to take effect. My guess is that each victim had the lye pushed far into the throat, probably in small cake or powered form, and then the mouth and nose were pinched tight to avoid regurgitation. This may be why duct tape was place over the mouth, or it could have been to keep the victim from screaming. The process was repeated until the killer thought enough of the substance had been swallowed." He shrugged at his conclusion.

"Anyone else?" Robinski asked as he stood to retake the head of the room. "Thank you, Dr. Sam. Special Agent Monroe, can you give us any idea of who or what we should be looking for?"

Monroe stood from his chair and cleared his throat. "What we do know, without a complete profile, is that the killer or killers seem to have a grudge against Realtors. It may be against woman specifically, but it's too early to tell. The fact that 65 percent of Realtors are female puts the odds in their favor of being in the wrong place at the wrong time. The two murders happened thirty-two miles apart, and it's a safe bet that the killer doesn't live in either of the locations where the bodies were found. Criminals tend to commit their crimes in places other than where they reside. More details are needed before we can be more specific. Today the FBI is sending out an electronic bulletin to all real estate companies in the Chicagoland area, warning of the potential risk. This is an enormous task, seeing how there are thousands of real estate offices, from the one-man shops to small mom-and-pop operations to medium and large national brokerages. We certainly don't want to start a panic, but the professionals in the industry need to be made aware of the situation."

The door at the north end of the conference room opened, and an officer stuck her head in and motioned to Chief Robinski. "Excuse me," he said as Monroe was finishing the last details of the victims and their crime scenes. All eyes watched him as he left the room. Two minutes later he reentered the conference room, looking more worn than before, if that were possible.

"Shit," he moaned as he stood at the front of the room. "Another body was just discovered, in Lawton." He slumped down in his chair at the head of the conference table. The room broke out in a dozen conversations. Liz flipped to a new page in her spiral. Lawton was two communities to

CHAPTER 14

"Good afternoon. This is Kurt Banning. May I help you?"

"Hi, Kurt,

"Wow," I said, "it hasn't even been twenty-four hours and you need a Kurt fix."

"Funny. Really, though. I would like to meet you somewhere, if you're available."

"A nooner?" I asked incredulously. I should have heard the tension in Liz's voice, but I was in my normal playful mood.

"Not funny," Liz replied in a hushed voice. "Seriously, we've got some interesting developments in the three Realtor murders."

"Three!" I shouted and sat straight up in my chair, feet planted on the floor. "Did you say three?"

"Another one this morning. It was announced while we had our first task force meeting. So, can we meet somewhere?"

"Sure. Where are you at right now?"

"I'm on my way over to Lawton to check out the crime scene."

"Lawton!" I was now sitting at full attention at my desk.

"Yes, Lawton. It's where the last victim was found. I'm going to see what information I can get from the LPD. Give me some time to get the details."

I was numb as I hung up with Liz. This was obviously some kind of serial killer on the loose and a little too close to home. Wilmington and now Lawton. I was confused and not sure what to take away from the recent murders, but I was sure Liz would fill me in later, as much as she could, at least. Liz and I had agreed to meet at Abby's in ninety minutes. I had some time to kill and needed a diversion from the information I had just received from Liz. I decided to call Mr. Schwartz, whose home I had just listed the week before.

"Hi, Ernie," I said when he picked up. "It's Kurt. Do you have a minute?"

"Sure, sure, Kurt. What's up?" Ernie Schwartz and his wife, Enid, had lived in the same house for forty-two years. A solidly built all-brick ranch with a full basement. It was loaded with stacks of newspapers, *National Geographic* magazines (does anybody ever throw those things out?), and a 1949 set of encyclopedias, Britannica, I think, complete with all the indexes and updated issues. The first thing I told Ernie when I came to talk to him about listing his home was to de-clutter the basement, which really was a rec room finished in a sixties motif. Peel-and-stick vinyl flooring, painted cinderblock walls, and a drop ceiling with twenty-inch soundproof tile squares. There were plenty of memories plastered on the walls and above a bar, which Ernie had built himself. It was nothing fancy but had served many New Year's Eve parties, birthday parties, and anniversaries. The three Schwartz children had been born and raised in the home at 20 Locust Street. Samuel was grown and living in a posh suburb north of Chicago. He was a well-respected surgeon of internal medicine. Melvin had graduated from law school but decided on trying his hand at writing. He currently resided in Sarasota, Florida, with his fourth girlfriend of the decade and had recently had a novel put to print with a well-known publishing house. Ernie was pleased for Mel but disappointed he never attempted to pass the bar exam. The love of his life, his daughter Rachel, lived two hours away, with his grandchildren, whom he thoroughly enjoyed but didn't see often enough. His son-in-law was a nice enough young man and had made the offer along with Rachel for Ernie to come and live with them.

Ernie's wife Enid had passed away just before Christmas, a year and a half ago. And although he was in good health, the family agreed it would be best for him to live closer to one of his children. Samuel had no children, and his wife, Charlotte, acted as if she had a broom handle stuck up her butt, according to Ernie. Mel was a free spirit, and besides, Florida was too hot in the summer and too full of old people the rest of the year. That left Rachel, his adorable grandchildren, and his tolerable son-in-law, Keith. So off to Indiana he would go, as soon as he sold his home in Hamilton. That was my job.

"I wanted to share the feedback from the three showings we had this past weekend," I said.

"Somebody wants to buy?" he yelled into the phone.

"Not yet, but I thought you might be interested in what the other agents and their clients thought of your home."

"If they don't want to buy, should I care what they think of my home?"

"Well, yes," I said, "it helps us make changes that might attract other interested buyers."

"Like what?" It sounded as though he was having a sandwich for lunch while we spoke.

"The first family loved your yard and all the wonderful landscaping you've added over the years. The fact that it is a ranch and all on one floor was a big plus, but—"

"But," Ernie interrupted, "they want to buy my bushes and trees but not the house. Okay, screw them. What about number two?" It must be wonderful to be eighty-five and not give a crap what anyone thinks, just cut through it and get to the point.

"The second family liked the floor plan. The second and third bedrooms were a little small, but they only have a baby at this point. Might have worked—"

"But," he interrupted again, "they want to buy?"

"No," I replied, "they felt there was too much wallpaper in the kitchen and bathrooms. They don't want a home they have to re-decorate."

"My Enid picked out that paper when we built the house. Kurt, it took me three weekends to hang that paper. And it wasn't easy. All those big flowers and vines."

"I know, Ernie. I'm sure it was very fashionable forty years ago, but it's not exactly what buyers are looking for today. We talked about that before we put your home on the market. Maybe we should consider—"

"Screw them too. What about number three?"

"First-time home buyers, just starting their search. A young couple. Not sure what they really are looking for but wanted to see what their money could buy."

"Them I like," he said.

"Well, we're still on their short list of homes they liked."

"Good. It was good enough for Enid and I way back when. I'd like a nice young couple to buy this house. It's a lucky house, Kurt. We had three great kids born in this house."

"I know it is, Ernie. I'll keep you up to date on future showings. Anything I can do for you?" I asked.

"Sell my house, Realtor man. Bye."

I love clients like Mr. Schwartz. I feel an extra responsibility to them to reach their goal so they can get on with their lives and whatever the next chapter holds. I'm not offended by their attitudes, as I prefer to know where I stand at all times. Ernie just let me know where I stood.

I tidied my desk, put away some files, locked my desk drawer, and headed off to meet Liz at Abby's. "See you later this afternoon, Molly," I said as I rounded the corner and headed for the main door.

"You're meeting *her*, the girlfriend," Molly said with mock jealousy.

"If by *her* you mean Liz, yes I am, and she's not my girlfriend."

"Well, you behave yourself, Mr. Banning," she said as the etched glass door was closing behind me. The dreary skies were clearing and the drizzle had stopped, but the temperature hadn't climbed out of the fifties from earlier in the morning when I arrived at the office. Margaret was tucked safely away from the elements in my garage behind the Prescott Realty building. I climbed into my Realtor Caddy and pulled out of the alley, headed west. I was told years ago, when I first went into real estate, that the best way to know what was going on in your market place was to drive around and keep your eyes open. Never take the same route home or to an appointment, Bard Holmes had told me once. Travel the side streets, go out of your way to see what's going on in the neighboring cities, drive slowly and observe, he had said often. His pearls of wisdom were never lost on me. I admired Bard and the business he continued to grow, of which Mr. Prescott had left him in charge. He continued to make Prescott Realty successful by being observant, asking questions and being honest.

When I first joined Prescott Realty as a rookie, Bard Holmes had taken me out for a drive one afternoon in early April. It was a lesson in prospecting. We drove the tree-lined streets and side streets of Hamilton. From the new homes in the south part of town to the historic homes in town to the dated small bungalows at the north end of town, he pointed out things that amazed me in my neophyte stage. We would pass homes with workmen's trucks in the driveway. Paint contractors meant the owners might be neutralizing their homes and getting ready to place their houses for sale in the spring market. Old rolls of carpet sitting alongside the driveway on garbage day was even a better bet for an upcoming sale than the paint trucks. Decorators, roofing contractors, and window companies meant those people were here to stay for a while, keep looking for clues. Unusually large quantities of junk on the curb meant the owners were in clean-out mode, another possible indicator of a potential listing. Garage sales in the spring and early summer were an open invitation to stop by, spend five bucks on a piece of junk, and strike up a conversation with the owner. "Looks like you've cleaned out the basement after a long winter," you might say. Which led to, "Yeah, we need to get rid of this stuff. It's been gathering dust for years, and it's time to sell it off." An inquisitive mind might then say, "Looks as if you're getting ready to move," hopeful of the response, "We've been talking about it, and the timing seems right." Out comes the business card with a smiling Kurt Banning, at your service. If you had a chance to make an appointment for a listing presentation, the five dollars was well spent. If not, you could collect enough junk to have your own garage sale.

A small do-it-yourself moving truck might mean a renter is moving in or out. If they were moving in, put the address on your mailing list and contact them just before a one-year lease was about to expire. You could help them buy their next home, at the very least, or find them another rental if they weren't happy staying put. If they looked like they were moving out and there was no For Rent or For Sale sign in the yard, you would look up the owner in the tax records and put them on your mailing list before following up with a phone call. Those incredibly cute and expensive giant wooden signs announcing births and milestone birthdays are like flashing neon signs to a Realtor. Just had a baby? You're going to need a bigger home in a year or two, especially when the second or third bundle of joy comes along. Look who just turned sixty, or retired. Might be time to downsize into a townhome or condo, or better yet, let's sell the old shack and more to the Sunbelt. A good Realtor is a good detective. The clues lay strewn everywhere if you just slow down, observe, and ask questions. Bard Holmes was a genius.

As I drove through the familiar neighborhoods of my sales territory, my mind was not on finding the next home to list or what homes my competition had on the market. I was thinking how in seemingly an instant, the small-town security that we all took for granted was being smashed like ice cubes falling on concrete. Wilmington and Lawton were facing a serious problem, and I wondered if Hamilton was soon to follow. And even though the local police departments didn't deal with such heinous crimes on a daily basis, I had the utmost confidence in their abilities to find the killer, but in the meantime how many more Realtors would turn up dead? I meandered the quiet residential streets, working my way to Abby's, where I hoped Liz would give me some news that would calm the anxiousness in my stomach.

Meanwhile Liz had arrived at the home at 2376 Willow Court in Lawton. The drive from the Wilmington Police Department had taken less than thirty minutes, even with the midday traffic. Police cars, an ambulance, the county medical examiner's van, and a handful of onlookers' cars were parked along the side street of Brookfield Avenue, which led traffic north and south, with the cul-de-sac court, Willow, dead-ending to the east. Three news station vehicles, with antennas extending from their roofs, were parked a block away. Liz pulled her unmarked squad car to the entrance of Willow Court and doubled parked near a black and white Lawton patrol car.

"You can't park there," a uniformed officer was saying as Liz got out of her car. When he saw the badge clipped to her belt, he motioned her over to the line of yellow tape that had been stretched across the driveway of 2326 Willow Court.

"Detective Colburn with the Hamilton Police Department," Liz said, shaking the hand of the young patrolman. Crowd control was a duty often given to rookies. Liz doubted the officer had been out of the academy for more than six months. His eyes had an innocence that looked as though he was frightened more than he ever had been in his life. His short-cropped blond hair was just visible at the side of his police-issued baseball cap. The dark blue hat had not yet had time to fade with the sun or pick up any sweat stains from the job. His voice was a bit uneven as he addressed his senior officer, Liz.

"Officer," Liz looked down and squinted at his badge, pinned neatly to his chest, "Logan, Chief Dougan, my boss, asked me to come over and speak with the officer in charge. Who might that be?"

"Um, well, I was the one who responded to the call from a dispatcher from the Metro Maintenance and Home Services Company at," he referred to his own small spiral notebook, "10:17 this morning."

"Then, Officer Logan, are you the one in charge?" Liz said curtly.

"No, ma'am. That would be Sergeant Lapinski. He's inside."

Liz ducked under the tape as the young patrolman held it up for her. As she went up the front steps to the already open door, the usual pandemonium was taking place inside. The covered body lay on a gurney. A plainclothesman was taking photographs, and two guys in jump suits were dusting with talc for fingerprints. A group of three men were talking in the middle of the room, making notes on pads.

"Sergeant Lapinski?" Liz asked to the room in general, not knowing which one was Lapinski.

"That's me. What can I do for you?" he asked, noticing Liz's badge.

"Lieutenant Colburn with the Hamilton PD. My chief asked me to get any details possible from the guy in charge. I was told that's you."

"That's correct, but everything at this point is confidential until I make a full report to *my* chief. What's Hamilton's interest in this case?"

"I've been assigned to the task force investigating the other two murders, which seem to be connected," Liz replied. "I'm acting on a direct order."

Lapinski was the only non-uniformed in the room. He looked veteran, with lines of experience crisscrossing his face. His skin was starchy white and his jaw line sagged with age. He had been on the force for quite a while and had topped out at sergeant. Liz gave him the respect he was due.

"If it's not too much trouble, you can have your chief call my chief to verify what I'm saying. I certainly don't want to ask you to tell me anything that might violate the confidence of your department. My sole reason for being here is to gather any information possible that might connect the other two crime scenes and help build a profile that will catch this son of a bitch."

Lapinski stared at Liz for a moment. He liked her attitude. "Give me a minute to finish with these two gentlemen and I'll share what I know with you. If you want to take a look where we found the body, the stairs are right over there." He nodded his head towards the open basement door.

And if as not wanting to seem too soft for agreeing to talk with Liz, he added, "And don't touch anything."

"Right, Sarge."

Liz headed down the stairs to the basement. There were numbered markers on the floor that corresponded with photos that the photographer from upstairs had taken previously. All the lights were on, illuminating the entire space of the unfinished basement. Bright 100-watt bulbs hung every ten feet, forming a grid along the floor. It was your normal basement, concrete slab floor, cinderblock walls, two well windows, and a variety of conduit, plumbing, and wires. The furnace and hot water heater had been installed at the far end of the basement, making it easier to finish but much less efficient for delivering heat and hot water throughout the home. Liz noticed a dried stain on the floor near the main water shutoff valve and little else. The basement had that faint musty smell that comes with years of curing cement and lack of ventilation.

"Lieutenant Colburn?" came a booming voice from the top of the stairs. It was Lapinski.

"Be right up." Liz took one last sweeping view of the empty basement.

"Chief Connolly says it's okay to share the evidence with you," Lapinski said when Liz reached the top of the stairs.

"Thanks, we really appreciate it. We all have to work together to catch a creep like this." So he had checked her out, she was impressed by his thoroughness.

Liz opened her black covered spiral notebook that she had been using earlier in the morning at the task force meeting in Wilmington. She looked at Sergeant Lapinski, poised with her pen waiting.

"The victim was a thirty-six-year-old white female," he began. "Her name was Ann Lawrence. She went by Annie. A service company employee that checks on vacant homes discovered the body this morning. A bank currently owns the home, and it is common for them to hire third-party companies to keep an eye on all the properties in their foreclosure inventory. The home is listed for sale by Marshal and Montgomery Real Estate Company," Lapinski read from his own notes. "Annie Lawrence worked for them. She evidently held an open house here yesterday. Her car was found in the driveway. We had it towed to the crime lab auto yard. The medical examiner didn't give us a cause of death, but the time of death was between 8:30 and 11:00 p.m. yesterday. Jose Benitez, who works for the Metro Maintenance and Home Services Company, discovered her around ten o'clock this morning. Based on his statement and what we found when we arrived, Ms. Lawrence was restrained by a black two-inch-thick belt. Her hands were tied behind her back, suspended from the water pipe. Her blouse was torn open down the front, and the pervert had written LYER on her chest over her heart, with what appears to be lipstick. She had duct tape across her mouth."

Liz was scribbling as fast as she could, using a shortened method she had developed over the years to gather a lot of information during brief encounters with witnesses, suspects, and other law enforcement personnel.

"And this last little bit of information is strange—" Lapinski said.

"Did she have her business cards taped over her eyes?" Liz interrupted.

"Yeah, how'd you know that?" Lapinski looked shocked.

"Same MO as the other two Realtors that were found during the past three weeks."

"Three?" asked Lapinski. "I heard about the one over in Wilmington, but who's number three?"

"Well, actually, your victim here is number three. The first one, which kind of went into the normal homicide file, was up in Glenburg," Liz answered.

"So, we got us a real wacko on our hands."

"Seems that way. Thank you, for your help Sergeant. If you get any more information from the lab or coroner, please call me," Liz said, handing him one of her cards.

"Piece of shit better hope I don't find him first." Lapinski was disgusted and had been around long enough to see the evil people can do. In law enforcement, if the guy wasn't guilty of what you charged him with, he was probably guilty of something else, so he should be put away. That was Sergeant Lapinski's motto.

By now, most of the official vehicles were gone. One news truck was still parked on a side street with an onsite reporter speaking into a camera, possibly filing a report for the five o'clock news. The ambulance was gone, as was the coroner's van. A dozen or so neighbors were standing around in small groups, talking among themselves, trying to guess what had

CHAPTER 15

"Hi, Liz," I heard Macy say as she enter Abby's Restaurant. Macy had been a waitress at Abby's for as long as I had been coming here. She always had a smile on her face and a pot of coffee in her right hand. The uniform was clean and starched, even if the apron wasn't. "Kurt's already here, down there," she motioned with the pot, causing a wake of coffee to slosh against the glass.

Liz looked tired and small in her black jeans and argyle sweater vest over a white collared blouse as she approached the booth. She was wearing an dark blue insulated windbreaker with H.P.D. across the left front. She gave me a weary smile and a halfhearted wave. All in all, she was a beautiful woman. I stood up and gave her a tight hug. She slid into the booth, across from me.

"You look beat," I said, "and it's only afternoon."

"Long day already. It's hard to believe just twenty-four hours ago we were driving back from a wonderful weekend in Wisconsin. What a difference a day makes, to quote the old standard."

A small smile turned up the corner my mouth when she had said wonderful. "So what's going on? You said on the phone there was a third Realtor found this morning.

"Well, it appears as though we have a full-force serial killer on the loose."

"No coincidence?"

"Nope, afraid not. What I can tell you, and please Kurt, keep this to yourself. Not a word to anyone, and that includes Dexter."

"Promise, Scout's honor." I held up the three middle fingers on my right hand.

"What can I get for you, hon?" asked Macy, appearing out of nowhere, standing at the end of the booth. I was already on my second cup of decaf.

"Just coffee," said Liz. "Too late for lunch and too early for dinner."

"Cops and their coffee, go figure." She turned to me.

"I'll take a refill and a piece of banana cream pie." Liz raised an eyebrow at me. "What? I have a little left over winter flab. I'm back on the treadmill and the extra five will be gone by the end of the month," I whined.

After Macy left, Liz continued, "I'm telling you this for two reasons. One, I think you can give me some insight on the real estate angle of the murders. You know how an open house is run—where someone could be vulnerable, timing, that kind of thing. Maybe you can see some similarities among the homes where the crimes were committed."

"Okay, sure. I'm at your service. The easiest time for someone to enter an open house undetected is in the beginning, when we set up, and at the end, when we're shutting everything down. After the directional signs are put into place, which I would do on the way to the home, I unlock the residence, go in and put my flyers, cards, and sign-in log on the table, usually in the kitchen. The vulnerable period is when you are going through the house, turning on the lights. You are away from the entrance, upstairs flicking on switches and ceiling fans and also when you go down to the basement to catch those lights as well. If it's a finished basement, it takes a little longer. All totaled, you're away from the main door three, four, five minutes, depending on how large the home is. Same goes for when you're finished and you repeat the process at the end of the open house, shutting everything off. Otherwise, it's pretty difficult for someone to enter without you knowing about it. Unless you doze off, which I've done twice. Most open houses are done on Sundays, sometimes Saturdays, which you already know. They usually last three to four hours and take place in the afternoons, which you also know. You can't date a Realtor very long without understanding the weekend routine, right? You said two reasons. What's number two?"

"I'm worried about you and the other agents at Prescott. You all do a lot of open houses, especially in the spring, and I would feel terrible if you weren't aware of what was going on and got hurt, or worse."

"Do I hear concern in your voice for 'little old me,' Lieutenant?" I joked.

"Kurt, it's not funny. This is real. There are three dead Realtors and no suspects."

"Sorry." I could see the anguish in her eyes and the stress that had hardened the usual soft line of her lips. "There are more than twenty thousand Realtors in the Chicagoland area. What do you really think the chances are of me meeting Mr. Psycho? Besides, with or without an extra five pounds, I'm still in great shape and can take care of myself." We men have to be in order to compete with the fairer sex.

"I'm sure you can," Liz reached across the booth and patted the top of my hand, another tired smile. "What about the sign-in log?"

"All Realtors use some type of system to keep track of who attends the open house. Every seller thinks his or her home will sell on a weekend open house. Wrong. On very rare occasion you may actually sell the home you're showing It's not the most efficient way to go about selling properties, but it is an effective way to pick up potential buyers with which to work. Many Realtors won't do an open house in their own listing because of the dual agency issue." I could tell that in an attempt to be thorough, I was bludgeoning her with boring stats. Liz looked as though she was staring straight through me.

"So our killer, or killers', name should be on one of these sign-in logs?"

"Ah, probably not," I said, amazed. "You think the guy doing this is going to tango into the house, write his real name down on a piece of paper, and then kill the Realtor? You have been trained in police work, right, Liz?"

"Ha ha. I meant that there might be a hand writing analysis that could be taken from the signatures."

"Truth is, a lot of people don't want to sign the log. At times, it's uncomfortable asking for a signature. I'm pretty good at getting the names and contact info from the people who come through my open houses. I treat it like a conversation, not a presentation. I write down their wants and needs in a home, ask if it would be helpful to send them homes that match their requirements, and when they say yes, I say, 'Great, can you please write down your name and address and the best way to contact you?' I have a pretty good success rate. But there are times when I say goodbye at the front door, thank them for coming and say I'll be in touch this week, and go back into the kitchen to review the list and make a couple of personal notes. That's when I find out that the "serious buyer" I just spent the last thirty minutes with are Mr. and Mrs. Mick Mouse living in Orlando, Florida. I then image them driving away, laughing their little ears and tails off."

"Sorry, Kurt." She made a pouty face. "Let's get back on track."

"All right, what have we got so far?" I sounded a little too eager, as if we were starting off on a treasure hunt.

Liz took out her notebook and flipped to the first page. "I have the details on victims one and two. I've added my own information for victim three after having just come from the crime scene in Lawton. All three Realtors were women. All had conducted a Sunday open house." She paused and looked up. "Shouldn't you be writing this down?"

I reached into my portfolio, tore out a page, and took the gold-plated pen from the inside pocket of my sports coat. I felt as if the teacher had just scolded me. If I were really bad, maybe she'd make me stay after school. My mind was drifting back to Wisconsin.

"Three women, three Realtors, three open houses," Liz continued. "Each victim has a different profile. One was in her forties, two were in their thirties. Two were divorced and one was married. Two had children, while the third apparently did not. Their experience in real estate varied from two years to fifteen years."

The pie arrived. Abby's pies are all homemade. The slice was perfect and huge. Thick slices of fresh white bananas lined the bottom of the crust—real crust, not graham cracker crust. The filling was smooth and just a tint off white, not the artificially yellow store-bought pie filling in a can. The topping was meringue, peaked and stiff, baked to the color of golden caramel. I might have actually begun to drool at the sight. "Enjoy," Macy said as she slid the plate towards me.

"All right, so we have three women Realtors killed during three open houses in three different towns," I began. "So what are the similarities, besides the fact they all shared the same profession? How did they die?"

"Poisoned."

"Poisoned? What is this, the eighteenth century? What does that say about our suspect?"

"First, he's my suspect, not yours, and second, all I want from you is your insight into what might be happening at these open houses. Got it?"

"Yes, ma'am, Lieutenant Colburn, ma'am."

"Seriously, Kurt, if you can give me solid ideas as to how this guy got to his victims, it would be helpful. Not necessarily why—the FBI is working on a profile—but how. At this point we're not sure if the killings were random or planned. We don't know if the suspect knew his victims, and if he did what the motivation might be. How is it possible to get that close to someone without any signs of flight or struggle? None of the crime scenes show any sort of struggle on the part of the victim."

"Okay. I'll check out the Realtors through the Association to see if there was any connection between the three. If you can give me the addresses of the properties, I'll check to see if there is any relationship from that angle. What else came out of your task force meeting this morning?" I asked.

"Mostly details about the first two victims and the crime scenes. We didn't know about the third victim until just before we broke the meeting."

"And you're sure about the poison?" I asked.

"Yes, Dr. Sam presented his findings as well as the Lake County Coroner, where the first victim was found. Some kind of lye was forced down each victim's throat. Kurt, they were forced to eat lye! Based on Dr. Sam's description, I certainly wouldn't want to experience a death like that. Slow, painful, and terrifying. Thankfully, the women would have gone unconscious, but not for a while. The acid in the lye causes bleeding in the stomach and internal organs. These women actually bled to death, Kurt."

I was losing my interest in the pie. I slid the half-eaten plate of banana cream towards the middle of the table. I would be willing to do anything to help Liz get this freak behind bars. My sense of humor, or lack of tasteful humor, which I used as shield and weapon, would be out of place from this point on.

"Whatever I can do to help," I said, flashing a reassuring smile.

"Thank you, Kurty."

Liz provided me with the names of the three victims so I could look them up via the Realtor Association's website, as well as the addresses of the properties—nothing confidential about that. All Realtors have the ability to look up our brethren. I had done it frequently for several reasons over the years, as do other agents. The obvious reason was to gain contact information, such as email, office number, cell number, or agent ID, which are required on all transaction documents. Other times I was curious about who I was dealing with on the other side of negotiating, for example, if it was an agent I wasn't familiar with or hadn't heard of before. I can also find a competing Realtor's volume. The information is broken down between sellers and buyers. It's nice to know how much experience the other side has with transactions. A list of credentials usually accompanies their stats, for example, are they a broker or a sales person? Do they hold designations such as CRS, CNC, ABR, SRS, CSC, and SFR, and on and on? Some agents' business cards look like a Scrabble tile were spilled across the front. One can assume that the more designations an agent has, the more schooling they have, and therefore the more knowledge they have. This is not always the case. Sometimes it means that the other agent just has a lot of time on his or her hands and likes taking classes. I have found myself on the other side of many a transaction with some pretty well-schooled idiots. You can also find out if a particular agent is a member of certain real estate–related groups or clubs. Are they relocation certified? Do they specialize in certain fields, such as short sales, foreclosures, or bankruptcies? If you think the US government has a lot of information on people, the Realtor Association might rival them for data.

Dex is fond of pulling up the photo of the agent on the other side of his transactions and taping a copy to his file. He mentally picks at their flaws to make himself feel superior when he's on the phone with them. Are they too old, too young? Big nose, big teeth, big hair? To Dex it's all a game, and he likes to win. He has gone as far as using the old public speaking trick of imagining them in their underwear while he's talking to them on the phone. It gives him a sense of superiority. He does enough business each year to pay his expenses and have a little pocket change left over. He basically lives on his trust fund, but he enjoys the atmosphere of the office and the camaraderie of his fellow Realtors. And honestly, he is a fine Realtor when he chooses to put in the effort. Plus, he has been expected to carry on in the family profession of real estate, even if his family's name isn't on the door. He's never intentionally mean and usually takes the high road. Thus his lovability.

Liz and I parted Abby's and went in opposite directions. I was anxious to get back to the office to start compiling any useful information for her. I told Liz I would call her as soon as I had gathered everything, by tomorrow at the latest, I hoped. The sun had come out to brighten the end of what otherwise was a very gloomy day.

I entered through the familiar etched glass door off Main Street of Prescott Realty. The top of Molly's blond head was visible behind the receptionist desk, sitting under a three-by-five-foot oil portrait of our founding father, James Prescott.

"You're just in time, Kurt," Molly said, looking up. "We're getting ready to sing Jimmy 'Happy Birthday.' Cake's in the break room."

"Be right there. Got to drop some files off at my desk." Cake on top of pie? I didn't think so, but I would be gracious and join the choir. Jimmy Burton was celebrating his sixtieth birthday and was one of the owner partners. At some point, Prescott was going to have to start recruiting a younger group of Realtors to continue the tradition of 'Exceeding Expectations,' in lieu of 'Hope We're Open Tomorrow.' When I had started at Prescott, I felt funny calling an older gentleman Jimmy. I would have preferred Jim or James, but very quickly the awkwardness left and Jimmy it was and has been. I really was more interested in starting on my project for Liz, but the birthday celebrations had been trimmed down to be an efficient chorus of "Happy Birthday to You," a division of cake, and a little small talk with people who weren't terribly busy. The tradition was intact, and I was back at my desk in five minutes, with a cube of chocolate cake with vanilla frosting resting on a paper plate, cluttered with balloon shapes in an array of colors.

My first task was to look up the Realtors to see if there was any interesting information that would link the three of them together. All three were in good standing with the Illinois Association of Realtors. Sara Donoghue, victim one, had been in the business for three years. Last year's production had been eleven home sales; all but one had been on the buyer's side. She appeared to be modestly successful and had completed her ABR (Accredited Buyer Representative) designation the previous year. All of Sara's transactions had been in the north suburbs of Chicago.

Barbara Miller was a fifteen-year veteran and had put together some impressive sales figures. She was a top producer at her company, sold extensively throughout the western suburbs of Chicago, and consistently held one of the top three spots at her firm. Her production ran close to sixty units a year, well balanced with both buyers and sellers. She was a broker associate.

Annie Lawrence was only into her second full year as a Realtor. She held a real estate sales license with no designations. Her first year had been a good learning curve apparently, and so far this year she had matched the previous year's number, all with buyers.

I sat and was staring at the information I had pulled up when Dex walked up to my desk. "How you doin', buddy?" he asked with a smile. There was chocolate cake stuck between his front teeth.

"Good, great. How about you?"

"Same old same old. Hey, how was the weekend in paradise with Miss Lizzy? Any stories you'd like to share with Dex? You know I live vicariously through you, Kurt."

"Nope, nothing to share."

"Pretty deep in thought there. Whatcha working on?" Dex glanced in the direction of my screen.

I clicked the close button on my computer. "Just running some stats for a community I'm thinking about farming," I lied.

"Farming?" He wrinkled his nose. "Really, at this stage of your career? That's for newbies."

"Got to keep the future pipeline filled Dex," I replied. "Never know when your old sources will start to dry up. I'm too young and too poor to retire, and I'm too old to start another career. Plus, it will challenge me to take some business from the competition." I actually had given recent thought to putting together a farming campaign, whereby you designate a particular geographic area, usually a subdivision, and market the tar out of it. You want to become the neighborhood specialist, the go-to guy for selling homes and a resource for the owners living in the neighborhood. It is a good strategy, used by a lot of freshman Realtors to jump-start their careers. It takes time, patience, and a continuity plan, plus a committed budget for mailings, promotions, and such. Once established, a farm can produce a steady stream of clients.

"Whatever," Dex said. "You gonna eat that cake?" He was eyeballing my five-hundred-calorie chunk of dessert.

Giving up Jimmy's piece of cake would move Dexter along and save me a half an hour tomorrow on the treadmill. "Sure, buddy. Help yourself," I said with a smile.

"Thanks."

He scooped up the paper plate and disappeared around the corner of my cubicle. Back to work. I reopened the window on my computer and compared the three agents. There was nothing unusual to my untrained eye, but I would print it off for Liz and give it to her when I saw her next. I clicked out of the agent profile website and entered the Multiple Listing Service site, the MLS. There is a plethora of information that can be found in the MLS. Most people think it is the data link between brokers for sharing listed properties. Well, yes it is that, but it's a whole lot more. You can find the style of home, age, square footage, and taxes, see an aerial view of the property, trace ownership, determine the mortgaged amount and who the lender is, view interior photos, get demographics on the neighborhood, and see who the listing agent is and the brokerage with which they are affiliated. Other helpful information includes past sales data, number of days to get a contract, and days until closing, original list price, final list price, sales price, and ratios between the prices. If you like numbers, you can spend all day wading through the carnage of the local real estate market. I do like numbers, and as soon as I get them to say what I need them to say, I stop. Massaging numbers is what makes the world go round.

I checked the three properties in the order Liz had given them to me. Nothing odd or unusual popped out. The first home, at 1214 Mission Court was located in Glenburg, Illinois. This was quite a ways from where I normally do my real estate business, and I was not familiar with the area's housing market. Built in 1984, it was a two-story colonial, four-bedroom, two-and-a-half-bath home. Full basement, unfinished. It had been on the market for almost nine months and had been reduced by $40,000 from its original list price. It was in foreclosure, and the owner of record was a T. Robbins. The photos indicated that the home was furnished and somewhat dated with older appliances, wallpaper borders, and a country motif. According to the showing instructions, the home was now vacant. All one needed to do to show the property was give a courtesy call to the listing agent, leave a message, and use one's Realtor key card to enter. Taxes were current through the previous year, and the mortgage was held by First Family Bank and Trust. It seemed pretty clear cut to me as I was sitting at my desk.

The second home, at 113 Tesla Drive, was an older brick ranch built in 1965, located in Wilmington, an area with which I was very familiar. It had three bedrooms and two baths and a two-car detached garage. I knew Tesla Drive to be a quiet tree-lined street running east to west. It had moderate rush hour traffic, but by 9:00 a.m. and before 5:00 p.m., there was very little activity. The interior photos showed a well-kept home that was neat and organized. The home had only been on the market for seventy-five days and was still at its original asking price. The showing instructions were normal: call the owner an hour in advance to provide notice before any showing. So, unlike the first home, which was vacant, the owners apparently still lived in the home on Tesla Drive. I did notice, however, in the agent remark section, which is not available to the public, that the contract would be based on a short sale. This meant that any offer brought to the seller would have to be approved by the lender, as the selling price would be less than the amount owed on the mortgage. These types of transaction were very time consuming, and unfortunately they were becoming more common due to the state of the economy and the current housing market. Whereas a normal resale might take forty-five to sixty days to close, a short sale could take months and months, some going as long as a year, if it closed at all. I checked the tax records to find the amount owed by the deed holders, Charles P. and Ellen A. Stuart. It looked as though a large amount had been recently refinanced. I thought this was strange. Based on the records available to me, it appeared that the home had been close to being paid off and then last summer, a huge amount of equity had been pulled out of the home, and it had been refinanced at two points above the prime rate. The mortgage holder was First Family Bank and Trust. Quite a coincidence, considering FFB&T, although a sizable banking institution in the area, was far down the list of large banking centers that came to mind for home buyers.

First Family Bank and Trust was at one time *the* small-town bank, located in dozens of suburban communities. In the early years, FFB&T's charter allowed them to operate only inside the state of Illinois. A decade ago, a large national banking firm was allowed to gobble up the much smaller seventeen-branch bank known as FFB&T. The decision at the time was to maintain the name of First Family Bank and Trust at all locations to give the good folks who banked with their local friendly banker a feeling that nothing had really changed. That effort fell flat on its C-note. Within months, customers of FFB&T saw fees that never before existed. Interest on savings and certificates of deposit seemed to be whittled away. The personnel inside the once friendly confines of the lobby changed. There was no more free coffee, and the Christmas Club Savings Program was canceled! FFB&T remained a fully-owned subsidiary of a large national banking conglomerate, but it was not exactly known as a powerhouse in the mortgage lending business.

I quickly clicked on the third property, at 2327 Willow Court, skipping all the data and going directly to the mortgage information in the tax records. I sat there staring at the page, feeling as though I was on to something but not quite sure what. First Family Bank and Trust held the mortgage for the foreclosed home. I printed out the records for all three homes, stuffed them into a file folder, and headed towards the front door, it was 5:30. I knew Liz worked until six. The trip to the Hamilton Police Department would take only ten minutes, even at that time of day.

CHAPTER 16

I pulled into the lot of the Hamilton Police Department at 5:47 p.m. The all-brick two-story building sat on a slight knoll. The city had built the state-of-the-art facility just four years ago. The setting sun reflected in the opaque full windows, shooting a blinding golden glare in my direction as I got out of my car and headed towards the entrance. I had been to the station only three or four times since the new building had opened, and I'm glad to report that each visit was social. The manicured lawn and the neatly trimmed hedges made the building look more like a modern office facility than police headquarters. The second floor, which housed the cells and booking department, had narrow slit widows across the front. There were twelve cells upstairs that could accommodate four prisoners each. During a crime spree weekend in Hamilton, there might be half a dozen people locked up, all drunks, sharing one large cell, with stainless steel goddess in the corner for whatever calls of nature might be needed. Most drunk and disorderly and DUI offenders were released during the third shift, which put them out in the wee hours of the morning looking for a ride home. For those with limited friends or family members who didn't care to venture out before dawn, one of Hamilton's dozen taxis stood waiting at the curb on most weekends. As I mentioned before, crime in our hometown is usually of the petty variety.

As I entered the building, the officer on door duty stood up from his high-backed stool. "Hey, Coach," he greeted me.

"Hi, Adam," I replied, "I'm here to see Lieutenant Colburn."

"*Sure* you are." The young patrolman winked.

Adam Rogers was a nice young man who I had coached for five summers in the park district's baseball league program. He had been an awesome third baseman, unfortunately, he wasn't much of a hitter. I threw him thousands of balls over the years, but he never picked up the rhythm needed to connect. Some ball players are born with natural ability, others learn it. Adam had filled out proportionately and had developed into a fine young patrolman, serving and protecting the citizens of Hamilton.

"How are your mom and dad?" I asked. I had sold the Rogers their home around the second year I began coaching. The parents of the kids I coached were a natural group of prospects. I would laminate the season's schedule and put my phone number and website on the reverse as a reminder of what I did when not coaching their kids.

"Oh, they're great. Thanks for asking. I think they may be getting ready to downsize to a townhouse. I heard Dad complaining about another year of mowing and outdoor painting. You should give them a call." And that's called being at the right place at the right time—and that's how real estate works.

"I'll be sure to do that," I said, handing Adam one of my business cards. "And tell them I said hi. Keep me in mind when you're ready to purchase something for yourself, Adam. All right if I go back to Liz's office?"

"Yeah, just sign in with the desk sergeant over there, Coach. Good to see you." Adam unbuttoned his shirt pocket and stuck my card inside.

"You too, Adam," I said as I walked across the marble-floored lobby.

The inside of the building had a two-story atrium, and from the lobby floor you could see the open hallway on the second floor. The full-length windows were tinted light gray, giving the illusion to those trapped inside working that it was a gloomy day outside. The main level held the reception area, desk sergeant's desk, and visitors' cafeteria. Behind double-locked steel doors were the squad room, officers' desks in an open pit area, the detectives' cubicles, chief's office, resource room, small meeting rooms, and locker room. There was also an all-purpose room that doubled as the lunch room.

"Hi, I'm here to see Lieutenant Colburn," I said to the desk sergeant.

"Is she expecting you?" he asked without looking up.

"Ah, well not exactly." He looked up from his crossword puzzle book. "She asked me to gather some information that I have right here." I held up the manila folder. He picked up the phone and dialed her extension. "There's a guy here." He moved the mouthpiece away and looked at me again. "What did you say your name was?"

"Banning, Kurt Banning." Jeez, for whatever reason, I felt like I was a criminal being brought in for questioning. I shifted from one foot to the other while he relayed my name. "She'll be right up. Take a seat." He nodded to a waiting area as he was hanging up the phone. I went over and sat in one of several black vinyl chairs that were built for discomfort. The back was sloped so you couldn't sit up straight, and if you pressed your back against it, you slid down, creating what my mother would have called "terrible posture." The magazines were old and of no interest to me, so I stared out into the gloomy day, which I knew to be clear with setting sunlight.

I heard the click of the automatic lock and turned to see Liz walking across the lobby. The clip clop of her heels echoed throughout the glass-enclosed atrium. She smiled and gave me a look of surprise. "What are you doing here?"

"I've got an interesting development in our case." Her eyebrow went up. "I mean your case." I held up the file folder. She reached for it, and I yanked it back. "Wait a minute. I want to go over this with you and explain it. I think this will give us a lead. Okay, give *you* a lead."

Liz looked at her watch. "I get off in five minutes. Come over to the house and you can fill me in on your exciting find, Sherlock. If you want a drink, you'll have to stop for olives. I'm fresh out. And if you're stopping for olives, why don't you pick up a rotisserie chicken from the deli. Get the meal combo, which comes with a couple of sides. I'll meet you there in thirty minutes."

"Okay, sure," I said as I headed back through the lobby. I felt like a dejected puppy.

"See ya, Coach."

"Bye, Adam. Good to see you again."

As I walked to my car, the excitement I had felt minutes ago had faded like the air in a week old balloon. Here I come, with potentially critical information that can break our case (yes, *our* case) wide open, and the next thing I know, I'm being sent off to the grocery like some errand boy to fill the lady's pantry. My ego was dented, but not for long. I often have kneejerk reactions to Liz. But by the time I had traversed the aisles of the grocery store, stopping at both the deli counter and the canned vegetable aisle for the olives, I was feeling much better about the situation. After all, Liz hadn't snatched the information out of my hand, said thanks, and disappeared into the bowels of the station. And she had invited me over to discuss our case. I guess I had overreacted once again to the sometimes charmlessness of one Ms. Elizabeth Colburn.

Liz's car was in the driveway when I pulled in a little past six thirty. Why she hardly ever parked in her garage amazed me. Actually, it irritated me. A perfectly good garage with no car inside—it didn't make sense. But a lot about Liz didn't make sense to me. That was one of the biggest reasons why we were no longer the happy cohabitating couple we once were. It was possible that at my age, I was becoming more like an oak tree than a willow. I certainly didn't think of myself as staunch and unbending, and I was pretty sure those who knew me wouldn't describe me that way either, unless it was Liz.

The front door was open and I could see Liz through the screen in the kitchen making Ketels. "Olives are here," I yelled through the house.

"Door's open. Come on in."

Duh, really. There was a homicidal maniac on the loose, an April chill in the air, and the front door was wide open! Just breathe and let it go. I walked through the small carpeted living room carrying a plastic bag with a whole chicken, seasoned with rosemary, a tub of mashed potatoes, and green beans. In my right hand I held a jar of queen olives, and tucked under my arm was the manila file folder with the breakthrough clues to solving the open house murders.

"You know your front door was wide open?" Obviously I couldn't let it go.

"Yeah, I know. I left it open for you."

No point in going any further down this road. I sat the bag of food on the kitchen counter, laid the file on the table, and opened the jar of olives. Two crystal glasses had been filled with ice and Ketel One. One was blushed with a drop of cranberry juice and the other sat waiting for the plop of two olives.

"Hi, honey. How was your day?" she joked. Liz seemed in a very good mood considering the seriousness of our meeting. She had apparently left the hard-shelled lieutenant back at the station. This bird was hard to figure.

"Oh, just peachy," I said. "It started out kind of slow—you know, paperwork, phone calls—and then another Realtor turned up dead in

Lawton. Just a typical Monday at the office. But by afternoon, I uncovered the clues to solve the biggest murder case in the county. And here I am, having cocktails with the prettiest cop in the county."

"Just the county?" Liz stuck out her bottom lip in a fake pout. She had changed into a pair of faded denim jeans and an authentic-looking fake rugby shirt. "Grab your drink and show me what you found out." I wondered if she might be bipolar.

"Great," I said as I dropped two huge pimento-stuffed green olives into my glass. I picked up both glasses and followed Liz into the family room, picking up my file as we passed by the kitchen table. The family room was cozy, Realtor-speak for small. It had hardwood floors covered by an authentic Persian rug in the middle of the room. A brick fireplace that saw little use was at the far end of the room, flanked by two built-in bookcases full of an eclectic collection of reading material. Liz's tastes ran from the obvious murder mysteries and thrillers to autobiographies of US presidents to leather-bound classics to self-help. A long, oversized sofa was positioned facing the fireplace with its back creating an artificial wall towards the eat-in area of the kitchen. Two upholstered matching chairs on the inside wall shared a side table between them with a lamp. The neutral colored walls held three expensively framed oil portraits of ballerinas in various poses. The bay window on the outside wall faced onto her fenced backyard. At this time of the year and at this time of the day, the fence was barely visible through the large picture windows. As we entered the room, Liz closed the drapes. We had spent hundreds of hours together in this room, cuddled on the couch watching movies, playing board games, reading, napping, and entertaining friends. It felt like home, although it had been several months since I had been invited to return. Liz sat in one of the two chairs, which was my cue to take the other. No snuggling on the couch tonight. After all, this was a business visit, not unlike meeting a potential client in their home to discuss the pricing and marketing of their property.

"What have you got?" Liz asked over the top of her glass as she took her first sip.

"Well, when I got back to the office, I started with the three real estate agents to see if there was anything similar in their profiles to connect them. Other than being members of the greater Chicago area real estate board, which has more than twenty thousand members, nothing. Their experience, production, designations—nothing even remotely connected." I handed Liz the printouts on each Realtor.

"That we kind of concluded," Liz said. Her glass was half empty, as I had been doing all the talking. I took a couple of large gulps to catch up. "We ran the three victims through our program, and nothing showed up on any of them, not even a traffic violation. FBI has been interviewing neighbors, friends and family and they have come up empty. Maybe that's what they have in common—they're founding members of the squeaky clean club."

"Anyway," I continued, "next I checked out the properties where the murders occurred. At first, I got the same kind of results as with the Realtors. Nothing stood out. They are different types of homes, different ages, in diverse neighborhoods. Two are vacant and one is occupied." I heard my voice rise an octave as I got near to revealing the investigative information that would break the case wide open.

"Yes, we know that too, Kurt. I thought you said you had some groundbreaking news to share with me."

Liz was staring at me. How long should I play her? I knew what I had was good, and I was fairly certain that neither the local yokels nor the FBI had stumbled onto the information I had uncovered. I felt like it was Christmas and I had the best present to give in the world and couldn't wait for her to open it. "Freshen my drink, please, and I'll show you what I found—actually, stumbled upon." I spoke intentionally slowly and held my empty glass out to her. I watched as she stood and took it, giving me a leery look as she walked into the kitchen. Liz had a great walk, the kind that turns the heads of men, and a few women too, as she strolls down the street. I watched her as she refilled the glasses with ice and Ketel. A few drops of cranberry went into hers and another two olives into mine. She stirred them with her index finger and sucked off the left over booze, glancing in my direction. I may not tell her again, at least not for a long time, but I love that woman and I really never stopped, even when we broke up, as hurtful as is was for both of us.

"Here you go," she said, handing my glass back, full. She retook her seat opposite me and tucked her feet underneath her. "Give." It sounded like a command to a dog. Sit, stay, rollover, give!

"All right, so I'm looking for links to the homes, right? The tax records are always interesting. They tell you nothing about the home, which is what I was trying to connect, but they do tell you about the owners. It shows what the taxes are, the assessments, exemptions, and mortgage information, such as amount borrowed, refinancing dates, and the lien holder."

"So, I'm listening." Liz sounded as though she were getting bored. I wanted to stretch this out and make it appear as though I had researched hours and hours, digging through files. I was also showing off a bit about my profession and abilities, demonstrating why one should respect the hard-working Realtor "Here's the connection. The homes are mortgaged by the same bank, and all three were in foreclosure or being foreclosed upon." I was waiting for Liz to jump up and hug me and call me her hero.

"Are you loco, Kurt? Eighty percent of the mortgages in this country are issued by the Big Five. This is the big break through you have been talking about?" She had raised her voice one full octave.

I was feeling smug. I knew the Big Five held the majority of the home loan business, but that's what made my discovery so much more important. "Liz, I know the banking statistics even better than you do; it's part of my job. The key is *who* holds the mortgage on your three crime scene properties."

She looked puzzled.

"It's not one of the Big Five. In fact, this institution wouldn't even raise a blip on the national radar. And in the Chicagoland area, they are a small player. So, the odds of all three properties being held by this one bank, and the fact that all three were in foreclosure, go way down."

"So who's the bank?" Liz asked, a little more interested than five minutes ago.

"FFB&T, First Family Bank and Trust." I said, beaming like a prize peacock.

"FFB&T," Liz repeated, letting it sink in. "I haven't seen one of those branches in years. There can't be very many in the area, right?"

"Eleven remaining offices throughout the Chicagoland area," I replied, still pleased with myself. "A small operation with one hundred percent of the homes involved in their portfolio. The connection is the bank," I almost shouted.

Liz sat staring at me—actually, looking through me—as she digested what I had just told her. Her mind was at work, mulling over the scenarios and possible meaning. "Let's eat," she said, getting up from the chair.

"What?"

"I'm starving. I never ate before or after I saw you today. I'll think better on a full stomach. Grab the plates, would you please? We'll eat in the kitchen."

Incredible. I followed Liz into the kitchen and pulled two plain white ceramic plates out of the cupboard and sat them on the dinette table, across from each other. Liz pulled the still warm food from the oven and sat it in the center of the table, still in their grocery containers. Thankfully the chicken had been pre-cut. Off came the lids and our delicious store-cooked dinner began.

"So what you're saying," Liz said with a swallow of chicken, "is that FFB&T owned all three homes and the odds of that are slim of that happening coincidentally."

"Well, really they owned two and were foreclosing on the third, but yes, they held the paper on all three. What do you think?"

Still mulling it over, Liz spoke slowly, almost as if she were talking out loud to herself. "The connection has nothing to do with the physical location of the homes, or the owners for that matter. It appears to have everything to do with the bank. Someone at the bank or someone who doesn't like the bank. This will lead us in another direction altogether." She refocused. "Good job, Kurt. Pass me the green beans, would you, hon?"

We finished the gourmet food and washed the few dishes we had used. I explained the short-sale foreclosure process to Liz. We talked about making application for home loans with lenders and the refinancing procedure. I told her about the number of people in really bad situations who could no longer afford their mortgage payments and what their options were. From mortgage modifications to equity lines to refinancing to selling to walking away, few offered any long-term relief or the possibility of restoring one's life and credit in any short amount of time. There was a myriad of reasons people got into these terrible situations; mounting medical bills, temporary job loss, skyrocketing college expenses for children, overextension on credit, and the occasional undisciplined spend thrift who burned through money like a California fire fanned by El Niño.

I left the file folder with Liz and started to leave. "Thanks, Kurt. This is wonderful information and will help us narrow down our search. I'll make sure Captain Dougan knows how much help you were and give credit where it's due," she said as she walked me to the door.

"You're welcome. Let me know what else I can do. I've got a couple of ideas that might be helpful in tracking this guy down." The business portion of the evening was over, but the feeling wasn't there for a good-night kiss. We had re-kindled in Wisconsin thirty-six hours prior, but we both had known that it was a getaway trip, not a get-back-together trip. We would continue our relationship as it was, whatever that might be.

"I'll let you know," she said, closing the door as I went down the steps to the driveway. My headlights shined on the rear of her car as I was backing out. Why in the hell didn't she park her car in the garage?

It was 10:30 as I headed home. It was a peaceful evening in mid-April as I drove the tree-lined streets of Hamilton on my short trip. The air was crisp, but I had the windows down and almost felt relieved to be going to the safe haven of my apartment. Alone is not always lonely.

CHAPTER 17

The wall clock behind the old scarred oak bar said a quarter to five and Randy was nowhere in sight. Hank Pilcher had wiped down the bar top for the third time while glancing over his shoulder at the clock. Damn that Randy. He was always late, paying no respect to anyone else's time. The ice container had been refilled to the top; lime and lemon peels had been diced and put into small square tubs behind the bar. Olives and maraschino cherries had been skewered with colorful toothpicks and were resting in deep glass dishes. The back bar had been restocked, and everything was set for the next shift at the Fifty-Fifth Street Tavern. Everything except the night bartender, Randy.

Hank had taken the daytime bartending job at the Fifty-Fifth Street Tavern six months earlier to supplement his dwindling income at Pearson's Plumbing and Supply. The fixture business had gone the way of the housing market, downhill. He could barely make ends meet with his living expenses, rent, and child support. The bar was located just a block west of Pearson's, and Hank had noticed a sign in the window two weeks before Thanksgiving that said, "Bartender Wanted." He had no experience with bartending other than sitting on the other side of the bar, more so in recent months. How hard could it be, he thought, as he went in to apply for the job. The interview had been brief. The pay wasn't great, not even minimum wage, apparently because he would make tips to supplement his hourly compensation. He worked what was called the dead man's shift, from eleven in the morning until the night shift began at five. Business was slow until things picked up when people were on their way home from work or coming back out later to enjoy their evening. The lunch crowd was a quick-turn group, and most didn't drink more than one beer. And there were the regulars who sat at the bar, nursing a whiskey or tap ale for a couple of hours, after which they would leave and float back later. Those drinkers weren't great tippers however, usually leaving the leftover change on the counter as thanks.

Fifty-Fifth Street Tavern was a dark, smoky shot-and-a-beer place that had been a neighborhood establishment since the early sixties. The menu was limited to frozen seven-inch pizzas that were heated in the ancient ovens in the back kitchen, along with hamburgers and several other grilled sandwiches. For those without much of an appetite, there were assorted bags of nuts attached to a board behind the bar. Little cups of a snack mixture were also set upon the bar for free snacking, if you didn't mind sharing with whoever else decided to dip their grimy hands into the bowls. The owner opened at seven in the morning and took care of the few early imbibers, cleaned up whatever mess was left over from the evening before, and did the book keeping and ordering. Billy White had owned the bar for the past two decades, buying it from the original owners after winning a lump sum total of just over two million dollars in the state lottery. Billy's dream had been to own his own bar in a thriving neighborhood, making it into the local hangout. Now, he had been the proud owner for almost twenty years. The beer always looks colder from the other side of the bar. The tavern business turned out to be much more work than Billy had originally thought. The glamorous life of a barkeep turned out to be eighteen-hour days, employees who pilfered from you, lousy friends who walked out on tabs because they were friends with the owner, and taxes up the wazoo from local, city, and state agencies, not to mention the occasional drunk who had to be escorted from the building. Billy eked out an okay living and didn't really complain—that would be bad for business.

Where the hell was Randy? Hank was getting madder by the minute as he looked up at the clock again. Five o'clock on the dot, but of course that was bar time, which meant it was only 4:50, but Mr. Billy White's rule was that starting and ending times were to go by the old schoolroom clock on the wall. Hank's anger issues were well documented by the few friends he had, as well as his ex-wife. He would start to spiral into a deep black hole, gaining speed as the ire got the better of him. And even though he realized what was happening, he most often could do nothing to stop his rage once it got started.

Hank had already cashed out the three patrons sitting at the bar, as well as his tip jar, twenty-eight dollars. Now it looked as if he would have to restart a tab for one of the patrons. A group of five men entered the bar, allowing daylight to spill into the darkness. Thankfully they took a table and would be Anna's customers.

The single door to the street opened again and Randy came half running in, clipping on his fake tie as he rounded the bar. "Sorry, man," he said. "Got caught in traffic."

Yeah, sure, Hank said to himself, "It's always something with you, Randy. I've got plans. I'm picking up my kids for dinner, and now I'm the one who's going to be stuck in traffic. This time of day, every minute counts beating the commute," Hank said in an irritated voice.

"Sorry, man," Randy repeated. He finished putting on his fake tie and turned his attention to his bar customers, putting on a fake smile. "How's everybody doin' today?" He clapped his hands and rubbed them together, ignoring the glare coming from Hank. Randy was a third younger than Hank, didn't have any kids or wife, and certainly didn't need the money as badly as Hank did.

He walked to the end of the block and turned the corner to the lot where employees parked. The late-model Chevrolet was backed into a space against the far wall of the parking lot. It wasn't much of a car and was on its last legs, but it was all the transportation Hank could afford. The door squeaked on its hinge as Hank opened the driver's side and slid in. He loosened his tie, a real tie, undid the top button of his shirt, and gave himself a look in the mirror. Life pretty much sucked, and there was no light at the end of the tunnel as far as he was concerned. This was his lot. Why? Hank had no idea. What had he done to deserve this hell on earth? Life had been good, and then one day, bam, it all fell apart. He was sinking in debt and felt less of a man for not being able to take care of his family. His wife had left him for the glamorous life that he couldn't provide and taken his children as well. He lost his home and was living in the squalor of a rundown apartment building. He was working two jobs, neither of which provided enough money to get ahead. The car he had bought new eight years ago was falling apart, and the jag-off he worked with at the Fifty-Fifth Street Tavern was an idiot punk. It gnawed in Hank's temples until he was far away from the bar, now thinking about his children.

Hank did have some self-worth. He was cleaning up the streets of lying, conniving Realtors who were selling homes out from under the struggling families who deserved better. Who did those banks think they were, anyway? Hard-working dads trying to shelter and feed their families and give their children a better life. Then along comes corporate America and the stuffed-shirt bankers in their three-piece suits, and tell Dad, "Hey, you owe us money, and if you don't pay up, we're taking your house away." Breaking up families, sending the wife and kids away to live a life he could never give them. Not anymore. So, Mr. Banker calls Mr. Realtor and says, "Sell the house and get those cheating bastards out of my property. We'll both make some money." Well, Hank wasn't about to let those responsible go unpunished. It would take a while, but they would get the message to stop. Otherwise he would leave a trail of lying, cheating, greedy, no-good Realtor carcasses all over the Chicagoland area.

Hank was a little disappointed in the lack of press his clean up jobs had created. There had been a small article in the local Glenburg paper about the death of Sara Donoghue and a tie-in article in the *Tribune* relating the murder of Barbara Miller in Wilmington. Both had referred to the incidents as "mysterious deaths, still under investigation." He hadn't seen anything yet about his latest accomplishment in Lawton, but soon people would understand what was happening and rise up in his support. He was the force of good battling evil on their behalf. He was a modern-day Robin Hood. The rich were getting richer and the poor poorer, but he would rescue the little guy and give him something to cheer about.

Hank thought about Sara Donoghue as he sat in the congested traffic, clogged at all the usual spots along the freeway as he and a hundred thousand others fled the city westward at the end of another workday. Sara had been an easy target on that brisk March Sunday. She had been pleasant and helpful as Hank toured the home with her. She seemed nice and full of energy, but greedy energy. Unfortunately for her, she was the enemy. Hank followed her into the master bedroom, took off the winter scarf that had been casually hanging around his neck, and simply flung it over Sara's head and around her throat. He had kept the vice-like pressure on until Sara crumpled to the floor, unconscious. He had tied her with rope from his jacket pocket before returning to his car to get his kit. When he re-entered the house, Sara was beginning to stir and making coughing sounds, clutching at her throat for air. She wriggled in the rope restraints, a waste of energy. He remembered the look of confusion on her face when he rolled her over into a sitting position with her back against the bedroom wall. Her protests were garbled through the duct tape. Hank calmly explained what was about to happen and why. He loved the wide-eyed fear that stretched the lids open to capacity. The whites were so white. One at a time, Hank fed Sara the lye tablets, washing them down with a forced swig of water. While he waited for her heart to stop, he had been stricken with genius. He had gotten Sara's car keys out of her purse and driven into the garage. At first he had been worried that a neighbor or passer-by might see him. But no, not a soul cared what went on at the house on Mission Hill Court. Well, Hank was on his own mission.

With the car secure in the garage, he went back into the house to see how his guest was doing. The early afternoon sun had melted the little snow left on the ground and washed away any foot tracks that Hank had made. Sara was all but gone, her pulse so faint that Hank had a hard time locating it on her wrists. Hank picked up Sara, still tied, and carried her down the hall, through the kitchen, and into the garage. She was very petite and light even as dead weight. It was easier than carrying a rolled-up piece of old carpeting on your shoulder. The trunk was popped, and he laid Sara down on her side. Hank had been impressed with the size of the trunk on the Continental. He could have easily stashed two or three Saras in the compartment. As he closed the lid, he had had no remorse. This was his first elimination. If anything, he felt a sense of pride in his accomplishment, a thrilling diversion to his sorry existence.

The blast of a horn behind him swept the image of Sara Donoghue out of his mind. He looked in the rearview mirror and smiled slightly. If they only knew who they were honking at. He was going to be late again. His ex-wife was getting use to Hank being late; he was so irresponsible, she had said over and over. Unfortunately, Samantha and Tyler were getting used to it as well. His children were all that really mattered to him. They were being cared for and supported by that arrogant asshole who had stolen his wife and showered his family with the luxurious lifestyle Lydia had always dreamed of living. Well, someday his children would be proud of him as well, when they learned how he had saved hundreds of families from being thrown out of their homes. Banks would fear him. Realtors would not dare take these listings from the banks, let alone advertise their gaudiness to the public. "Hey, come on out on Sunday and see the beautiful home we just listed from the bank, who threw the Smith family out on their ass with only what they could carry. Yes, sir, quite a bargain. See for yourself, and bring the whole family." Hank Pilcher would see that this came to a stop. And his children would once again respect and love him. He might have failed them, but he would be the rescuing saint to hundreds of Samantha and Tylers.

Traffic was starting to thin as Hank put distance between himself and the city. He traveled a triangular route on Wednesdays as he went from his bartending job in the city to his ex-wife's house in the southwest suburbs and then finally northeast to his grimy apartment in Gilbert. Wednesday evenings had been designated, by some stuffy old judge who could give a squat about Hank's life, as the night he would pick up the children and take them out to dinner. This meant a close-by restaurant so he could get the kids back in time for homework and bed. Nothing fancy, usually one of several family-style restaurants within a few miles of his kids' home. This had been his routine for almost a year. Less frequently were the twice-monthly visits to his apartment; some months, he was lucky to have them just one Saturday and Sunday. It was always his responsibility to pick up Samantha and Tyler. The wicked witch wouldn't even think about bringing them to him, or even meeting halfway for the exchange. No wonder his car was falling apart, with all the miles spent traipsing back and forth across three counties.

Traffic had come to a stop again. The flashing red and blue lights were visible through several layers of windshields in front of Hank's Chevy.

Barbara Miller had been a little easier than Sara Donoghue due to her age, but somewhat more difficult because of her size and weight. Hank had given Barbara the boot, literally, as she led him to the finished basement. A quick shove to the small of her back and she had tumbled down the stairs like the first rocks of an avalanche. When Hank reached her at the bottom of the stairs, she was semi-unconscious from the fall. That was the easy part. However, dragging her fat ass across the basement floor to the sump pump closet and hoisting her up on the chair had been a struggle. After he had sat her upright and tied her in position, he had to slap her awake so he could explain what was going to happen. She remained groggy, and this only incensed Hank even more.

"Wake up, damn it. Don't you want to know why you're going to die?"

Hank still wasn't sure Barbara had fully understood what was happening. The insertion of the lye tablets had been disgustingly easy. Her pudgy little lips were slippery with saliva, which made the lye slip nicely into her mouth. The wide-eyed struggle came about five seconds after the first tablet had reached her tongue. Even more tears came pouring out of the red-rimmed eyes, but the whites, oh my, they were so white. Barbara shook her head back and forth violently. The duct tape was secure and held the foam and screams inside. It had taken eight cakes to put down poor, sweet Barbara. When Hank was sure that she was well on her way to Realtor hell, he made the decision to leave her where she sat. Dragging her across the basement had taken a toll on his skinny six-foot frame.

Another horn blast brought him out of his daydream. "All right, all right, I'm going," he said to himself. Everyone's in a hurry. He was only two miles from his exit and was anxious to see his kids, even if it meant listening to the dressing down Lydia was going to give him about being late. It was full dusk and headlights were popping on in the cars headed toward him, snaking out of the suburbs like a mile-long Chinese dragon. Another fifteen minutes and he would be pulling into the pavered drive of the McMansion where Samantha and Tyler lived with the Witch and Asshole.

Patience was what the world needed. He had exhibited the extreme in patience tracking down the homes for sale that First Family Bank and Trust were in the process of foreclosing. Hank had spent endless hours at the library using the common computers to search through public records. He had identified ninety-six properties in the greater Chicagoland area that were headed to market and for which FFB&T held the mortgage. Not all properties were listed, of course. It was a process, and it took time. Banks, including FFB&T, couldn't just release all those foreclosed upon homes into the market. Even Hank understood the economic consequences on housing market supply and demand. If people thought that home prices were low now, just image what would happen across the country if hundreds of thousands of homes were dumped into the marketplace?

Hank kept his list of ninety-six FFB&T homes on three sheets of lined notebook paper, folded in half, in the inside cover of his family Bible on a bookcase in his apartment. Every Friday when the *Tribune* published the open houses for the weekend, he would sit at his little kitchen table under ugly florescent lighting and cross-reference the lists. Once a month, he was back at the library checking for new homes to add to his list. It was a big job and time consuming, but Hank was up to the task, and he had plenty of time and motivation. After all, it was First Family Bank and Trust that had forced a short sale on his own home, leaving him with no proceeds, a taxable situation on the debt forgiven, and ruined credit. The hole he was standing in was dug by FFB&T and the scumbag Realtors who profited from the sales of the homes after the bank took them away.

The gaslights flickered atop the three-foot-square and five-foot-tall brick pillars at the entrance to the Essingtons' home. Cobbled sound came from the tires on Hanks car as he rolled over the paver brick driveway, stopping in front of the five-panel birch wood garage doors. There were four of them. The matching paver sidewalk wound around the extensive landscaping, which included rose bushes, a stand of clump birch, and perfectly trimmed yew hedges. A coach light matching the ones at the driveway entrance flickered next to the arched front door. As he reached for the bell, Hank felt like throwing up. The door sprang open before he could push the button, giving him a start.

"Do you know what time it is, Hank?" Lydia yelled. Before Hank could answer, Lydia said, "It's past 6:30. You were supposed to be here at six."

"Sorry, I got out of work late and the traffic was terrible." Hank's voice was small and apologetic. He thought he sounded like Randy.

"Well, the kids were expecting you at six," Lydia continued while Hank stood on the porch, hands stuffed into his pant pockets. He could see down the hall through the partially opened door. "They were hungry, so I've already fed them. Plus, Samantha has an English test tomorrow that she needs to study for."

"Well, let me take them out for dessert then," Hank said in a begging voice.

"It's too late now, Hank. You'll just have to wait till next Wednesday to see them. Why don't you get a cell phone, for God's sake? At least you could let me know when you're going to be late."

"I can't afford a damn cell phone with the way you bleed me dry with child support. Do you and Mr. High and Mighty really need my eighteen hundred dollars a month?" Hank yelled back, his small voice becoming larger. "I don't think so," he answered his own question.

"That's not the issue, Hank, and you know it. You are so irresponsible it just drives me crazy."

"Fine, what time do you want me to pick them up on Saturday?" Hank asked, frustrated.

"Thad and I are taking the kids into the city this weekend to dinner and a play, and we'll be staying over at a hotel. You'll have to take them the weekend after next."

"God damn it, Lydia. I asked for this weekend off from work."

"Goodbye, Hank," Lydia said, closing the front door. Hank could hear the tumblers click as she turned the deadbolt.

Hank walked briskly back to his car, fuming. He slammed the door shut and started the engine. He jammed the car into reverse and squawked to a stop in the street. He dropped the gearshift into drive and laid rubber, speeding out of the cul-de-sac. He knew it was childish, but for a long second it gave him a small amount of satisfaction.

Hank wound his way out of the subdivision and headed east, back towards the interstate. His heart was pounding in his chest with rage. He slapped the steering wheel with the palm of his right hand. *By God, they're all going to pay, the bankers, the Realtors, the lawyers, the title companies, every damn one of them.* And he'd find a way to deal with the Witch and the Asshole eventually. He raced home, exceeding the speed limit most of the way, weaving in and out of traffic and being rewarding with numerous horn blasts and hand gestures. He was looking forward to reading his Bible when he got back to the apartment.

CHAPTER 18

Hank Pilcher was up early Friday morning. He always got up early on Friday mornings and walked to the corner convenience store to pick up his copy of the *Tribune*. Most days he skipped the paper, but never a Friday issue. It was filled with weekend events, movie reviews, the weekend sports schedule, and of course the real estate section. This Friday was an exceptionally warm and sunny morning. Birds sat in the newly foliated tree branches and whistled good morning. The spring weather had put smiles on strangers' faces as they passed on the sidewalk. Hank even found himself smiling back. The store was only four blocks away, and it took Hank only a few minutes to make the trip.

The open sign was flashing, as it did twenty-four hours a day, as Hank pushed open the glass door. It was a popular place to pick up odds and ends and last-minute needs. The silver on the push bar had rubbed off from the hands of all the patrons over the years.

"Good morning, Mr. Hank," greeted the short Asian clerk from behind the counter.

"Hi ya, Chen," Hank said back.

The newspapers were piled just inside the door, on vertical wire racks. There must have been a dozen papers to choose from. The colorful *USA Today* was on top, followed by the locals and on the bottom shelves financial papers like *Barron's* and the *Wall Street Journal*. The *Tribune* was stacked high from the floor up the side of the rack. Normally it was just a paper that Hank bought, but today he decided to splurge and add a chocolate glazed donut to his purchase. The baked goods were in a lit glass case at the rear of the store. There were maybe six short aisles of overpriced products on the short list of items people ran out of and for which they would pay a premium. Hank thought the store always smelled like lemon cleanser. The store was in fact very clean, but the linoleum floor, which had been swept and mopped a million times, was cracked and faded and even seemed to slope towards one side of the store.

As he waited in line to pay for his purchases, he glanced around the store, seeing things for the first time in his almost two years of patronage. Usually Hank walked in the door, turned immediately to his right, picked up a paper, and laid down three-quarters on the counter, even if there was a transaction going on ahead of him. "Thanks, Chen," and out the door he would go. But now, standing in line, his eyes fell on state lottery signs, banners for Marlboro cigarettes, the newest flavor of Gatorade, racks of impulse items, hung with beef jerky, disposable lighters, and energy packets. As Hank edged closer to the register, he looked behind the counter: condoms in a variety of colors and textures, rolling papers, adult magazines that were covered so you could just make out the names: *Jugs, Men's Delight, Dirty Talk*. There were plastic tubes holding instant scratch-off lottery tickets. Oh, my God, Hank thought, how many ways are there to throw away your money? When it was finally Hank's turn to pay, he noticed a spit going around like a Ferris wheel, with dried up hot dogs stuck on metal spikes. It was 7:30 in the morning, and the dogs looked as if they had been left over from the night shift.

"That all, Mr. Hank?" Chen asked.

"That'll do it."

"Dollar fifty. You want bag?"

"No thanks, I'll eat it on the way."

Hank left the store and headed east towards Humphrey Arms Apartments. He munched on his chocolate glazed donut as he squinted into the sun, the *Tribune* folded under his arm. Round trip, he was gone for fifteen minutes, including his standing in the checkout line.

Back inside his tiny apartment, Hank switched on the overhead light in the dark kitchen and waited for the flickering bulb to come to life. He heated a mug of water in the counter top microwave and spread the newspaper on top of the table. He hung his lightweight wind breaker on the back of his chair and retrieved the family Bible from the one-shelf book nook around the corner. Hank was giddy with anticipation. The buzzer sounded on the microwave. Hank removed the steaming mug and dumped a heaping teaspoon of instant coffee crystals into the boiling water, followed by two scoops of sugar.

With the *Tribune* open to the real estate section, primarily the weekend list of open houses, Hank removed the folded sheets of paper from the inside page of his family Bible. His system for identifying and cross referencing open house properties and First Family Bank and Trust foreclosure properties was unique. The well-worn creases in the sheets of lined paper had been folded and unfolded dozens of time. The hand-written list on three pages of lined notebook paper had been color coded; those circled in red were not yet listed for sale, green were listed and available for sale, and yellow were homes that had been listed but which were too risky to carry out his plan. The unmarked properties of listed homes had not yet been checked out to see where they fell. Three homes on the list were crossed out in black. Mission accomplished. There were sixty-six homes circled in red, seventeen were in green, and ten were yellow, and the rest had yet to be investigated. Hank had driven by the green and yellow properties to assess his mission.

Every week, now that the spring real estate market was in full swing, there were more than two hundred open houses advertised for Saturdays and Sundays via print and Internet. Hank was limited to those in print. That made the search easier but not as efficient. The number this weekend was 102. Most real estate companies were moving away from the print media and to a fully electronic ad campaign. After all, it was the twenty-first century, and most twenty- to fifty-year-olds weren't perusing newspapers to get information. It was old news by the time it was printed and delivered; you had to wait until mornings to get the hard copy, and the newspaper had a one-day shelf life.

Even if Hank didn't find any new properties to circle, he still had dozens of homes he hadn't had time to check out. Two hours later, nothing new had surfaced. Hank replaced the *Tribune* with a Chicagoland area map and his unmarked list on the kitchen table. By noon, he had narrowed it down to four homes he would check out later in the day. It would have to be today. Hank had called Roy Emerson, his boss at Pearson's, and asked to switch weekends after the snafu with Lydia regarding the kids' schedule. He was set to work the next day at Pearson's Plumbing and Supply Company from open to close. Two homes were slightly west and south of where he lived, one was due south, and the other was north and east about half an hour away.

The grumbling in Hank's stomach reminded him that the donut breakfast had long ago worn off, and he didn't want to spend the afternoon driving by one fast food place after another with the aroma of French fries filling his car. In the refrigerator was a carton of leftover Chinese noodles and Peking chicken. They followed the same route as the mug of water had earlier in the day. Smart little bastards, those Chinese, he thought while his food was being nuked. Take rice and noodles, throw in lots of cheap vegetables, and add chicken that came from God-knows-where and sell it to the round eyes for big money. Twelve different chicken dishes on the menu from his local carry out and every one of them was exactly the same if you broke it down by ingredients. Just the presentation was different, depending on what tumbled out of the carton first. Steamed, sautéed, grilled, deep fried—it was still the same lousy chicken. Very clever, those little people.

Hank opened the fridge to grab a cold beer to go with his lunch and realized that the freezer compartment door was being held open by an inch-thick ring of ice. Damn it, he thought, time to deice the freezer, again. The new home he had built for his children and that two-timing bitch had had a deluxe side-by-side stainless steel frost-free twenty-five-cubic-foot-capacity refrigerator with water and ice in the door and a night light. *What the hell?* Hank thought. He felt as though he were living in the Stone Age, with a freezer full of ice that would take hours to defrost. His cheery mood was fading as the microwave announced that his lunch was ready.

The most efficient route from his apartment to the target homes was to drive south, then north and west to the other two homes, and hit the home farthest north last before heading back to the apartment. It was a lot of driving that would require a lot of gas. But the mission had a price, and he was willing to pay it. He had been born in Chicago, attended public schools, and moved to the suburbs for his first job. When the Pearson's Plumbing and Supply Company job opening came along, he began his many years of commuting into the city. He was much more comfortable getting around in the city, but he knew enough to find shortcuts and avoid the major highways. He figured his round trip this fine Friday would take him about four hours, including surveillance. With luck, he would be back home before the real rush hour happened. The grind started about four in the afternoon, building to mass escape at five and total log jam by six. Although his commute would be going against the flow of traffic as he headed home at the end of the day, if he left now, he would be tucked cozily in his apartment by five o'clock. Hank tossed out the empty wax carton, hand washed the single plate and fork, folded the map, took his written directions, and went down the stairs of the apartment building to the lot where his car was parked.

Hank's car was parked near a faded red snow fence, leaning over near a garbage dumpster. His car sat on a cracked, weed-sprouting asphalt slab with the last fading images of once bright yellow painted lines to identify where you should park. Hank noticed another small spot of rust, this one behind the rear driver's side wheel. The Chevy Malibu was eight years old, with over 117,000 miles on the odometer. The inside was clean, although the carpet was worn where the heel of his right foot rested while on the gas. The steering wheel grip was worn smooth, and the seat upholstery on the driver's seat had a small tear beginning in the stitching where the natural seam occurred. Half the outside mirror on the passenger side had broken off years ago, giving only a partial view of anyone coming up on your right. Several minor dents could be detected if you knew where to look along both side panels of the dark green Malibu. These had been caused by careless sons of bitches who had no respect for other people's property. They flung open their doors, not caring if they hit the car parked next to them. They were probably Realtors and bankers. They were going to get their new cars every two years anyway, so why worry about a little dent or ding here or there? Hank had sanded and bonded several rust spots on the fenders over the years. From a distance, the car didn't look so bad, he thought. But he knew exactly where to look to find every little scratch and ding.

Hank wound through the side streets leaving the Humphrey Arms and headed for the southbound expressway. Traffic was light and easy at noon, and he made good time to Rose Wood corporate limits. A mile and a half from the exit ramp, off from the frontage road was Primrose Drive. He drove slowly down the street, checking out foot traffic, the distance of the homes from each other, and the number of other vehicles on the street. It wasn't the best test at this time of day, but Hank had a gut feel for these situations. The street was quiet, with stop signs posted on the corners of the dissecting streets. This was good in terms of leaving the property quickly after disposing of one more blight on the face of the earth. What Hank didn't like was that Primrose went back out to the frontage road, paralleling the expressway but with no easy access back to an on ramp. Number 313 Primrose Drive was also located on a corner, which Hank preferred not to visit, not yet anyway. Too risky. Traffic came from two streets, both foot traffic and cars, in addition to neighbors that might see him. It didn't feel right, and Hank wasted no more time in the neighborhood. He returned and headed north to the bypass that would take him out to the western suburbs.

The radio was tuned to talk. He was particularly interested in the political discussions. His attention today was not on the speaker, who was currently ranting against forced redistribution of wealth in America, but rather on Annie Lawrence. She had been interesting to deal with last weekend. Medium height and slim, she hadn't given him much of a fight. He found it comical when she had thought that she had fallen down the stairs and apologized for being such an oaf. It wasn't until he had planted the toe of his boot in her side that her eyes filled with the realization something was wrong. There was confusion, then recognition, the fear, then fight, and finally submission. How odd, all the emotions the eyes could convey. He loved the look of fear, as it indicated his victims knew that their punishment was near. He was amused thinking back at her panic, followed by her vain attempts to get tough, followed by, finally, the begging. He didn't like the begging. It was pathetic and undignified. The only challenge with Annie had been the lack of props to use in finishing his mission. Regrettably, he had to forfeit the new black belt he had purchased just a week before. A small price to pay to remove one more weasel.

The trip west to Pine Brook took a little over thirty minutes. It was a small community of 25,000 people that gave the impression that everyone knew everyone else. He drove the length of Main Street until it curved and turned into Summit Avenue. Summit dead-ended at the railroad tracks. The home at 3 North 125th was a crumbling two-story colonial. The For Sale sign hung at an angle from past winds and looked as neglected as the house itself. *Why in the world would anyone hold an open house at a shit box like this?* Hank thought. That and the fact that it was a dead end street, with only one way out, made the decision an easy one. His spirits were dropping as he headed east out of Pine Brook towards more familiar territory. He was headed to Hamilton, Illinois.

Hank felt comfortable in this neck of the woods. After all, he had made earlier visits to the neighboring communities of Wilmington and Lawton. He liked the serenity of the western suburbs. It was more peaceful and less tainted than the city or the rich northern suburbs. The south and southwest communities were more working class and blue collar. The west felt inviting and safe and controlled. The people living here basked in a sense of security; no harm could befall this upper middle-class community. The security was false. His mood improved as he revisited the areas of his past good deeds. Did these folks realize that a hero was in their midst? For now he was anonymous, but someday he would be hailed as a fighter for the little guy, who stood up against the tyranny of big banks and the lowly real estate industry. They might even commemorate a holiday in his honor, on which day school children would stay home, banks would be closed, and there would be no mail service. It brought a smile to Hank's whisker-stubbled face.

He passed through Wilmington, heading east towards Hamilton. The two cities shared a common boundary, which was a major fourteen-mile north-south stretch of highway that led to two separate interstates at either end. After traveling through the more commercial areas, he entered the quaint downtown area of retail and restaurants lining both sides of the brick paver streets. People were out on foot, taking advantage of the dry, mild April weather. As he crisscrossed the main intersection of First Street and Main Street, his eyes fell upon the Prescott Realty sign hanging over the sidewalk, mid-block on Main. Fancy location for the fancy pants-Realtors inside, laughing and counting their money. Well they wouldn't be laughing for long. The smart ones would be scared shitless and find a more honorable profession than preying on innocent, hard-working families just trying to survive. Three blocks north of First, Hank turned east on Fourth Street and drove past an elementary school with buses already lined up to take the little tikes home. A shiny silver flagpole stood in the semi-circle walkway to the front door of the building. The flag lay limp against the pole as the sun reflected from the glass windows of the one-story building. Hank thought about his own childhood and fifth grade and immediately shook the thoughts from his mind.

At the end of Fourth Street, five blocks from Kennedy Elementary School, Hank turned north onto Sunset Drive. In the middle of the second block stood his next target. He felt it in his gut. A beautiful split-level home. The yard needed a little work, and the shutters could stand a coat of fresh paint this spring, but it was perfect. A half-brick front topped with red cedar boards running horizontally and a cantilevered second floor hanging over the windows of the lower level family room. A side driveway led past the house to a detached garage in back. As Hank slowly rolled by, he noticed a side entrance to the home, as well as the front door. He backed up and got out to take a flyer from the brochure box attached to the wooden staked sign. That was the beauty of stalking these homes. They were for sale, right? People didn't think twice about seeing someone parked in a car at the curb staring at the home, or even getting out to take a brochure. It wasn't even suspicious if someone actually got out and walked around the house to the backyard.

A young mother pushing a buggy and walking a small, fuzzy white-haired dog came towards him on the sidewalk as Hank was headed back to his running car.

"Beautiful day, isn't it?"

"It certainly is, just a beautiful day," Hank said, showing off his brilliant salesman's smile.

"Are you thinking about buying the Huffner house?"

"Well, it is a beautiful looking home. Can you tell me anything about the house, or the family who owns it?"

"Oh, the Huffners don't own it anymore," she said, suddenly turning sad. "They were great neighbors. Lived here six, maybe seven years. They were here when we moved in down the street." She pointed with the hand holding the leash. "Their oldest, Katie, babysat for my two kids two or three times a month. Nice family."

"What happened?" Hank asked as if he didn't already know.

"Sad story. Pete, that's Mr. Huffner, was a computer tech with a local company. Was with them over twelve years. Anyway, he was laid off just a little over a year ago. He looked for another job, but he was either overqualified or there were no openings. He started back to school at the local community college, going for his elementary education degree, so he could become a teacher. Male teachers at the elementary level are supposedly in high demand—you know, with so many being women, they like to balance out the role models. Anyway, Pete is half a semester away from graduating when he gets broadsided by a drunk driver on the way home from school. Right in the middle of the day! Can you believe that, someone drunk at 2:30 in the afternoon?"

"Oh, I am so sorry to hear that." Now it was Hank's turn to sound sad. He had seen plenty of drunks stagger out of and into the Fifty-Fifth Street Tavern at 2:30 in the afternoon. "Then what happened?"

"Well, Pete's okay, but he spent three weeks in the hospital, racked up a ton of medical bills, and couldn't finish his semester. Julianne, his wife, got herself a part-time job, but it wasn't enough. After making up his time at school, Pete missed the time period when schools were hiring teachers for the next school year. Anyway, long story short, they fell behind on their house payments and couldn't make up the difference. They put their home up for sale to try and salvage something, but the markets been slow. Even when they tried to make good on some of the back mortgage payments, the bank said, "Sorry, it's too late," and began foreclosing on their home. They finally moved out and just up and left about two months ago. It's really a shame. I am so sorry for going on and on. You must think I'm the neighborhood gossip. It's a wonderful home and a wonderful community."

"Don't be silly. I feel terrible for the … Huffners, was it? You obviously are a caring person and your compassion is touching. You would make a wonderful new neighbor."

"Well, thank you," she said, blushing a shade. "I must go. It was nice talking with you and enjoy the rest of your day."

"Bye now," Hank said as he headed to his car. Hank couldn't believe his good luck. He was thrilled with this next target. He took one last glance at the For Sale sign, hung stylishly on a four-by-four wooden post, and noted the same real estate company he had seen when he drove through town, Prescott Realty. The agent, Dexter Bradley, displayed his number prominently in six-inch-high characters. A rider hanging from the bottom of the sign announced "Open Sunday." *Well, Mr. Bradley, I'll see you Sunday.* Hank smiled. He had been lucky so far, encountering only female Realtors in the open houses he had visited. But he was prepared to surprise and overtake whoever he found inside the homes. Up until now it had been easy, but Hank looked forward to this new challenge. He was curious as to how a man might die versus a woman. Would he plead and beg and cry like a baby? Or would he be dignified and die like a man? Well, he would find out in about forty-eight hours.

He decided to skip the house in the far north suburbs, for now anyway. He drove home, listening to the talk on the radio. The experts were debating the market on Wall Street, discussing hedge fund managers and the risks they took with other people's money. As always, the radio host had the final say and simply disconnected those who disagreed with his point of view. Traffic was still light but building as he headed home, driving against the flow. A very good day, Hank decided, well worth the trip. He arrived home with plenty of sunlight still glowing in the west. He whistled as he climbed the stairs to his third-story apartment. Usually he came home depressed, but not today. He looked forward to his house-hunting trip on Sunday and was even mildly excited about his Saturday at Pearson's Plumbing Supply Company. That night, Hank dreamt about a parade in his honor, a multicolored ribbon with medals hanging around his neck, sitting in the back of an open convertible as it passed cheering folks along the parade route. And on his left, in the crowd, were Samantha and Tyler, waving and throwing him kisses. There were dozens of black notches painted on the side of the white Cadillac, one for each Realtor that Famous Hank had disposed of during his reign of power.

My cell phone rang Saturday morning just as I was getting into the shower. At 7:20 a.m. it was too early for a business call, so I assumed it was social. I hadn't heard from Liz since we had met on Monday, although this was typical of our relationship. Plus, she had been busy with the task force and wading through information on the open house murders. She had emailed me to say the information I had given her regarding First Family Bank and Trust had been helpful and that they were tracking down any other connections that might be pertinent. She had signed off with a thanks. Why I wrapped a towel around myself to retrieve my phone, I wasn't sure. I enjoyed a casual stroll through my apartment au natural. I checked the caller ID before picking up the phone.

"You're up early," I said.

"Can't sleep, 'ol buddy," said a nasally Dex.

"You sound terrible, Dex. What's going on?"

"It started yesterday with sneezing and a sore throat, and when I woke up this morning I was drenched in sweat and ached all over."

"Poor baby," I teased. "Do you have me confused with the doctor's office?"

"No, but I need a favor."

"Want me to bring you some chicken soup?"

"Even thinking of food right now would make me puke."

"Okay, seriously, what can I do for you, Dex? You name it and I'm there."

"I need someone to cover my open house tomorrow on Sunset. The ad already ran and it's posted on something like twenty websites."

"No can do, Dex. I'm already set up for my own open house Sunday," I said, feeling bad. "Maybe I can find someone else to help you out."

"Naw, that's okay. I'll find someone in the office to cover. Just thought

I'd give you first chance at a premium opportunity." Dex coughed into the phone.

"You sound terrible. Have you been to the doctor?"

"Got an appointment this morning at nine."

"Tell you what. I'll pick you up at 8:30 and take you there myself."

"No need to bother," Dex said.

"No bother. You're my friend and you don't sound as if you should be driving. It'll be good to have an advocate with you. Plus, you'd do the same for me, right?"

"Sure I would. Okay then, see you at 8:30." Dex hung up.

Dexter and I met my first day at Prescott Realty just over ten years ago. He had guided me through the office, showed me where things were kept, and introduced me to the office staff and other Realtors. He was my goodwill ambassador. We clicked from the start and became fast friends. After the first day in the office, I felt as if I had known Dex my entire life—it was that kind of relationship. He had watched as my real estate career had taken off quickly and offered valuable advice on how to keep it going strong. Although his career, if you could call it a career, was slow but steady, that's the way he liked it. Just enough business to cover his costs with a few bucks left over to spend on his sinful pleasures. He was a fixture in the office and was more of a social butterfly than a productive Realtor. He was always available to help me with a project or market analysis when I needed him and to cover my business on those rare occasions when I left town for a getaway.

Our relationship was odd and puzzled those who didn't understand the chemistry. We were complete opposites in every way. Dex came from old money and lacked for nothing. He lived quite comfortably off a trust fund set up by his grandfather. I, on the other hand, came from a hard-working family that would have been classified as middle income. My parents earned every dollar they had ever made. Dex was flashy and even eccentric in his dress, whereas I preferred simple, stylish, well-cut cloth. Dexter was terribly out of shape, not obese but pudgy. And he did nothing to improve his image. Health was not a priority with Dex. Besides, he had longevity on his side. His grandfather and grandmother had both lived into their nineties, and his father and mother were now in their late seventies and in perfect health. I had encouraged Dex to ride with me as a form of easy exercise. He had gone out and bought a top-of-the-line touring bicycle, which he sat upon maybe half a dozen times before it ended up in his garage, parked next to other expensive toys of which he had grown tired. I, on the other hand, felt compelled to work at maintaining my current weight of 180, which fit nicely on my six-foot-two-inch frame. My hobbies included biking, golfing, crossword puzzles, and following my beloved Detroit Tigers. Dexter's hobbies included eating out, drinking expensive alcohol, reading historical biographies, cooking, and ogling pretty girls. When we were out together, we resembled Mutt and Jeff. My straight blond-haired conservative appearance clashed against his five-foot-seven, 212-pound figure, with dark curls, always in disarray, dressed as if he was in a theatrical production, including his trademark green socks. But we were bonded and enjoyed each other's company and the backgrounds that we brought to the party.

The trip from my apartment to Dexter's fabulous rebuilt home in the historic section of town took less than ten minutes. I could have walked it in twenty, cutting through alleys and parks. Dex had purchased an old Cape Cod on an impressive lot seven years ago and torn it down to make way for his present abode. Until then he had lived with mother and father, who thought it was high time their thirty-something (closing in on forty) son move out and onto his own. Without being gaudy and over-building the lot, Dex's architect and contractor created an elegant home to match the lifestyle that he portrayed. Thirty-five hundred square feet of high-end everything! A chef's kitchen with walk-in pantry and commercial-grade appliances. A beautiful sunroom off the back of the house with Byzantine tile from Mexico. The first-floor master bedroom offered tray ceilings, recessed lighting, and two walk-in closets with a built-in steam presser for his extensive wardrobe. The master bathroom included heated floors and a built-in television in the mirror high enough to be viewed from the whirlpool tub. The towel racks were heated and a bidet had been installed next to the toilet. The first-floor den on the west end of the home had a coffered ceiling, wainscoting in cherry wood, and built-in bookcases. His collection of books, which numbered in the hundreds, ranged in subject matter from the *Mayan Agricultural Calendar* to *What Ever Sailor Needs to Know about Trade Winds*. There were plenty of first-edition classics as well as current spy novels. There were three guest rooms upstairs, each with its own bathroom. The finished basement was a true man cave. Dex had spared no expense in finishing off the lower portion of his home. The amenities included a theater room, complete with seating, surround sound, and a popcorn cart. He had installed a custom-built oak bar with brass rails, stained glass, wine cooler, and refrigerator. The flat-screen plasma television hanging above the bar offered four hundred channels of viewing! A billiard area of the basement was finished off to resemble and Irish snooker room, with high tables, neon Guinness signs, and a lead stained glass light above the red velvet table. The entire home was wired for Internet, sound, and security. A camera at the front door allowed Dex to determine if he wanted to answer or not from monitors throughout his home. A three-car attached garage sat at an angle behind the home. From the outside, Dex's home looked updated and comfortable, but once inside you realized that you had stepped into elegance.

Dex came out the front door as I pulled into his driveway. Obviously he had been waiting for me. He had on a full-length cashmere coat, even though it was in the high fifties, pulled tight across his chest as he ambled sluggishly towards my car. He got in with a huff and puff. His dark curls were stuck with sweat to his forehead, and his color was missing.

"You don't look so good," I said as he fastened his seatbelt.

He turned his head with effort and looked at me through yellowish eyes. "You think? I feel like shit, Kurt. I thought I was getting a cold, or it was my allergies, but I think I have the flu," he snuffed.

"Where we headed," I asked.

"Doctor Bennet, over on Bristol."

"Got it. She'll have you fixed up in no time. Hey, didn't you date her once?"

"No. I asked her out, but she gave me the 'no dating patients' bit. Cute, though. I would have enjoyed playing doctor/patient with her."

"There's the Dex I know and love. At least you haven't lost your sense of depravity."

We drove the short distance to Doctor Bennet's office in silence. Well, kind of. I could hear the rattle in Dex's lungs as he labored to breathe. Poor guy really did look like shit. I helped him out of the car and up the steps to Doctor Bennet's office. The receptionist had him sign in and take a seat. We sat amidst month-old magazines, along with two other coughing, wheezing patients waiting for the doctor. I absolutely detest waiting rooms in clinics and hospitals. After all, they're full of sick people, and the disinfectant stings the hairs in my nose. We are fodder for the airborne germs just waiting for an accommodating host. I am very lucky in that I rarely get sick. Maybe a cold now and then, but I've never been really sick. Chalk it up to my stubborn German heritage.

"Did you find anyone to take your open house for tomorrow?" I asked while we waited.

"Not yet. I sent an e-blast on the intra-office website just before you picked me up. I'll check when I get home."

Fifteen minutes later Dex was called back to an examination room. I sat in the lobby and read a six-month-old copy of *Reader's Digest*. Had I planned ahead, I would have brought my own reading material from home. At least those pages aren't infected. One more patient entered the waiting room while I waited for Dex. She was eleven and was brought in by her mom. Attractive woman, in her mid-thirties, I guessed. I smiled politely when our eyes met. She returned the smile and then busied herself with paperwork for the receptionist. I didn't see a ring on her hand and wondered if she might be a single mom. The little girl had dried snot on her upper lip and kept shifting from one foot to the other. They took a seat across from me on plastic formed chairs.

"Hope it's nothing serious." I nodded towards the little girl.

"Me too. Her mom is out of town for the weekend and I'm taking care of Lila. I love my niece, but I don't really have much experience with kids."

Bingo! "I'm sure she's in great hands. Are you from the area?"

"Just visiting my brother and his wife for a couple of weeks. They went into the city for an overnight getaway, and I said, 'Oh sure, I can take care of Lila. No problem,' and now here we are. Timing is everything"

"She'll be fine. Probably just a bad cold," I said. Where are you from?"

"Tampa."

"That explains the beautiful tan. How long will you be visiting?"

"I'm leaving on Monday. The time just flew by."

"That's a shame, about leaving on Monday, I mean. My name's Kurt, Kurt Banning." I stood as I introduced myself.

"Joanna," she said and extended her hand. Her touch was smooth and cool, and I held her hand for a second too long as we looked at each other. She blushed, and I quickly glanced at the floor.

"Lila," the nurse said, holding a file in her hands, standing in the entrance to the examination rooms. Damn!

"Well, it was nice meeting you, Kurt Banning," Joanna said, flashing an unbelievable smile as she stepped around me. Her white teeth looked brilliant against her smooth, tanned face. The large brown eyes, hooded by magnificent long lashes, had a sparkle I hadn't seen in a very long time. I felt my temperature go up a couple of degrees and hoped it was Joanna and not an airborne bug looking for a landing strip.

"It was all my pleasure." I fumbled to get a business card out of my wallet. "When you're coming back for another visit, call me. I'll give you a tour of our fine city."

Joanna took my card, smiled again, dropped the card into her purse, and disappeared around the corner into the examining room with Lila.

I felt a bit guilty about the innocent flirting. Joanna was an attractive woman, and I would have loved to spend some time getting to know her better. The image of Liz leaped into my head. It was as though I had those two little people on my shoulders, the devil and the angel.

"What were just doing?"

"He was exercising his right to engage in conversation with an attractive woman."

"But what about Liz?"

"Liz schmiz. They're just friends."

"But they have history; they're still in a committed relationship."

"Oh no they're not."

"Oh, but I believe they are."

"Well, Liz sure doesn't treat us like we're in a committed relationship; she hasn't even spoken with us since Monday."

"She's been busy."

"Yes, and I say our boy here gets busy too."

I was sitting in a trance listening to the two Kurts arguing when I heard Dexter cough behind me. "What did the doc say?" I said as I stood.

"She says I'll live, even if I don't want to. It's not the flu or a bad cold. I have a bacterial infection. She called in a prescription that should knock it out in five days or so. Can we stop by the pharmacy on the way home and pick it up?"

"Sure. Let's get out of here. All these sick people give me the creeps."

We drove to the Family Drug Emporium. The prescription wasn't quite ready, so we strolled the aisles looking for essentials for Dex. Tissues, throat lozenges, an oral thermometer, *Time* magazine, and an assortment of Dex's favorite candies: M&Ms, Twix, Brach Malted Malt Balls.

"What did they give you?" I asked.

"Moxifloxacin," he said reading the label. "Suppose to be good. According to the pharmacist, I should start feeling better in a couple of days. No booze though while I'm on this stuff. Says on the label that it may make me dizzy, sleepy, cause diarrhea, headache, cramping, loss of appetite, rash, or a milky discharge. Ooh! From where, I wonder?"

We talked in general about the case Liz was working on during the drive home. Nothing confidential, just the facts known by the public and speculation by the Realtor community. "You said you have an open house tomorrow too. Where at?" asked Dex.

"My new listing on Concord. It's an awesome two-story with a huge backyard. The Randalls put in a new kitchen last summer and the bathrooms have all been updated. It should move pretty quickly where we have it priced. That's one of the reasons I wanted to get an open house done early in the listing period. I don't think it'll last long on the market. I'm not wasting time this spring. I've got open houses scheduled for the next four weekends."

"Aren't you nervous about the crazy person going around killing real estate agents at open houses?"

"Dex, there are thousands of homes on the market and hundreds of open houses every weekend in the Chicagoland area. What are the odds? Plus, would you stop driving just because you know people have car accidents? I don't think so. Whoever is doing this has already hit the area. It's random and seems to be spread out. Liz told me they are working on narrowing down the field of suspects and the FBI is involved, putting together a profile. It's just a matter of time before they get caught. And look at us, big burly he-man types. Who's going to screw with us, anyway?" I left out the fact that I had dug up valuable information that would help Liz's case.

I parked in Dex's driveway and we went in through the front door. He tapped the beeping pad on the inside wall to disable the alarm system. I carried his bag of goodies into the kitchen and set it on the gold-flecked Italian granite countertop.

"I'll take you up on that soup you offered earlier, if you don't mind," Dex said while removing his coat and throwing it on the high-backed Queen Anne rosewood chair. "I want to check my email before I fall into bed for a long nap."

"Go ahead. I'll fix the soup. I know my way around your kitchen." Dex had hosted dozens of dinner parties in this house and I had been lucky enough to attend many, mostly with Liz. On two occasions I came stag, one of which was a setup. Dex wasn't even subtle about it. When I arrived, Dex took me by the arm and had introduced me to Ashley Thomas as her date for the evening. That's Dex, get right to the point. He always hosted the parties as a single, showing up in silk ascots or smoking jackets or thick velvet slippers, while the guests were donned in sports coats or turtlenecks and simple dresses. He was born in the wrong century and would have fit right in with Louis the Fourteenth. Those who didn't know Dex like I do often misunderstood his sexual orientation. But as his wing man more times than I can remember, I would never question his masculinity. He preferred to keep his escapades private, behind the closed doors of his castle. Conversely, the "boy's night out" affairs in his basement were entirely different. Denim and flannel with gallons of single-malt Scotch and imported fifty dollar cigars. We rotated around the pool table or lined up for darts or at the bar. Some evenings we lounged in overstuffed leather sofas in front of the big screen and watched war movies or pay-per-view boxing. Dex loved the fights, as a spectator only.

I rummaged through the cupboards and found a variety of cans of Progresso. My choice was Italian noodle with chicken stock and vegetables. Unlike most pictures on the containers of food, the soup actually looked as good as the label. While the soup was heating, I found a loaf of Italian bread and sliced off two large chunks, along with a tab of butter, and poured a glass of green tea over ice. Dex had quite the setup here, and I was happy for him, not envious like most of his acquaintances. I heard him moan something from the bedroom and yelled back that I'd be right there. Bowl of soup, silver tablespoon, plate of bread and butter and silver butter knife, and a crystal glass filled with iced tea all went onto a hard leather-bound serving tray. I walked through the family room, past the enormous two-story stone fireplace, down a short hall, and into the master bedroom. Dex was ready for me, propped up in bed, lying under layers of sheets, blankets, and coverlets.

"Smells good," he said through a stuffed nose.

"How can you smell anything through that plugged-up red thing on your face you call a nose?"

On the computer sitting on a small desk at the bay window in his bedroom, the browser was still open to the Prescott Realty intranet site. This was available only to employees and Realtors at Prescott. It was invaluable as a way of sending information and requests to each other, not quite as efficient as texting, but better than phone calling or trying to catch someone in the office. The company also provided a plethora of resources, tools, links, and forms online to enable us to be the most professional and effective Realtors out there. Pretty high tech for a small boutique operation.

"Found somebody to do your open house?" I asked as I sat the tray down across his lap, noting the open computer.

"Yeah, Jane's going to handle it for me. Emailed me back this morning and said she'd be happy to do it since she didn't have anything else going on Sunday. What is she, a hundred years old?"

"No, Dex. I don't think so. Not a very respectful way to talk about a nice lady who did you a favor and got you off the hook." Jane Stark had been at Prescott Realty longer than anyone could remember. When Mr. Prescott had died and left the company to the original founding and existing members, Jane had refused her stake in the company. As rumor had it, she didn't feel worthy of the position and didn't want any responsibility for the success or failure of the company going forward without the leadership of James Prescott. Jane had been a Realtor for over forty years, more or less. So long, in fact, that she was grandfathered in from paying any more Realtor dues or fees. She was a guest of the Association and Board of Realtors. Except her first five years in the business, she had spent her entire career at Prescott. The changes she had seen were an amazing testament as to just how far the business of buying and selling homes had come. When Jane had begun her career, listing agents showed and sold their own properties. There were no buyer's agents, and everyone was a dual agent. Listings were advertised in the newspaper and by yard sign only, that and word of mouth. There had been no organized Multiple Listing Service. When the MLS did arrive, it came with oversized ten-pound listing books, covered in cheap thirty-pound stock paper, issued once a month and then eventually every other week. Mimeograph machine had been replaced by copiers and then by fax machines and finally email. When Jane started, there had been one telephone in the office that everyone shared. These were followed by the desk phones, mobile bag phones, and smart phones of today.

Jane Stark had never married but was a great aunt several times over. You knew when she had just walked through the office. Her perfume was heavy and floral and reminded you of the old lady you sat behind in church on Sunday mornings as a kid. Her hair was snow white and thick as a ball of cotton. I'm sure she had worn the same style since high school. Jane was prim and proper and always dressed like a lady. Long skirts, sweaters, or blazers to keep warm, even in the summer, and black thick-heeled schoolmarm shoes completed her ensemble. And mind your manners and tongue around Ms. Stark; she didn't go in for any of that off-color humor or "blue language," as she called it. She owned cats and lived in the house she was born in, and almost everyone loved her. She was Grandma to those of us who worked with her, and I think she was closer to eighty than one hundred.

"You're right. It's the fever talking. Thanks for taking care of me today. You're a good friend, Kurt."

"Yes, I am." I smiled at my sick buddy. "Eat your soup, get some rest, and call me if you need anything. I put your cell phone on the nightstand next to your bed. It's plugged in and charging."

I set the alarm, locked the door, and pulled it tight. On my drive home, I drifted back to Joanna and how refreshing even those few moments of conversation had been. I had enjoyed interacting with a woman who wasn't a coworker or client, or Liz for that matter. Something to ponder. After all, I wasn't sure where Liz and I were headed. I knew where we had been, but the future was unclear. In fact, I wasn't sure there was a future. We both seemed to be fine with whatever it was we did have and it never came up in conversation. So, for the time being, I would leave sleeping dogs lie. Eventually, though, I would have to establish the rules for my own sanity and direction. Who wants to wake up one day, retired and alone except for a wrinkled, aging, on-again-off-again girlfriend?

***

Sunday, at a quarter to four, as Jane Stark was turning off the lights in the lower level family room on Sunset Drive, she heard the front door open and a man's high voice say, "Hello, anybody here?"

"I'll be right there," Jane said, turning the lights back on. Hank was surprised by the voice. He thought she sounded like Mrs. Doubtfire from the eponymous movie. He heard the clumping of heavy square shoes coming up the half flight of stairs from the lower level family room. Jane turned the corner, facing the foyer, puffing a bit from the climb.

"What a surprise!" Hank said, and he truly meant it. Mr. Dexter Bradley was an old woman.

CHAPTER 20

I had been dreaming about being on a cruise. The weather had been picture perfect all day, where the blue of the sky meets the blue of the ocean at the horizon. No clouds, no waves, no kids, nothing but blue surrounding fit, tan bodies. Cocktail waitresses wearing white go-go boots delivered festive drinks on bamboo platters. The sound of Motown blared through overhead speakers on the Lido deck, and a naked female water polo team splashed in the main pool. The chop came out of nowhere and the ship was lifting and rising. I remembered that I had missed the lifeboat drill after we left port. Liz and I had hid under the covers in our stateroom, too cozy to go up on deck. The tossing of the ship now was sliding tables and deck chairs into the pools, and plastic souvenir glasses with palm trees stenciled on the sides rolled back and forth across the deck and fell overboard. I was frantic to find Liz as the "abandon ship" bells went off. I was running against the flow of vacationers that knew exactly where their lifeboats were stationed. I was yelling Liz's name into a strong wind that put the words right back into my mouth and the bells kept ringing.

I sat up in bed, eyes open, realizing it had only been a dream, but the bells kept going off. It was my cell phone, lit and ringing next to my bed. The clock said it was one-forty in the morning on Monday.

"Hello," I croaked. The rapid breathing from the dream had dried my throat.

"Kurt, it's Bard. Something awful has happened." Bard Holmes was not just a principal at Prescott Realty; he was the managing broker and a father figure to the younger and newer agents. A call from him would be rare, but in the middle of the night as unlikely as winning the lottery.

"What is it, Bard?" I asked, rubbing the fog from my temples.

"It's Jane. They found her about two hours ago. She's dead, Kurt!"

"What?" I was standing in the dark of my bedroom, illuminated only by the screen of my cell. I was sure the dream had ended. "Are you sure?" A silly question. "What happened?" I asked, still not comprehending Bard's words.

"I received a call from the Hamilton Police Department about thirty minutes ago. They got a call from the neighbors on Sunset Drive saying that lights were on and there was a car parked in the driveway."

My heart jumped in my chest and I felt as if I was going to be sick. I walked through my apartment without turning on the lights and opened the back door for air. The early morning was crisp, and I shivered standing in the doorway, looking into a starlight sky. "Oh God, no," I said, almost too faint to be heard.

"Mr. Wallace, who lives next door on Sunset, let his dog out before going to bed, a few minutes before midnight. He knows the house is vacant, so when he saw lights on, he called the police."

I already had guessed the rest of the conversation as Bard continued.

"When the officers arrived, they found the front door unlocked and went in to investigate. Jane was sitting in the kitchen." Bard's voice began to crack. "And she was—sorry, Kurt—she was tied to a chair, and she was dead. They couldn't find any family contacts, so, knowing she worked at Prescott, they tracked me down to give me the news. I'm on my way to the hospital. They've asked me to come in and identify her in person." Bard's voice trailed off.

I was back in my bedroom, getting dressed. "Bard, do you want me to meet you at the hospital?"

"No, no, that's all right. I wanted to call as many of the office people as possible so they're prepared when they come into the office today. I'd rather be the one to tell them about Jane. I don't want them hearing it on the news or reading it in the paper. Just wanted you to know, Kurt, from me." Bard disconnected, sounding weary and beaten.

I slammed my fist down on top of my dresser. I should have known, I said to myself. Damn it! I didn't even think about the open house as being a target. I went to my office area and turned on the computer. While it was warming up, I called Liz. I knew she'd be asleep, as she was currently working the day shift.

"Do you know what time it is?" Liz mumbled. "I hope you and Dex are not on a drunken binge and now you need someone to talk to, 'cause if you are, you've got the wrong number, mister."

"Liz, this is serious," I said with a stony voice. "That psycho you're chasing just killed Jane Stark from my office." My voice became louder with each word I said. "That son of a bitch killed a sweet little old woman who wouldn't hurt a soul and couldn't defend herself. What kind of asshole kills little old ladies?" I was screaming into the phone at this point.

"Slow down, Kurt," she said, all the sleepiness gone from her voice. "When did this happen and how did you find out?"

"Bard Holmes called me five minutes ago with the news. He got a call from someone at the department." My computer was booted up and I was going into the MLS. "I didn't have to wait to get any details from him; it's got to be the same person. Jane was found tied to a chair at a house where she did an open house for Dex earlier today. Today's Monday ... I mean yesterday." I clicked through a few pages until I came to active listings, I punched in the address on Sunset Drive, went to the tax page, and there it was. "Shit!"

"What?" Liz asked into the phone.

"It's right here. I'm such an idiot! I'm telling Dex that we have nothing to worry about. 'What are the odds?' I said. 'Slim to none, too many possibilities. Better odds of getting hit by lightning.'"

"Whoa," Liz said, "what are you talking about? What does Dexter have to do with this?

"Dex is sick and couldn't do his open house yesterday. He put out a notice on the company bulletin asking for assistance. He asked me, but I was already booked. Jane volunteered to sit the open house for him, and now she's dead, Liz. How careless of me. I should have known."

"You couldn't have known, Kurt." Liz was trying to be consoling. She was up and getting dressed for the office, holding her phone between her neck and shoulder.

"Well, here it is," I said, looking at the tax records on my screen. "You want to take a guess as to who holds the mortgage on the property? It's First Family Bank and Trust," I said before Liz could answer.

"I'm going into the office. I'll call you when I get more details."

"Let me come with you."

"No, Kurt. This is police business. I'll call you as soon as I have more information."

"The hell it is. I knew Jane. I worked with her. This is my office they're messing with, Liz. I want to help."

"I know you do, but not yet. Listen, you gather what information you can from the real estate side, and I'll be in touch as soon as I can. I've got a call coming in from the station."

"I want in on this, Liz." She had already hung up.

I paced around the apartment, not knowing what to do. It was three in the morning. I made a cup of coffee and sat at my computer, wondering what information I could pull that would be helpful. Details about the house, the past owners, and current showings all seemed worthless. Dexter would have all that information, anyway. It was his listing. I wondered if Bard had called him yet. Dex needed to know. It was his listing, his friend. He was going to feel every bit as sick to his stomach as I did. I hated to bother him if he wasn't awake; he was still recovering from his infection. And if he did know, Dex would have already called me. I decided to do nothing for the time being.

I rotated from sitting in front of my computer to pacing from the front window of my apartment, which overlooked Main Street, to the kitchen, which had a small window above the sink that looked down onto the alley behind the building.

I thought about the last time I had spoken with Jane. It had been a brief discussion while the office had been celebrating Jimmy's birthday, just one week ago. Conversations with Jane had always been superficial. I'm not sure anyone really knew much about her other than she was a Hamiltonian, lived in her childhood home, and had been at Prescott Realty since the beginning of time. She was a wealth of knowledge regarding the local real estate scene. She had seen the same homes sell over and over, knew the string of owners, and possessed many interesting facts about the history of Hamilton. She would have been the top winner if they had ever invented a trivia game about Hamilton, Illinois. I was embarrassed to admit that I couldn't even remember what we had spoken about at the party. I wondered if she was lonely. I wondered if she never married, by design or chance. Had she ever had a love interest? For God's sake, I didn't even know when her birthday was, or exactly how old she was. I felt shame that I hadn't taken more time to get to know Miss Jane Stark, and now I would never have the chance. It was all so depressing, and nothing adds to depression more than being awake in the wee hours of the morning with turmoil swirling in your stomach and brain.

I took a quick shower and changed into jeans and a loose sweater. I decided to go downstairs to the office and go through the listing file Dex had for Sunset Drive. We all have keys to the office so that we can conduct our business whenever the opportunity arises. That's the kind of office Prescott Realty ran, with total trust and accessibility. I'm not sure anyone even locked their desk drawers. I would normally ask Dexter if I could look at the listing file, but I wasn't going to call my sick buddy before the sun came up to ask.

I wondered how Liz was making out at the police station as I went down the back exterior stairs from my apartment to the back entrance of Prescott Realty. I knew she would call when she could, but right now, I was pretty sure she had her hands full. I opened the steel security back door to the building and walked through the kitchenette, flipping on the lights as I made my way through the empty office. I enjoyed the peacefulness of the office without the chatter of other agents, phones ringing, the paging of Realtors over the intercom, and fax machines and copiers humming away. When I first got into the business I didn't have my own computer, so I spent many an evening in the semi-lit solitude of this place. Community desks and computers were arranged in the middle of the office in an open area. This was affectionately referred to as the "pit." Occasionally I would run into another agent, working late, enjoying the same serenity of the empty office. I doubted I would run into anyone that morning. The file cabinets where the official files and records were kept were in fact locked, according to rules and regulations. No problem. The keys to the file cabinets were in Molly's unlocked top desk drawer.

I pulled the listing file for 913 Sunset Drive and took it to my desk. I pulled the chain on the green and brass bankers light that sat on the corner of my desk. It was much less harsh than the overhead fluorescent lights. I pulled the stack of documents out of the legal size folder and began going through them. There was the standardized listing agreement showing First Family Bank and Trust as the property owner. An officer of the bank, Marcus Weinberg, Senior VP, Loss Mitigation, had signed it. I made a note of his name and phone number on a separate sheet of paper. The usual disclosures were also attached indicating that the bank had no knowledge of radon gas, lead paint, or mold. The real property disclosure had been signed with the box checked indicating that FFB&T had not occupied the property for the previous twelve months and had no information pertaining to latent defects. Additional addendums were included as well references to the property as a foreclosure that was being sold "as is." I didn't find anything unusual or helpful other than Mr. Weinberg's contact information. I reassembled the file and replaced it in the cabinet, locked it, and returned the key to Molly's desk. I looked up at the large wall clock. It was half past four in the morning and still as dark as black paint outside.

I strolled over to the desk that Jane Stark had occupied for decades and sat down. I could smell the bouquet of her perfume. There were numerous thank-you notes pinned to the corkboard on the wall next to her desk. The curled edges and yellowed corners gave a clue as to how long they had been displayed. An old black-and-white photo in an antique oval frame held the picture of a mustachioed man and a woman wearing a high-necked laced blouse. They must have been Mr. and Mrs. Stark, her parents. A blotter calendar sat perfectly square in the middle of her desk, with neatly hand-printed appointments and dates in the little cubes marking the days of the month. This Tuesday was a sales meeting, the note said, nine o'clock. Well, Jane, at least you wouldn't have to sit through any more of those. Her desk was sparse except for a holder for paperclips, pens, and sticky notes. A bottle of hand lotion sat on the right-hand corner of her desk. Her wastepaper basket under her desk was a third full of miscellaneous papers, tissues, and several bite-size candy wrappers. Maybe Miss Stark had a weakness for sweets.

I went back to my desk and caught up on routine reports and overdue correspondence with my clients. I worked until the morning light began to replace the darkness of night. It was 6:30. The past five hours had seemed to take days to pass. The surreal feeling of Jane being killed and the quiet peacefulness of Hamilton about to be rocked had sunk in, and I was exhausted as well as famished. Abby's would have been open for half an hour, so I turned out the lights and exited the rear door and headed to my car, which was parked twenty feet away in a spot that had a sign above it that read, "Tenant Parking Only."

"Good morning, sunshine. You're up early, or are you just coming home?"

"Morning, Marcy," I said, entering Abby's. "I've been up since early this morning working."

"Really? Must be some clients you're working with. What are they, vampires? And since when does the impeccably groomed Mr. Banning go to work unshaven and wearing jeans?" She said, smirking.

I instinctively reached up and felt the stubble. "Lot of questions for so early in the day. What are you, a cop?"

"Sit anywhere, hon." Marcy motioned with a pot of coffee to the mostly empty tables and booths.

I picked up a fresh copy of the *Hamilton Riser* from a stack sitting on the glass countertop by the cash register and headed to a window booth. Of course there would be nothing in the local paper about poor Jane Stark. There probably weren't two dozen people in all of Hamilton who were even aware of what had happened the day before. By noon, the city would be ablaze with discussions about a murder that would spin us on our axis. Grocery clerks speaking in hushed voices to shoppers. Teachers whispering in the faculty lounge. Post office clerks giving the latest news to stamp buyers. It would spread faster than a Hollywood gossip story.

Marcy arrived at my table with a steaming mug of decaf. "What'll it be, hon?" she asked.

"Two eggs, scrambled, a side of bacon, whole wheat toast, and a short stack of buttermilk pancakes."

"Quite an appetite this morning." With a wink, she disappeared with my order.

I perused the thin copy of the Monday issue of the *Riser*. The headlines were about an upcoming school board meeting to resolve redistricting and balancing the growing elementary school population. A weather infograph was on the bottom of page one, partly sunny and a high of fifty-six. Not bad for mid-April. The rest of the week was forecasted to be the same. Pages two through eighteen were filled with social events, an editorial about the loss of morality in America, letters to the editor, a half page of obituaries, a human interest piece about an area dog that had traveled over two hundred miles to be reunited with his owners after having been lost during a weekend vacation in southern Indiana, recipes for meatloaf, lasagna, and something funky that could be done with chicken. The pages were full of advertisements for automobiles, a new dentist in town, a doctor who could make your breasts larger or smaller, furniture sales, and the grand reopening of Walter's Bait and Tackle A-Lure Store. The final three pages were devoted to local, college, and professional sports. At this time of year, the main topics were the NBA, the beginning of the MLB season, cross country, girls' high school softball, and boys' high school baseball. I had read the entire newspaper from front to back and had begun to go through it again in hopes I had missed something of interest the first time when Marcy delivered my three-plate breakfast.

"Enjoy," she said, refilling my cup.

The eggs were fluffy and fresh and the bacon was perfect, crisp without being burnt. There was too much melted butter on the toast for my taste, almost as if it had been applied with a paint brush. I poured the excess onto the two giant buttermilk pancakes sitting on a separate plate and covered them in real artificial maple syrup.

I thought about the mind of the person with a vendetta against Realtors, or FFB&T, or both. Three of the homes had been in foreclosure, and one was being foreclosed upon. This creep obviously had a thing for the bank. Possibility one: he worked for FFB&T and was eliminating inventory. No, the homes would still be there, even though the selling of the properties would be suspended for a time while the investigations continued. Possibility two: he or she had a grudge against the bank itself and was out to send a message. Possibility three: the suspect was making a social and political statement about the current economy and housing crisis. But why just FFB&T properties? Possibility four: the jerk hated Realtors, but again, why just homes owned by the bank? All possibilities kept coming back to First Family Bank and Trust. I planned on calling Marcus Weinberg as soon as the bank opened.

I was sopping up the last of the syrup with a wedge of cold pancake stuck on my fork when my cell phone started a vibrating dance across the tabletop. "Hello," I said, swallowing the next to last bite of pancake.

"Did I wake you?" Liz said.

Now that was a laugh. Bard Holmes calls me in the middle of the night to tell me one of our fellow Realtors is dead. I call Liz and then just roll over and go back to sleep? Incredible! "Just finishing breakfast."

"Breakfast? How long have you been up?"

"Oh, I guess it has been, I don't know, since I was awoken after one o'clock in the morning and told that Jane Stark had been killed." My voice had raised more than I had intended, and drew looks from the few early risers sitting in Abby's. Luckily they didn't understand what I said because of my mouthful of pancakes. "It's kind of hard to get back to sleep when you hear news like that," I said in a more hushed voiced. "Anyway, I was starving, so I came into Abby's for an early morning breakfast. You know, eat and get it out of the way so I can spend the rest of the day helping you with *your* case."

"Actually, I am calling to ask you to assist us. I told Chief Dougan about how you connected the dots on the homes with First Family Bank and Trust. He thought you might be helpful, and he's got an idea that might help us catch this guy. So, what do you say? The case needs a Realtor on board."

I was stunned. For all of the times I had hoped to get involved with solving Hamilton's crimes, petty as they were, she had always rejected me, saying that it was "police business." Now, the biggest crime in years comes along, and suddenly I was invited. "Of course, whatever I can do," I said enthusiastically.

"As soon as you're through stuffing your face, come over to the station. The desk sergeant will be expecting you and show you back to the briefing room."

"On my way." I threw my napkin on top of the empty plate and headed up front to pay the bill, even though Marcy hadn't given me the check.

It took me a little longer than usual to get from Abby's to the Hamilton Police Department. Eight o'clock Monday traffic was filling the secondary streets as I headed west to the station. Cars full of commuters were headed for the expressways and train station, a scene that normally does not involve me. The parking lot was full when I arrived, so I decided to take a visitor's spot, even though I was now an official member of the Open House Murders Task Force. I swaggered across the lot to the front door and opened it with authority. I nodded nonchalantly at the officer at the door and headed directly to the desk sergeant.

"Good morning, Sergeant. The chief's expecting me." I sounded like a pompous ass straight out of the movies.

"Name please."

"Oh right, sorry. Banning. Kurt Banning." Now I sounded like a spy in Her Majesty's Secret Service. Get it together, Kurt. I couldn't help but feel important, but I needed to keep my enthusiasm in check. The sergeant picked up his phone and punched in four numbers. He announced me to someone at the other end. As he was hanging up, I went to the steel double doors to be buzzed in.

"Take a seat, Mr. Banning. Someone will be out to take you back in a few minutes."

Reality check. I slinked over to the same set of plastic chairs where I had waited for Liz one week earlier. I was just a commoner with no permission to enter the inner sanctum without an escort. My ego was bruised but not destroyed. Two minutes later, I heard the familiar click unlocking the bolts on the door and saw Liz coming towards me. It was just past eight o'clock in the morning, and she looked stunning. She wore black jeans and a light blue HPD cotton blouse under an unsnapped black down vest. Her hair was pulled back and up instead of its natural cascade down onto her shoulders. She stopped halfway across the lobby and waved for me to follow her in. As we passed through the double doors, the relative serenity of the lobby was replaced by the low hum of people at work. Telephones were ringing, half a dozen phone conversations were being held simultaneously, fingers were tapping keyboards, and rubber soled shoes squeaked on freshly polished linoleum floors. I followed Liz in silence down the corridor to the next to the last room on the right. Sitting at a round conference table were Chief Dougan, two uniformed police officers, and a plain clothes gentleman I did not recognize.

Liz made the introductions and we shook hands all around.

"So, I'm looking through the records," I began, talking a seat, "and I noticed all the homes involved are held by First Family Bank and Trust. This morning I checked the listing file on Sunset and got the name of the bank officer who signed off. I'll give him a call as soon as we're done here. I don't know if he's the same individual on the other homes or not. Then I'm thinking about the potential scenarios for each property ..." I was yammering on like a six-year-old who just found a turtle in the back yard.

Chief Dougan raised an eyebrow and glanced at Liz. Interrupting the report of my breakthrough, he said, "This is your guy?"

"Yes, Chief. He gets a little excited at times. Kurt." She directed her attention to me. "We asked you to come in this morning to give us some advice on open houses. You know, how they're run, what a Realtor does to prepare, a list of do's and don'ts, a run down."

Open houses. Did she just ask me about open houses? I sat there looking back and forth between Liz and Chief Dougan. Surely they needed more from than a basic open house tutorial. "Ah, yeah, sure, I can give you a rundown on how to set up an open house and what takes place during there, but aren't you interested in the bank connection and the possibility that it's a—"

"Mr. Banning."

It was Chief Dougan. He had a commanding way about him, even in silence. He looked older than his fifty-eight years and had permanent scowl lines on his face from thirty-four years of police work. His white hair, or what was left of it, was cut close on the sides and almost non-existent on top. Dougan was as wide as he was tall and carried an air about him that said, "Don't screw with me." He was dressed in dark slacks, a wrinkled white shirt, and a loose tie that had probably never been cinched up to begin with. His shirt was two sizes smaller than his neck.

"Kurt, call me Kurt."

Chief Dougan stared at me. "Kurt," he said through a tight jaw, "we've asked you here, at Lieutenant Colburn's suggestion, to guide us through the steps in conducting an open house. We have discussed an idea that needs your input. This murdering son of a bitch has now stepped into my city, and that's all the reason I need to go after him. The FBI is working all the Chicagoland crime scenes, and I'm sure they will be in Hamilton by noon today. They are working their cases, and of course will have the coordinated effort of the joint task force. But I'll be damned if I'm going to watch as this asshole walks into Hamilton to do his dirty work. We need your help to set the trap."

I doubted if they would give me a gun, but they might let me carry a badge.

CHAPTER

I took a seat next to Liz at the table as Chief Dougan laid out the plans for nabbing the open house killer. I was sworn to secrecy and told in no uncertain terms that what we discussed in this room stayed in this room. I was made privy to a plan that the chief, Liz, and the other three members of the Hamilton Police Department had been working on since very early that morning. The success of the operation depended on no outside leaks and the commitment from the six of us not to share any details.

"Mr. Banning, what we need from you—"

"Kurt, call me Kurt."

Chief Dougan rubbed his forehead with a liver spotted hand and let out a slow exhaust of air. He once again glanced at Liz. "All right ... Kurt, what we need from you are the details and setup for an officer of HPD to successfully pose as a real estate agent and conduct an open house without making anyone suspicious."

"I can do that."

"Good. Our plan is to find a home for sale in the market that is owned by First Family Bank and Trust. We need you to identify which home can be used as the target property. Next, I want you to set up whatever notifications you use to advertise an open house on an upcoming Sunday. Preferably this Sunday—the sooner the better. I want that home splashed across whatever media you use."

I was anxiously listening to Chief Dougan, anticipating my involvement in the case. I was full of suggestions, but based on how I had entered the room earlier, like a stoner on speed, I decided to wait until I was asked for specifics.

"That's easy enough. We have plenty of time to put the notices into place. What else?" I asked.

Chief Dougan continued, "Mr. ... ah, Kurt, I would like you to work with Lieutenant Colburn and get her as prepared as possible to be the Realtor on duty in that house this Sunday. Fast track the learning curve. She needs to be as believable as possible."

I turned my head and stared at Liz. She gave me an affirmative nod. "Chief, with all due respect, you're asking Liz to be a target for some lunatic out there. Have you thought this through?" I asked stupidly. Of course they had thought it through. They were the police department, after all.

"I assure you, Kurt, we have been thinking of this strategy since before this latest murder and we've spent all of the morning going through the possibilities and details. We have done a risk evaluation, and although there is a risk, we have deemed it to be minimal. Lieutenant Colburn is a well-trained police officer, and we will have backup staked out in the neighborhood. In fact," Chief Dougan turned to Liz, "it was her idea. She volunteered. After much debate about our available options, this plan makes the most sense. She recommended we bring you in as the instructor, so to speak."

"Let me sit in the open house," I almost begged. "If there's backup, I'll be fine. And I don't have to fake being a Realtor. If I feel something odd is going on, I'll give you the high sign or a whistle or shoot up a flare, whatever you want me to do."

"I appreciate your offer, Kurt, but we can't risk the life of a civilian in a police operation. And unless you've forgotten, this guy seems to go after only women. You don't fit the profile."

"But—"

"Besides, all the victims have been women. If the killer walked into your open house and saw a six-foot-two male who looks like he can take care of himself, I doubt very much that he'd make a move. No good."

"But—"

"Listen, Kurt." This time it was Liz who spoke up. "We have gone over the plan numerous times. The house will be under surveillance. We have safety checks in place, and it's the best plan to capture this guy before he gets to another Realtor in another house. He has hit our area twice, and the statistics suggest that he is becoming more comfortable with Hamilton and the surrounding area. Odds are he'll be back." She reached out and put her hand on my arm. It was a touching show of emotion in such a professional setting, especially for Liz. "What I need from you is a rundown of dos and don'ts to hold an authentic open house. It has to feel real for me to pull it off. The suspect cannot be tipped by some error or mistake I make. After all, he seems to understand the open house environment. Any deviation will spook him when he shows up."

If he shows up is what I was thinking. For Liz's sake, I hoped he didn't.

"Can you do that?"

Now she was appealing to my sense of pride. Of course I could do it, and she knew it. I was one of the top producing agents at Prescott Realty. I could hold an open house in my sleep. I had mentored new agents when they began working at Prescott, and training was something at which I was rather good.

"You know I can," I said, a little put off. "But I want to go on the record as saying I don't agree with the plan." Now I sounded like a character in a television crime drama. "When do we get started?"

"I'd like you to work with Lieutenant Colburn this week and have her ready to go by Friday. Any questions, Mr. Banning?"

Great, back to Mr. Banning, I guess this was the signal telling me I was still the outsider. "Ready when Lieutenant Colburn is ready."

"Fine, you'll get started today. I want you to go through the area listings of homes for sale and identify which ones are held by First Family Bank and Trust. Our department will contact the real estate brokerages representing those homes and ask them to suspend any future activity on properties associated with FFB&T. We appreciate your assistance, Mr. Banning. We're counting on you to turn Elizabeth into an authentic, first-class Realtor this week."

Chief Dougan stood up, indicating that my portion of the meeting was over. We shook hands and Liz walked me to the meeting room door. Before I left, Chief Dougan added, "We could use that list of homes as soon as possible."

Liz and I walked down the corridor in silence. I was thinking the nightmare was just beginning. An hour ago my stomach had finally returned to its normal place, and now it was back up in my throat, resting on my gag reflex. We stopped at the double locked doors and just looked at each other. I was the first to break the silence.

"Liz, are you sure about this?"

"Absolutely," she said with conviction. "It's a good plan, Kurt, and we have safety checks along the way. This is what police officers live for, to get the bad guy. Besides, have you forgotten how good I am at hand-to-hand encounters?" There was a faint smile. "Don't worry."

"Sure, famous last words from General Custer, the Captain of the *Titanic*, and Wile E. Coyote," I said, trying to cut the tension. "I'll get to work on the listings, but it'll take a while. We have more than 250 in our office alone. Come by the apartment after six and we'll get started at turning you into a first-class real estate agent."

"Thank you, sweetie." Liz reached out and touched my arm again. She turned, her shoes squawking on the linoleum. With a smile I couldn't see, she said over her shoulder, "See you at six. I'll bring Chinese."

I walked out of the police headquarters with a lot less enthusiasm than I'd had when I'd entered an hour earlier. I drove back to the office and decided en route that I didn't feel like working with people hanging around and discussing Jane Stark. Too many questions to which I had answers I couldn't share. It wouldn't be a productive environment to do the work I needed to do before meeting Liz at the end of the day. I re-parked my car in the "Tenants Only" spot behind Prescott Realty and climbed the back stairs to my apartment. I would spend the day working at home and trying to ignore the phone. It felt like afternoon as I unlocked the back door and walked into my efficient kitchen. The clock on the microwave said 9:48.

I took another shower to clear the fog in my head. I wasn't comfortable with Liz being the target, but it had been pointed out to me that my opinion wasn't under consideration. I put on fresh clothes. Even though I wasn't going downstairs, I dressed in dark slacks and a yellow long-sleeve dress shirt. I threw on a geometrically patterned sweater vest to take off the chill that was being created from within.

I spent the next few hours on my computer, going over listings. There were twelve hundred plus in our marketing area. I started by eliminating the obvious, which included any commercial properties and multi-family attached properties. Condos, duplexes, and townhouses got tossed. I put the work "vacant" in a search parameter to give me a more likely list. I took listing from all five communities in the county. Although I was looking specifically for homes in Hamilton, I widened the search to be thorough. I searched the listings of every real estate company no matter the size. By early afternoon, my eyes were burning from the strain of staring at a blue screen for hours. I had a short list of five homes that were in foreclosure and were held by FFB&T. Four of the properties were in the surrounding areas, and one was located in Hamilton, a listing by Rodgers Realty. I stood up to stretch and realized how stiff I was. Surprisingly the phone had not rung once. I grabbed a bottle of unsweetened tea and went up on the roof to get some air and to get away from the glare of my computer. I could never work a job where I sat in from of a computer all day, every day, all year long. I often thanked God for the flexibility he had given me in my life, which allowed me to wander aimlessly through the universe doing this and that and never getting into trouble financially. I have been fortunate to live a life where employment has never been an issue. It helped that I lived beneath my means. Not that I scrimped—on the contrary—but I always paid myself first and invested wisely. Money was not the most important thing in life, far from it, but what it did do was to me choice. Having choices was a lesson that my parents had taught me early on, and it had served me well over the years. Many times, choice is the difference between feeling trapped or feeling liberated. How many people did I run into every week that were caught by a job, or a mortgage, or a home that held them captive? Choice of career, where to live, how to live, and with whom to live were all important factors in the life of Kurt Banning.

On most days, the view from my rooftop was a quaint scene of a growing major Midwestern city with a small-town feel. I looked over the treetops that lined Main Street. I could look both east and west and see the thriving businesses that attracted shoppers and diners from outside Hamilton as well as the locals. Colorful awnings gave respite from the bright spring sun. Tasteful neon lights lit up the sidewalks in the evening. Several restaurants offered courtyard dining and dancing behind the brick facades. My view gave me a two-block vista in either direction. The clouds were large and puffy on that day, like cotton balls floating in a lake. The only thing that separated me from falling to the sidewalk below was a four-foot-high brick wall, three stories up. I was one of the few who actually had a downtown apartment. Many of the other buildings had been renovated, turning second-floor spaces into offices for attorneys, accountants, and architects. People below me strolled in the mild weather in light jackets, glad to be rid of the heavy coats and gloves of the most recent winter. The aroma of coffee drifted up from the Roast Bean directly across the street.

Most of the Prescott agents took their clients across the street to the Roast Bean to treat them to a five-dollar cup of gourmet coffee. When there were no clients, we consumed the watered-down weak brew from our cozy kitchenette. Hamilton offered old fashioned head-in angled street parking. No parallel parking was necessary, to the relief of the many student drivers that cruised the streets during summer. By mid-afternoon, as I peered over the four-foot wall, only a handful of spaces remained unoccupied.

I climbed the stairs back down to my apartment and made a peanut butter and jelly sandwich. Smooth peanut butter with grape is the only way to go. I had loved PB&J since the days of brown bag lunches in elementary school. Nothing melted a hard day like a lunch break of cold milk, potato chips, and a homemade PB&J, my comfort foods.

I took my late lunch to the dining room table, which sat in the eat-in area between the kitchen and living room. I lived in a building erected in the very early 1900s, but with twenty-first-century comforts. My apartment was spartanly furnished, but the few items I owned were high-end amenities. The living room, which had a large picture window, faced south and let the low winter sun warm the entire front half of my apartment. The window looked down onto the street, mimicking the view from the roof. A three-person leather couch faced a sixty-inch flat screen television, mounted on the wall. The television was rarely used, but it had seemed like a good idea at the time of purchase. An oversized wing chair that doubled as a recliner sat next to a mahogany side table, topped with a Frank Lloyd Wright stained glass lamp. This was the usual resting spot for my derriere and where I could read in comfort. Standing in the corner was a replica of an authentic Crosley floor-model radio from the thirties. I enjoyed listening to baseball games on the old machine while basking in the yellow glow of its large dial. I grew up listening to Ernie Harwell and George Kell giving play-by-play coverage of the Detroit Tigers on the radio, and to this day, I still preferred listening to a game and using my imagination rather than sitting in the crowded stands of a stadium.

The middle of the worn hardwood floor was covered by a handmade Persian rug, which I had purchased while vacationing with my ex-wife many years ago. We had spotted the rug in a bazaar, haggled over the price, won, and had it shipped back to Illinois. It was one of the few items I had requested in the divorce decree over fourteen years ago. It looked great and was a big help with the acoustics inside the echoing room. The hundred-year-old building retained a tin-paneled ceiling. Two abstract paintings were the wall's only adornments. Quite a contrast to the ballerina oils that decorated Liz's walls. On a low mahogany table, which matched the side table, was my Bose entertainment center, complete with an iPod docking station. This was usually playing during the hours I was at home and held an eclectic collection of music. My musical tastes range from the Beatles to Dean Martin and Vivaldi to Aerosmith.

The guest room doubles as my office away from the office, some ten feet directly below me. An old futon makes it possible to accommodate the occasional guest. A small galley kitchen opens to the dining area and living room, giving the apartment a much bigger feel. Other than the countertop microwave, the other appliances feel neglected. The master bedroom, which has its own bathroom, takes up the back fourth of the apartment and has a box window overlooking the alley below, my "Tenant Only" parking space, and the garage where Margaret is safe and secure. My bedroom holds a California king-size bed with no headboard, a cherry wood dresser with attached mirror, and a matching armoire that hides a thirty-two-inch Vizio high def television. This was the television that got the workout. I turned it on each night when I went to bed, falling asleep within the first five minutes or during the first commercial break, whichever came first, and then I would fumble in the dark for the remote in the wee hours of the morning to turn it off. This was another contrast in lifestyle between Liz and me. When it was bedtime, Liz had to have total silence, no harsh glare from the television, no lighting whatsoever, and all the drapes drawn to prevent any early morning ray of light from seeping in before she was ready to rise. I, on the other hand, loved the glow and the noise of the TV, the shine of a full moon through an open window, and the break of dawn. The sun was my alarm clock, a ritual I missed while Liz and I had been cohabitating. As much as we had wanted to live together, the compromises for both of us had been too much and added to the strain of the relationship. Sometimes lust becomes love and turns to loathing. We never made it to loathing, but we had gotten close.

My bathroom has a single vanity, as does the hall bath, both covered in the matching granite of the kitchen, which I had installed five years earlier during a minirenovation. The counter is clean and empty except for an electric toothbrush, badly in need of a new bristle head. Everything else is hidden neatly away in cupboards and drawers. No night creams, hairspray, nail files, or long hairs in the sink occupy my bathroom, at least not anymore. Liz and I had shared her home back then because of the space, but remnants of sporadic stays above Prescott Realty and weekends at the apartment had been common.

I sat eating my sandwich at a sturdily built mahogany dining room table, which sat six comfortably, contemplating the short list of homes I had compiled thanks to my morning efforts. Only one was actually inside the Hamilton city limits, and it seemed to be the logical choice for the stakeout. Number 503 Boswick Lane had been built five years earlier in a newer subdivision, Switch Grass Ponds, in the southwest portion of Hamilton. The ponds were manmade, by the developer, maintained with the help of natural underground springs that ran through the neighborhood. According to the tax records, 503 Boswick Lane had been built for Joseph and Bernadette Wagner by First Class Customs Homes. For whatever reason, the Wagners had stopped making their mortgage payment to FFB&T twenty eight months ago and had been evicted four months previously. The home sat vacant and was now listed for sale by Rodgers Realty.

The home was a traditional two-story brick-front Georgian style house on a quarter acre lot, nestled between similar houses in a four-hundred-home community. There was a clubhouse, a swimming pool for residents, and an elementary school located at the far south end of the subdivision. Switch Grass Ponds was quite a contrast to the more mature neighborhoods closer to downtown Hamilton.

The Boswick Lane home boasted four bedrooms, three and a half bathrooms, a three-car garage, and a finished basement that had been completed the year after the home had been built, according to the tax records. The thirty-eight hundred square feet offered a first-floor den, sunroom, and gourmet kitchen to die for, according to the listing sheet. The first-floor laundry and mudroom had a built-in locker system for hanging coats and hiding boots and stashing mittens, gloves, and scarves. The all-hardwood first floor had nine-foot ceilings, with a step-down tray ceiling family room that actually was fourteen feet from top to bottom. A fully landscaped yard included a brick paver patio with accent wall and fire pit, gazing out onto a lush new yard with play set. The photos in the MLS showed that the Wagners had taken great care of their home while trying to hold on for a miracle. The finished walkout basement was unusual for the flat lands of suburban Chicago. There was little terrain allowing for such a luxury. I wasn't keen on Liz sitting in a home as a decoy that had an additional point of entry. I made some notes on the pad next to me.

After finishing lunch, I moved to the wing chair and made some more notes on how to turn Liz into a credible Realtor by the weekend. My eyelids started sagging as I reached the end of page one. I glanced at my phone—4:30. No wonder my eyes were heavy. I had been up for fifteen hours and the sun was still shining brightly through the living room window. Would this day never end?

"Kurt." I heard my name before I felt the hand on my shoulder, gently shaking. "Kurt." I was coming up from a deep sleep and struggled to focus my eyes once they were open.

"Kurt, it's me." I looked up from being reclined in my chair to see a blurry Liz standing next to the arm. I could smell cabbage-stuffed egg rolls.

"Whaa time zit?" I slurred.

"Six-thirty, sleepy head. Now get up while I dish out the Chinese. I'm starving."

Liz had let herself in using her key. I had never asked for it back when we went "off again." To my recollection, this was the first time in over six months that she had used it. On the other hand, I clearly recalled returning *her* key. I was standing at her door, in the foyer, taking it off my key ring and handing it to her six or seven months ago. I had dropped it onto her open palm. Now, as I was coming out of a foggy sleep, I couldn't remember if she had asked for the key or if I had offered it up like some pouting child.

No matter. She was here now, and so was the food. I heard her getting plates out of the cupboard and silverware out of the drawer as I leaned forward to a sitting position. My neck was stiff as I stood up, probably from being hunched over my keyboard most of the day. Liz had already scooped rice and mandarin chicken onto two plates, along with a crispy egg roll, by the time I got to the table. She sat two bowls of steaming egg drop soup next to the plates. I sat staring at the delicious looking food, shaking off the last of the cob webs.

"Want a beer?" Liz asked with her head stuck in the refrigerator.

"Sure."

Liz brought two Blue Moons to the table. Mist was rising from the mouths of the just opened bottles. If anyone had been looking through the window, they would have assumed they were watching a happily married couple about to discuss their days at work.

"Here I am, working all day long on a murder case, and I come home to find you napping the afternoon away," she joked.

"Hey, I've been up working since the wee hours, and I got a lot accomplished. I earned that little cat nap," I said.

"Kidding, Kurt. Don't get so defensive." Liz became more somber as we began to eat. "I read the crime scene report on Jane Stark. Same MO as the other three. She had been restrained in a kitchen chair, nondescript duct tape had been place across her mouth, dry white powder residue found on her lips. No tox report yet, but we're pretty sure it's the same substance that was used on the other three victims," Liz said as she shoveled a forkful of rice into her mouth. *Geez, how can you eat while talking about this stuff?*

"Two of her business cards were taped to her wire-frame glasses. No photo on her business cards, just a slogan that said, 'Go with Experience.' The buttons on her floral dress had been undone to the waist, her camisole top was slit open, and her bra had been cut between the cups."

"What a pervert." I was so angry, I could feel my heart beginning to pound in my temples.

"LYER was written on her chest over her heart. No signs of sexual assault, thank God." Liz swallowed a bite of chicken.

Liz was so nonchalant, spewing out the details with no emotion. The description of poor Jane Stark's fate, alternating with the memory of the last time I saw her in the office, made my stomach twist. I slid my plate to the side and wiped my mouth with a paper napkin emblazoned with a red-dye dragon.

"Not hungry?" Liz asked, shoveling a forkful of sautéed vegetables into her mouth.

"I ate a late lunch," I said, washing the taste of teriyaki sauce out of my mouth with a gulp of the cold Blue Moon.

"So what did you find? Any homes that match our needs in Hamilton?"

"It turns out there are five that fit the profile. You know, foreclosure, vacant, listed and owned by First Family Bank & Trust. One of those homes actually is in Hamilton. That ought to make Chief Dougan happy. This way he doesn't need any authorization from the neighboring communities to set the trap, right?"

"He runs the show in Hamilton. Good job, Kurt. We appreciate your help with this. You know that." It sounded like more of a question than a comment.

"Anyway," I said, "we should take a drive by the home tomorrow, check out the neighborhood. It's listed by a small agency, Rodgers Realty. If it looks like a good subject, I'll make an appointment for us to go into the home, presenting you as a potential buyer. I know the owner, Phil Rodgers. He runs the company with his wife, also his office manager, and his daughter and son-in-law, both licensed Realtors. I don't know how he stays in business running such a small shop."

"Well, his overhead is low, right?"

"True."

"I'll give the details to Chief Dougan in the morning and let him handle the details for Sunday. But sure, we can check out the house tomorrow."

"Home."

"What?"

"Never mind. I don't think your chief likes me."

"Don't worry about him. He comes off all gruff and hard ass, but he really is warm and fuzzy underneath. Just overworked, like the rest of us."

Liz and I repacked the leftover Chinese food and put it in the refrigerator. We washed and hand dried the few dishes we had used and exchanged the beer for two Ketel Ones, one with a splash of cranberry and the other with two olives. We moved into my office in the back of the apartment, where I had spent most of the day whittling down the list of homes. This is the one area of my home where I allow a certain amount of messiness. Stacks of files line the floor. Works-in-progress are scattered across the credenzas, as well as the small space on my desk that's not taken up with my computer. My high-backed leather executive chair with brass rivets outlining the ends of the arms sits on a plastic mat so I can roll to and fro. The futon is usually littered with mail, newspapers, and a few magazines to which I subscribe. The top of my four-drawer file cabinet has a large pot with a fichus tree has been trying for years to commit suicide.

I carried in a dining room chair for Liz so she could sit next to me at my desk. I showed her the Multiple Listing Service sheets for each of the five properties, with the pertinent information highlighted in yellow. I had put a giant red star at the top of the sheet for 503 Boswick Lane. The listing broker and mortgage information were included for each.

My cell phone rang for the first time all day, highly unusual. I left it on the table in the living room next to my chair. I excused myself and left Liz going through the thin file I had composed.

"Hey, Dex," I said into the phone, recognizing his number, "how are you feeling?"

"Appears I've slept through a whole lot of excitement. After you tucked me in on Saturday, I didn't wake up until early Sunday afternoon. I only got up to reheat my soup, pee, take my medication, and went back to bed until this afternoon. My cell phone died on the nightstand, so I've been out of touch. What the hell's going on, Kurt?"

"Poor Jane. It doesn't seem real. A lot can change in twenty-four hours."

"I know," Dex said, sounding slightly better but still stuffy. "I spoke with Bard about half an hour ago. I feel shitty about this, Kurt. I was supposed to be the one sitting that open house. If I hadn't asked for help, Jane would be alive. I should have just canceled the damn thing."

"It's not your fault, Dex. You had no idea about the connection between the murders and the bank."

"What? What are you talking about? What bank?"

Uh oh. "I did some digging for the police department and discovered a link between the other three murders and First Family Bank & Trust," I confessed. "They asked me to keep that information confidential." There was silence on the other end of the receiver. "Dex?"

"Why didn't you tell me?" he shouted into the phone. "When I asked about someone doing my open house on Sunday, why didn't you say something. Kurt, seriously? You knew and kept your mouth shut?"

I could almost see the vein on his forehead standing out. Now I was the one silent on the phone. Dex was my best friend. A few seconds passed and then I said, "I wasn't supposed to mention it to anyone. The truth is I really didn't even think about it. If I'd known it was an FFB&T property, you know I would have stopped this," I said in a quiet, bashful voice.

"I gotta go, Kurt. I think I'm going to throw up, again."

"Dex, wait." Too late. He had disconnected.

When I returned to the office, Liz looking at some of the framed certificates on the wall. "You're pretty impressive, Mr. Banning." She nodded towards the real estate shrine I had built for myself. I wasn't feeling very impressed with myself at the moment. I gave a half smile and sat back down in my chair.

"Okay, now what?" Liz asked.

"We work on setting you up as a knowledgeable Realtor and get you ready for conducting that open house on Sunday," I said. I was getting angry now. I was angry with myself. I was angry with Dex for getting sick. I was even angry with Jane Stark for having volunteered to help out last Sunday, thirty-hours ago. I was determined to do whatever Liz and the Hamilton Police Department needed me to do to catch the rotten son of a bitch who had turned our lives upside down.

CHAPTER 22

Liz and I spent a portion of the next three days going over scripts a Realtor might use while conducting an open house. It would have been helpful to have her attend an open house that I was running as an observer, but Chief Dougan wanted her up and running by Sunday. There was no time for on-the-job training.

I gave Liz the low down on the subdivision, Switch Grass Ponds. After years of planning and countless city council meetings, the developer, Midwest Development, had been approved to create a four-hundred-home housing tract in the southwest section of Hamilton. The inclusive community would offer twenty acres of green space and parks, as dictated by the city fathers. There would be a clubhouse, swimming pool, and six tennis courts for use by the residents. The facilities would be covered by the association fee charged to each homeowner annually. The minimum lot size would be a quarter acre, with some as large as a third of an acre, depending on location and boundaries. Prices for homes in Switch Grass Ponds would start at $500,000. Midwest Development had a reputation for conscientious developing and had handpicked a dozen builders to construct the homes.

Switch Grass Ponds was located in what had been one of the last remaining farms in the township. Anderson Farms had sold out after the patriarch of the family had passed away and, the adult children were more interested in their inheritance than farming and maintaining a generational tract of land. The property was just over four hundred acres of rich tillable soil, which had a meandering creek running through the southeast corner. Soon, silhouettes of framing and roofs began to distort the skyline. Wheat and corn were replaced with two-by-four studs and concrete foundations.

The clubhouse and pool were completed while the first builder models were being erected, to entice potential buyers and give them a vision of the upscale feel of the neighborhood. The winding streets and parkways were lined with young maple trees, which were a nice contrast to the other newer developments in Hamilton, which seemed obsessed with placing the streets on boring north-south grids. Switch Grass Ponds was anything but a boring tract development, and it drew a flock of new homebuyers during the early stages of growth. The community had been built out in three phases over thirty-eight months during a building boom in the real estate market. There had been no shortage of people wanting to move on up. I personally had sold over a dozen homes during the initial phase and countless more on the resale side of the business. I made an appointment to show 503 Boswick Lane to Liz on Wednesday afternoon.

"Hi, this is Kurt Banning with Prescott Realty," I said into the phone on Wednesday morning. "I would like to show your listing at 503 Boswick Lane later today, between two and three o'clock."

"The home is vacant and on electronic key box," said the receptionist, Mrs. Rodgers. "You are confirmed. Anything else I may help you with, Mr. Banning?"

"Thank you, that's all for today."

Liz and I talked about the neighborhood as we drove by the clubhouse at 2:15 Wednesday afternoon. Several joggers were out on the asphalt paths that wound through the subdivision. An elderly gentleman was bent over, exposing his bony butt as he picked up his dog's poop from a neighbor's yard with a plastic bag turned inside out into a glove. Minivans were beginning to line the curb in front of Hauser Elementary School in anticipation of the 2:30 dismissal bell. The wind had picked up, and there was a chilly breeze coming out of the north, even though the sun shone brightly.

"Potential buyers coming to you on Sunday are going to want to know how much turnover there is in the neighborhood," I said while driving. "They will want to know the state scores for math and science for Hauser Elementary School. Others will want information about the homeowners association—you know, the dues, what they include, whether the budget is funded and in good standing? Standard stuff. It's not just about the home they're standing in but the whole package."

"Can you make me a cheat sheet?" Liz asked.

"Already done," I said, pulling a typed sheet of paper out of my black portfolio, which was wedged between my seat and the console."

"Do people really ask all these questions?" Liz said, rolling her eyes at the lengthy list.

"No, I just researched all that stuff 'cause I was bored. Of course they ask. Not everyone, but the more questions a person asks while in the home, the more interested they tend to be. The more interested they are, the more likely they are to buy. You need to be prepared. If you forget something, look at the list. Tell them you're new." Liz gave me a look that indicated a newfound respect for the field of real estate.

We drove down Primrose, turned left onto Hartfield, took it to the end, and turned left again onto Boswick. The home at 503 was the second house from the last and backed on to an open field, with a walking path cutting a ribbon of asphalt between the backyard and the elementary school in the distance. The end of Boswick rose gently up a knoll, giving the last three homes walkout basements. The sign in the yard was a blue metal panel with "Rodgers Realty" block printed in white. The two-legged sign leaned slightly away from the direction of the wind. I parked in the driveway. Liz gave a thoughtful glance up and down the street, assessing the landscape. She was in police mode.

"Okay," she said, unbuckling her seat belt, "let's go in."

I used my key card to unlock the electronic box on the front door and remove the house key. The key card looks like a hotel room key, a great improvement over the bulky tools we used when I first entered the business.

I unlocked the front door, made from a wood-stained fiberglass material with no storm door. As we entered the foyer, the air was stale and cold. I wasn't sure if it was cold because no one had been living in the home for the past four months or because of my feeling that I was walking into a future crime scene involving someone for whom I cared very much. Our voices echoed off the naked walls and the tile flooring in the foyer as we walked down the hall towards the kitchen. Half a dozen Realtor cards sat on the island counter top from previous showings. Rays of light shone through the partially closed window blinds in the back of the home, and I could hear buzzing from the sleeping flies that had been awakened by the warmth of the afternoon sun. The occasional chirp coming from the upstairs smoke detector indicated the need for a new battery.

It was a traditional floor plan, with kitchen, eating area, family room, and den strung along the back of the home. This particular home also had a sunroom jutting out from the kitchen eat-in area, with 180 degrees of windows looking out onto the tall grasses of the open green space that separated the yard from the school, maybe a five-hundred-yard stretch. There was a sliding glass door from the sunroom to the deck, whose paint was beginning to flake along the top rails. The butler's pantry led to a large dining room, with tray ceiling, crown molding, and a chair rail. Opposite the dining room, across the foyer, was the formal living room. This is the second-least-used room in today's homes.

"It seems pretty clean for a vacant home," Liz said.

"The banks don't spend much money on these properties, but they do have to go to some lengths to keep them in a marketable condition. A thorough cleaning after the owners move out, mowing the lawn in the summer, that kind of thing. But when they say the home is sold 'as is,' they mean you get nothing but the keys and a clear title.

No repairs, no survey, no warranties, no tax proration, nothing."

We went upstairs, where the four bedrooms were located. The three secondary bedrooms all had walk-in closets and access to a bathroom. All the windows were bare. From what used to be a boy's room, decorated with baseball decals on the wall and a ceiling fan with paddles resembling baseball bats, you could see the children streaming out from the side and back doors of Hauser Elementary School across the field behind the home.

There was a humungous master suite, a popular design feature with modern home builders. Recessed rope lighting was hidden at the lip of the tray ceiling, double-stack windows framed the north wall, and a bank of electronics were mounted next to the double entry doors off the landing. The heating and air conditioning controls for the second-floor zoned climate control were placed next to the security pad for the alarm system, which was next to the controls for the ceiling fan and lights, just inches from the intercom/AM/FM radio/CD player with speaker unit. It was a sterile, futuristic look, which collided with the warm and welcoming look of the rest of the room. There were more wires running through the wall than an old fashion telephone pole.

The master bathroom had both a whirlpool tub and mud set tile oversized walk-in shower with body jets. The closet had been built out over the garage and was noticeably cooler than the rest of the bedroom and bath. The entire second floor was void of window treatments, giving a clear view of the outside world of Switch Grass Ponds.

Looking at Liz's reaction, I realized we were touring the home with completely different points of view. I had kicked into Realtor mode and was looking at the selling points, features, benefits, and potential for resale. On the other hand, Liz was searching for blind spots, escape routes, and vulnerabilities. As we descended the stairs, I said, "Never enter a room ahead of the client. Keep them in front of you, whether you're going into a room or down the stairs or out into the back yard. Stay behind them."

"Got it." She was only half listening while continuing to size up the home. We were eerily quiet as we finished the second floor. Unusual for a Realtor, not to be yakking away about this and that. After all, I wasn't with a client, trying to sell a home. I was with a cop who would be risking her life in a vacant home, trying to entrap a crazed animal intent on killing her. The home suddenly felt colder than when we had entered.

We returned to the first floor and checked out the garage through the entry door in the laundry room. It was a basic three-car garage, with no service door to the outside (thankfully) and small daylight windows in the three individual garage doors. The sliding glass kitchen door opened to an expansive deck that was ten feet above the ground. The stain was still good and the wood looked impeccable. We went back into the house, I double checked the sliding door to make sure it was locked and replaced the wood dowel in the track for extra security.

Next we headed to the open staircase going down to the basement. The online photos had looked great, but they didn't do justice to the real thing. It was obvious that the owners, in better financial times, had gone over the top in finishing off the two thousand square feet of below-ground living. Liz let out a soft whistle as we reached the bottom of the stairs.

"Wow, now this is living." She turned in a circle, taking in the amenities. While the above-grade living spaces were typical of the homes Switch Grass Ponds, the basement was astonishing.

"I think even Dex would be envious of this place," I said.

The heated floors were seventeen-inch tumbled quarry tile, laid diagonally. The built-in bar looked as though it had been plucked from the set of *Cheers* and dropped into the basement, including the overhead rails. A mix of oak and mahogany woods had been used, and the back bar wall held a large ornate mirror. We counted seven televisions that were either built in or mounted to something. A one-hundred-gallon recessed aquarium sat empty, with dried water scum along the glass front. A plastic frogman lay on his side at the bottom, along with various fake sea foliage. A small door in the drywall to the side gave access to the back of the aquarium for cleaning, filling, feeding, adjusting the heater equipment and of course, adding fish. There was a separate theater room, complete with tiered seating, low lighting sconces, and a deluxe sound system. The exercise room came complete with rubber mat flooring, mirrored wall, and a small television mounted in front of where treadmills, elliptical machine, and stationary bikes might have once stood. There was a large bedroom with a curtain covering the window in the exterior wall. The closet was cedar lined, and the adjoining bathroom offered a dry heat sauna in addition to the walk-in shower, sink, and commode. The dry heat prevented the growing of mold.

Eight pool cues stood in a rack near an eight-foot billiard table covered in regal red felt. Obviously this was left behind due to the cost of moving and storing it. There were sconces and movie posters from old black-and-white films, expensively framed and hanging on the walls. The natural lighting from the full-sized windows and exterior door gave the impression that one was in an upper-floor living space rather than a basement. The door opened onto a red brick paver patio. All very impressive.

"I'm sure I don't need to remind you that two of the four victims were found in the basements," I said with some concern in my voice.

"No, you don't," Liz said, preoccupied with looking at the door and window lock construction. "The dead bolt on this door is one of the best they make, but the windows are pretty flimsy. The top locks on the sash windows will give in with the right amount of force, at the right pressure point. Not the worst I've seen, but not the best either, especially for home like this one."

We again walked through the home and I pointed out the vulnerable places an attack could take place. Liz, being an officer of the law, knew as much as I did, even more, about vulnerable positions.

"You need to provide yourself with escape routes other than the front door," I said. "I don't like the idea of leaving the basement door unlocked;

someone could enter without your knowledge. But I would definitely unlock the slider in the kitchen for an escape onto the deck." The second floor offered no escape for someone who felt trapped. There were no balconies or roof access.

We went outside and strolled the perimeter and to the neighbors. I'm sure we looked like an interested buyer and her Realtor. From the front of the home to the rear lot line, the yard sloped dramatically, obviously enough to provide for a walkout basement. The paver patio was the landing area coming down from the wooden stairs of the deck. The narrow patio ran horizontally to the home and connected to that portion of brick at the exterior of the basement. A three-foot accent wall around the patio made it feel smaller than it really was. There was a freestanding fire pit towards the center of the yard. It appeared to be homemade, with falling brick and an uneven ground location. It had not been built by the same brick layers who had done the patio—this was obvious by the lopsided tilt and lack of mortar between the bricks.

After spending almost an hour in and around the home, Liz was satisfied with the layout. As we drove out of the subdivision, she noted the access roads into and out of 503 Boswick Lane.

I couldn't stand the silence in the car as we headed back to the downtown area of Hamilton. "What are you thinking?"

I croaked, startled by the dryness of my own voice.

"I'm thinking about Sunday. I'm anxious, but in a good way. It's a good edge to have, you know? Unlike his previous victims, I'll be anticipating everyone who walks through the front door as a possible murderer."

Great, Liz was excited about meeting a murderer on Sunday! "We don't even know if he'll show up." I was hoping he wouldn't. "I wish you would let me in on this, in some way."

"And how would that work, Kurty? He's not going to make a move with you hanging around. Who are you supposed to be, my partner or a potential buyer? The scene has to feel natural to him. He's done this before and knows what to expect. If there's anything that looks or feels unusual, he'll bolt."

Liz was determined to do this thing on her own, and it was obvious that she would take no involvement on my part.

"I'll be wearing a tiny ear piece and microphone," she continued, "and the surveillance team will be able to pick up on everything that goes on inside. Boswell and McGee will be sitting in an unmarked car just a block away. Don't worry, Kurt. I'll be well protected."

In silence, we drove back to the Hamilton Police Department, where Liz had left her car. Chief Dougan had met with Mr. Phil Rodgers, owner and managing broker of Rodgers Realty, earlier in the day. He, as I had been earlier in the week, had been sworn to silence regarding the operation to catch the Open House Murderer. They arranged to use his listing on Boswick Lane as the bait. He placed the open house ad in all of the normal venues, in addition to some websites. It would be hard to miss if the killer was looking.

No one at Prescott Realty was aware of my involvement or knowledge of what was going on. I had been purposely avoiding people in the office all week, feeling that any change in my personality or mood might cause undo questions. Luckily, Dex was still recuperating from his illness and had not been back to the office. He was still feeling guilty about Jane Stark, and I was pretty sure he was still mad with me about the whole mess. I held enough shame and guilt for both of us, but that didn't change the fact that poor Jane was no longer with us.

Liz and I pulled into the employee parking lot at HPD a little before five in the afternoon. We had an appointment with the booking photographer to get pictures of Liz for fake Realtor business cards. This time, escorted by Lieutenant Elizabeth Colburn, I walked the length of the lobby and straight through the steel double doors without any delay. The desk sergeant peered at me over the top of his reading glasses without lifting his head. We turned right and went to the elevators to the second floor.

The second floor of the station held the cells, attorney visitation rooms, and the booking department. Officer Les Kaufmann was sitting on the edge of a desk, speaking with another officer and holding a cup of coffee as we entered the frosted-glass doorway, above which was stenciled "BOOKING."

"Hey Lieutenant, right on time," Kaufmann said, sliding off from the desk.

"Hey, Les. This is a friend of mine, Kurt Banning. He's a local Realtor. We shook hands and gave the obligatory smiles and nods. A friend? It made me feel like an also-ran. Couldn't Liz have said, "One of Hamilton's top-producing real estate agents" or "the guy who's going to help us solve the Open House Murders," or "my very best friend in the entire world, who I was once engaged to"? Apparently not.

"All right, let's get started," Officer Kaufmann said. We followed him into a smaller room off the main office. Liz had worn a white pointy-collared blouse with a dark blue blazer, at my suggestion. Below that, she wore jeans and black boots, which didn't matter as this was going to be a head-and-shoulder photo shoot. The room was stark—one tin-topped table and no chairs. The far wall of the rectangular room was decorated with a height chart, ranging from four feet to seven feet. A smirk crossed my face as I imagined a usual-suspects lineup of four-foot-tall criminals. Stacks of book-size tablets, made out of slate board material, sat on the table along with erasable markers with which to write. On the floor, about a foot from the wall, was two sets of footprints, decaled to the floor. The edges were still crisp, indicating that there had not been a lot of criminal feet standing in this location. One set of footprints faced directly towards where Officer Kaufmann would be taking his pictures. The other pointed towards the side wall. Lovely, Liz was about to get her mug shot.

Les pushed a silver button on the wall that resembled an old doorbell, and a screen came down from a slot in the ceiling behind Liz, covering the height chart. The screen was a swirl of muted shades of browns, tans, blues, and greens.

It reminded me of the kiddy photographers in the local department stores. I wasn't even going to ask why they had it here to begin with.

Les saw me staring at the screen and said, "We sometimes need non-criminal photos for press releases, public relations, advertising, that kind of thing."

Advertising? What kind of advertising could the police department possibly do? "Looking for a comfortable cell? Join us downtown Hamilton for state-of-the-art incarceration. This Saturday only. Hurry, space limited."

"Okay, Liz, stand on the mark facing me. Turn your shoulders slightly to the right. Nice smile, not too big." Les pointed the digital camera, the flash went off and the camera geared for the next shot. Click, click, two more photos. "Tilt your head a little to the side. That's it, hold it." Click, flash.

"Would you like any slinky photos for your personal collection Kurt?" Liz purred. "Les is a great photographer and not just crooks and corpses but a little skin too. Isn't that right, Les?" She winked at the cameraman.

I couldn't believe it. This was serious business and these two were yucking it up at my expense. "Thanks, I'll pass," I said, at a loss for a snappy comeback. It was surreal, standing there while a police photographer took shots of what might be the last photos of Liz—at least alive. I could only imagine how it felt being a drunk driver or participant in a bar room fight, standing here listening to Les the Comedian taking pictures of them with bloodshot eyes and bruised faces.

Liz pulled out her service revolver and did an Annie Oakley pose. Click, click. They were both laughing as I grew tired of their immature antics. I just wanted it to be over and done so we could leave.

"I'll upload these and you can pick the best one," said Les Kaufmann. "Just the professional ones. I already deleted the fun ones. I'll have them to your email in less than thirty."

"Lighten up, Kurt," Liz said as we rode the elevator down from the second floor.

"Liz, this is serious. You're about to walk into a home with a crazy person who loves killing Realtors, and you're acting like a schoolgirl on a class trip. I'm worried about you, and I have a bad feeling the more this plan unfolds."

"How many times are we going to go over this? You're walking a fine line between being helpful and being a pest. In fact, I'm done for today. I have other work to finish. I'll walk you out."

"Don't bother. I know the way."

I pushed the double doors to the lobby a little too hard, banging the wall with the handle. Eyes from visitors, the desk sergeant, and the front door duty officer all looked in my direction. I could feel the heat building in my cheeks as I went through the glass doors, a bit more gently this time, to the escape of the fresh air. I stomped across the parking lot like a kindergartener having a tantrum and jerked open the door of my Cadillac. I sat down in a huff and jammed the key into the ignition, but before I turned over the engine, I sat a moment taking in some deep breaths. I was pissed, but had no idea at whom I could direct my anger.

It was too late in the day to start on a new project, although my files and phone calls had been piling up while I was helping Liz and Chief Dougan and the HPD and the whole damn town of Hamilton. The breathing helped. I had done my civic duty, and it was plain to see that my role was coming to an end. I had one more day of prep with Liz, on Friday, and then it was over. Actually, I would be glad to distance myself from the chaos that had taken over my life recently. My sales funnel was suffering as a result, and it would be good to get back to normal. Whatever that was.

I didn't feel like going home. In spite of my earlier years of self-abuse, it was too early to start drinking, although I was certain I could justify an adult beverage. I pulled out my cell phone and called Dex. I was hoping he was ready to forgive me for the breach in our friendship. No answer. This was not helping my mood.

Friday morning Liz arrived at my apartment at a little after eight o'clock. She had brought six chocolate glazed donuts. I had the coffee brewed.

"Peace offering?" she said, handing me the grease-stained bag.

"Accepted." I had cooled off considerably from Wednesday and had a chance to put things into perspective. This was a police investigation with highly trained professionals, doing what they did best, even if it wasn't often. I was out of my element. And besides, I would have been a little put off if the local law enforcement officers had walked into my office and tried to tell me how to sell real estate. My concern for Liz, however, was as real and strong as ever. She wasn't my fiancée anymore, or even my girlfriend. We were friends, best of friends, and I knew we always would be. Sometimes we were lovers, and other times we fought like Republicans and Democrats.

There was comfort and tension in our relationship, whatever that relationship happened to be at the time.

We spent the morning going over information Liz would need to have handy for Sunday. She wrote as I gave her data that would be helpful. We discussed the current trends in housing and where interest rates were hovering. I printed out a list of other homes for sale in Switch Grass Ponds so she would be ready to answer questions about the neighborhood. I had also printed sales brochures for the home on Boswick Lane the prior evening, on the office color copier. We put together an open house registry to log in the people that would be coming through on Sunday. Liz showed me the business cards, which had been printed on heavy stock at the police station. I had to admit they tuned out well, in spite of being taken by a guy who regularly took photos of the dead or derelict. I had checked the websites to be sure that the open house notices had been posted on all the usual sites and confirmed the few print newspaper locations as well. All signs pointed to a successful open house for Sunday. Liz was ready, the home was ready, and the forecast called for perfect spring weather. I was the only ingredient in the mix that wasn't ready. I had a perpetual ache in my gut. It had been a long day, finalizing tiring and sometimes boring details. Nine hours later, I walked Liz down the back stairs to her car. We looked at each other for one intense second before she drove off. No words were exchanged, or needed to be.

Saturday evening, about ten o'clock, my phone rang. The footloose, fancy-free lifestyle of a bachelor found me at home, sitting in my recliner, reading a biography of Thomas Woodrow Wilson. A two-olive Ketel One was at my side. The caller ID told me it was Liz calling.

"Hey, what's going on?" I asked when I picked up the phone.

"Wondered what you were doing actually."

"Having a party. I'm surprised you can hear me over all the noise."

"Want some company?"

I pushed the footrest down with my legs and sat forward. "Everything okay, Liz?"

"Oh yeah, everything's fine. In fact, I'm having my own party, but it's getting stale. Thought I might join yours if you don't mind me inviting myself over?"

"Are you kidding? Come on over. There's still plenty of food."

"See you in fifteen."

The call had been unexpected, but I was thrilled to be seeing Liz. The apartment was neat, as always, so there was nothing to do for fifteen minutes but wait for Liz to arrive. I topped off my drink and added fresh olives and made a Ketel with cranberry for Liz. I wasn't sure the reason for her visit. There had been no urgency in her voice. Fifteen minutes to the second, there was a soft knock on my kitchen door. I let Liz in and handed her a highball glass with vodka. She looked stunning and smelled of fresh soap. Her hair was still damp from a recent shower, and she smiled at me in a soft, sleepy way. Before I could say anything, she took the drink in one hand and me by her other hand and guided us to the bedroom.

We never said a word to each other, at least not for the first hour. We made love slowly, as if neither one of us wanted to finish. It was tender and gentle until the power to resist failed us both.

"What would you call our relationship, Kurt?" Liz asked after we caught our breath. We lay twisted in the tangle of warm sheets. We were resting on our sides, facing each other; a strand of her dark hair was stuck to her damp forehead.

"Good question. I've thought about that, especially lately. I don't have the answer. But I do know there is no other person who I care about as much I do you."

"Do you love me, Kurt?"

So there it was. The reason for the visit. I stared into her alert brown eyes, looking for a clue. "Of course I love you, Liz. I have never stopped loving you, but we seem to be so different, I can't always tell what kind of love we share. There's nothing I wouldn't do for you, you know that." Then I broke a rule and let my guard down. "Do you love me?"

She didn't answer. A tear rolled out of the corner of her eye and ran across her temple to the pillow. Liz pulled my face close to hers with both hands and kissed me a long time. I wasn't sure if that was the answer and, if so, what that meant. We untangled from the sheets and Liz rolled up on top of me in one smooth motion. Our bodies rejoined as they had been twenty minutes ago.

Sometime after 1:00 a.m., I heard the deep sleep breathing that comes after exertion. Liz was curled into the crook of my neck with her right leg thrown over my waist. The moon was a perfect pale circle in the sky. I watched it through the bedroom window, clouds drifting across the face of it, as I lay holding Liz securely to my side. Our breathing had matched rhythm without me realizing it. Liz had never answered my question. I supposed the answer didn't matter. It was my last conscious thought before my eyelids lost the battle and I fell asleep.

It must have been a deep sleep, because I never woke once during the night. That was unusual for me. I'm more of a cat napper, getting two to three hours at a time and then falling back to dreamland for another two or three hours, and so on throughout the night. When I woke, I was on my side facing the window. The morning light was full, and I sat up with a start thinking I was late for an appointment. There was no appointment, and there was no Liz. I had thought she might be in the kitchen preparing a post-coital feast, although I didn't smell the beginnings of breakfast.

I retrieved my bunched up boxers from under the covers at the foot of the bed and went into the kitchen. Liz had set out my mug, a jar of instant decaf coffee, and a teaspoon. Next to it laid a note. It said, "Please don't call me today. I need to stay focused." It was signed, "Liz." Not "Love, Liz," just "Liz."

CHAPTER 23

Hank Pilcher had been distracted from his present task, and he was frustrated, very frustrated. His battle for the little guy, the persecuted homeowner, had been temporarily sidelined, but he was determined to get it back on track. It was one o'clock on the first Sunday in May, and he stood on a one-inch-thick black rubber mat, washing beer glasses behind the bar at the Fifty-Fifth Street Tavern. The crowds on Sundays had improved, mostly due to the weather and the fact that the baseball season was a month in. The forty-two-foot scarred oak bar was divided almost equally between Sox fans and Cubs fans. The cheering drinkers were gathered at either end of the bar, where televisions were mounted high enough to give even a standing patron a good view of his or her team.

Hank had discovered that the Cubs fans preferred beer and were less likely to leave a generous tip, versus the Scotch- and whiskey-drinking Sox fans, who let their change build up on the bar and gladly donated the proceeds for good service. Hank catered to the black-and-white wearing drinkers a little more than the blue-and-red capped crowd. He did his best to cover everyone, but in a pinch, when it got extra busy during commercials, he flowed with the tips. He had become a very efficient bartender, and as a result, weekend tips had greatly improved. There was no need for small talk, which Hank disliked immensely, to build rapport during a ball game. Hank wasn't a fan of baseball, or any sport for that matter, but the games brought in the fans. He was good at his job, which he took pride in, even if it wasn't his most important job.

Ever since that little shit Randy had gotten fired for pinching the cash register during his shifts by not ringing up all the drinks, Hank had been working overtime, which included weekends. The extra hours were good, and he enjoyed the bump in tips, but it was interfering with the job at hand.

"Two more Buds down here," a guy wearing a blue baseball cap with a red capital C yelled from the far end of the bar. He sat near the television showing the Cubs in a close game with the Cardinals. No "please," and nothing but the two quarters in change left on the bar for Hank after delivering the cold bottles of brew.

"Hey, when you have a chance, could I have another Jack and Coke please?" That was the difference. A request, not a demand, plus another dollar bill floated to the bar top in Hanks direction from the Sox fan.

A week ago Friday morning, Hank had followed his normal routine of picking up the *Tribune* from the corner convenience store. And although the number of open houses was not as great, he had found two good prospects by wading through the posted ads and cross-referencing them with the list hidden in his family Bible. Late that Friday afternoon he had driven by both homes. The first one was located in the town of Bellgrove, near the west side of the Chicago city limits. It was an established neighborhood that in the past decade had been devoured by a large population of mostly second-generation Polish who were leaving the poorer south side of Chicago. The homes were small, closely-packed brick bungalows with neatly trimmed patches of grass in the front and alleys running behind the homes giving access to the detached garages. Hundred-year-old oak trees lined the streets in the parkways, converging at their tips and creating a canopy that blocked out the sun during summer. A variety of metal mailboxes hung next to the front doors, with faded numbers identifying the addresses. Although quite old, the homes had been proudly maintained.

Number 440 Oak Street sat on a corner lot facing south. The driveway into the alley was the boundary on the west side of the yard. Many young families lived in the neighborhood, based on the number of Big Wheels, tricycles, and bicycles parked on sidewalks and walkways. There were no cycles of any kind parked in the yard at 440 Oak. No sign of life at all, just a shiny metal pole with a square metal sign hanging on rusted hinges, squeaking in the low breeze, announcing to the passing world that it was For Sale. Hank once again decided that a corner lot, with front, side, and rear exposure was too risky. He drove away, with his map on the front seat, taking surface streets that would eventually lead to an access road that took him to one of the many expressways that cut across the five counties making up the suburbs of Chicagoland.

Thirty minutes later, Hank's old Chevy exited a ramp that promised to take him to Fennelville, home of the Soaring Eagles high school team. It was a "Community of Change" according to the sign at the edge of the city limits. Fennelville had been settled in 1856, and as of the last census, it was home to 59,602 people. The main drag through downtown was a mix of retail, commercial, and occasional apartment buildings. Hank thought the town looked old and tired. Paint was peeling from storefronts, letters were missing from marquees, and parking lots had sprung weeds through the cracks of asphalt. Hank didn't see the Community of Change that the welcome sign announced, unless that change was poverty.

According to his directions, Division Street was three more blocks and a right turn away, after which he'd be at the home of the latest poor bastard thrown out on the street. The hustle of cars and foot traffic came to a halt as he drove slowly down Division Street looking for the home at 6407. In contrast to Bellgrove, the homes in Fennelville were mostly two-story clapboard with large sagging front porches, some of which were screened in. The tired-looking home was third on his left, in the second block. Left over garbage from a recent wind had swept debris under the overgrown shrubs trimming the front of the home. The screen door was missing from the porch, an invitation for more trash and stray cats to move in. The concrete driveway that ran past the home to the rear garage was cracked and buckled and dotted with oil stains. It was the most neglected home on the block, and Hank could just imagine how disgusted the neighbors were with the appearance. Hank parked his Chevy in front of the home and got out to take a closer look. He cupped his hands and peered into the home through the window in the front door. Some pieces of furniture remained. He saw a table and four chairs in the dining room, which was off the front living room. A floor lamp stood next to a rocker and an old sofa with a huge tear in the upholstery sat up against one wall. *It's got possibilities*, Hank thought. He glanced back at his car and then took a quick trip around to the side of the house where the driveway ran past. No entry into the home from the side and only one door in the back, which had a padlock on the knob. A deep, rumbling bark from the fenced yard next door gave Hank's heart a leap. He scowled at the mutt through the faded wooden fence and muttered, "Shut the hell up."

Yep, this was the perfect project for Sunday, Hank decided as he returned to his car. One way in, middle of the block, probably nothing but old deaf people living nearby. His target was set, and he looked forward to meeting the Realtor from Star Real Estate Company the day after tomorrow. He headed out of Fennelville with great expectations.

Hank decided to allow himself a rare indulgence. He stopped at a liquor store on his way home and bought a six-pack of Miller Genuine Draft beer. He had nothing against drinking; it just wasn't his thing. In the past it had clouded his judgment, and after one especially robust Christmas party at Pearson's Plumbing and Supply years ago, when business was thriving, he had woken with such a hangover that he swore never to imbibe again with the hard stuff. Most people usually forget that promise to themselves by the following weekend party, but not with Hank. A promise was a promise, to himself or anyone else. An occasional beer was not breaking the oath he had taken. It was only beer, and he was in a celebratory mood and happy to be on the hunt once again.

When Hank got home, he took a cold bottle and his week's worth of dirty clothes and went down to the laundry facilities in the basement of his apartment building. No matter what time of year, the laundry room was always humid. Four old white Kenmore washing machines were lined up against one wall facing three matching white Kenmore dryers. Two loads of wash and one dryer cost him $4.50 each week.

On Saturday Hank drove to the suburbs to pick up his children from the wicked witch and her husband. He arrived a few minutes before noon and waited in the driveway. He had planned a fun day for he and the kids, and the weather couldn't have been more perfect. They would start the afternoon at their favorite restaurant, Spools, which offered an assortment of pastas with a variety of sauces and cheeses as toppings. Who knew pasta came in so many shapes: spirals, elbows, tubes, thin noodles, thick flat noodles, shells, and on and on.

Hank supposed they all tasted the same and were made from the exact same ingredients, just like the sneaky Chinese.

Samantha always ordered the baked mac n cheese, while Tyler loved to slurp up traditional spaghetti with red sauce. After that they were going to play a round of miniature golf at Timber Mountain, followed by ice cream at the DQ. And instead of dinner, they would be munching their way through bags of popcorn and chocolate covered peanuts at the movieplex, where the new Pixar animated film had just been released. It was suppose to be such a box office hit that he had already bought the tickets to avoid the disappointment of a sellout. The movie was over at 9:00 p.m. and he would have the kids home before 10:00, as promised. Hank knew it was a lot to cram into one day, but he had the entire day, and he hadn't seen his children in over a week.

The sun felt warm on Hank's face as he waited in his car until both the big hand and little hand were straight up at twelve o'clock. He loved his children more than anything in his measly life. He was also getting use to the idea of another man raising them; after all, Thad Essington could give them things that were beyond Hank's reach. Besides, it wasn't how much time he and the kids spent together; it was what they did with the time they shared.

At the appointed time, Hank strolled up the winding curve of the paver sidewalk to the oversized double front doors. He rang the bell and waited. He could hear the sound of heels on the tanzanite floor tile headed his way. Lydia opened the door looking especially pleasant. Hank was leery of the rare smile on her face.

"Hello, Hank," Lydia said a bit too friendly as she motioned him into the foyer.

Now Hank was suspicious.

. He couldn't remember the last time he'd made it past the front door and actually inside the mansion.

"Hi," he responded, hands shoved into his pockets. "Kids ready?"

"Just about." Lydia looked behind her as if expecting to see the kids standing there. They weren't. "I know we set today up as a full day until this evening, but I completely forgot about the picnic."

"What picnic?" Hank asked, taking his hands out of his pockets.

"Well, you see, every year Thad puts on a family picnic for all the employees, staff, and their children, plus a few important clients." Lydia gave a small frown that meant "I'm sorry," but Hank was too busy trying to keep his rising temper in check and not grab Lydia by her skinny little white neck and slam her head into the wall.

Hank was now rubbing his balled hands together. "So, what are you saying, Lydia?" Before she could answer, Hank said, "Are you saying I can't spend the day with my kids? Are you telling me that you've decided at the last minute to change the schedule?" Hank's voice was becoming louder.

Lydia turned and looked down the hallway once more, as if expecting the children at any moment. "No, that's not what I'm saying, Hank. You can take Samantha and Tyler." Her voice was extra quiet in hopes of getting Hank to lower his as well. "But I'll need you to drop them off at Memorial Park later so they can join us."

"How much later?" Hank said through a clenched jaw.

"Well, it would be nice f you could have them there by three o'clock."

"Three o'clock!" Hank shouted. "For Christ's sake, Lydia, I have a whole day planned with them." His voice was at the high end of its range.

"Everything all right here?" Thad asked, coming into view down the hall.

"No, it's not all right!"

"What's wrong, Henry?" Thad had never referred to Hank as Hank but always used his given name.

"What the fuck do you think is wrong, Thad? I have a day planned with *my* kids, and now Lydia tells me at the last minute about some bullshit picnic. Today is my day!"

"Henry, I do not appreciate that language, and I will not stand here and talk to you if you continue to speak that way."

"Fuck you!" It came out of Hank's mouth as a scream. He turned and yanked on the door handle and flung it open so hard it banged off the foyer wall.

"Wait, what will I tell the kids?" Lydia yelled after him.

"Tell them the truth: that their mother is a lying little whore who screwed the boss and broke up a happy family, you bitch!" Hank said over his shoulder as he stormed to his car. A neighbor who was planting spring flowers in her front yard looked up in amazement, her mouth hanging open.

"What are you looking at?" Hank shouted.

She just stared at him as he backed out of the driveway and sped away. He drove like a madman all the way home, cutting in and out of the maze of cars on the freeway, nearly causing two accidents. Hank blew his horn at the drivers going too slow and flipped off the ones who got in his way. The adrenaline from the scene at his ex-wife's homes was pounding through his body. By the time he arrived back at the apartment, he was still steaming. Hank had worked himself up into a lather and didn't know what to do to release the pressure. He paced back and forth across the worn wooden floor, which creaked at the same spot at each turn. He drank the four beers left over from the from Friday's six-pack. If Saturday had been a train wreck, Sunday turned out even worse.

Hank showered and shaved Sunday morning after fixing a big breakfast of white toast, thick slab bacon, two eggs over easy, and a leftover donut from Friday morning's trip to the convenience store. He washed down the feast with a cup of instant coffee and a glass of orange juice. He put on a freshly laundered brown plaid shirt over a V-neck white tee shirt, both of which he tucked into the waistband of a pair of khaki pants, whose crease had long ago faded.

He had his plan to arrive and carry out the next extermination in his head. He would leave the apartment around twelve and get to the house in Fennelville around one o'clock. The ad had said the home would be open to the public from noon to four. He would scout out the property and hoped to get a glimpse of whichever lucky Realtor would be holding the open house. Hank would park at the end of the block for an hour or so and watch the foot traffic in and out of the home. Then he would find a nearby restaurant and eat a light lunch. He preferred to work with a little food in his stomach. Weather permitting, he would spend some time in the fresh air, sitting on a bench in a park or plaza. Around four o'clock, closing time, he would return the open house and introduce himself to the lucky agent who would think he or she had a live prospect. Hank smiled at the irony.

At eleven o'clock the kitchen wall phone rang in Hank's apartment. He didn't get that many calls, mostly solicitors with worthless offers or Lydia calling to complain about a late child support payment. Once he cleaned up the Realtors, maybe he could beautify the world by starting to eliminate solicitors and ex-wives. Out of curiosity, Hank picked up the phone. It was Billy White, the owner of the Fifty-Fifth Street Tavern. He begged Hank to come into work. Yes, Billy knew it was Hank's day off, and it would be inconvenient, but the new bartender who had replaced Randy, had called in sick at the last minute and Billy needed to cover the shift. He was really in a bind. He offered to pay Hank time and a half if he could help him out. Hank could have said no, but he really needed the money. He had prepared for the open house, but the truth was, he was still smarting from the incident with Lydia from the day before, which was sucking the joy out of his upcoming mission to Fennelville. There were hundreds of Realtors and open houses out there, and there would always be next Sunday. He told Billy fine, he'd be there in time to start the noon shift. As Hank drove into work, he thought about Randy. Sick? Hank doubted it. He was probably still drunk and horny and shacked up with someone he had never met before last evening. Never mind, he told himself. He would take the shift and the overtime and the tips. Screw Randy.

That had been last weekend, and now here he was at the bar again on another Sunday filling in until Billy White could hire another bartender. Mid-week, Billy had met Randy coming through the door at five ten to start his five o'clock shift and immediately had taken him into the office. Billy confronted Randy about his tardiness and the shortages in the till during his shifts. Of course Randy denied any knowledge of skimming. Nonetheless, Billy fired Randy on the spot, paid him what he owed him in cash, and showed him the door. Now another Sunday was passing without Hank being able to resume his priorities.

"Barkeep, another brewski down here."

"Coming up."

Next week was going to be different. He would tell Billy that no matter what, he needed next Sunday off. New bartender or not, Hank was not going to be stuck behind this old oak counter a week from today. He had work to do.

The week progressed uneventfully for Hank. He has spent three days working at Peterson's Plumbing and Supply Company, as well as two days and two evenings at the Fifty-Fifth Street Tavern. Wednesday Hank caught Billy before he left for the day and told him there was no way he could work this coming Sunday.

"I don't mind helping out, Billy, and I sure do appreciate the extra money, but Sunday is the only day to be with my kids this week," Hank lied.

"Not a problem, Hank. I hired a new bartender yesterday and she's coming in for training tomorrow and Saturday. I don't think she'll need much training, though. She worked bars on and off for the past twelve years. I was hoping you could show her our setup on Saturday afternoon. I've scheduled her to overlap with your shift for a couple of hours."

"Sure, no problem," Hank said, relieved to be getting back to his routine. "Whatever you need, boss. I'll do my best."

"I know you will, Hank. You've been great taking up the extra hours and I really appreciate it."

Hank's mood immediately improved. He actually began whistling behind the bar while cutting up fruit, getting ready for the afternoon crowd.

Thursday was a Peterson Plumbing and Supply day, and Friday was Hank's day off from both jobs. Hank was feeling better about his world. For the past two weeks, life had felt out of kilter. His work schedule had been rearranged, he hadn't seen Samantha and Tyler since the blow up with Lydia and Thad, and his trips to the suburbs on Sundays had been suspended. That was all changing now. Back to his regularly scheduled life.

"Good morning, Mr. Hank," said the clerk behind the counter.

"Hi, Chen. Beautiful morning, huh?" It was Friday, 7:30 a.m. Hank bought his copy of the *Tribune* as usual and glanced at the front page as he walked back to the apartment. Same old same old: crooked politicians, subway ticket price hike, crime on the rise. He stopped at the corner before his building and pulled the magazine-style real estate section from the paper. Hank dumped the rest of the *Tribune* in a sidewalk trash bin before entering the lobby of the Heritage Arms Apartment building. In Hank's opinion, the real estate guide was the only portion of the paper worth keeping.

Back upstairs, Hank sat at the old kitchen table with his red marker and began the time-consuming task of cross referencing the weekend's open houses with the First Family Bank and Trust list of foreclosures. The previous two weeks of targets were no longer on the radar. Of course not; that would have been too easy. After a couple of hours, Hank discovered that there were only two homes out of more than a hundred that were FFB&T properties. The first one was far north, in Lake County, almost at the Wisconsin border. That would take over three hours, round trip, depending on the traffic. The other home was located in the familiar western suburbs, in the town of Hamilton. He smiled. Hamilton was his old stomping grounds, kind of his own personal Sherwood Forest. Hank was getting pretty familiar with this area, having recently visited Wilmington, Lawton, and Hamilton during the previous month. Was this a sign? A call back to clean up the remaining scourge of the west?

Hank made a bologna on white bread sandwich, a glass of milk, and the few stale potato chips left in the bottom of the greasy bag. After washing the plate and glass and putting them on the dish strainer to dry, he went into his bedroom closet to check his supply of equipment. The black plastic tool box had a top tray that, when removed, left a spacious storage compartment inside. The bottom compartment held several pairs of latex gloves, size medium, a large roll of silver duct tape, and three round plastic tubes, eight inches long and containing sodium hydroxide tablets. Each tube held eight tablets, except the third tube, which contained two tablets. Four ten-ounce plastic bottles of pure spring fed glacier water lined the bottom of the tool box. A small ball peen hammer rested on top of the water, and a partial roll of paper towel and three dust rags were tucked in the side. In the top tray were a pair of heavy duty scissors, a roll of Scotch tape, and old metal forceps that had long ago lost their luster. There was a coil of rope, medium thickness, a box cutter, and miscellaneous screwdrivers. And for whatever reason—Hank couldn't remember—there was an old red Bic lighter that still lit a flame. Hank was satisfied that the kit was complete and would not need any restocking for several more weeks.

Hank pulled his Chevy out of the parking spot next to the building and headed west towards the target. He was giddy with anticipation, and the slight drizzle that had begun did not dampen his spirits. The drive to the Hamilton exit had taken only fifty minutes, in light midday traffic on a Friday afternoon.

By the time Hank passed the sign welcoming him to Hamilton, the rain had stopped and rays of sun were peeking out from under the bellies of the remaining clouds. He followed the directions written in the margin of the real estate section of the *Tribune* until he reached the entrance to Switch Grass Ponds.

It was a lovely neighborhood and a nice change of pace from the deteriorating areas he had been scouting. On this Friday afternoon the sprawling subdivision was alive with children walking home from school and moms headed to meet them. There was also a lot of street traffic, mostly minivans. It felt right as he turned onto Boswick Lane and drove to the far end of the dead-end street. *A perfect setup*, Hank thought. Hardly any traffic, since it was not a through street, and far enough from the main entrance to go unnoticeable. He had spotted the home before he actually saw the address. A four-foot-by-three-foot metal For Sale sign with a rider sat leaning slightly in the front yard. Rodgers Realty—Open Sun. 1–4. He whistled at the sight of the home. *Nice digs*, he thought. Not exactly the type he was use to seeing while on his assignments. Even the wealthy got stung by those bastards at FFB&T, and now Mr. Rodgers was in charge of disposing of this once family-friendly home. Hank smirked at his private joke of being in Mr. Rodger's neighborhood. *Watch, boys and girls, while I make the bad man disappear.*

Hank knew this was a keeper. He turned into the driveway, backed up, and headed in the direction from which he had come. When he neared Hauser Elementary School, he pulled his car over to the curb and watched as the children continued to spill out of the building. Some headed to bright yellow buses, others to waiting minivans, others still to bicycles that had been left unlocked all day in the racks of this naive community. Some poor kids were lugging twenty-pound backpacks. Eventually we would become a society of hunchbacked people, who by the time they were thirty wouldn't be able to stand at attention for the playing of the national anthem.

Hank's car didn't exactly blended in with those of the parents in Switch Grass Ponds picking up their little Einsteins. He reflected on his own children, who also would just now be getting out of school for the weekend. All that innocence and unlimited dreaming. He hoped—no he, prayed—that Samantha and Tyler would have much better dreams and lives than his own. His dreams had exploded like a popped balloon when the economy had taken a tumble. The truth was he could not afford Lydia's dreams. His life now was seeing his children grow up from a distance. Thad seemed like an okay guy, and it was obvious that he loved Hank's children. It was a hard thought to swallow, and it nagged Hank most days. But it was for the best—for them anyway, right?

As the last yellow bus pulled away from the school, Hank continued his drive through the neighborhood and out of the entrance to Switch

Grass Ponds. Unlike previous drives home from his scouting trips, where he had been either elated or angry, this ride home was thoughtful and melancholy. Hank spent most of the trip thinking about Samantha and Tyler, whom he had not seen in over two weeks. He wondered what type of adults they would grow into and what they would think of him. He wondered what part he would play in their lives other than the occasional visit from their absent father. Hank imagined all kinds of distortions about him their mother would have planted in their heads and hearts. Someday, however, they would know the truth and be proud of who their father was and what he had done. A champion of the misfortunate, a righter of wrongs, even a hero. Hank drove the rest of the way home in silence, no radio, just floating, a one-man conversation going on inside his head.

Saturday morning, Hank woke up feeling rested. He brewed a pot of real coffee and relaxed in front of his 21-inch Sony Trinitron. He had bought the television a few years before he and Lydia had been married. It was one of the few items that he had taken from the house when they had divorced. And even though one side of the picture was starting to go black, it worked as well as the day he had bought it seventeen years ago. Those Japs really knew how to make electronics, Hank thought to himself.

The day was gray and drizzly, a calming kind of day to Hank. He reflected on his miserable existence but slowly drifted back to his life. He had had visions of being an artist when he was younger and in school. His preferred medium was charcoal. Sparked by nostalgia, he took the stairs to the basement of his apartment building and went to his storage locker. He unpacked the box marked MISC and retrieved his old sketch pad, pens, pencils, and charcoal sticks. Surprisingly, the charcoal was dry and appeared to be in useable shape. Back in the apartment, Hank cleared the kitchen table and set out the pad and colored sticks. In a short while, his right hand was flowing smoothly across the page, making outlines and filling in rough shaped objects with varying shades of charcoal. Hank had not been so content in many months. With old habits and training returning, he flipped to a new page and began, in great detail, drawing a portrait of Samantha that filled nearly two-thirds of the page. When he was satisfied with his work, smearing and brushing to give shading and depth to her mouth and nose, he drew in Tyler at the top left of the page.

Two hours had passed before Hank realized the time. He stood and stretched and walked around the tiny kitchen to work out the kinks in his back and neck from hunching over the table for so long. The clock on the stove said it was three o'clock. In an hour he would leave for his five o'clock shift at Fifty-Fifth Street Tavern. He propped the drawing up against the kitchen wall and repacked his art supplies. He admired his creation from different angles and then went to shower and shave before work.

Hank arrived for his shift at the tavern ten minutes early. If nothing else, Hank was punctual. Billy White was standing behind the bar with a blonde. Billy waved him over for introductions.

"Hank, Jody. Jody, Hank."

"Nice to meet you," Hank said, holding out his hand.

Jody gave a nod. "Same here."

Under the dull bar lighting, Jody might have looked twenty-five, but close up, the makeup couldn't conceal that she was closer to forty. Her shoulder-length hair was dark for the first inch coming out of her scalp. She had a long-handled bottle opener stuck in the back pocket of her short, tight denim skirt. Her low-cut blouse showed ample cleavage and was guaranteed to generate more tips in an hour than Hank would make during his entire shift.

"Jody will work with you for the first two hours of your shift."

"Sure, no problem."

"She's been around the bar business before and she's doing great, a real quick learner." Billy flashed a smile in Jody's direction.

I'm sure she has, Hank thought. "Well, whatever she needs, I'm happy to help out." Hank's smile was forced and not nearly as brilliant as the one Billy White had plastered on his face. A customer at the Cubs end of the bar signaled for another beer.

"I've got it," Jody said, throwing on a smile and gliding down to the waiting patron.

Hank noticed a tramp stamp on Jody's exposed waist as she passed him. Without the three-inch cork wedges she was wearing, she probably wouldn't be able to reach across the bar.

The next two hours idled by with small chit chat between Jody and Hank. She was originally from Nebraska and had tried making it as an actress in L.A. with no luck. Jody had been engaged twice but had never made it to the altar, and she was currently available, if Hank knew what she meant. Hank divulged very little of his personal life other than showing her recent school pictures of his kids.

Jody picked up most of the counter business, and Hank filled orders at the service bar for the waitresses. A little after 7:00 p.m., Jody cashed out her tips, gave a little girl wave, and told Hank to have a good evening. Jody was harmless, Hank decided, although a bit full of herself. Anything was an improvement over Randy, and as long as she was on time for shift changes, he supposed they would get along fine.

"See ya, hon," Jody said over her shoulder as she headed for the door. It didn't require a response, and Hank didn't offer one. The rest of the evening was standard for a Saturday and the bar closed at 2:00 a.m. The fruit was covered, the glasses were drying in the rack, the back bar was restocked for Sunday, and everything was wiped down. Sal, a sort of assistant manager for Billy in the evenings, locked the door behind Hank as he left. Sal was a cousin or brother-in-law or some other connection of Billy's wife. The streets were quiet and the air was brisk as Hank drove home at quarter to three on Sunday morning.

After a good seven hours of sleep, Hank was up and ready for the day. He showered and shaved, combed his stringy hair straight back, and added a dab of gel to keep it in place. He should have been anxious, but there was a peace that gave Hank a sense of confidence he had not felt before one of his Sunday outings. He was alert and keen, but there were no butterflies gathered in his stomach, as there had been in the past. He took this to mean he growing confident in his skills. He was getting good at what he did. *Yes*, Hank thought, *I'm coming into my own*. I am a professional, trained to be efficient and competent.

At a little past noon, Hank left the Heritage Arms Apartment building and headed west to Hamilton. In less than an hour, in light afternoon traffic, he would be parked, scoping out the home on Boswick Lane. The day was full brilliant sun, the sky a shade of robin's eggs blue and not one puffy cloud to spoil the view.

CHAPTER

"We'll give it one more try," Captain Dougan had said to Lieutenant Colburn on Thursday afternoon. Liz was getting bored sitting in Sunday open houses at Boswick Lane with no action. Although she had gathered half a dozen buyer leads for me over the past two weekends, there had been no encounters with the open house killer. If the police thing didn't work out, I told her she'd make a decent Realtor.

The first Sunday open house after Liz and I had inspected the property on Boswick Lane had been a flat bust. It had been an exceptionally cold day, with rain and a stiff breeze. Only three couples had ventured out in the terrible weather to tour the home. Luckily for me, one couple was a type-A prospect and were on the hunt for their "move-up" home. Liz had told them someone from her team would follow up on Monday. Imagine, *her* team! Even in her make-believe world of real estate, she playing the one-up card on me. Russell and Katherine Cheshire did receive a phone call from me on that following Monday, and in fact I already had them preapproved them with a preferred lender and we had made one house-hunting trip to view potential homes. Way to go, Liz! After spending a good portion of March and April with first time home buyers, townhome buyers and condo buyers, it was nice to be moving up in price range.

As requested by Liz on that first Sunday, I had not called her during the three-hour open house, but I must have paced five miles, wearing a path between my apartment and the office downstairs. I had purposely not scheduled an open house of my own on that Sunday for a couple of reasons. One, I wanted to be available in case Liz needed me. Two, the weather forecast had looked crummy. I busied myself with paperwork, reports, prospect phone calls, and anything else I could find to do until I got a call from Liz, which came sometime after 4:30 that Sunday. We had a light dinner together at my apartment that evening, and she gave me the highlights of the open house. There really wasn't much to tell, having had only three couples come through the home, but she had obviously enjoyed her brief time with the non-criminal population.

We went over questions that she had not been prepared to answer, such as, "Will the seller consider a lease to own?" Once it was disclosed that the home was bank owned, the question was "How long before the bank will respond?" The real estate field was rife with unrealistic timeframes by financial institutions seeking an agreement on contract conditions. Some said it took a year to get an answer from the ivory tower managers. That data wasn't far off, although it was a bit inflated in the current climate of foreclosures and short sales. Liz had stumbled on questions about latent defects, back taxes, and potential liens. We prepared for the following Sunday by gathering additional information.

That next week unfolded with no news of any new crimes against Realtors at open houses or any other venues. I was busy negotiating an offer on Mr. Ernie Schwartz's home. It wasn't a great offer, and it took me two days to convince Mr. Schwartz to make a counter.

"Mr. Schwartz, it's not where we begin but where we end up that counts," I had told him. Gruffly he agreed to make a counter-offer to the potential buyers, through me to their agent. We discussed strategy and points of the contract that we could negotiate. "You know, Mr. Schwartz," I had said, "it's not just the price but the other conditions that are important as well."

"Like?"

"Well, there's the closing date and the strength of the buyer's financing. We can consider any personal property they may want, and of course we would like to see a reasonable amount of earnest money. I know it's not the price you're looking for, but we can work them up to something closer to a number that will make you happy. This is just their initial offer. Are you okay with the closing date? That will give you sixty days to pack and move. We'll give them their date and ask for more money on our side."

"Okay, sure." I could almost see Ernie standing in his wallpapered kitchen with his arms crossed over his chest, scowling. At least we had agreement on the date. That was something with which I could work.

"Their financing had been preapproved with a reputable mortgage lender at a reasonable rate, amortized over thirty years, and the earnest money is sufficient."

"Thirty years! Holy Christ! Do they have any idea how much they'll be paying back in interest?"

"I'm sure they do. They've already spoken with their lender. I have a copy of their letter in the file."

"Pretty sure you're going to get me to agree if you've taken time to start a file," Mr. Schwartz barked.

"Ernie ..." now it was time to be diplomatic and assure him I was working in his best interest "... I want what you want. I am not trying to talk you into anything. It's your home. I'm here to help you do what you want to do." There was silence on the other end of the phone. After what seemed like an eternity, I continued, "They are still asking for your washer and dryer, along with the wicker furniture on your screen porch and the gas grill. What do you think?" More silence. I was about to ask if he was still there.

"What do they want with the washer-dryer?"

I could have been a wise guy with some smartass remark, but I checked the impulse. "They don't own a washer and dryer, since they've been renting for the past three years. This is their first home purchase."

"Them machines are old and I'm not guaranteeing nothin' about em." Ernie was softening.

"That's fine. I'll let them know you are happy to include them, but they are in 'as-is' condition. Happy?"

"I didn't say I was happy, but okay."

"Let's hold on to the wicker furniture for now," I continued, "we can use it as a bargaining chip later. Or maybe you would like to take the furniture with you."

"Not sure yet, but nice to see you're on my side now," he huffed.

"Of course I'm on your side, Ernie. You're my client. I'm advising you as to what I think is best given your situation, the time of year, and the market in general."

"Go ahead, what else I got to decide? I'm missing my shows."

"I think we should go back and give them the washer-dryer, agree to their close date, and counter the price at five thousand less than where we are now. Their financing is strong and the earnest money is fair. What do you think?"

Again silence. I've learned you should rarely interrupt silence.

"Tell you what, Kurt. You tell them they can have the washer and dryer. Give 'em the wicker stuff—it's uncomfortable as hell anyway. My late wife loved it, but it gives me a pain and I can hardly get out of the chair when I sit down. I want to close by the last week in June, and I'll come down four thousand dollars from my last price. Fair?"

"Fair. That I think I can sell."

"You'd better be able to sell it, 'cause that's my best offer. Call me back. Let me know when it's done." He hung up.

By the end of the week, Ernie Schwartz had finalized all the details of his sale and was lining up moving companies. By early summer, Ernie would be living in Indiana with his daughter, son-in-law, and those wonderful grandchildren. I wasn't sure who was going to enjoy it more.

The next Sunday rolled around with great expectations from Liz and the Hamilton police force for nabbing a killer. It was such enticing bait, what killer could resist? They were so excited that you would have thought they were planning a surprise party for the mayor. I really didn't get the excitement, other than the prospect of removing a criminal from the streets, but this was dangerous and the atmosphere was out of sync with the task at hand. Nonetheless, I wished Liz good luck, whatever that meant, and booked my own open house for the same Sunday.

The weather couldn't have been better than it had been the previous weekend. Unseasonably warm for May in Chicagoland, blue skies with cotton ball clouds and the promise of a good day in real estate. Liz promised to keep me updated with text messages throughout the afternoon. She had told me not to worry. She was being monitored by Officers Kaufman and Lindell, who would be parked not more than two blocks away, just as they had been the previous Sunday. And in case I had forgotten, she would be on the lookout for a killer, which took away the element of surprise on his part.

I had scheduled my own open house on the opposite side of Hamilton. Nick and Connie Williams had finally decided to put their home on the market, ugly carpet and all. They had taken to heart some of the staging suggestions, such as touching up the paint in the bathrooms, removing the clutter from bookcases, and rearranging pieces of furniture to create a better traffic flow and open up the rooms. I had put the home on the market earlier in the week and was truly excited about the amount of traffic that could be generated from a successful open house. This was one of those rare homes that might actually sell during an open house. I would worry about the dual agency if the opportunity arose.

I arrived at the Williams' home at a quarter to one, after having set up four directional signs, guiding the buying public as well as curiosity seekers to the front door of Winston Street. I had trained the sellers well. All the interior lights were on, even though it was midday, low soft music was coming from the home's built-in intercom system (light jazz, not my taste), and the home shone from the tiled foyer to the first-floor den to the master suite.

At two o'clock I texted Liz with a simple "how's it going." I got a quick response: BUSY. PEOPLE EVERYWHERE. LIKE DIETERS ON A 100 CAL. CUPCAKE. I smiled and clicked my phone shut. I was having a busy day as well. Its success would be determined over the next five to seven days when I saw the responses I received from my follow-up. Four families had come through during the first hour of the open house, and only one had been a nosy neighbor. I run a relaxed open house. I greet guests, hand them a flyer about the home, give them a few quick details, and then send them off to enjoy the home. I put small tent cards throughout the home that say things like, "Ask me about the pool membership," or "Interested in a home warranty?" or "Don't forget to ask me about the traveling youth soccer league." They usually meet me back in the kitchen, which is a great room to finish up and answer questions. It's a naturally inviting room and welcomes everyone like family, which is the environment I try to create.

After hour one, two of the families turned out to be good future prospects, and one was definitely giving buying signs. They had arrived with their lenders' preapproval letter in their hands and were scouting potential areas in which to purchase their new home. Three hours yielded no sale but over a dozen guests and at least five potential customers that I hoped to turn into clients.

I closed up a little after four o'clock, picked up my signs around the neighborhood, and sent a text message to Liz before pulling out into the late afternoon traffic. I typed, "R U still alive?"

A few minutes later: "Alive & well. Will send you new clients tomorrow via email. Am I getting a referral fee? LOL."

At least she still had her sense of humor, although I knew she was disappointed that once again no one had tried to take her life.

I called Dex on my way home to see if he was up for a beer. Things had been icy between us since Jane's death, but gradually he had forgiven me for leaving him in the dark about the open house murders and the connection with FFB&T. He has stopped blaming himself and me for the death of Jane Stark.

"Hey, Dex, feel like grabbing a beer and some nachos at Rocky's on the River?"

"Is that the new place that just opened?"

"Yes. It's supposed to be a nice place. I haven't been yet. What do you think? Catch the end of the Sox game?"

"Ah, sure, give me thirty minutes and I'll meet you there. And the Cubs are on, playing the Dodgers."

"Great. I'm sure both games will be on. I'll see you there."

Dex and I had known each other for ten years and the bond we had built would survive. Jane Stark's death had affected everyone in the office. The cloud was slowly lifting, and laughter could be heard again, but almost with guilt. Odd when we think about our contribution to the little world we occupy. And when we're gone, the world spins a little slower until it picks up speed and then it goes on without us.

I arrived at Rocky's on the River first. As the name implies, the sports bar sits on the banks of the Abson River, which runs north to south on the far western edge of Hamilton. It is a natural border between Hamilton and Wilmington. The parking lot was impressively filled for a late Sunday afternoon. Apparently there were plenty of sports to view. The NHL playoffs had begun, the NBA was winding down its season, and of course MLB was in season as well as the PGA. NASCAR was screaming from a corner screen as I walked in. I'm sure badminton and croquet were being played somewhere in the world, and if they were, Rocky's was well equipped to broadcast them. I found a booth and ordered a Blue Moon with an orange wedge and waited for Dex. I was halfway through the beer when he slid into the booth opposite me.

"Hey," he said with a head bob. "Been here long?"

"Half a beer." I raised the now unfrosted glass to show my accomplishment. "What do you think of this place?"

Glancing around, Dex said, "A little too 'franchise-y' for me. But I dig the waitress uniforms." The waitresses wore tight faux-referee striped tops and black mini shorts. Each nametag said, "I'll make the call!" followed by their names printed in magic marker, making it easy to replace the nametag when the waitress quit or got fired. The inside of Rocky's was littered with pennants from Big Ten colleges and West Coast teams. Jerseys bearing autographs of Gretzky, Pele, and Pete Rose adorned the walls. Soccer balls, baseballs, and basketballs were perched in Plexiglas trophy cases, along with wooden bats and a set of golf clubs from the early 1900s. NFL helmets from every team lined a shelf above the back bar. I counted twenty-two television screens of varying sizes mounted around the bar. There was not a bad seat in the house. We heard the squeak of new tennis shoes on linoleum before we actually saw Ginger.

"What'll it be, handsome?"

"I'll have what he's having, and bring my friend another one too, please."

"Sure thing. Would you like to see a menu, or are you on your way home to have dinner with your wives?" Ginger winked at Dex.

"Why not," I said. "Our wives threw us out, so we're all yours." I winked back.

Ginger snapped her gum, smiled, and laid two menus on the tabletop.

I had let Dex in on the sting by the Hamilton Police Department, in which Liz was being used as bait. I knew I wasn't supposed to, but I felt I owed it to him. It went a long way to restoring his trust in me.

"Any news from Liz today?" he asked.

"Another bust of a Sunday according to her last text message. Although she is feeding me a plethora of potential clients. Now she wants a cut of the commissions."

We made small talk and occasionally glanced at the various monitors. Cars zoomed by, basketballs were slam-dunked, and golf balls were flying onto greens. It was quite an exciting afternoon in the world of sports. Ginger returned with two frosted glasses of fresh beer, each holding a sliced orange on its lip. When she bent to set down the beers, the uniform that management required the waitresses to wear, gave us a clue as to why Ginger may have been hired. Working the tip!

Dex and I enjoyed the House Burger, which came with a fried egg on top, more orange slices, and several more views of Ginger's twin peaks. The friendship was definitely on the mend. We parted with a bro-hug and headed to our separate homes.

The following Thursday was when Chief Dougan gave Liz her third and final attempt at luring the killer of Real Estate Agents into his trap. She had called me on that Thursday to say she was giving it one more try. It was becoming almost commonplace to think of Liz as a helpless target for a murderer. I again wished her good luck, which sounded odd, wishing someone good luck that a killer would cross her path. "Well, I hope your killer friend shows up this Sunday. Kind of boring around here without him," I had said sarcastically. With any luck, Sunday would be another bust of a day and Liz would finally be off decoy duty. The forecast for Sunday was sun, no clouds, and mild temperatures.

I was scheduled to work with the Middleton family on Saturday and Sunday. They were relocating from Pittsburg, Pennsylvania. The Middletons were a personal referral from Mike Cotswood, a past client who I had helped buy a home and get acquainted in Hamilton three years ago. Mike and Chuck worked for the same company, and Mike had told Chuck that I was the best Realtor in Hamilton. Thank you, Mike. If fact, Mike had sent me four referrals in the past three years. I had spoken with Chuck's wife, Erin, earlier in the week and had gathered all the specifics she was looking for in a new home for her family. I narrowed the field to nineteen homes that I thought would give Erin a good feel for life in Hamilton. It would be a jammed weekend for the Middletons, as we were set to see ten homes on Saturday and the remaining nine homes on Sunday before they flew back to Pittsburg on Monday morning. In two weeks, when they returned, it would be a buying trip, having learned the area and narrowed the list of homes to their top three. I had mentally moved into buyer's agent mode from listing agent duties with Ernie Schwartz. His contract was signed and in the hands of the attorney. We were now waiting for any home inspection issues that might arise.

My route was set for the Middletons. It was going to be just Chuck and Erin on this trip, no kids. Thank you God! It's not that I don't like children.

I do. They taste just like chicken, as my grandfather use to say jokingly. But it's much easier to view properties without screaming, hungry, bored kids distracting their parents and irritating the Realtor. I had included a planned lunch stop for Saturday and a tour of all Hamilton had to offer while viewing single-family homes with Chuck and Erin.

The call came in late Friday afternoon. "Kurt, call on line one. Kurt, line one," Molly's soft voice came through the office intercom. Erin Middleton's grandmother had passed away the evening before, and they would have to cancel their trip to Hamilton for the weekend. I extended my sympathies, telling her not to worry and that we would reschedule whenever the timing was right for them. I lined out the Middletons on my calendar. Last-minute changes are a fact of life in real estate. Sometimes a last-minute cancellation gives you relief and sometimes it's a disappointment, but either way it means down time and potential loss of income. Instead of scurrying through my files and trying to replace the Middletons on my calendar, I decided to enjoy the bonus time. A free weekend is a rarity for a Realtor, especially in May. I started planning my time off in my head. Pay the bills, pick up dry cleaning, and replenish the pantry, laundry, and other dreary chores. I thought about calling Father Mike to schedule a round of golf on Saturday and then remembered it was his preparation day for Sunday Mass. I wasn't worried about filling the days. I was excited by the possibilities.

Saturday morning I called Liz to thank her for the leads she had sent me. She asked if I would like to catch a matinee with her later in the day. Matinee? What were we, seventy years old?

"There's a new romantic comedy that I've been wanting to see."

"Love to. What time?"

"Starts at four o'clock. I'll meet you at the movieplex a few minutes before. Sound good?"

"I'll see you there."

Four o'clock! Maybe we'd be done in time for the blue hair special, meat loaf and mashed potatoes at the Past Your Prime restaurant.

Going to the movies is a once-a-year event for me. And it didn't take long to remember why. Between the lack of comedy and obvious plot, the constant munching of popcorn by starving people, the chatty teenagers, and the occasional cell phone going off, I was relieved when the final credits rolled. Really, who needs a gallon of soda and a tub of popcorn as big as your head? The floor was sticky as we made our way through the throngs of moviegoers waiting for their show to start. The movieplex had sixteen screens and was constantly busy from the time the doors opened until the last show ended well after midnight. Two of the theaters within the movieplex even doubled for church services on Sunday, until the growing congregation could afford to build its own house of worship. I wonder if they used unbuttered popcorn and grape soda for their communion. It's the worship that counts I guess, not the where.

It was 6:15 and the sun was shining brightly as we left the theater. I asked Liz if she would like to go to dinner, if you can call dining at 6:15 dinner.

"I don't think so, Kurt. Thanks for keeping me company today. I thought it was a good movie, didn't you?" Liz seemed subdued.

"Yeah, great, good acting, and wow, what a storyline, "I lied.

"Well, see you later," Liz said as she headed to where her car was parked. I watched her as she walked away. We both had gotten excellent parking spaces. Of course that hadn't been very challenging at four in the afternoon. Liz and I had spent more time together recently than we usually did. The old relationship habits had crept back into our lives. One of us seemed to be quiet and distant at times, or stressed to the point of arguing about something foolish. The closeness had created a sense that we were taking each other for granted, and the familiarity smoothed off the exciting edge of the newness we felt when having been apart for a while. When we didn't hang around each other, I missed Liz and our conversations and the little excursions, not to mention the wild sex. That part of us never got old. But when we spent too much time together, the floor sometimes felt as if it were covered in eggshells, and the goal was to get across the room and out the door without breaking any. She got bitchy and I got quiet and sullen. Liz hated when I didn't argue back. She detested my quietness when there was an elephant in the room. Someday we might find a common balance where we knew just the right amount of Liz and Kurt time that both of us could tolerate.

Sunday morning I slept in and felt guilty for not going to church. Father Mike never asked where I'd been or how long since he had seen me when I missed services. I tried to make it a priority, at least one day a week, but like many sinners, I often fell short. If I was working I rationalized that it was okay to miss church. God would forgive me and understood that I had to work. I prayed a lot, tried to live a good life, was nice to others, and committed only small sins, I kept telling myself. But on the rare Sunday without clients, it was more difficult to enjoy the morning, lazing around with the newspaper, doing the *Tribune's* crossword puzzle, or watching an old movie on the television. In two or three weeks, Father Mike and I would begin our annual tradition of an eight fifteen standing tee time every Wednesday morning at the River Bend public golf course. We had been playing together, from the first Wednesday in June through the last Wednesday in August, for the past five years. I looked forward to the competition and enjoyed seeing that a man of the cloth was as human as I was when it came to knocking the little white ball around a seven-thousand-yard course.

We all have that inner voice. There are times to ignore it, thinking it foolish, and then there are times that we listen because the roar is so loud. By the time I had finished reading the newspaper, done three-quarters of the crossword puzzle, and washed the breakfast dishes, it was a little before noon. What's the point of playing hooky if you can't enjoy it? I had a queer feeling about Liz's open house that afternoon, and I decided I needed to be nearby. Why? I wasn't sure. Maybe it's because we'd been spending so much time together again. Or maybe I felt deprived of the action after all of my involvement with the setup. Whatever it was, it was pulling me hard in the direction of Lieutenant Elizabeth Colburn's open house, scheduled to begin in less than an hour. I had to be discreet. If Liz caught me in the vicinity while she was working, I'm not sure the firestorm would ever blow over. It was a chance I would have to take, but cautiously. I knew Officers Kaufman and Lindell would be in the area, if not within eyesight of the home on Boswick Lane at least within microphone range. I wasn't sure either of the officers would recognize me, but it was a small town, so I wasn't going to chance it. I would need an excuse and a disguise to be near Liz.

I took a quick shower and skipped the shave. I found a navy blue warm up pair of striped sweat pants and a matching lightweight button-up jacket that I put on over an old college jersey that I hadn't worn in years. In the bottom of my closet was a pair of black high-top Converse sneakers that I wore when I bicycled. Throughout high school I had been an above average athlete but never the star standout. I played three sports and continued with golf into college, where I was also short of being a star. It felt good to be back in the athletic clothing. I grabbed a stocking cap from a drawer full of winter clothes. The temperature outside was a balmy fifty-five degrees and full sun.

I went down to the garage where Margaret was stored and rummaged through a large mildewed cardboard box that hadn't been opened in a decade. Inside was a bright orange official-size basketball. The nubbed texture felt good in my hands, and I gave it a spin on the tip of my finger. The Spalding orb immediately fell, bounced off Margaret's side, and rolled into the alley before I caught up to it. I had spent a lot of Friday nights in the high school gym, passing the basketball from hand to hand while sitting on the bench, waiting to get the call from coach to get into the game. This was back when shorts were short and didn't cover your knees and expose the crack of your behind. I threw it to the ground in anticipation of a springing bounce back and got a splat instead, like dropping a pumpkin on the pavement. The ball held less air than a vacuum-packed bag of frozen peas. On a shelf next to where my ten-speed touring bicycle hung was an air pump, and I began breathing life into the dead Spaulding. I couldn't help but think of the Tom Hanks movie, *Castaway*, and his friend Wilson. I now had his cousin in my hands, filling his lung with air. In minutes, the ball was full and the bounces echoed off the garage floor and walls. After reacquainting myself with a few ball-handling maneuvers, I locked Margaret safely in the garage and climbed into my nondescript Realtor-mobile, headed for Switch Grass Ponds.

At 1:15 I pulled into the rear parking lot on the north side of Hauser Elementary School. There was one other car parked at the edge of the crumbling asphalt lot and three bikes balanced in the metal rack near the rear of the building. I hadn't anticipated having company. I parked in a white lined space near the back of the lot where the teachers normally park during the school week. I got out, put on my sunglasses, and pulled a knit cap down over my ears. I grabbed the now inflated basketball and walked around to the backside of the school, where I remembered seeing the court the day Liz and I had inspected the home on Boswick Lane. From the worn yellow circle in front of the hoop, I had a clear view of the back of the home across the open green space, some five hundred yards away. I carried a small set of sports binoculars in the zipped pocket of my warm-up jacket.

My companions turned out to be a dad with two young boys flying kites in the field and three other boys, around ten and eleven years old, swinging and climbing on playground equipment. No one seemed to notice my arrival. I hadn't thought about what a forty-year-old white guy shooting hoops would look like to a crowd. Hopefully no one would mistake me for a pervert and call the cops. The dad was running back and forth across the grassy field, pulling on the string to keep the kite aloft. Once they were sky high, he would hand over the ball of string to one of his boys until the lack of a strong wind sent the nylon triangle zigzagging towards the ground. Again and again, Dad would take off, pulling and yanking until the little kite with SpongeBob's face on it was gliding high, only to have it fall slowly back to earth. After a half hour of this routine, dad and the boys packed it in. Although it was a beautiful day, it really was not kite-flying weather. The dad smiled at me as they passed by the court where I was practicing free throws. The two boys looked dejected and dad looked exhausted.

My final three companions also gave up after a short time of climbing, laughing, and chasing each other around in small circles, calling out names like "dumb ass" and "boner breath" as well as a few others that made no sense, except to ten-year-olds. It was the first time I had a chance to pull out the binoculars and take a look at the rear of the home on Boswick Lane. From the back, the home was three stories high. All the lights were on, including the ones in the walkout basement. Good girl, Liz. I could see between the houses that there were cars parked on the street. With the binoculars I could even make out people passing by the windows on the main floor. I kept an occasional eye on the home while I continued to practice layups and jump shots. The rust fell away pretty quickly, as I began sinking shots from twenty feet out.

***

Hank arrived in Switch Grass Ponds just after one o'clock on Sunday afternoon. He had followed the open house signs from the entrance of the subdivision even though he knew where the home was located. It was a beautiful day with sun reflecting off from the window panes as he drove through the neighborhood. Hank drove past the home and noticed three cars parked in front. He assumed one of those belonged to the Realtor. He turned around at the dead end and drove westward towards the outlet street, then continued straight for another two blocks. He turned his Chevy around again, facing the direction from which he had just come, and parked on the side of the street. From Hank's position, he could see who was coming and going. His only concern was that a neighbor might find it curious as that someone was parked in front of their home. He left the engine running.

At two o'clock he decided to move to avoid drawing attention. As he passed by the elementary school, he saw a tall white man playing basketball. Hank laughed to himself. "White Men Can't Jump" he thought, remembering the movie title. There was really no other vantage point from which to see the house, but he parked where he could watch cars turn onto Boswick Lane. When he left his first spot, only two cars had been in front of the open house, and now one of those, the red Toyota Camry, was headed his way, having just left. That left the Realtor alone in the house, but it was too early to strike. Hank always anticipated meeting the Realtor. He never knew what he would encounter when he walked through the front door. So far, all had been women and the last one had been as frail as a piece of dried kindling. The open house was advertised until four o'clock. It was barely 2:30. He would wait

***

I was pretty impressed with my free-throw ability. Where was this in high school? I had made thirteen in a row before sculling one off from the front of the rim. Liz seemed to be consistently busy without being swamped, based on the movements from the windows. I took a break and retrieved a water bottle from my car. The air was crisp, but the sun warmed me enough to break a forehead sweat while shooting baskets. I looked at my watch to discover it was a little before three o'clock. In another hour Liz would be finished with the open house and safely out of Boswick Lane.

***

Hank moved his car to one more location, a side street across from Hauser Elementary School, and set out on foot, following the sidewalks. He looked like any other resident taking a stroll on a beautiful Sunday afternoon. His hands were shoved deep into the pockets of his lightweight brown jacket, the front unzipped. He saw the white dude leaning against the hood of his car, eyes closed, enjoying the sun on his face, holding a bottle of water.

Hank walked at a steady pace down to the corner of Boswick Lane and Spring Grass Parkway. His heart rate had increased, not due to his brisk walk but rather with the excitement of the task at hand. Someday he would be hailed as a titan for the common man, bringing justice to the unjust. He walked down the opposite side of the street from the open house. As he passed by, he looked into the home as much as he could. When he got to the dead end, he crossed the street to be on the same side as 503 Boswick Lane. He slowed his gait as he neared the driveway of the home with the For Sale sign in the yard. He caught a glimpse of the real estate agent through the open front door. The storm-door glass threw off a reflection of the woman standing in the kitchen, which Hank could see down the hallway from the front sidewalk. She was of medium build, and the silhouette made her look petite. She didn't appear to be much of a challenge, and Hank looked forward to introducing himself to her in about thirty minutes. He picked up the pace on his return trip to his parked car.

***

The sun felt stimulating on my cheeks. I could feel my hair matted with sweat under my cap. It had felt good to get a little exercise and fresh air, and I smiled, thinking that summer would soon be all the way here. I scooped up the basketball with a roll and flick of my foot and walked back around the corner of the school building to the asphalt half-court. I had planned on timing my departure so Liz would not catch sight of me on her way out of the subdivision. Things were settling back into normal weirdness between us, and I wasn't about to light a fuse. I knew Lindell and Kaufman were parked somewhere in the neighborhood, but I hadn't seen them during my time of basketball spying.

My watch read quarter to four. I shot a few more baskets and took several more glances at the house through my binoculars. At five to four, I saw the upstairs lights go out. Liz would be finishing up and locking the front door in another few minutes. I took one last jump shot, banged it off the front of the rim, and ran into the grassy playground area to retrieve my ball. When I got to my car, my keys were not in the unzipped pocket of my warm-up jacket. Damn! I knew they must had fallen out somewhere near the court around behind the building. Now panic set in at the thought of being discovered by Liz as she was exiting Boswick Lane. As I was searching the grassy area I had just run through, sun sparkled off from a shiny key ring in the unmowed grass. I carried few keys on my ring as a matter of comfort and weight. There was my house key, a key to the office, a key whose use I couldn't remember but was afraid to throw away, and of course my car key. They all hung together neatly, teeth facing in the same direction, on a round metal ring attached to a shiny steel Ketel One emblem. The key ring had been a give-a-way at the local liquor store four Christmas' ago. Before that, I simply carried the keys looped through an old non-descript ring.

I stole one more quick view of the back of the house. The lights on the main floor had been turned off and the curtains had been drawn shut in the family room, dining room, and sliding glass door in the kitchen. The walkout basement was still aglow with wattage. I hoped Liz remembered to turn them off before she locked up and left.

***

"Lieutenant Colburn," Officer Kaufman's voice came through Liz's earpiece, "everything all right? Just checking in." Lindell looked at his watch.

"Everything's fine, Dave," Liz said loud enough to be picked up by her tiny concealed microphone. "It looks like another busted Sunday. Sorry for wasting your time for the third week in a row. I'm turning off the lights and will be out of here in a couple of minutes. No reason to wait around. Go home and enjoy your families. Thanks again. See you Monday."

"Are you sure, Lieutenant? It's no problem. We can use the overtime." Kaufman chuckled.

"No, you guys are relieved. The captain is already complaining about the budget on this case. Thanks for being nearby today. It's nice knowing you were just a shout away."

"At least let us pick up your open house signs for you on our way out."

"Sounds great. I'll get the one in front of the house. Thanks, gentlemen."

Kaufman and Lindell disconnected their surveillance equipment and pulled out of their parking spot of the past three hours. They drove down towards Boswick Lane and picked up the open house sign on the corner, then drove through Switch Grass Ponds, plucking the remaining four directional signs from corners and intersections and stowed them in the oversized trunk of the navy blue Crown Victoria. As their unmarked police car left the area, an old Chevy rolled to a stop in front of 503 Boswick Lane.

Hank noticed the upstairs lights were off, and the first-floor lights were going off systematically from room to room. He took the brick steps two at a time up to the front door, which was still open, with only the storm door separating himself from the Realtor inside.

***

I waited for the basement lights to go out, but they remained on. It was a couple of minutes past four, and I assumed that Liz was shutting down the open house. I had seen the two men in a dark Crown Vic stop at the corner past the school and hoist one of the open house signs into the trunk. Really, who did they think they were kidding? The car itself screamed, "Don't look at me. I'm under cover." Although I had never met Kaufman and Lindell, I knew it was them. Plainclothes policemen still looked like cops. And even though the outside of the car was plain, I'm sure the inside was packed with gadgets and gizmos right out of a James Bond movie.

It wasn't like Liz to forget something as simple as turning out the lights, although I had done it myself on a couple of rare occasions. I decided to give it a few more minutes.

***

Hank took hold of the storm door handle and pulled it open, stepping into the foyer.

"Hello?"

Liz heard the squeak of the dry hinges of the storm door. She was coming around the corner from the front room den, where she had just turned off the lights. She practically ran into Hank, standing on the entrance rug with a drooping smile on his face.

"Well, hi," Hank said, reaching out his hand.

Liz was processing a million bits of information. The man standing in front of her was the killer. She knew it by his demeanor. The smiling attempt to be disarming, the milky glaze of his stare, even the slicked-back thinning hair gave him a criminal look. A flicker of doubt and recognition shot across Liz's face as she started to speak. She hoped Kaufman and Lindell were still within earshot. The rotten bastard was right in front of her, and even though she had let her guard down, she was now surging with adrenaline and ready to take the next step. Liz didn't have a chance.

Hank noticed quite obviously the change in Liz's eyes and the expression that crossed her face. The draining color from her cheeks was starting to replenish. He reached back with his right fist and threw a punch square into Liz's jaw. She saw it coming but much too late. A quick jab sent Liz crumpling to the tiled foyer floor. Her fleeting thoughts as the blackness engulfed her flowed out in slow motion. She thought about her best friend from second grade, Sandy Hillman, of her father, and of Kurt. She hadn't told Kurt she loved him, and now she never would have the chance. She imagined the embarrassment to the department of having set a trap that had gone terribly wrong. Liz thought about the coroner saw-cutting through her chest bone during the autopsy. Then everything was gone.

Hank slid Liz's small framed body with his boot, enough to close and lock the door behind him.

***

Come on, Liz.

I hadn't seen her drive out of Boswick Lane, so I had to assume she was still in the house, turning off lights, putting away brochures, packing up her brief case, unplugging her laptop, dozens of tiny little things that take time. Closing drapes and blinds can take a while. I was sure she was just being thorough, but the basement light deal was bothering me. I returned to my car and tossed the basketball on the back seat, along with my empty water bottle. I walked back to the corner of the building and looked through the binoculars at the rear of the house. Nothing had changed. I was starting to get an itchy feeling. If I burst in and Liz was okay, it would be the end of any trust we had recouped. We had stayed professional while working together on her case. The old adage is *Trust your instinct.* Mine was telling me to go and check on Liz, regardless of the consequences. I put the binoculars in my jacket pocket, along with my keys, zipped it shut, and casually began walking across the field behind the school building. I headed for the open green space that separated the homes from the school.

***

Hank rolled Liz onto the foyer rug and dragged her limp body away from the door, down the hallway, and towards the center of the home. As was the custom with bank-owned properties, the home was not furnished, and there were little items available to assist him with his task. Hank left Liz and ran up the stairs to the second floor, looking for an appropriate place for his ritual. Nothing but four empty bedrooms and bathrooms. Not so much as a shower curtain had been left behind.

Back on the first floor, Liz hadn't moved. Hank opened the door to the basement and took the stairs down. The finished basement was a perfect setting and was fast becoming his signature death scene. Back on the main floor, Hank stepped over Liz, checking to make sure she was still unconscious on his way out the front door and to his car. He needed to retrieve his kit from the trunk. Still a perfect day, with plenty of sunlight and no one on the dead end street. Inside, Hank rolled Liz up in the floor rug and carried her fireman style over his right shoulder down into the basement while carrying his toolbox in his left hand.

Hank tied the unconscious Realtor's hands behind her and her feet together at the ankles using a heavyweight nylon rope. He leaned her up against the wall where an entertainment center had been, based on the indents in the carpet and all the wires and cables protruding from the wall. He laid out the tools from his kit on the carpeted floor in front of him. *Nice carpet. Actually, nice kick-ass basement,* he thought as he took in the full view for the first time since they had descended the stairs. How many happy evenings had this family spent down here? Laughing, watching movies together, eating popcorn—and where were they now? Out on the street because some greedy bank wanted their money back, and they wanted it *now*! And this bitch lying on the floor was helping to get that money back by selling the house right out from under them. Well, Hank was here to even the score, if only a little. Yes, sir, one home at a time, one Realtor at a time. Hank would be sending a big message. *You can't screw with people's lives, assholes,* Hank's inner voice shouted.

Hank had cut the correct length of duct tape to cover Liz's mouth, then set out a tube of sodium hydroxide tablets and his forceps. He was already wearing a fresh pair of latex gloves. Based on her size, Hank didn't think it would take more than three or four tablets.

The Realtor was still out. Hank hadn't meant to hit her so hard, but the adrenaline rush had added extra gusto to his punch. He splashed a little water on her face from one of the bottles. He patted her cheeks lightly, almost in a nurturing way. They must be awake and aware of what is going to happen and why. That was half the fun after all. His reward for a job well done. A lesson to be taught.

Liz gradually began to moan and move her head from side to side. She was rising up from a dark abyss and coming to the surface when she felt the pain in her jaw. When she finally opened her eyes to a squint, the room was angled and fuzzy, and she felt as if she was going to throw up.

Through the haze, she saw a man sitting on his haunches. She recognized the droopy smile and immediately tried to stand up. Only then did Liz realize that she was tied by her hands and feet, immobilized.

"Welcome back to the living—for now." Hank's smile was genuine this time. She could feel the warmth of his breath and smell the staleness from his mouth.

"I know who you are," Liz mumbled through a tight, sore jaw, clear enough for Hank to understand.

"I'm sure you do. I've been in all of the papers. My reputation precedes me. I'm flattered." Hank did a slight mock bow from his squatting position. "I suppose you know what comes next." It was a statement, not a question.

Liz was still trying to get the fog out of her skull so she could deal with this maniac. "I know who you are," she repeated, "but you don't know who I am."

"Oh, sure I do," Hank said. "You're one of those high and mighty judges who take it upon themselves to decide who gets to live in their house and who gets thrown out. You're just a whore for that corporation pimp, First Family Bank and Trust. The homeowner's late with their payment, throw them in the street. We need our money. Sell it for what you can, and do it quickly. We need our money. You should be ashamed of what you do, but you're not. You want your money too!" Hank was speaking with implacable control as he opened the tube of lye tablets and got another bottle of water ready. The forceps already lay on the carpet.

Liz eyed the collection of tools and realized she didn't have much time. Thinking clearly was a challenge as her head pounded from the earlier punch.

"Listen. I'm not who you think I am. My name is Elizabeth Colburn. Lieutenant Colburn with the Hamilton Police Department. Right now there are several squad cars headed directly to this house. You're cooked, my friend." Liz gave it her best convincing voice. She didn't really know if Kaufman and Lindell were still in the area or if they had picked up any of the short conversation before the lights had gone out.

"Funny, I don't hear any sirens, Lieutenant Elizabeth Colburn." Hank cocked his head in a mock listening position. "And we've been together for what, ten or twelve minutes. What are the police doing, coming by dog sled? Nice try."

Liz knew Hank was right, of course. She wasn't sure how long she had been knocked out, but certainly if her backup had heard, they would have been there by now.

"Now open up your pretty mouth, nice and wide." Hank came towards her with an inch-thick white tablet held between the ends of the long, tarnished forceps. Liz shook her head violently back and forth to avoid the tongs, but Hank grabbed her fiercely by the mouth with his open hand and squeezed. The pain was excruciating, and when Liz let out a cry, Hank stuffed the round tablet into her mouth. The burn was instantaneous. She tried to spit it out and did manage to push a large chunk out on her lip.

"Naughty girl. Hank doesn't like it when people don't take their medicine."

Liz's eyes were beginning to tear up from the burning in her mouth. Hank squeezed her cheeks and added a few drops of water. Before Liz could say or do anything, Hank replaced his hand with a six-inch piece of duct tape, which he slapped into place across her mouth.

***

I moved from a stroll to a quicker pace, taking my hands out of the jacket pockets and swinging them to help stride me forward. I stopped to take out the binoculars once more, thinking I had caught a glimpse of movement through the basement's walkout sliding glass door. I couldn't see anything, but I could see through the window curtains that the basement lights were still on. I picked up the pace and moved across the five hundred yards of untamed grass. From my angle, I could see, between the homes, the front end of a late-model car parked in the street in front of the open house sign. I didn't know if it was a neighbor's car or how long it might have been parked there, but it gave me an extra push in my step. I felt the burn in the back of my thighs from three hours of dribbling and shooting baskets as I covered the uneven ground.

***

"Who do you people think you are, taking homes away from hardworking families?" Hank said as he took out another tablet. "You're scum, you know that? You took my home away, broke up my marriage, and gave my kids to another man—a Realtor at that—to raise as his own. I'm working two dead-end jobs just to afford the rent on a crummy little apartment, and I'm driving a ten-year-old car that has more rust than these forceps." Hank held up the tweezers with a tablet clinched between the ends. He pulled back the tape from Liz's mouth and squeezed her cheeks one more time. Her jaw was still very sore, and her mind was reeling as it considered her options. Time was running out, and it was clear that the cavalry was not coming to the rescue.

When Hank leaned in, forceps in hand, Liz spit lye soaked saliva in his face.

"Bitch!" Hank yelled as spittle landed in his right eye. He doused water from another bottle on a clean rag from his tool kit and blotted his eye. The sting was not as bad as it could have been if he hadn't instinctively blinked. Most of Liz's spit ran down his cheek, but it still burned. "I ought to kill you right now," Hank snarled as he continued to wipe his watering eye.

"I'm a cop, you asshole! You want to go to jail for killing a cop? Liz was screaming at Hank through burning, numb lips, saliva spraying into the air with each word. She had held most of the foaming liquid in her mouth and tried hard not to swallow. The searing sensation was filling her mouth, stinging her gums while her cheeks puffed out trying to contain the liquid as it was expanding to beyond containable. Hank picked up the forceps from the floor, with the tablet still wedged in its teeth, and shoved it into Liz's mouth. He slapped the tape back into place.

For the first time, Hank was unnerved, and doubt crept into his mind. What to do next? He paced in small circles in front of Liz's feet, mumbling to himself. In frustration, he kicked a hole in the drywall next to Liz's head. Talking out loud, mostly to himself, Hank considered his options. He noticed the hundred-gallon aquarium built into the wall to his left and opened the small door next to it. Inside, he removed the large lid by standing on a small wooden chair that had been placed there to access the tank.

Liz had managed to roll onto her side, desperately trying not to swallow. She knew from the toxicology reports presented by Doctor Sam that the other victims had died from internal bleeding. A slow, agonizing death. Liz intended to hold on as long as possible, not swallowing. The tape was not as tight as when first applied, and she pushed at it with the tip of her tongue, attempting to loosen the seal and allow as much of the foam in her mouth to dribble across her cheek and onto the floor. She didn't know where Hank was, and she held onto a brief thought that he may have fled.

She felt Hank's hands grab her by the waist and hoist her up into the air. The movement caused her to choke, and she swallowed a gulp of the poison saliva. He carried her roughly into the small room, banging her elbows on the door jamb as they went. Clumsily, Hank dragged her up onto the chair. Liz felt the little wooden chair teeter as he stepped up. For a slightly built fellow, Hank was surprisingly strong, or maybe the fear or anger and adrenalin had increased his strength. He lifted Liz onto the edge of the aquarium and tossed her over into the empty glass container. She hit her head on the way down and saw stars but didn't lose consciousness.

Hank was a mass of confusion by now. Things had gotten out of control. His control, which he had lost. He was panicky to the point of rage. He stumbled over to his toolbox, breathing heavily from the exertion of depositing Liz into the aquarium. He threw the scattered contents into the top compartment and tried to latch it shut. Only one latch clicked shut. He glanced around hastily and headed for the stairs, not worrying about left behind evidence. He took the stairs two at a time.

Liz was struggling to get on her knees from a lying position. The burning was impossible to contain, and she vomited into the tape, which held the contents of her stomach in her mouth. Tears were running across her face, and sudsy snot was burning her nostrils as it oozed from her nose. The exertion of trying to right herself, along with the sodium hydroxide, was giving her a light head. She felt as though she would faint at any moment. It was hard to breathe. If she passed out, Liz knew she would be added to the list of the Open House Murder victims.

***

I heard the car's engine rev. The late model car parked in front of Boswick Lane, which I now recognized as an old Chevrolet, jerked to a start as the driver slammed it into gear. The tires squawked on the pavement as the stranger sped down the street well over the posted speed limit. I caught glimpses of the car between homes as it flew down the street. I dug my cell phone out of my jacket packet and dialed 911 as I moved at a sprint towards the back of the house. Please God, don't let Liz be dead. A million

Liz and Kurt moments flooded through my mind as I closed the last fifty yards to the house.

"Nine-one-one, what's your emergency?" a female voice said.

"This is Kurt Banning. There's been a murder, or attempted murder, in Switch Grass Ponds. I'm not sure which. I need an ambulance to 503 Boswick Lane. Hurry!" There was panic in my voice as my imagination ran away with me. I hoped—no, I prayed—that Liz was fine. I'd come around the corner and she would be there, putting the open house sign in the trunk of her car. I didn't care if she was going to be mad because I breached our agreement. I just wanted to see her alive.

"Sir, are you with the victim now?"

"No, but I'm on my way there right now," I huffed into the phone.

"If you're not with the victim, or apparent victim, then how do you know—"

"Lady, I just do, so please get an ambulance here now. Please! Also, the person responsible just drove through the subdivision. He's headed towards the main road, driving a dark Chevrolet."

"Did you get the license plate number?"

"No. I was too far away to see as he drove off." I panted as I ran. "The victim is a police officer. Please contact the Hamilton Police Department *after* you send for the ambulance."

"This *is* the Hamilton Police Department, and I'm on it now, sir. Dispatch is on its way."

I flipped my phone shut and ran with all the energy that I had left. *Don't be dead, Elizabeth, don't be dead,* I kept saying in my head as I ran faster than I would have thought possible. I wasn't sure if it was the wind on my face or the panic in my heart, but tears were flying at the corners of my eyes as I pushed through the last one hundred feet, up a small incline towards the back of the home.

I ran to the sliding glass door of the walkout basement and cupped my hands to the window. I looked in through my own reflection, frantically searching. It took me a couple of seconds for me to see Liz, kneeling in the aquarium, head slumped down, leaning against the side wall of glass. I could see that her feet and wrists were bound. I jerked on the doorknob, but it was locked. I pounded on the door with the palms of my hands and yelled her name. Nothing. I looked around for something to break the glass. Nothing. I ran up the slope of the side yard and around to the front of the house. The door was shut. I tried the handle, and it miraculously was unlocked. The murderer had left so quickly that he had neglected to lock up. I threw open the door and caught the rebound after it hit the wall. I hardly notice the the smack into my shoulder, I was just relieved to be inside. I rushed through the home towards the basement stairs. Just before I stumbled down the stairs, I thought I heard the faint sound of a faraway siren. I hoped it wasn't my imagination. I skipped steps and almost tumbled down as I leaped over the final three steps.

I ran to the aquarium and pounded on the glass. Nothing. Liz was still in the same position has I had seen her through the basement door. She was leaning against the back wall of the empty fish tank. The siren, now multiple sirens, were much louder and closer. I went into the adjacent little room—that door too had been left open—and saw the small wooden chair. I realized before even getting on it that I would never be able to lift Liz up and over the tank wall. I kept yelling her name. Nothing. *Dear God, please don't let her be dead.* I was making all kinds of deals and promises to God if he would allow Liz to be alive. In her slumped position I could see her face.

I carried the wooden chair with me out of the room and stood facing the front of the giant aquarium. I slammed it into the wall of glass, but the tempered glass only shook, and the reverb went up my arms to my elbows. I swung again, harder. The scum-caked glass cracked from the point of impact and spread out in a honeycomb pattern. One more swing and the glass let go with a shatter. I reached in and took hold of Liz under her tied legs and waist and dragged her through the broken glass. I didn't feel the razor sharp edge rake my cheek as I leaned in. As I sat her on the basement floor and yanked the tape from her mouth, I heard footsteps upstairs.

"Down here, in the basement," I yelled as loud as I could. "We're in the basement!"

I was untying Liz's ankles and hands when I saw six black boots standing next to me. Her eyes were closed, and she was cool to the touch. The skin on her lips and cheeks appeared to have a chalky hue.

"We'll take it from here, sir. We've got her," one of the paramedics said.

I looked up with blurred vision and saw three EMTs standing in front of me, one holding an emergency kit and another already on his walkie-talkie in contact with the hospital. I was reluctant to give up my spot but stood aside as they lay Liz flat and began checking for vital signs.

"Shallow breathing, Captain, and I've got a faint pulse."

I bowed my head. *Thank you, God.* I stood to the side as they began administering aid. "She's been poisoned with lye," I told them.

All three of them looked at me. "How do you know that, sir?" one asked.

"It's a long story, but believe me. She is Lieutenant Elizabeth Colburn, working a sting operation with the Hamilton Police Department. The guy who did this has done it before. He got away before I could get here, but I saw him driving away like a lunatic."

"So that's what that was all about," the captain said to the other two paramedics. They nodded and seemed to know what he was talking about.

"What what's about?" I asked.

"On the way into the subdivision, we saw two squad cars next to a dark green automobile that had apparently clipped a telephone pole on a curve in the road. Must have lost control and rolled his car onto its side. They had him in the back seat of one of the cars. He was staring out the window with a blank look on his face. He must have been in shock. His face looked pretty messed up from the crash. A second ambulance was dispatched just after us to this same neighborhood. At first we thought it was a duplicate call-in, but the dispatcher confirmed one was an automobile accident and the other had been a frantic call, talking about a murder."

I stared at them and took a gulp of air. "Is she going to live?"

"I would say her chances are extremely good, especially now that you've told us about the poison. Her pulse is weak, and she needs oxygen. We'll neutralize the acid in her system and get her to the hospital for a complete check-over. All indications are that we made it in time for the Lieutenant to make a full recovery, although I imagine it will be a while before she's feeling very good."

By the time the paramedics had Liz on a stretcher and were headed up the stairs, she half opened one eye. She asked in a quiet, muffled voice what was happening. The man in charge told her she was on her way to the hospital and that she would be just fine. Liz rolled her head in my direction, saw me, and attempted a small smile before her eye closed.

CHAPTER 26

I had trailed the ambulance to Jonas Memorial Hospital after retrieving my car from the school parking lot. By the time I had weaved through Sunday afternoon traffic, parked in the visitors' lot at Jonas Memorial, and run into the emergency room, Liz had been taken back to a trauma room and was being attended to by a team of very capable technicians. It took a little white lie that I was her husband to gain entrance to the exam room. She was surrounded by concerned people in an array of colorful medical uniforms. It was obvious that I was in the way as I kept moving around the tiny room to get close to Liz. Her eyes were closed, but her chest was rising and falling on its own.

"She's going to be fine. Why don't you get a cup of coffee or go home and come back in a couple of hours," said the emergency room doctor. "We have tests to do, and until then we won't know anything other than she's stable and the prognosis is good. We'll call you if there's a dramatic change, Mr. Colburn. Get some rest."

I smiled and laughed inside. Mr. Colburn! Liz would have gotten a kick out of that. I did as the doctor ordered and returned to the safety of my second-floor apartment, exhausted. Another one of those days that had seemed to last for forty-eight hours.

Liz stayed in the hospital overnight for tests, rest, and observation. I called her attending nurse twice during the night for updates. I was reassured that she was resting comfortably. I returned the next morning carrying a stuffed lizard with multicolored stripes around its midsection. A red tongue made of felt stuck out between its parted lips. I had never understood Liz's fondness for reptiles, there was a lot about Liz I didn't understand, but I hoped that it would make her smile.

There was a large bouquet of flowers sitting in a vase on the side table from Chief Dougan and the Hamilton Police Department. It was large enough to block Liz's view out the window of her third-floor room. She was sleeping, with her arms on top of the blankets, an intravenous tube trailing along her right side, and a finger clip on her index finger was monitoring her oxygen level. The covers had been pulled up snug to her neck.

I sat in the only chair available, which seemed, based on its lack of comfort, to have been designed to keep visitors to a minimum. Even with matted hair and a pale complexion, I thought she looked beautiful. Her dark hair fanned out over the starched white pillowcase under her head. When I thought about how close I had come to losing my Liz, air caught in my throat and made a small gasp.

"You're not crying now are you, Kurty?" Liz had opened heavy eyelids and was looking in my direction. I stood up and went to her side and gave her a huge kiss.

"Ouch! She grimaced. Liz's lips were swollen and had second-degree chemical burns on both the top and bottom.

"Who me, cry? What are you crazy?" I smiled down at her. "How are you feeling?"

"Like someone broke my jaw, poisoned me, and threw me in a fish tank. Just another day at work on the Hamilton Police force," she mumlbed. "The doctors have been making me drink some terrible liquid that looks like milk. They took an X-ray of my lungs and did a scope of my trachea and stomach lining. Nothing too serious or permanent. I have some blistering in my throat and on these." She pointed to her lips. It will take a time to heal, but I should be good as new in a couple of weeks. Looks like you'll be drinking Ketel solo for a while."

"Liz …"

I didn't know where to go from there. I had so many conversations in my head that we had never had, I just didn't know where to start. I smiled instead. "Get some rest. I'll be back tomorrow afternoon to take you home after your discharge." I gave her a kiss, on the forehead this time, and walked to the door.

"Kurt," she said before the door closed, "me too."

I left the hospital feeling worn out. It could have been all the basketball, but I doubted it. I drove home thinking of the surreal events of the past six weeks and six hours. Scientists say that there is a reaction for every action, and sociologists tell us that we are a product of our environment.

These being true, I was curious who I would be when I woke up Tuesday morning.

I made one phone call before I had turned in on Sunday evening. It was to Dex. I definitely didn't want him reading this in the paper. Our conversation was short, and I did most of the talking. At the end of the conversation, he made a wisecrack about my ability to shoot baskets and then run a five-hundred-yard race.

As tired as I was, sleep did not come as quickly as I had hoped. I turned on my old standby remedy, the television. The second story of the late evening news came from the suburb of Hamilton, thirty-two miles from downtown Chicago. Apparently the killer, known as the Open House Murderer, had been captured by local police on Sunday afternoon, according to the network reporter on the scene. The suspect, Henry Hank Pilcher, was apprehended leaving the home of an attempted murder of a real estate agent holding an open house in this upscale neighborhood of Hamilton. The cameraman panned the Switch Grass Ponds marquee as the reporter continued with his story.

"Official word here is that the suspect was fleeing the area when he lost control of his car and struck a utility pole. Police arrived on the scene after receiving an anonymous tip from a Good Samaritan. Henry Hank Pilcher, a thirty-eight-year-old white male, was in the hands of the local authorities after having been examined, treated, and released from an area hospital for minor injuries suffered in the automobile accident. He would be transferred from the Hamilton jail to the regional FBI facility in Chicago on Monday. Reporting from the western suburbs, this is Hal Watkins." Good night, Hal.

Tuesday morning, to my chagrin, I awoke as the same old Kurt Banning. I was famished and prepared myself a feast of eggs, bacon, and a stack of whole wheat toast. Liz wasn't scheduled to be released until three o'clock, which gave me time to get some much neglected real estate work done, even though I was sure it would be difficult to concentrate.

"Well, good morning, Mr. Banning," Molly said as I came through the front door. "How was your weekend?" She gave me a sheepish stare. "Must have been amazing, huh?"

To the best of my knowledge, other than Dex, who wouldn't be in for at least another two hours, no one was aware of the goings on at 503 Boswick Lane, or my involvement. At least not yet.

"Yeah, had a great weekend. You know, real estate stuff, the usual. How about you?"

"Not as good as yours obviously. Something for you on your desk arrived first thing this morning." Molly gave me a wink.

That Molly is an odd girl at times, I thought as I headed to my desk. I got a few stares and sly grins as I made my way around file cabinets and other people's desks and headed to my cubicle. I was puzzled, thinking the whole world had gone daft, until I rounded the corner of my center form and saw a three-foot-high floral arrangement in a vase on my desk. Exotic was the first word that came to mind. A card was tucked inside, and by the look of the envelope, it had not been opened by nosey Miss Molly. On the outside it said, KURT BANNING, typed by the local florist. On the inside was a short note from Liz.

It said simply, "Love You! L."